AHREN

The 13th Paladin

Volume 1

Dear Reader,

If you enjoy my books, spread the word and tell your friends.

There's nothing more enjoyable for a book than new readers experiencing it...

www.tweitze.de

www.facebook.com/t.weitze

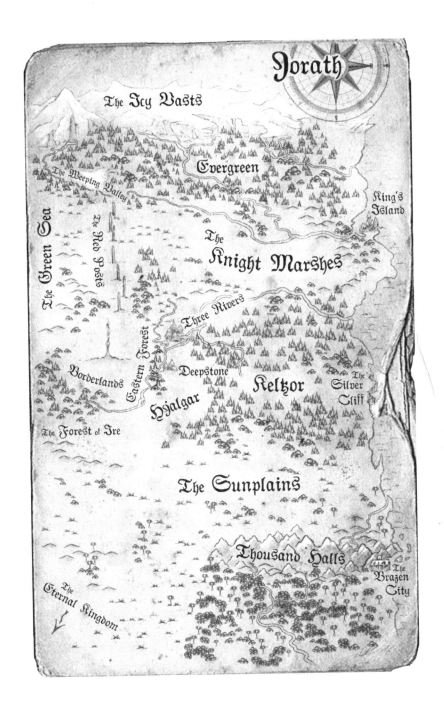

Jorath

The Icy Vasts

Evergreen

King's Island

The Green Sea

The Weeping Valley

The Red Posts

The Knight Marshes

Three Rivers

Eastern Forest

Borderlands

Deepstone

Keltzor

The Silver Cliff

Hjalgar

The Forest of Ire

The Sunplains

Thousand Halls

The Brazen City

The Eternal Kingdom

764 years earlier

The figures slowly peeled away from the soaring column of smoke, which was becoming denser. They were different shapes and races but they all exhibited the same facial expressions which fluctuated between exhaustion, satisfaction and confusion. They clambered up the last few paces of the newly formed crater and turned around. They looked up for a while in silence at the pall of smoke, a good thousand paces in diameter, which rose smooth and dense, like a black wall in front of them. It hid the being within from the eyes of creation.

One of the figures asked in a tired voice, without looking away, 'will it suffice?'

'It must suffice', another answered. 'We cannot do more, so long as one of us is missing'.

There was a short pause before the voice continued, 'if everything goes according to plan, it will only be for a short time'.

One by one, the bedraggled forms turned away, leaving the pillar of smoke in their wake. It pointed towards the heavens like a warning black finger, defying the wind and the time.

Chapter 1

It was the sudden croaking of an ogre frog that woke Ahren up from his slumber. Startled, he looked down at the creature, a good forearm in length, which had woken him so rudely. With a frown and a wave of his hand he shooed the troublemaker away, and with an almighty leap the frog found the safety of the river some distance from the drowsy youngster.

'Stupid frog', Ahren muttered to himself, as he reached for his fishing rod. It was only then that he noticed the waning intensity of colour in his surroundings, which could only have been caused by the encroaching dusk. 'The THREE be with me!' blurted the youngster, now fully awake, as he suddenly realised that he'd slept the afternoon away. A closer look at the rod revealed that a fine big creature must have taken the bait because the line had been snapped. With a sigh he imagined the splendid specimen and wondered how he had slept through the tugging of the fishing line. A look around him answered his question. Here, in the bend of the river, he was protected from the wind, far away from all the other villagers and their activities. The river was four paces in width and the willows, hanging low over it, afforded shade from the sun without covering him to the point that it would be cool. The sluggish stream lapped gently around stones that stuck out of the water and lulled anyone who was a good listener to sleep. The soft, grassy bank had done the rest, and so the idyllic surroundings had carried him away to the land of nod. Ahren stood up slowly. But now he was in for a rude awakening. As he stood there and looked around, he noticed that his bait box with its rare and coveted Godsday flies was lying knocked over, on the ground. These

5

flies were used to catch the equally coveted and delicious blueshoal fish, which always fetched a handsome price at the market. Master Cossith always took one off him whenever Ahren managed to catch some and paid him with a large chunk of the delicious cheese he made so well. Ahren bent down to look for the flies and was startled to see tooth and claw marks on the wooden box. Martens had feasted on his bait! Unfortunately, these pests had just as much a weakness for the Godsday flies as the blueshoal fish. They were called Godsday flies because they only hatched on the Day of the gods and died the same night, but if you caught them in the day and locked them away so they couldn't see moonlight, then they would survive until the next Godsday. Unless of course, they served as bait for blueshoal fish. Ahren realised with exasperation that his full supply of flies was gone, which would have provided him with another three days' fishing. Snorting with anger he flung the useless box into the river and put his rod on his shoulder. As he reached for his bucket with the day's catch, a despondency, such as he hadn't felt in a long time, came over him. His catch had been stolen too! He thought of what his father would say once he arrived home with no fish and no flies, not to mention a snapped fishing line, and felt a lump in his stomach. His backside was already sore at the mere thought of it.

With slumped shoulders he made his way homewards, a journey that suddenly felt terribly long. He beat his way through thick bush and came out onto a small path which led from his home village of Deepstone and ran through the Eastern Forest. This was a small, dense forest which snaked alongside the river like a green ribbon. While it took hardly any effort to reach the west side of the wood from the river bank in less than an hour, it took two or three days of marching to get through it by sticking to the river. At least that's what Falk, the Forest Guardian said anyway. A feeling of imminent disaster, caused by his father's scorn,

6

hung over him, and it seemed to the thirteen-year old that the wood was stretching itself out. An hour became a small eternity as he walked between the trees towards the sound hiding that was waiting for him. The sun set slowly in high summer and accompanied him on his return journey.

It still wasn't dark when he stepped out from the trees and paused on the edge of the village. Deepstone clung to the edge of the forest and mirrored the Eastern Forest in its form. It was more than ten times longer than it was wide. Each house was no more than a bowshot from the wood, for it hadn't taken long for the inhabitants to realise that the trees offered protection from the cold wind that swept over the hills of Eastland. A few had tried to build their wooden houses further away – with little success. In the best-case scenario, this meant that twice the amount of wood was needed for heating in winter, and in the worst case, a family member would succumb to the Blue Death. Old Vera, the village Healer, said the winter wind would then no longer want to leave the afflicted person's lungs, and indeed, the howling of the winter wind could be heard again with every wheezing breath that passed between the blue lips of the victim. Ahren's mother had died in this way, shortly after his birth. Too weak, her body could offer no resistance to, nor defy the Blue Death.

Not one of the Wailing Houses, as they were called by the other inhabitants, was in use for more than one winter. Each and every family abandoned the house the following spring and build a new one in the shelter of the wood instead.

And so, the little village resembled a small version of the protecting wood. The houses stood in a row, like a wooden pearl necklace along the edge of the forest in groups of no more than four or five houses together. The village population of Deepstone would never have amounted to its current two hundred inhabitants were it not for the fact that the land here was fertile and yielded a good harvest every year. Everything seemed still. It was high time for supper, and of course it would have been blueshoal fish on the table at home today, if Mother Nature hadn't kindly lulled Ahren to sleep with her peace and quiet, only to make him then pay such a high price.

The boy trod with a sigh to his father's hut and stood still. The house his father had built that time had a compact structure that reminded him of a gnarled, dead tree stump, and gave a general appearance of ugliness and depression. The windows were small and the wood almost black. The hut had been coated with such a heavy layer of tar that in the dusk it resembled more a withered root that had pushed its way up through the earth than a place you could call home. The villagers used to say that after his wife had died, Edrik, Ahren's father, had poured all his pain and sorrow into building this house. But later it became clear to Ahren, that his father's only aim had been to build a house that was completely wind-proof. He had succeeded in this and Ahren was sure that his house was the warmest in the whole village. Secretly though, he had to admit that the other villagers had a point. Ahren was young but he already knew that there was more than one kind of coldness that could trouble a person. This brownish-black wooden fortress provided no refuge. Shivering inside, Ahren stopped studying the house and opened the door.

It was no surprise that Ahren was still in bad form the following day. His father had reacted as expected and used his belt. Sitting was not an option now and Ahren stole away from the house before his father thought of a more severe punishment than the wood-cutting he had been ordered to do. At least that could be done standing up. He walked smartly into the wood to cut branches off one of the marked trees. Falk, the Forest Guardian, hunted the woodland animals, but he also knew which trees could be felled without damaging the forest. Unlike the practice in other villages, the Deepstone villagers could not cut wood willy-nilly. The protection offered by the forest was too important, and so the woodcutters often went deep into the forest to fell the trees that Falk had specially marked. He had singled out a small group of trees the previous week and Ahren made his way there. Even before he reached the clump of trees, he recognised the loud voices of Holken and his friends. Holken was the son of the local blacksmith and the strongest boy in the village. Ahren realised with a sigh that today was threatening to turn out even worse than yesterday. Although he wasn't particularly slight for his age, he certainly couldn't compete with that muscular bully, and for some reason, Holken always seemed to want to prove this. Naturally this led the other boys in Holken's gang to see Ahren as nothing more than fair game. He avoided the blacksmith's son as much as possible, but this was probably not going to be possible today. The next nearest group of marked trees he knew of was half an hour's march away, and he would also have to carry the chopped wood back to the hut, so he would have to make the journey four or five times, laden down with wood. If he didn't want to double his workload, he would simply have to make use of the clump of trees in front of him. Just as he was about to move to within sight of the young gang, he heard a familiar voice in the undergrowth.

'Psst, Ahren, over here'.

'Likis!' Ahren nearly screamed with relief but stopped himself at the last minute with a low-voiced exhalation. He gave a start, afraid that the gang had heard him, and with two quick steps to the left he was behind the bushes where his best and indeed only friend was waiting. Likis looked the same as ever. A half smile on his narrow face, and a cheeky sparkle in the blue eyes that flashed from under his black hair. Added to that, there was the dirty clothing, which had doubtless been new and

9

pristine a few days earlier, but which was now torn in several places. No jerkin in the world could survive Likis' propensity to crawl through the undergrowth and hide. Ahren himself was of a somewhat lean build and a typical Midlander with his nut-brown hair and green eyes. But compared to Likis, he was stocky. And slow. Because if Likis was nothing else, he was certainly fast.

'I was hoping you'd come here today. I've been sitting in this bush for half an hour already, wondering how I can get my hands on some firewood without having such a backache tomorrow that I won't be able to stand', said Likis in a low voice.

'How did you know I'd be coming here?' asked Ahren, surprised. Likis smiled mischievously and Ahren's face turned bright red. Of course, his father hadn't exactly been quiet the night before, as he vented his feelings regarding his son's failings. Likis' family were immediate neighbours and must have heard everything.

'Don't worry about it. Everyone can have a bad day. But you really do have to tell me later how it's possible to lose the fish, the flies, *and* the rod, all in the one day, without having been set upon by robbers', said Likis with a chuckle.

'Only the line, not the whole rod!' said Ahren defensively, which only provoked the usual half-smile from his partner. Sometimes Ahren hated him for that grin. It seemed as if his wiry friend would meet every situation with this crooked smile, no matter how serious or awkward things became. One time, Likis had gone so far with his pranks that the bailiff had seriously considered dragging him before the village council. This was one of the most humiliating things that could befall a person in a community as small as Deepstone. Likis had simply adopted this half smile and begun to talk the bailiff out of his plan. Half an hour later he was let go. Old Mara, who had seen the whole thing, had said to Ahren:

'that young boy has a gift, no doubt about it. In ten years, he'll either be sitting on the village council himself, or he'll have been banished'. She had shaken her head kind-heartedly as she watched Likis scampering away.

'I see, I see, just the fishing line. Then it's not so bad. That could happen to anyone', said the wiry boy, referring teasingly to Ahren's misfortune.

'Just leave it, will you? I'll tell you everything later', Ahren responded, giving in. He knew his friend would give him no peace anyway if he didn't. The word 'curiosity' took on a whole new meaning when you were in Likis' company. Maybe, thought Ahren, that was why he combined stealth and chattering so well. What the merchant's son couldn't find out through cajoling, he did through stealth. Yet he never used this acquired knowledge to his own advantage. Yes, he got up to tricks, but he never harmed anyone unless he was forced into a corner. Maybe that's why he got away with so much, thought Ahren to himself. He said to Likis, 'but first I need firewood, and preferably without being nabbed by Holken. Two beatings in two days are just too much' and with a grimace he rubbed his backside.

'That's exactly what I thought too, when I saw Hammerhead here', said Likis. Hammerhead was a nickname he had invented for the budding apprentice blacksmith because he was firmly of the opinion that the big bully wouldn't need a hammer for his handiwork, his head would do just as good a job – it was of no use for anything else anyway. The fact that Holken really did possess a somewhat angular head just added insult to injury. Likis relished picking the right words and thereby really infuriating the target of his scorn. Not that he was ever brought to book in this regard. Likis was small and slight, but besides his ability to be stealthy, he was also the best sprinter in the village and used his surroundings artfully to his benefit. Any time he was in imminent danger of being eventually hunted down and caught, he would find refuge among several sympathetic villagers. He would have plausibly convinced them that it was certainly not his fault that at that moment he was being chased by a gang of ruffians. That was just as well, Ahren thought to himself, for Holken would certainly tear the younger boy apart if he ever caught him.

Ahren valued his friend for these very reasons. His sharp humour, his quick-wittedness, and of course his fleet-footedness (which saved him from the consequences of the other two qualities) were a combination of all the things lacking in Ahren. For some reason his hands and feet were always getting in the way, and even if he never considered himself to be stupid, he never had the courage or the presence of mind to find the right words at the right time. Now Likis was grinning at him and formulating his plan on how they could get to the firewood as quickly as possible without having to do the heavy work themselves or without falling into the hands of the other youngsters.

'It's really very simple', he whispered. 'I'll lure them away from the clearing and you grab the firewood. Hammerhead is so hell-bent on getting his hands on me that he'll give chase as soon as he sees me. The other idiots will follow him for fear of getting a tongue-lashing if they don't help and then I'll give him the slip.'

'Yes, that sounds great. Let's go!' agreed Ahren enthusiastically. The thought of not having to spend hours on end cutting wood, but of snatching the fruit of the others' hard-earned labour, appealed to Ahren so much that he agreed without giving it a second thought. Yesterday's misfortune had wounded him deeply and the thought of outwitting the world in general and the village boys in particular, seemed to him in his present state of mind to be poetic justice.

'Good, get into position over there and grab the wood as soon as they're all gone. Best bring it to *Safehold*, it's not so far and you can easily hide there'. *Safehold* was a tree-house the two boys had built the previous summer. Falk was the only other person who knew about it – the pair had asked him about a suitable tree because they wanted to be sure that their tree-house wouldn't be chopped down one fine day.

'Sure, I'll do it. Just be careful nobody catches you'.

'They haven't managed it yet', chuckled Likis, and disappeared among the trees.

'That's exactly what worries me', muttered Ahren and stared at the place where he had just seen his friend. The day would come when fortune wouldn't smile on the crafty boy and then it could end in tears. Already Likis' plan didn't seem like such a good idea to him. But his nimble friend was already gone and Ahren crept into the undergrowth with an uneasy feeling in his stomach. He pushed himself into the designated position and had to admire Likis' trained eye in such matters. From here he had a good view of the cluster of trees in question and of the four youths toiling away, without being seen himself. As long as he didn't draw attention to himself with sudden movements, he'd be able to lie here unnoticed for a good while.

He contemplated the scene before him. Holken dominated the picture of course, with his bulging muscles rippling under his sweaty skin as he worked on the thickest branches with forceful swings of the axe. With a derogatory snort Ahren observed that the show-off had taken off his shirt so that he could be admired more. He did this for the benefit of the four other youngsters. Besides, Holken was the eldest in the clearing so the others looked up to him anyway. Ahren was almost sick with envy as he watched them joking around. He'd have given anything to be part of their group, instead of having been chosen to be a whipping boy by a stupid twist of fate. Maybe that's why he couldn't stand Holken.

Before he could give this any further thought, Likis darted into the clearing, grabbed a few thin branches from the impressive pile that the five had already cut and crowed a merry 'thanks, you snails!' to the stunned onlookers, only to disappear again into the undergrowth. Ahren suppressed a laugh with difficulty and pressed himself hard into the ground to avoid being spotted.

'Right, he's done for, grab him!' screamed Holken, his face red, and he and the others gave chase to the timber snatcher. That was almost too easy, thought Ahren, as he slipped towards the clearing, after giving the mob a few seconds to head off. With his heart pounding and with sweaty hands, but also with a wonderful feeling of exhilaration in his stomach he strode quickly into the clearing and grabbed a big bundle of fire-wood. He quickly piled as much wood into his arms as possible until he almost collapsed under the weight and stumbled into the undergrowth, fearful that he would hear a scornful cry or feel a hard fist in his back. With relief he realised that neither had happened and after a short trot he reached *Safehold*. Panting, he hid the wood in some nearby shrubbery and looked up at the one place in which he had really felt comfortable in his young years.

As always, he was filled with pride when he looked at the wooden construction, well hidden and studded with twigs, five paces high, concealed in the tree's thick foliage. In reality, *Safehold* was a wooden box, three paces by three, nestled in the crown of the tree and only visible through keen observation. The tree itself was ten paces high with expansive branches and carried the additional weight effortlessly, even in stormy weather. Falk had helped them with the complicated knots and lent them the hoist with which the youngsters had lifted the wood into the crown of the tree, but generally they had built it completely by themselves. Ahren would never have thought that the Forest Guardian would have been so supportive, but it seemed he understood their yearning for a hiding place and with a lot of patience and good advice he had given them regular feedback on their progress.

Frowning, Ahren thought back to the knots Falk had made to tie the main beams together. Although both Ahren and Likis had watched carefully, neither could say with any certainty how exactly these knots were tied and a thorough examination of them, after Falk was finished, hadn't shed any light on the matter. It almost seemed as though the knots had only one end, but that was surely only because of the clever binding. When Ahren asked him once about it, a thin but warm smile appeared on the Guardian's leathery face and he only said, 'every craft has its secrets, and this one is mine'.

The youngster wanted to climb the tree now – they had deliberately done without a ladder, so as not to endanger the secret location of their refuge – when a daring thought came into his head. Why not make another trip to the clearing? There was a good chance he would be able to take the same amount of wood again. Then the two friends would have a considerable amount of wood to boast of and the others would end up completely empty-handed. If he was going to risk it, he'd have to be quick! Without hesitating, he started heading back. It wasn't long before the pile of wood was in sight again. A quick look confirmed that no-one was there. Ahren picked up the rest of the wood with a triumphant grin when suddenly Holken leapt into the clearing, roaring furiously.

'You! I should have known that you and that little weasel were in cahoots. I'm going to give you such a belt in the face, you'll remember it every time you look in the mirror!'

Ahren was frozen to the spot but his mind was racing. Holken must have lain in wait for Likis, hoping to pounce on the nimble youngster if he came back, which was a surprisingly subtle tactic for a muscleman like him. But Likis had been far too clever to fall for something like that. Unlike me, thought Ahren drily, as he flung the wood at his opponent and spun round on his heels.

There were maybe three paces between them and Ahren's heart was in his mouth. He started running towards *Safehold* as fast as his legs could carry him; behind him both left and right, he could hear scornful shouting as well as the crashing of branches and twigs. The others must be right on his heels! It would end in disaster! Terrified, Ahren sprinted on through the wood. He could barely breathe. The roots of the trees were treacherous. One false move could be his undoing – and then he'd really be in for it! He ran on aimlessly through the wood for some minutes, trying to escape from the blood hounds' field of vision. He may not have had Likis' natural talents, but he had certainly learnt from his friend. Low-lying branches whipped his forearms as he protected his face and he could feel his breath beginning to burn in his chest. The cries of his chasers were still close behind and the young boy knew he'd better not slow down, even though he was beginning to see black spots before his eyes. Hurriedly he searched for a hiding place or some indication of his present location. He could see a fallen oak tree in front of him. Its bare crown was being held up by two healthy trees forming a sort of knotty ramp. With a joyful yelp he began half-climbing, half-running up the oak's rough bark until he arrived among the leaves of the other trees, and then fought his way through the crown of the tree towards the right. The others were also clambering up and shouting threats, thinking they had trapped him, but Ahren remembered the spot, having been there often enough with Likis. If you weren't being chased by an angry mob, you

16

could have great fun climbing around the treetops! The additional branches of the fallen oak offered countless opportunities for holding on. To put it simply: it was a wonderful playground. Ahren climbed higher and higher into the crown of the tree and moved to the other side of it, and in his hurry, as well as because of his increasing tiredness, he grazed himself in several places – on his hands, his elbows and his knees. He prayed that none of them knew this spot, because it had one peculiarity: there was a little pond within reaching distance of the tree on the right as long as you sprang from one particular branch. Actually, it was perfectly safe – the distance wasn't great. But Ahren was tired, his knees were shaking and he could hardly breathe. He pulled himself onto the wide branch that always served as his jumping-off point, paused for a second in order to look down at the dark, murky pond-water at least ten paces below him.

A quick glance over his shoulder confirmed that the others were slowly clambering up the oak, turning their heads in search of him with their faces grimacing and full of scorn. It looked as if they'd lost sight of him among the leaves. This was his chance. Ahren took one more deep breath, filling his lungs with as much air as possible, and threw himself off. His tired legs protested and his jump was far from perfect. He flew through the air at an angle so that he landed in the water on his side. The left side of his body burned like fire, the abrasions and little cuts he had picked up as he had fled stung unmercifully, and he was also winded. He thrashed about rather than swam until he finally reached the surface. Breathing heavily, he looked back at the tree, then at the opposite bank which was edged with low reeds. Clearly, the others hadn't noticed him disappear. With a little luck he could vanish among the trees before anyone spotted him. He swam quietly to the bank and had just pulled himself onto dry land when he heard a chorus of surprise behind him.

Ahren stumbled away – he was simply too tired to run any faster – but still managed to build up a sufficient lead, so that his chasers couldn't see him anymore. It seemed as though none of the blood hounds were willing to take the shortcut through the pond, which meant they had to clamber back down again. Feeling himself to be safe now, he made his way towards *Safehold* and prayed that the village boys would soon tire of the chase. He realized with relief that they too had run out of energy – their angry calls some distance away indicated that he had maintained his lead. After a short jog, Ahren, gasping for breath, touched the tree trunk, his place of safety. If the tree house had been only a hundred paces further on, he would probably never have reached it in time. With one last effort he heaved himself up into the safety of the den, lay flat on the floor and tried to bring his breathing under control. His legs felt like rubber and he was sure he couldn't take another step. As the noise of his chasers came closer, he turned on his tummy with a suppressed groan and peeked through a gap in the branches. One after another, three of the angry boys ran under his hiding place. After a few seconds he could hear confused and angry cries – they realized that their prey had given them the slip.

'He must be here somewhere!' shouted Holken and stopped, barely six paces away from *Safehold*. 'He must have hidden himself, look for him!' Cursing silently, Ahren watched how the boys began searching through undergrowth and in the trees for him. What had he got himself into? Now they'd find the treehouse too! Ahren closed his eyes and held his breath, hoping that the camouflage would fool the boys.

'Look! There's the firewood! He must be very near!' shouted one of them.

A feeling of hopelessness overcame Ahren. He saw Holken staring over at the pile of wood before beginning to search everything meticulously. The others followed his example and Ahren scolded himself silently. He should have put down the bundle of wood further away, or at least hidden it better. Terrified, he watched the commotion below him. Even if the boys were to give up, he thought it would be wise to stay put until the gang had calmed down. He hadn't forgotten the threat Holken had uttered in the clearing and he was in no mood to lose a few teeth by running into him on his way home.

After a while Sven went over to Holken and whispered something into his ear. The miller's son was no danger on his own and even rather quiet and shy. But he had the habit of pitching in if his victim was incapable of offering any more resistance. Holken never got carried away like that, but the unwritten rules of the village boys meant nothing to chubby Sven. It was rumoured that even the village elders had discussed the miller's son's bad behaviour. Ahren saw the coldness in the eyes of the miller's son from the tree-house and a shiver ran down his spine. Meanwhile a smirk appeared on Holken's coarse face as he listened to his companion's suggestion.

'Come here boys, we'll head back. Sven thinks he knows where we'll find Ahren's sneaky little friend. Then we'll give him his due'. They gathered together the stolen firewood again and disappeared into the forest as they headed for the clearing.

Ahren was terrified of what the boys had planned. What should he do? On the one hand, he didn't want to leave his friend in the lurch, but on the other hand, he just didn't have the courage to climb down and to surrender to the village boys. The adults were too far away and he had angered Holken too much, and anyway, there was Sven with his cold eyes. He always had the most vicious ideas. Not to mention excellent powers of observation. If anyone could root out Likis' hiding places, then it would be him. Ahren sat there for a while, as if spellbound, and feverishly considered his options. He was torn between self-preservation and loyalty. The scene kept flashing in front of his eyes: Likis, discovered in one of his hiding places by the angry mob. Horrified, he imagined what Sven would do with Likis, once he had a chance to act out his darker impulses with nobody stopping him. Suddenly he was more afraid of the miller's son than of all the other boys put together.

'You can come down now, they're gone'. The deep, growling voice sounded from below. Ahren couldn't believe his ears. Falk! Relief came over him like a wave. Peeking down over the edge of the tree-house he recognized the weather-beaten face of the Forest Guardian. He was casually leaning against the tree-trunk and looking up at him. The boy hadn't been aware of his approach. Nobody in the village could hear Falk, if Falk didn't want them to. He made an impressive appearance, dressed as always in buckskin garments, with the long bow over his shoulder and the hunting knife on his belt – weapons of any sort being something of a rarity in the little village. The tall, broad-shouldered frame of the Forest Guardian with his closely-cropped grey hair and full beard completed the picture. A few heartbeats passed by with Ahren not daring to move. He simply stared at Falk until the latter finally boomed from below: 'now, come on down. Some of us here still need to earn a living!'

Groaning and red-faced, Ahren clambered down the tree and looked up at the Forest Guardian with a mixture of gratitude and anxiety. How much had he witnessed? Falk eyed him with a serious face and a questioning look. 'And? Everything alright with you?'

Ahren nodded but his opposite number's face darkened noticeably. 'What did they want from you? That didn't look like the usual teasing. Holken might be a ruffian, but today they were really angry'.

'Well, actually it was really quite harmless. Likis and I just stole a bit of firewood from them, that's all'. Ahren was trying to defend himself.

'Firewood? You *stole* it? I must be hearing things! You were too lazy to cut some for yourselves, and you robbed them of the fruits of their labour? No wonder they want to tan your hide!' Shaking his head, Falk looked down at him with a serious look. 'Even if they often cause trouble, at least they've done their work and been diligent, two things that can't be said about you, if you ask me'.

During his short sermon, Falk's voice was growing louder and Ahren's face redder. His voice shaking with remorse, he could only utter a simple 'I'm sorry'. Falk had always been friendly towards him, and the fact that he was furious about something Ahren had done, weighed heavily on the boy. The Forest Guardian's summary of the events was right, of course, which only made it worse.

'What? Do you mean you're only sorry when you're caught letting others do your work while you shirk off? The Apprenticeship Tests are next week. Which master craftsman or woman will pick you as an apprentice now?' Ahren winced and the old man continued. 'And by the way, those boys you were stealing from are the sons of the miller, the blacksmith, the fisherwoman, the seamstress and the dyer. Five bosses who will on no account take you on. Likis will start as an apprentice with his father. He doesn't need to give it a second thought, but you...' Falk didn't finish the sentence, but Ahren could imagine the rest. His father had played his last sympathy card within the village a long time ago due to his constant drunkenness. As he was only a labourer on Trell's farm, he couldn't train Ahren. Not that the young boy would have wanted it. The gaunt farmer Trell, who had more cows on his large farm than any of the other villagers, didn't employ apprentices either and paid all his workers an equally miserly wage, and with the best will in the world, Likis' father, the only merchant in the village, really didn't need *two* apprentices. So, if Ahren was to learn a trade, he was dependent on one of the village master craftsmen and women. If news got out of what he'd done, even if it was only seen as a prank, he might be turned down by all of them.

'Master Falk, I…' he began, but the big man cut him off with a terse gesture.

'Alright. I won't say anything. The others will spread the story around anyway, but they're only young boys. If you're lucky, you might just get a few disapproving looks. I know your father. I know it isn't easy for you, but if it happens again, I will personally mark this tree here and then fell it. Is that clear?' Falk's piercing grey eyes now resembled two freezing mountain lakes and Ahren's heart became even heavier.

'Yes', Ahren swallowed, 'thank you for your understanding'.

'Oh, I don't *understand* your behaviour. but if I were to report you to the council, you wouldn't learn any more from your mistake, would you?' the Forest Guardian growled. 'And bear this in mind', he said, 'for the sake of two armfuls of firewood, you're now covered in grazes and cuts and probably aching muscles as well. Also, your clothing is ripped, that'll probably take you two hours to mend. Not to mention the load of trouble you're going to have with those other boys. If you'd just stuck to cutting your own wood, you'd only have the aching muscles.'

Taken aback, Ahren stared at the older man. This sober analysis made him realise how stupid and pointless his prank had been.

'I'd be better off going and cutting my own firewood' said Ahren, trying to get out of the conversation. Any more of Falk's unvarnished truths and he'd burst into tears. The last time that happened was years ago. His father had taught him one thing at least. Tears never helped, and anyway, thankful as he was that the Forest Guardian had protected him, he had a tiring day of wood-chopping ahead of him and had to hurry if he wanted to be finished by evening.

I don't want to renew my acquaintance with father's belt, he thought to himself.

'That's the right attitude', Falk nodded, pacified once more. 'Don't forget today's lesson. I've lost the track of a magnificent buck, and I don't want that to have happened for nothing'. The Forest Guardian turned and prepared to disappear into the undergrowth but then he hesitated and turned around again to face the cowed youngster. 'It's strange that the boys chased you so deep into the forest and are looking for your friend now. It seems a little…drastic. Especially as they have their wood again', he continued.

Ahren knew what the Forest Guardian meant. Even if the blacksmith's son was the undisputed king of the village boys and a complete ruffian, trouble with him would only ever amount to a few scuffles. A song and dance like this, wasn't his way of operating. 'It was Sven. He goaded Holken on', Ahren replied, remembering when the situation had escalated.

'Well, that would explain it. Much as I don't want to get involved, I'm going to have to talk to his father', grumbled Falk. And without another word, he turned again and disappeared into the thicket. Thanks to his camouflaged clothing, he was invisible after a few steps. A silence descended in the clearing, leaving a thoughtful, crestfallen young boy who had a mountain of work ahead of him.

Ahren spent the rest of the day chopping wood and lugging it to his father's hut. His whole body ached, his cuts burnt like fire every time sweat ran down them, and he was so tired he could hardly walk straight. While he worked, he pondered over the morning's happenings and the Forest Guardian. This distracted him from the physical pain and helped him to keep going.

Falk was not known for involving himself in village matters. He'd been living in the Eastern Forest for as long as Ahren could remember. Nobody really knew much about him, except that he was a blow-in. Which, in a village like Deepstone, meant anyone who wasn't at least third generation there. The Forest Guardian lived off the beaten track in the woods, liked to keep himself to himself, and lived by the motto: 'live and let live'. Hardly anyone in the village took any notice of him. Except for four years earlier when for once. he was the talk of the village. One of the five seats on the council had become vacant and he was offered the position. He had recently killed a particularly large Fog Cat called Grey Fang, who had been a danger to the village. There was great consternation when the Forest Guardian turned down the offer as no-one remembered anyone rejecting this honour before. Since that time this silent man was left to go about his work unhindered and they respected his solitary way of life. The villagers considered him austere and serious, so Ahren was doubly grateful for what he had done for him today.

Panting, Ahren dropped a heavy branch on the woodpile behind the house and went into the wood once more. He had picked a tree far away from this morning's clearing and so the journey was twice as long. The sun was low now, but he still had to bring back two more branches. He could cut them up into smaller pieces tomorrow. His mind wandered to the Apprenticeship Tests that would be taking place the following week. His prospects really weren't good and he had tried not to think about it for as long as possible. These tests were held every year among the thirteen-year-olds of the village. This made it possible to determine who would be suitable for one of the available trades. The master craftsmen and women might be looking for an apprentice or might wish to promote a particular talent. Being an apprentice had many advantages. You got a little apprenticeship money, you were allowed to drink alcohol,

24

could go to dances, and of course you learned the basics with which you could make a name for yourself later. After some time, you could work as a journeyman or even become a master craftsman. Plus, you belonged to the apprentices, no longer to the everyday village boys. Then Ahren would be free of his adversaries. Nobody messed with an apprentice – out of respect for the master.

No-one knew yet which masters had registered their need for an apprentice with Keeper Jegral, the village priest. Likis was thirteen too, so he would go to the test with Ahren, but it went without saying that his own father, Merchant Velem, would take him on. Holken too would be standing in the village square next week, but it was equally certain that his father wouldn't officially apply and simply claim him as an apprentice during the ritual. Making a claim in this way was frowned upon, as it meant circumventing the suitability test. There would be no risk of another candidate endangering the chances of your child getting the apprenticeship. Likis' father, on the other hand, believed his son had to *earn* the position. As he was a traditionalist, he made an official search, which didn't stop him from preparing Likis as thoroughly as possible beforehand.

That left only Rufus and Ahren as genuine candidates, as no girls were applying this year. Ahren could only hope that at least two more master craftsmen or women would officially register a search. Of course, it wasn't certain that a master who registered would necessarily pick one of the apprentices, but there was a very good chance – as long as you didn't reveal yourself to be hopelessly inadequate in the relevant trade. If you came away empty-handed, you'd be hired by one of the farms or businesses, from where it was almost impossible to get one of the desired apprenticeships. Deepstone was simply too small. Some of the disappointed candidates moved away in order to find work for themselves in a strange place, but most of them moved back within a short time. It was no better in the other villages. A few went off to the big towns, for example Three Rivers, and were never heard of again. A last resort was the army, but the recruiters were notorious for paying a miserable wage.

Hjalgar didn't have a traditional standing army – the country was simply too small, and surrounded by powerful kingdoms. No-one wanted to end up a soldier. One look at the dilapidated border stations and the bored faces of the few soldiers with their dull eyes and you understood exactly how the proverb *'useless as a Hjalgar soldier'* came about. The fact that the small country in the Eastern Midlands had never been seized was due to its peculiar location. It was a buffer zone between the three kingdoms of the Midlands and none of its neighbours dared to invade as that would immediately start a war with Hjalgar's two other neighbouring states. No-one wanted this area to fall into the hands of the other and so Hjalgar had remained one of the safest places on the whole continent for the previous three hundred years. Also, because it had no army, it proved no threat. Lost in thought, Ahren brought the last heavy branch to the hut and admired the sizeable pile of firewood. Then he went in to prepare supper so his father's mood wouldn't worsen.

The next few days flew by. Likis burst into laughter when his friend told him about his little adventure with Holken and his gang, and he dismissed Ahren's worries about him. Of course, the wiry boy had had all the time in the world to safely bring his share of the wood from the clearing to the merchant's hut, and he had spent the rest of the day in one of his secluded hideaways on the river, hoping that Ahren would turn up again. Sven couldn't frighten the feisty young boy. In fact, he wasn't fit to hold a candle to him. The two friends enjoyed themselves with all sorts of silliness, knowing full well that the carefree days of their childhood

26

would be over forever once they had completed the Apprenticeship Test. The children of the village only had to do a few jobs and usually had the full day to do them. If they completed whatever they'd been given to do quickly, then they had a lot of time to play. This would all change the following week. Likis was excited and his eyes shone when he talked about his forthcoming apprenticeship in the merchant's shop, while Ahren pondered his uncertain future. One afternoon the two friends were walking along, deep in conversation, on the main street towards the village square, when Likis tapped Ahren on the shoulder. With a wink and a little nod, he indicated to his friend that he should look around discreetly. Casually turning his head in the direction his wiry friend had suggested, he quickly understood what his friend had noticed. A familiar muscular back could clearly be seen protruding over the rough picket fence of one of the many vegetable patches found beside almost every house in Deepstone. Holken, it seemed, was trying to stalk them.

'Well, hiding isn't one of his strong points', Likis whispered quietly. Then he added loudly, 'Am I glad I'm not in Holken's shoes. His father's been looking for him for ages. Called him a "lazybones" and is really furious. If Hammerhead doesn't make an appearance soon, he'll be in for a real hiding'. Suppressing giggles, the pair leaned against the wall of a hut, clearly visible but at a safe distance from Holken's hiding place, and pretended to be engaged in a quiet conversation. In reality, however, they were watching the ruffian with glee as he became increasingly nervous in his hiding place. Finally, the big boy jumped up and ran towards the blacksmith's, his face a picture of fear, while the two friends doubled over with laughter before running from the scene. They wanted to be gone before Holken realized he had fallen for one of Likis' tricks again. The blacksmith's son never stalked them again.

Two days before the test Ahren and Likis were lying on the riverbank, their fishing rods in the water. The weather reflected Ahren's mood. Dark clouds moved across the skies, the sun occasionally breaking through for a moment.

'Likis?'

'Yes?'

'Is it known at this stage which master craftsmen and women have registered a search?' asked Ahren, his voice a mixture of hope and fear.

'Father proclaimed his quest to the Keeper today, and he also asked who else had visited the priest at my request'. Likis looked mischievously at his friend and continued, 'Master Pragur and Mistress Dohlmen were there. I don't think anyone else will turn up'. Mistress Dohlmen was the village shoemaker. It was true that Ahren had nothing in particular against shoes, and the mistress had a good reputation, but he was also aware that Rufus was very poor at sewing so the selection wouldn't favour him. Yet Ahren too was clumsy with his fingers. Anyway, Ahren knew which Master *he* wanted to impress. Pragur was namely the village bailiff. A bailiff, yes, being a bailiff was something Ahren could easily live with. Everyone respected you, and your armour was made from cured leather. You also had a short sword *and* a truncheon. You trained with those weapons, and only the village council could set aside your rulings. Bailiffs enforced law and order and chased away bandits and other riff-raff. A bailiff was a hero in Hjalgar – or at least what was the nearest thing to a hero in Hjalgar.

As he lay on the riverbank, Ahren imagined himself outdoing Rufus in the Apprenticeship Test and eventually being picked by Pragur. That man was one of the few people in Deepstone who had time for Ahren. He was often called upon to lay down the law whenever Ahren's father became too loud. The peace keeper was always friendly and compassionate to the young boy on these occasions. If he were to become a Bailiff aspirant, he himself could perhaps make a stand against his father. This thought put Ahren into the best of moods.

Likis prodded him in the side. 'And? What do you think, shoemaker or bailiff?'

'Hmm, bailiff would be great', said Ahren. 'All I have to do is beat Rufus in Pragur's test. He isn't particularly strong or fast, so I should be able to manage it'.

'Oh yes, you as a bailiff, then you could always keep an eye on our shop. And your father would have to be nicer to you'. The two friends began building castles in the air and by the time the midday sun had won its battle with the clouds, they were imagining themselves as town council members leading Deepstone towards a glorious future.

It was the evening before the summer solstice, the day when the Apprenticeship Tests were traditionally held, and Ahren was so excited that he could hardly sit still at the supper table. Again, and again he imagined his triumphal election to bailiff, persuading himself that he alone was the correct choice, that Pragur had taken to him kindly, that…

His father, dark rings around his eyes and no longer quite sober, growled, 'Stop fidgeting, boy. Tomorrow you'll be able to do your bit for our livelihood at last. I've had a word with Trell. You can work on his farm for half a crown a week and give me a hand. Good news, isn't it?'

Ahren froze. All his images of the following day vanished in front of his eyes. 'Bu…but the test tomorrow' he began.

'Yes? What about it?' his father interrupted. 'Do you think anyone will take you on with all the mistakes you keep making? You're useless as a fisherman, your shoulders aren't broad enough for heavy labour, and you're always in a world of your own. Just be thankful that I'm able to get you on to Trell's farm without fuss. At least you'll be spared the humiliation of not being selected by anyone'.

The matter-of-fact way in which Ahren's father shattered his dreams filled him with a feeling of hopelessness. Not only was he condemned to working beside his father, but he'd be working for a pittance as well. The thought of having to spend days and years in his father's company horrified him but this made him bolder than usual. 'And what about the position of bailiff?' he ventured.

'I suppose you think you're better than I am? I get a job for you and this is my thanks?! If the work is good enough for *me*, then it's good enough for *you*. You're coming to the farm with me tomorrow and beginning your new job, understood?' The threatening undertone in his father's voice made it clear that any objection would result in a beating.

But Ahren didn't care, not this time, not with these terrible pictures in his head of himself, broken, sitting beside his father with a pitcher in front of him, both waiting in cold silence with bitter looks on their faces, waiting for another day of endless, monotonous work. Ahren was nearly in a state of panic. 'I'm going to be in the fairground tomorrow, and I'm going to take part in the test and become a bailiff and then you can look for someone else you can let off steam at'. No sooner were the words out of his mouth when Ahren recoiled. One look at his father and he knew he'd gone too far, much too far.

'Let off steam?' he roared. 'I'll show you what letting off steam is!' He threw over the table with a crash and grabbed his belt.

If he catches me now, the boy thought horrified, I won't be able to go tomorrow, never mind pass the test and I'll spend the rest of my life here. His eyes bulging with fear, he rushed to the door and pushed the heavy latch to the side. His father locked the door with it every evening and normally Ahren found it very difficult to push the heavy latch aside, but now he was possessed by a hot wild panic and with his first attempt it slipped open. Feverishly he tried to evade his father's drunken fingers while simultaneously opening the door. The whole hut suddenly seemed even darker and more threatening than before. The tar that filled in the joints seemed to be stretching out in an attempt to pen him into the house. He had just managed to open the door widely enough to slip out, when his father's hand grasped his arm and yanked him back inside. With a triumphant yell, the drunken man pulled his own arm backwards, holding the belt ready to chastise his son.

He's not even looking at where he's going to lash me, Ahren realized in shock. It was clear to him that the leather belt would hit his face. In a flash he raised his arm and with a loud slap, the leather strap hit his left hand. Ahren heard a crunching noise as a fiery red pain shot through his wrist. His father raised his arm again only to slip on a plate that had fallen to the ground with the table, and tumbled to the floor.

'The Three be thanked!' Ahren thanked his lucky stars, gathered himself up and quick as a flash disappeared into the forest. The coarse insults of his father rang in his ears as he pushed his way through the undergrowth, scratching his skin all over, and ran to the only safe place he could think of, his tree-house, his *Safehold*.

The cries of his progenitor grew ever fainter, but the final, babbling, tortured cry would remain with him forever. 'It's *your* fault. *You're* the reason she's dead!'

This cry echoed long through the night in Ahren's ears as he lay in a ball in his tree-house, his injured hand pressed against his chest, sobbing uncontrollably for a mother he had never known but whose death he had caused, however unwittingly.

Chapter 2

Midsummer's day began in glorious sunshine which provided a ceremonious invitation to the festivities. Every self-respecting person was there, spending the day mingling on the village square with the other villagers. The village innkeeper served beer and the miller's wife offered her famous little cakes, which were so tasty that it was rumoured the miller had only married her on account of these little delicacies. A look at the miller's portly figure and the plain features of his wife only added credibility to the rumour. The centre of the village community was dominated on one side by an enormous oak tree, whose heavy branches offered protection and shade. Deepstone's vast warehouse dominated the other side. The communal village supplies were stored there and it also served as temporary accommodation for festivities such as this. The two other sides of the village square were lined by the most important buildings in the community. Here you could find the tavern, the forge, the grocer's, the Village Hall, and of course the village chapel. It was the only building made of white stone, and it dominated the area. All the houses surrounding the square had been festooned with cloth garlands that morning and these were fluttering colourfully in the breeze. The Village Hall was the only two storied building on the north side of the square and with its hard-packed clay walls it lent the scene a certain grandeur.

Apprenticeship Day was always filled with laughter. Stories of past Apprenticeship Tests were told and the merits of the new candidates compared. One or two even placed bets on the possible outcomes of the day ahead, although this was officially prohibited by the village council. Everyone was finely dressed, in clothes they would otherwise only wear on the Days of the Gods, when they would stream into the chapel to listen to Keeper Jegral's prayer service. And indeed, here he stood now in full regalia on the festively decorated square, chatting with the council members before striding to the centre.

Three tall poles were rammed into the earth, on top of which were three wooden flags, the symbols of the respective guilds. On the first pole was a wheel with twelve spokes, a symbol of the twelve trading towns that were scattered around the whole continent and that made up the merchants' council. The second flag displayed a leather hunting boot with spurs, in front of a stylized coat of arms. These shoes were only worn by the nobility and only a guild shoemaker had permission to make them. And, last but not least, a short sword in front of the locked town gate, the bailiff's sign, which stood for protection and order.

The priest turned around and recited the opening formula. 'May HE WHO MOULDS hold his guiding hand over this Apprenticeship Test and show to all, what sort of people he has created out of the young members of this village. May the inner form he has given them enrich our community, and may it bring to light today, which calling they each should follow'. His tunic, woven from shimmersilk, glittered in all the colours of the rainbow and lent the thin, bald man with the friendly eyes the impression of constant movement. Every time Keeper Jegral moved. the colours were rolling like waves over his regalia, changing ever so slightly. Spellbound by the interplay of form and colour within the robe, even the smallest children remained still when they saw the traditional clothing of the priest. 'May the young men now step forward to give the future of this village a new shape.'

The three boys stepped forward, all in their best clothes. As if underlining the priest's words, they were quite different from each other in appearance and demeanour, as though the god of forms was showing the gathering how varied mankind could be.

But Ahren was nowhere to be seen.

Likis was cloaked in feast day clothing, which displayed the colours of the merchants' guild – yellow on blue. He stood there, small and slight, and glanced around with a worried look. His friend not turning up couldn't be good, and of course he'd heard the uproar the previous night and was now greatly worried.

Holken was standing beside him, his big, brawny frame forced into a robe much too small for him and which he was wearing with obvious discomfort.

Finally, Rufus, with his nondescript face, stood there shyly in simple but clean clothing.

The clergyman looked at the three youths with surprise. 'Well now, where is Ahren? There should be four boys here, ready to show the world their form'.

A snort could be heard from the beer stand. Edrik, who was celebrating in his own way and was already quite tipsy, shouted 'the young boy won't be coming. He'll be starting tomorrow as a labourer on Trell's farm'. With these words a murmur rippled through the crowd while Likis gasped in shock. An embarrassed Trell meanwhile, stepped from one foot to the other. The gaunt landowner wasn't very popular anyway and he really didn't want to play an unwitting part in this little scandal.

'Oh, well then, if he's already made his decision, I don't want to stand in the way of the Moulder's decision'. Piqued that his ceremony had been thrown into disorder, Jegral was just about to continue when unrest broke out on the fringes of the crowd. It was Ahren, who pushed his way through the crowd, until quite out of breath, he positioned himself beside

Likis. He was filthy, full of badly healed scratches, and his left hand was terribly swollen. He had woken up late from an exhausted sleep, and with a pounding pain in his hand he had dragged himself to the village square. His friend looked at him anxiously. 'Did a carter's wagon roll over you?' Likis followed Ahren's eyes as he looked meaningfully at his father, who had made himself comfortable at the beer stand. Edrik examined his son with a suspicious look and Likis murmured, 'I understand'.

The villagers had recovered from their initial shock and were now whispering intently among themselves. Annoyance at the boy's unseemly conduct was mixed with pity. A feeling of cold contempt began to spread, for a man who hated his son so much that he would shame him in public.

'HE WHO MOULDS will now accompany these young men to achieving manhood. May out of them be moulded men of whom we may be proud', intoned Keeper Jegral, trying to keep the ceremony on the right track. 'Which master today seeks the advice of the MOULDER?'

Likis' father stepped forward. 'Master Velem seeks a boy who can be moulded into a merchant', at which point he looked steadfastly at his son and gave him a wink.

Then it was the shoemaker's turn. 'Mistress Dohlmen seeks a boy who can be moulded into a shoemaker'.

And finally, the bailiff stepped forward. 'Master Pragur seeks a boy who can be moulded into a bailiff'. Jegral made the sign of the THREE in front of each of them and continued.

'The masters and the mistress may step forward and present their tests'.

With measured steps the two masters and the mistress stepped forward and positioned themselves behind their respective guild signs. In unison they uttered the ritual, 'May HE WHO MOULDS guide our process'.

At this point Likis' father stepped forward. 'As merchants you must master the art of counting, so I shall give each of you three problems you must solve'. With a few short words he gave each of the boys three sums to solve. It quickly became clear that Likis was the mathematical genius in the group, as he answered all his questions quickly and correctly. Ahren needed a little longer, but he was surprised to see that he too could answer all the questions. Likis had helped him, of course, when they'd practised together. Every answer was a struggle for Holken, while Rufus could only answer one question. Yet he didn't seem too bothered.

Likis' father turned to Keeper Jegral. 'The boys Ahren and Likis can be moulded into merchants'.

The priest responded. 'Which should be your apprentice, so that he may be finally moulded into a merchant?'

The merchant gave Ahren an apologetic look and said, 'the boy Likis should be a merchant, by the mercy of the MOULDER'.

A cheer rose up from the crowd of villagers, even if the outcome of the choice had never been in doubt. Everyone had assumed Likis would be next in line, and today's ceremony was simply a formality that needed to be observed.

'Then apprentice, take your place by the side of your master,' Jergal intoned and Likis, brimming with joy, went over to stand beside his father, who looked at him proudly as he positioned himself under the merchants' symbol. When Ahren saw this, his heart sank and he almost broke down. He stole a glance at the beer stand and saw his father staring listlessly into space.

A pity that the innkeeper wasn't recruiting this year, thought Ahren. After years of experience, the boy could tell by looking at anyone, how much beer they would tolerate before falling asleep. This black humour helped to cheer him up. He smiled sincerely at his best friend who beamed at him with joy.

Then Mistress Dohlmen stepped forward. 'As a shoemaker you have to be skilled with your hands and know how to handle the leather correctly. Each of you will now, to the best of your ability, put soles on the boots we have ready for you here'.

Three footstools were put before the boys, with needle, thread, boots and soles on them. Ahren struggled to clamp the boot between his legs and to feed the thread through the needle, and soon realized he couldn't hammer well with his bruised hand. Clenching his teeth and ignoring the pain, he did as well as his talent and injury would allow. He took even longer than Holken, and his boots were no great shakes. Mistress Dohlmen examined the boot with a frown and then shook her head. Holken's boot provoked the same reaction. Rufus' sample, on the other hand, showed even, clean stitching. Indeed, while the boy was working, he had been humming quietly to himself, moving the needle in a steady rhythm and everyone could see clearly that the shy young boy must have been secretly practising for weeks. After a few seconds the shoemaker gave a smile of surprise and said with scarcely concealed joy, 'young Rufus may be moulded into the trade of shoemaker'.

Great! Good for her and good for me, thought Ahren. If Holken's father steps forward and calls him to his side as apprentice, then I'll get the bailiff's job. Then I just have to pass the test, and there won't even be any competition. Full of expectation he glanced over at the blacksmith, but he only looked over to his son and gave him an encouraging smile. Crucial seconds passed by with nothing happening and a cold shiver ran down Ahren's spine as the realization suddenly struck him. Holken didn't want to become a blacksmith, but a bailiff! The terrible thought flashed through his head.

Suddenly, the bailiff stepped forward and spoke: 'he who wishes to protect this place and keep the peace must have the necessary skills in combat and be in the appropriate physical condition. As there are only two candidates left, they must take each other on, with wooden sword and shield, and put their abilities to the test'.

Gloomily Ahren observed how Holken nonchalantly took up the sword and shield and held both of them easily, although the shield alone must have weighed at least eight stone.

Now Ahren received his weaponry. Awkwardly he strapped the shield to his injured left hand, and with his right, he clumsily grasped the rough, wooden sword handle. Holken's sword, held with a firm grip, pointed steadily towards the skies while his own continually fell towards the earth. It took all his energy to raise it upwards.

He was in a cold sweat already. He thought of all the tales where weak but nimble warriors defeated mighty but cumbersome monsters. Now, standing opposite the blacksmith's son with the midday sun beating down and the whole village looking on, he didn't believe any of these stories anymore.

'Are you prepared?' asked Pragur.

Holken thundered a powerful 'yes!' Ahren, however, only managed a timid nod, which was greeted with a snigger from one of the village boys. Ahren glanced around once more, looked in the faces of the onlookers and saw pity in almost all their eyes. They had already written him off.

And then Ahren became angry.

They had given up on him, just as his father had given up on him.

Just as he had almost given up on himself!

He gripped his weapons more firmly, felt a painful stabbing in his left hand, and looked resolutely at Holken. His opponent was taken aback by his change of demeanour and gave him a respectful nod.

'He who first drops his sword or surrenders, either through defeat or agreement, is the loser', called Pragur. 'The victor shall be my new apprentice. And now, begin!'

The bailiff had hardly finished speaking when Holken sprang forward and swung his sword down on Ahren. He just managed to raise his wooden sword and parried the blow after a fashion towards the right. His right arm began to hurt with the force of the impact. The shield, Ahren thought, use your shield! The next blow was already coming towards him. Because his left hand was already in pain from just holding the shield, and his right was still slightly numb, Ahren instinctively ducked, and Holken's blade whizzed over him. For his own part, and quite instinctively, Ahren swung his sword towards Holken, just as the latter was preparing to begin a powerful swing of his own. With a loud clash, Ahren's blunt sword landed on his opponent's shield.

A murmur rose from the crowd. Nobody had thought that the delicate boy would last for more than a few seconds, never mind go on the attack. Even Holken seemed surprised and hesitated, giving Ahren the opportunity to hit him a couple more times. These blows were rather ineffective however, as they were repeatedly repelled by the other's shield. Nevertheless, a feeling of triumph grew in Ahren and he fired himself up by thinking: I can do it. I can beat him. I'm going to be a bailiff. I…

Holken brushed Ahren's last sword thrust to the side and rained down a series of punishing blows on the young boy's shield.

Ahren could see stars in front of his eyes. Something went out of place in his hand and suddenly the feeling of a thousand hot needles exploded in his arm, but strangely, his hand now felt totally numb. When he looked down, he could see that his shield was hanging loosely from his arm and his hand was dangling uselessly. The villagers around him were gasping. Another second passed and despite the shock, the feeling in his hand gradually returned. Panting he sunk down on one knee.

Holken took a step backwards. 'Do you yield?' he asked loudly.

An eternity at my father's side, echoed in Ahren's head, and he painfully stood up again. 'Never!' Ahren gasped. The pain was getting worse. 'I can stand, so I can fight!'

The first cries to abandon the fight could be heard from the crowd and Pragur was just moving into position, but Holken had heard Ahren's answer and shrugged his shoulders. He took two steps towards the injured youth and clipped him with his sword, a movement which Ahren wearily parried. But this was only a ploy.

For at the same instant Holken smashed the edge of his own shield with full force down on the injured hand of the stunned youth.

Ahren fell to the ground as if struck by lightning, while an overpowering darkness came over him and washed all sensation away.

He was in the pond again. In the forest and under water. Water which surrounded him and comforted him. It took away all his pain, all his feelings, leaving him comfortably numb. Time was unimportant in this wonderful, cool place. Then he noticed a movement in the pond. Something from below was coming towards him. Something that was bigger than him. The spectre became clearer as it approached inexorably. With horror he recognized the figure of his father, felt how he was being grasped and pulled into the depths. Ahren fought back. Fought with all the strength he could muster, floundered and raged and kicked and somehow tore himself away, but the figure of his father grasped him firmly by his left wrist and pulled him into the depths again. A fiery pain began to rage under his skin, in his hand, where his father was grasping him. Ahren paddled and floundered, but his father's grip was too powerful, the saving light of the surface too far away. The more he pulled, the greater the pain, but Ahren did not want to give up, did not want to go into the darkness his father had prepared for him. Pragur's face loomed on the surface and Ahren thrashed upwards with all his strength, fought his way up from the depths, his left arm in excruciating pain. Then he broke through the surface and opened his eyes.

'He's awake again', said Pragur and disappeared from Ahren's view. Ahren looked around him, totally disorientated. He was surrounded by faces. Holken, Dohlmen, Rufus, Pragur and several more. Dust tickled his nose and the sun stung his eyes. The one constant was the unbearable pain in his left arm. Ahren was afraid to look. To see what had become of his arm. Nightmarish pictures raced through his brain, of him as a cripple, fighting his way through life.

Keeper Jegral's voice intoned, 'Make room, make room I tell you, all of you!' He carved out a passage through the crowd with untypical aggression, and knelt down beside Ahren. 'You'll be alright, young man, you'll see', he said in a friendly voice and took Ahren's mangled hand in his own. 'This day is under the protection of HIM WHO MOULDS, and no-one shall come to grief, if it be not HIS WILL'. Closing his eyes, the gaunt man started to recite in a singsong voice as he manipulated Ahren's injured hand and pushed the damaged bones back into their correct position.

Ahren watched all this as through a veil. The priestly song seemed to vibrate in his head and no pain seemed able to penetrate the movements. The young boy watched with grim fascination how Jegral, with eyes closed, put all the bones under his skin to rights, as if playing with one of those wooden puzzles, where you always had to push the correct piece so that the next one would slot into place.

41

The priest finished his song and a profound silence hung over the village square, broken only by Ahren's heavy breathing. But that too began to ease off as the boy realised that the pain wasn't returning, although the Keeper had finished. Slowly, he tried to move his hand. To his amazement, it felt as if the injuries of the last two days had never occured.

While the boy was staring fixedly at his hand, Keeper Jegral stood up and spoke in a firm voice. 'HE WHO MOULDS has determined the hand of this youth be healed. Let us pray'.

The whole village intoned the litany of the THREE, and Ahren had a little time to recover. Of course, he had heard of the healing powers of the Keeper before, but he had never seen such a miracle healing, never mind experienced it on his own body. Following the death of his mother, his father had broken off all contact with the Keeper. He was bitter that the priest had not been able to heal her. Jegral had tried to explain that the Keepers could only put things into shape. Mend broken bones or re-attach limbs, for instance. The curing of diseases was beyond their competencies, however. An infected lung or a gangrene-infected leg was damaged in its substance, not in its form. But Edrik didn't want to hear of it. And for this reason, Ahren had only spoken to Keeper Jegral about half a dozen times in his life, each time more or less by chance, and only briefly. There would be a beating if his father saw him with the charlatan, as he called him.

Can charlatans cure limbs? he asked himself. His hand was answer enough. He knew why his father hadn't stopped the healing. A quick glance to the beer stand confirmed that Edrik had fallen asleep long ago.

The villagers had finished their prayer in the meantime and Jegral began to speak again. 'Now, Master Pragur, what say you?'

The strong man with the steel-grey hair pushed himself forward and said, 'young Ahren and Holken can be moulded to the position of bailiff'. Ahren's heart jumped for joy.

'As, however, I need only one apprentice, and as I determined the rules beforehand, I select Holken', said the bailiff and turning towards Ahren he continued more quietly, 'you're a brave boy with an impressive will to fight. I would have taken you on as an apprentice too if I could have. But Deepstone is too small for so many bailiffs, and my apprentices would have to move on'. With a last apologetic look to Ahren, he grasped the law enforcer Holken by the arm and placed him by his side in the place of ritual beneath the bailiff's guild symbol.

Ahren slumped down as Jegral began to utter his closing words. Words that would seal his fate. 'HE WHO MOULDS has shown us today how the youths assembled here shall become members of our society…'

'*Forgive the interruption, but we're not quite finished*', a deep, full-bodied voice intoned from the edge of the square. Jegral looked angrily in the direction of the trouble-maker but could see nothing, other than an unusual wooden shape that looked like a crooked sign. The construction started to move and then Falk stepped from behind it and into the middle of the square. He wore the cloak he had made from Grey Fang the Fog Cat. Ahren remembered the beast's reign of terror only as a succession of tedious days. He, like all the other village children, had not been allowed to leave the house until the Forest Guardian had killed the Dark One. He had only seen the Guardian wear this cloak on one other occasion – when Telem, a farm labourer had been sent into exile for robbery. The Guardian had worn the same clothing that time as he led the banished man a day's march to the east and left him there. For weeks after he didn't make an appearance in the village. There were rumours that Telem had tried to win him over and this had really bothered Falk. Yet this somehow didn't fit into Ahren's picture of Falk – the man was simply too stern. A frightening thought struck him. *What, if he wants to lead me into exile. Maybe the village council had judged our prank to be robbery, and as I was the only one to be caught…have I really made so many enemies?* He looked around furtively while fear ran through his youthful veins. But he saw only curiosity in the faces of the others – with the exception perhaps of Jegral. His attitude veered between surprise and annoyance.

'What does this mean?' he asked firmly. 'Why are you disturbing this sacred ceremony?'

'Disturbing? Surely not. I'm lengthening it, in fact'. With that, Falk spun the wooden construction around. It was clear that he had taken his spear, attached Ahren's practice shield (which looked quite the worse for wear) to it, and painted a bow and arrow onto the shield. Ahren saw it in a flash. The Forest Guardian's symbol!

Falk walked briskly until he was beside the bailiff, rammed the spear into the ground and stood in front of it.

'Master Falk seeks a boy who can be moulded into a Forest Guardian', he said in a festive voice before continuing in his normal grumpy tone. 'Apologies for the delay but I had to improvise a guild stake first'.

Jegral gathered himself together after this unexpected entrance while a wild hope sparked within Ahren. The priest began to speak. 'You didn't register your search beforehand. Technically this may not be absolutely necessary. However, it's quite…unusual. What has made you change your mind?'

Falk snorted. 'You can't pick a Forest Guardian over one afternoon, I've said that many a time. We are the one line of defence if a Dark One wanders our way'. As he said this, he stroked his cloak and the villagers shivered. 'With all due respect to the bailiffs who look after security

44

within the village', Falk shot Pragur a look, 'chasing a Grief Wind or a Swarm Claw alone in the wilderness is quite different from throwing a drunkard out of the tavern'.

The Keeper interrupted him brusquely. 'All well and good, but you still have not answered my question. So far you have only repeated the reasons you give every year to justify your refusal to take part in the ceremony'. Jegral sounded annoyed and Ahren hoped that Falk wouldn't goad him any further or his chance would be gone and he'd have to work the fields with his father.

'This year I have found a suitable candidate', Falk continued calmly. 'He has proven to me that he can climb, move swiftly through the wood, and that he is a very competent swimmer. He understands how to camouflage a shelter, and he has shown great stamina and tenacity here today. He has also exhibited valour in taking on a larger and stronger opponent, even while injured'. He turned and looked directly at Ahren. 'There is only one thing missing. The supreme Forest Guardian discipline is archery. And I thought this would be a fitting test for this ceremony'. He bowed slightly towards the Keeper.

Jegral looked like the cat that got the cream. With a delighted look and a friendly voice he said, 'Well, that being the case…set the test!'

Falk approached Ahren and gave him a hunting bow and a quiver with three arrows. Then he called out, 'archery is a difficult art and so I will give the boy three chances to hit the target. It is the alarm bell sounded by a Forest Guardian if the village is in danger. Hopefully, after today, we will not hear it for a long time'. With that, he pointed to the large bell, positioned three paces high in front of the Village Hall. Only the bailiff, the Forest Guardian and the town council could sound this bell. No others were allowed, on pain of severe punishment.

A young boy had sounded it a few years previously as part of a prank. His punishment had been to sweep the village square at the first cock crow in wind, hail or snow. Everyone had steered clear of it since then. Even walking under it meant bad luck. All this went through Ahren's head as he took the bow in his left hand. He placed the arrow on the bow string with his right.

An eerie silence descended on the village square. But there was an almighty racket in Ahren's head, so great was his fear. His young spirit had gone through so much already today. He raised the bow awkwardly as if in a trance. Trying to keep his trembling hand still, he aimed at the bell, twenty paces away. As soon as the arrow left the bow string, Ahren knew it wouldn't hit the target. The arrow bored into the ground three paces short of the Village Hall. A disappointed groan went up from the crowd. Ahren stood there in a cold sweat and Falk looked thoughtfully at him. Then he turned towards the Keeper. 'The young boy is terrified and exhausted. May I have a word with him?'

'Certainly', said Keeper Jegral, giving an understanding nod.

Falk placed his hands on the young boy's shoulders and fixed his eyes on him. 'I know you're afraid, you're tired, and to top it all everyone is looking at you, but you must concentrate. You already shot with a bow, don't you remember?' Falk asked quietly so no-one else could hear.

'Only during the Autumn Festival', Ahren answered shyly. The Autumn Festival took place once the harvest had been brought in and the village prepared for the winter. The adults and apprentices would dance while the children would take part in all sorts of games of skill such as sack races, running competitions, climbing, apple-bobbing or wrestling. During the last three Autumn Festivals, Falk had set up a target range on the edge of the fair. He would let the children shoot with a short bow and practice arrows with cloth balls attached. Ahren had spent a lot of time

46

there, far from the beer stand where his father would make himself comfortable. And far from Holken and his gang. That was how he had first met Falk. But it seemed so terribly long ago now.

The Forest Guardian shook him and whispered, 'it's perfectly natural to be afraid. Everyone is afraid of something. When I encountered Grey Fang, I was afraid too'.

'You were afraid?' Ahren was stunned.

'I'll show you a trick now. Where do you feel safest?'

'Why?' asked the young boy, confused.

'Trust me and do as I tell you. You'll have to get used to obedience anyway, as soon as this is behind you, so you may as well start now'.

Ahren tried to concentrate on the Forest Guardian's question. Where do I feel safest? He immediately thought of the tree house. It was quiet and peaceful there at night and his father couldn't find him there, as he knew nothing of its existence.

'*Safehold*. The tree house I mean', responded Ahren.

'Good. Now try and imagine how you feel when you're there. What it smells like there, what it feels like. What you hear and see whenever you're there and how safe it is there'.

Ahren closed his eyes. His thoughts were whirling around. The hurtful words of his father, the danger of a future on the farm, his injured and now marvellously healed hand. All these thoughts swirled around his mind and he found it impossible to concentrate. He tried thinking of the tree house, looked at it with his inner eye, but the memory of Holken's raging face kept pushing through. No, no! It's safe there, thought Ahren. He clung to the thought. Imagined how it felt when he was there at night. He thought of the late summer breeze wafting from the east, how soft it felt on his skin. Felt it as it passed through the exposed walls. He heard the nightly concert of the forest creatures, as they moved around in the dark. Felt the silence that only a place empty of people brought forth.

'Right, boy, now you have it!' said Falk. 'Now breathe in, hold your breath, draw the bow and shoot'.

The crowd was silent and concentrated completely on the young boy, but he hardly noticed them.

Ahren raised the bow, this time more calmly, though still clumsily, but now not shaking. He drew the bow. He shot.

The arrow ricocheted with a dull clack off the door of the Village Hall, barely a pace from the bell.

Ahren's veins ran cold with panic once again. Not even Falk himself could flout the ceremonial rules. Were Ahren to fail again, it would all be over. Falk would not be able to take him on as his apprentice. The images and fears were tormenting the young boy again. Falk carefully took the bow from his hand and asked him something. But Ahren was in such a state of panic and there was such a roaring in his ears he couldn't understand him. The tree house, think of the tree house, he kept repeating to himself, as if speaking to another person. Slowly the image of *Safehold,* which had only now been smashed and scattered, formed itself again in his mind. With clenched fists he forced his fears away until they existed only on the outskirts of his consciousness. He could feel his legs shaking. Even if he were allowed to take a fourth shot, he sensed he only had reserves for this one last attempt. He was on the point of bursting into tears and knew he wouldn't be able to calm down and hold it together for another attempt.

Falk continued to speak quietly to him and this time the words sank in. 'You did everything correctly, in fact. The shot ought to have hit the target'. Falk rubbed his chin thoughtfully. He was like somebody trying to solve a complicated puzzle. 'Which hand do you use for buttering your bread, boy?'

At first Ahren thought he'd misheard. The question was absurd. So pointless. His mind must be playing tricks on him. He was hearing things. But no. His mind was calm. The picture of the tree house was still intact.

Peace and quiet. A grasshopper chirping.

'Which hand do I cut my bread with? My right, of course. My good hand'.

'Your *good* hand?' Falk's voice had an edge. 'Have you always cut with that hand?'

Ahren was confused again and then he remembered something. Normally it would have embarrassed him. But he was way beyond embarrassment now. After all, this would be his last attempt. 'No. When I was very small, I always used the dull hand', and he raised his left hand. 'But I haven't done that for years', he added quickly. He may have had to make this admission in front of everyone but he could at least reassure Falk that he had been brought up properly. His father had driven out his tendency to use the dull hand through much scorn and endless beatings. As was only right.

But Falk was angry and let out a curse.

I shouldn't have said that. Now he'll think badly of me and won't want me anymore. This thought flashed through his mind. Quickly he concentrated on the inner peace that the picture of the tree house brought about in him. But the picture was beginning to fray and wear away. He could already hear the sound of the other thoughts that wanted to carry him away.

'Damn superstition!' cursed Falk and grabbed Ahren by the shoulders. 'Ahren, this is very important. Now listen to me very carefully. Hold the bow with your right hand and place the arrow on it with your left'. Falk was smiling now. 'Trust me. Everything will be fine'.

Ahren was beyond all emotion now. Nothing made sense anymore. Mechanically, he took the bow that Falk handed to him with his right hand and placed the arrow on it with his left. It felt strange but somehow more fluid. He gathered together all his strength once more and conjured up the tree house in his head. He suppressed all other thoughts. A peaceful calm descended on his spirit. He inhaled and held his breath. Not even his breathing disturbed the inner silence. Everything seemed far away somehow, and unreal.

He raised the bow, tautened it, aimed and let the arrow fly. All within two heartbeats. Then he closed his eyes and breathed out.

The ensuing silence was broken only by the clear sound of a solitary bell toll.

Chapter 3

The ruptured eyes of the two-headed calf foetus looked accusingly up at him as he withdrew his bloodied hands. His efforts were once again in vain. The unhappy animal had been stillborn two days previously and now, to stop the stench, he raised a silk cloth to his nose. A servant scurried by, taking away the ritual bowl along with its gruesome contents. The magic had failed. The circumstances that had led to this bad omen no longer recognizable. The death of the poor creature too long ago. This was the tenth creature in as many months that had come into the world beyond the Border Lands, and none of them could deliver him an answer. The Dream Mirror remained silent and the elves too were baffled, no matter how much he pressed them. A bad feeling had been nagging him for years, like a stone in a shoe. At first, he had put it down to the increasingly fierce power games of the others. But now the cause seemed to have far darker roots. With a sigh he cleaned his blood-soaked hands in rose water and took a piece of black chalk from one of his servants. He would cast a large magic net and hope for the best.

The events that followed were a blur for Ahren. The villagers congratulated him heartily before Keeper Jegral eventually managed to regain control of his ceremony. For the next hour Ahren's ears were ringing and he found it impossible to concentrate on anything for more than three seconds. Every so often Falk would look at him and mumble something to himself. It took a good hour, with the priest's devotions coming to an end, for his head to clear a little. Falk noticed the change in the young boy's expression and whispered to him, 'you'll feel better soon'.

Ahren could only nod. He was still too tired to answer and what answer could he give? A thousand questions whirled around his head, all important and pressing. But when he tried to concentrate on an individual one, it would vanish. There was nothing for it but to stand there and listen to the priest.

'And so, we call for the blessing of HIM WHO MOULDS for the young men tested today, may they always find their place in our community. May they absorb the knowledge of their masters. May they mould it afresh in new forms of knowledge'. With that Keeper Jegral cupped his hands before his chest as a potter moulds his clay. It was the ritual greeting and farewell of the priests.

The devotions ended and the villagers burst into life once more. There was a lot of shouting and laughing, many ran into the Village Hall to bring out tables, long benches, food and drinks. The part of the day the villagers had been looking forward to most was about to begin – the feast. The festive square was ready in no time at all. The villagers settled at their tables, in family groups, surrounded by friends. Ahren felt somewhat uneasy, as he always did on such occasions, and looked for Likis' face in the crowd, hoping he could sit down near him. If his father found him beforehand, he would drag him to a place near the bar. He would then have to spend the rest of the evening sitting there quietly, ready to fetch his father a beer every time he had finished his tankard.

Ahren was hopping from foot to foot, keeping an eye out for Likis, when he heard Falk beside him: 'Come with me and let's sit down'. He marched determinedly through the crowd to a long table where Likis' father was standing with other revellers. Taken by surprise, Ahren followed the Forest Guardian. He had forgotten completely that as an apprentice he could now sit with his master.

Falk came to a halt, and immediately Ahren felt two wiry arms embracing him and heard Likis' voice. 'Wow, Ahren, what a surprise! You and the Guardian!'

Ahren turned around to his friend and looked into his beaming face. He himself must have started smiling too and to his surprise he couldn't stop. I'm going to be a Forest Guardian, thought Ahren. This thought was only now beginning to sink in. 'It's going to take a long while to get used to it', he answered his friend, 'I'm only glad I've escaped the farm'.

Likis grimaced. 'Where is your father by the way? What has he to say about it?'

Ahren shuddered. His father knew nothing of what had happened but the fledgling apprentice didn't want to imagine how he would react. 'He fell asleep during the trials. He probably knows nothing about it'.

'Well, being a Forest Guardian is an honourable profession. I'm sure he'll be delighted for you', answered Likis comfortingly.

Ahren wasn't so sure but kept this thought to himself. He needed more time to come to terms with all the changes that were going to happen in his life. Yet he had no more time, for at that moment Likis' father leaned over to congratulate him. 'You really gave us a fright there, young man, in your fight with our newest bailiff. Congratulations on your new master - there are few people from whom you can learn more'. Then he turned back to Falk and began conversing with him. The two boys exchanged surprised looks for they had never known that the merchant held the Forest Guardian in such high esteem.

Next, Likis' mother pushed her way through the revellers and held Ahren firmly in her arms. 'I knew everything would work out in the end. Rania would have been so proud of you'.

His late mother's name brought tears to his eyes. The thought that she'd be proud of him warmed a place in his heart, a place that had been cold for too long.

'Thank you', he mumbled and could say no more. He had pulled himself together somewhat when she released him from her embrace but the warmth within remained and gave him strength. He sat down beside his master and suddenly realized how hungry he was. Everyone had already started eating so Ahren didn't need to hold back and took everything that he could lay hold on. Mature cheese of a golden-yellow hue, sweetened bread with honey, boar stuffed with wild berries, and plenty of the dark sauce Likis' mother made so skilfully and that she always served when he stayed for dinner.

'It seems expensive times lie ahead for you, Master Guardian', one of the villagers called out, looking at the enormous portion of food Ahren had piled on his plate.

Falk looked at his apprentice with raised eyebrows. 'Well, if we fail to bag the next Dark One, I can always ask Ahren to eat it up. And if that doesn't work, then I'm stumped'.

While the table companions were laughing uproariously, Falk added quietly, 'Your body is trying to compensate for all the energy you expended during the healing, the combat and the Void. Try not to eat too quickly or you'll get sick and throw it all up. Your body needs strength but your stomach must keep pace. So, eat as much as you want, only slowly'.

Ahren didn't quite understand what Falk meant by 'Void' but followed his advice. It wouldn't be a good idea anyway to disregard his master's orders at the first time of asking. To the amusement of the others and to the young boy's own surprise, he took two more helpings – and the portions were no smaller. Once Falk was convinced his protégé had adopted a slower eating pace for the day, he left him in peace with a satisfied contented mumble. Likis, on the other hand, jumped at the opportunity to tease his friend. 'If you keep eating like that, you'll only amount to a bog trotter', he said grinning broadly. 'Falk says it's because of the healing', said Ahren with his mouth full.

'That's true, now that you mention it. I was starving for a week after Keeper Jegral patched me up that time'.

Likis had broken his leg four years previously during one of his climbing escapades. He had fallen three paces from a tree. Vera, the village Healer, told Likis' parents that his bone was shattered and he would probably be limping for the rest of his life. However, Keeper Jegral intervened and summoned the strength of the MOULDER. Ahren had heard horror stories from other villages where the priests would only undertake healings if they received donations or sometimes wouldn't perform them at all, but this was shrugged off as only a rumour in Deepstone. The few disabled villagers were the unlucky ones whom even Jegral's powers couldn't fully heal, and yet there was no ill-feeling among them towards the priest – for he had indeed saved most of them from certain death. Like old Tohl with his missing arm. He had been the one and only victim of the Fog Cat that Falk had killed. The monster had ripped the farmer's arm off and disappeared into the forest with it. Jegral had prayed for many hours and managed to close up the gaping wound and thereby save the farmer's life. Ever since then old Tohl never failed to assist the priest in his ceremonial duties. In fact, Ahren could think of only one person who showed animosity towards Jegral - his father.

Ahren was brought right down to earth when he thought of Edrik. He looked cautiously around for his father but he was nowhere to be seen. He was probably sleeping off his drunkenness or he had made himself at home at the beer barrel without his son. That was fine by Ahren. With a sigh of satisfaction, he pushed the empty plate away and looked around the table. Everyone was deep in conversation. Likis' mother had taken on board her son's attentiveness towards Ahren, who was now feeling quite calm and at ease. The meal had strengthened his body but his friend's friendly words and those of his family had strengthened his soul. He listened to the laughing and joking of the others with delight, saw the genuine closeness among the villagers and watched the torches being put into position. He had lost all sense of time, and only when he looked up at the sky, did he realise how much time had passed by. Darkness was slowly drawing in and soon the torches would light up the festive square. The celebration normally went on late into the night and this one would be no exception.

On an impulse, Ahren spoke to Keeper Jegral as he was passing the table. The Keeper wasn't averse to good food and the occasional tankard but he was a stickler for observing his religious obligations. It was getting dark and so he was returning to his chapel to hold evening prayers as he did every day. It didn't seem to bother him that he sometimes held them without any attendees and he always had a friendly word for the villagers.

'Keeper Jegral?' Ahren asked the priest shyly.

The priest stopped in surprise and paused. Then he spoke. 'Ahren, my congratulations to you on your formation into Forest Guardian. What can I do for you?'

Ahren blushed slightly. He wasn't used to addressing the priest. 'I just want to thank you, Keeper Jegral. Without you my hand would...' He couldn't say the words. He would never have become Falk's apprentice without a healthy hand and would have remained a cripple by his father's side. The priest had saved far more than a boy's limb today.

Jegral nodded patiently and came to Ahren's rescue as he struggled to find the right words. 'It wasn't me that healed you, it was HE THAT

MOULDS. You must thank him. You could do this by attending prayers on Godsdays'. Before Ahren could apologise the Keeper continued, 'I know it wasn't your fault in the past but perhaps I shall see you more often in the future?'

Ahren was still too embarrassed to answer and could only muster a nod. The Keeper gave him an encouraging smile and continued on to the chapel. The young apprentice turned to the table again and Falk, who had been involved in a lively discussion with the others asked curiously, 'what happened there?'

'I just said thanks', he answered.

The Forest Guardian's face softened for a moment and he said, 'that's good. I wouldn't be happy if I took an ungrateful apprentice under my wing. How did the priest answer?'

'I should go to Godsday prayers'.

'Well, that's only right. Remind me in good time'.

Likis' father, Velem, looked over at the two of them and said, 'There's one other thing you two should do to finish the formalities'. Likis' father drew his knife from his belt and passed it to Falk.

'Sit down over there', he said and pointed Ahren to the seat opposite his master's. The boy changed his place obediently. 'You seem to have recovered sufficiently, so now it's time to make the bond'.

As the apprentice sat down, he asked, 'the bond? I've never heard of that'. The conversations around the table had now come to a halt and everyone was looking at the pair.

Likis' father answered, 'It's an old custom that we rarely perform here in Deepstone. In days of yore the pact between master and apprentice was sealed in this way. It was a promise never to leave the other in the lurch, even in the most difficult of times and to make the training the strongest bond until it was deemed completed. In those days it was necessary in order to overcome feuds between families or class distinctions between master and apprentice. It's an important tradition and one worth retaining'.

Falk looked at the knife in his hand and replied, 'But nowadays the position of the master is generally seen as untouchable and he doesn't need to slash his apprentice as part of an old ritual'.

He looked at the merchant reproachfully, who, however remained unimpressed and replied instead, 'my master completed the bond with me and I won't treat his memory with contempt by ignoring his teachings. Likis and I will likewise complete the bond even though we are father and son. You should heed my advice in this matter'.

Once Ahren had heard the word 'slash' he had stopped listening and could only now look at the knife in horror.

Falk gave the merchant a searching look, rubbed his chin as he thought and then said determinedly, 'right then. Let's do it'. He turned to his frightened apprentice and sighed.

'Look at the young boy, we're frightening him to death'. He shook his head and spoke reassuringly to Ahren. 'You have no need to fear. Look', and with a quick cut Falk scratched his palm until a little blood appeared. 'And now you. Put your arm out'.

Ahren obeyed reluctantly.

'You must trust your master', said Falk. Then the fledgling apprentice felt a slight pain as the blade cut his skin.

'Now, put it there!' said Falk and stretched out his hand. Ahren gave his master his hand, the old Forest Guardian gripping it firmly before announcing, 'Now we are master and apprentice'.

'Now you are master and apprentice', intoned Master Velem. Turning to Falk he murmured, 'even if you think this form of ritual is outdated, it's important to do it properly'. He turned to the surrounding tables, all of whom were looking at this point, stood up, and called loudly, 'I as a neutral master witness the bond between Master Falk and Apprentice Ahren. Do any other masters bear witness?'

Many of the assembled seemed baffled at first. This form of ritual was indeed older than Velem had indicated. After a few moments however half a dozen mistresses and masters had raised their hands. Velem sat down again contentedly and turned to the two Forest Guardians.

Falk looked Likis' father in the eyes and nodded once. Whatever was going on between the two of them, Ahren couldn't figure it out. All he knew was, if Falk didn't loosen his grip soon, he would definitely lose his right hand. At this point it had stopped tingling. Falk finally released his grip and fished two clean towels from his cloak. 'Here, press that on the cut. It will stop bleeding in a few minutes.'

Likis got involved now. 'You say it was a spontaneous decision to seek an apprentice, yet you still brought suitable bandages for the bonding with you. We see through you, good Master Forest Guardian!' He beamed at everyone and many nodded in agreement.

'Admit it. You planned it all along'.

'Likis, as a Forest Guardian you always need to have bandages with you. You never know when you need them', Falk responded unmoved.

The others laughed and clapped Falk on the back, and Likis and Ahren exchanged looks. 'Am I glad I'm becoming a merchant', the wiry boy whispered to his friend. Ahren looked at his bloody hand and the bandage and at this moment could only agree.

Two hours later and Ahren had really joined in the merriment the table. There was much laughter. Falk had passed around a bottle of wine and Ahren was allowed to drink too – after all he was now an apprentice – and several songs had been sung. Ahren had only been an observer at these feasts up until now. He had never been a part of them. This feeling of security was remarkably pleasant and he felt a warm glow inside.

Suddenly he felt a calloused hand on his shoulder, and an overpowering smell of beer and stale sweat filled his nostrils. 'So, this is where you've been hiding yourself'. His father's speech was slurred. 'Come on, we're going'. The grip on Ahren's shoulder became even more painful, as was always the case when Edrik's movements had been numbed by alcohol. This hand seemed to be sucking out all the warmth and affection, and the sense of belonging Ahren had experienced over the last few hours. He hardly had time to react when his father turned around and started to leave without loosening the grip. Before the boy had pulled his second leg back from the table, he lost his balance and fell to the ground. His father lost his balance too and crashed against one of the tables. Cursing and swaying, he planted himself over Ahren, when he heard Falk's voice. 'That's my apprentice you've thrown to the ground. You'd do well to help him up'.

The drunkard squinted owlishly as he prepared his words. 'Apprentice? Him?' Edric laughed disdainfully. 'That's my son, and I'm taking him with me now'. With an almighty yank he pulled Ahren to his feet by the hair.

Ahren gave a pleading look to everyone around him and saw Velem whispering something to the Forest Guardian. At which point Falk slowly rose and said in a quiet voice, 'you will leave my apprentice alone or I will defend him according to the old law'. His arms tensed up and Ahren saw muscles like cables bulging under his leathery skin. The older man's posture had completely changed and his whole appearance radiated enormous danger – like a predator sizing up its prey. The question didn't seem to be *if* he would attack his opponent, but *when*. A fire blazed in the eyes of the Forest Guardian such as Ahren had never seen before and judging by the shocked looks of the other villagers, he was not the only one. Only Master Velem gave Falk a satisfied look.

Ahren's father, meanwhile, strengthened his grip. He was too drunk to notice the danger he was in, and began hauling his son away from the light of the torches into the darkness. 'I'm this boy's father, and I decide what's to be done with him until he comes of age. The village will never allow the father's rights to be questioned'.

In the meantime, the bailiff had stood up with his apprentice and quickly approached them. With a slick hand movement borne of years of experience dealing with tavern brawls, Master Pragur freed the young boy from the drunkard's grip and gestured to Holken to step between the adversaries.

Falk calmed down visibly once Ahren was free and resumed his normal, relaxed attitude. Ahren was just as surprised by this transformation as he had been by the first. His master turned and with a quiet voice addressed the bailiff. 'I hereby declare a feud with Edrik the farmworker. As his son is my apprentice, I will take him according to the rights of my bond until his apprenticeship is complete or the feud ended'.

Pragur stroked his moustache and stared at Falk with narrowed eyes. 'The bonding. Yes, I saw the ritual earlier. As did half the village. So, it looks like I can't do anything about it'. He gave Ahren a quick smile before turning to his father. 'The master will take the young boy with him as is the custom. And you, my friend, will sleep off your drunkenness and let the good people here carry on with their festivities'.

Pragur and Holken grabbed Edrik and brought him, despite his loud, drunken protestations, to the bailiff's barrack room. It had a room where troublemakers could sleep off their intoxication. It wouldn't be the first night Ahren's father had spent there.

'That young boy is going to be a first-rate bailiff', mumbled Falk as he watched Holken go off. 'Did everything correctly and reacted well, even if he doesn't particularly like you. You'll really have to match up to that, after all the trouble you've caused'. The twinkle in his eyes softened the blow of what he had said and he laid an arm on Ahren's shoulders, 'We'd better take you home. That's enough excitement for one day'. The villagers had begun having quiet conversations among themselves again and occasionally looked over at the master and his apprentice. Most of them gave Ahren smiles of encouragement. Falk went to the table with the young boy to pick up the rest of his belongings. Master Velen, with his arms clasped in front of his chest, looked up at the Forest Guardian and grinned broadly. He nodded to the merchant once and said, 'I should listen to your advice more often. That was a clever way out you gave me. That wouldn't have worked without the bonding, and Ahren's father would have been in the right. Thank you'. Likis looked up at his father in awe, who shrugged his shoulders and said, 'it stood to reason that Edrik wouldn't let his son go. I was only too happy to help. For years I've had to listen to how that awful man treats his own son. Sometimes it only takes a few well-placed words to emerge the winner in a particular situation. Look on it as your first lesson, Likis'. At that point Velem began to explain to his son and apprentice the finer points of trade negotiations. Falk nodded goodbye to the revellers and led the exhausted boy to his new home.

Chapter 3

The sun was already a hand's span over the horizon when Ahren woke up. There was no sign of Falk and so the young boy looked around the hut which would be his home from now on. He had been worn out the night before and the Forest Guardian had led him to a corner of the room with a mattress and a blanket. The boy had fallen asleep straight away. He could see by the light of day that the hut was quite big enough for one person. It was completely finished in wood. At first glance there didn't appear to be any joints in the wood but when Ahren went closer to the wall and looked more closely, he saw that each beam was cut perfectly into the next. He had never seen such accurate craftsmanship. The furnishings in the hut, on the other hand, were very plain. A simple stool adorned a round table. There was a shelf on the wall, with a few wooden bowls and cooking utensils. The massive chest in the corner of the room was padlocked, so it probably contained all the Forest Guardian's worldly belongings. The cooking area consisted of a pot on a tripod, over which a hole in the ceiling was visible. No fireplace. No oven. Ahren pulled the blanket back and stood up. The bed on which he had spent the night seemed to be made out of some kind of fibrous material which he didn't recognize. The mattress was only two fingers thick and yet the young boy had slept better on it than on the usual straw mattress two hand spans thick. He was still puzzling over the material and design of the mattress when the room darkened. He turned his head and saw Falk standing in the door.

'Good morning, Ahren. It's good that you're awake. I wouldn't have let you sleep much longer'.

'Good morning, Falk…I mean, Master Falk', Ahren caught himself.
'We actually get up much earlier, but because you had to go through rather a lot yesterday, I've decided on a more leisurely start to the day so I went to get a few things. As you can see, I'm not set up for guests, never mind an apprentice'. Ahren was taken aback and had another look around. There really were no more mattresses. 'Where did you sleep?'

Falk pointed with his thumb over his shoulder. 'Outside. If it's warm and dry enough, I feel better in the open air'.

Ahren glanced through the window in the direction indicated. Five paces from the house there was a broad fir tree and at its feet there was a blanket. His master didn't seem to place much value on comfort.

'First we eat', Falk decided and brought over a newly constructed stool which he placed opposite the other one. Then he took a bundle wrapped in an oilcloth from his back and slowly laid it on the ground.

'I can imagine you have a few questions. If you have too many questions in your head, there comes a point when you can't hear the answers anymore'.

With practised movements Falk quickly lit a small fire under the pot. 'Unpack your things while the stew is warming'. Falk stirred the spoon in the pot with one hand and pointed with the other at the bundle he had put down on the floor. Ahren went over to it with curiosity and opened out the oilcloth. He gasped in surprise. He saw a pair of boots, a jerkin and leggings, all made from buckskin. There was also a hunting knife in a buckskin scabbard.

Wide-eyed he stared at the treasures in front of him. The boots alone looked better made than anything he had ever worn. His father had never brought much money home and had drunk most of it, leaving Ahren very often dependent on the charity of the other villagers. And so, he often wore the cast-offs of the other village boys, and these were continually

64

patched up until he had grown out of them. He had never seen clothes like those lying in front of him. He looked up at his master with gratitude, but he had turned his back and was fully occupied with the stew.

'You're lucky that I placed an order for a new set of clothes with Mistress Dohlmen. I collected them earlier. The woman is up almost as early as I am. Her new apprentice Rufus doesn't seem too happy about that.' Falk laughed heartily before continuing, 'what you're wearing at the moment would have been in tatters by the afternoon. Not that they'd be much of a loss, but you'd have lost half your skin as well'.

He could have given me his old clothing and held onto the new for himself, thought Ahren.

'Thank you', he said. 'But I'm afraid I'll have to remain in your debt'. He wanted to keep things clear between them before he even touched the clothing. The Forest Guardian turned around and looked at him with raised eyebrows.

'Don't worry about that, you'll be earning those clothes. I meant what I said on the village square yesterday. You have what it takes to become a Forest Guardian. I don't take on apprentices lightly. In fact, you're the first. It will be a learning experience for the two of us', said the Forest Guardian with a twinkle in his eyes and turned again towards the fire. 'You should put on the things and see if they fit. Mistress Dohlmen did make a few alterations early this morning. That woman really has a good eye, but we want to be sure, don't we? What's important is that you can move well in them but that they're not too big. Oh, and behind the house is a stream if you want to wash yourself first'.

Ahren nodded and disappeared behind the hut with his things. A small stream, perhaps two paces in width, gurgled along behind the house. The current was gentle and Ahren stomped, snorting, into the water until it reached his hips. The clear, cold water banished all tiredness from his bones, and after he had dried himself with his old clothing, he slipped into his new. The leather was supple and had already been oiled, and everything fitted well, apart from the shoulders and the leggings. The boots were a little big but Ahren had experience in making clothes fit. He stuffed the front of the boots with strips of cloth he had cut from his old shirt, he rolled up the leggings and cushioned the shoulders. Within a few minutes he was finished and went back into the house. Falk was already waiting for him with two steaming bowls of stew. The Forest Guardian offered him a bowl and eyed him critically. 'It'll do for now. You'll have grown into them soon. Now eat and ask what you have to ask'.

Ahren took a spoonful of the stew which consisted of rabbit, vegetables and several herbs he couldn't identify. In an effort to win time he tasted the food, chewed it slowly while he tried to think of what he wanted to know first. The food tasted amazing and Ahren noticed that the same hunger came over him that he had felt the previous day at the feast. His body still needed to compensate for the healing process of the previous night. In order to eat his food in peace he threw the first question he could think of into the room.

'Why did you decide to take part in the apprentice search in the end? Why are you going to so much trouble on my account?'

'As I already said, you have what it takes to be a Forest Guardian. There's a girl in Two Rocks who would also be suitable but her Apprenticeship Trial isn't until next year. I saw how you fought your way through the tests. You did your best without complaint or excuses in spite of your injury and you didn't give up. But it was something else that tipped the balance'.

Ahren froze, his spoon half way towards his mouth, 'and what was that?'

Falk studied the boy for a moment before he spoke.

'Bad people are not born that way, they are created. By us. By all of us. What we experience, shapes us. And in a permanent way. Throw enough weeds into a well and it becomes poisoned. Clean it regularly and fish out the weeds, you always have clear water. Sven, the miller's son? He was always a timid boy, but that doesn't make him into a bad person. Yet if his parents don't take the fear away from him, but stoke it up so that they can keep him under control, then he'll continue to hide behind every strong back he can find and use every bit of power he can lay his hands on'.

Ahren shuddered as he remembered the look Sven had given him at the tree house. Could fear really create so much anger?

'I've seen and heard how your father treated you, and so far, you've put up a great fight in order not to be influenced by it, or at least not much. But the thought of what would happen to you if no-one intervened was unbearable. Sometimes we create the biggest monsters by doing nothing'.

Ahren was both confused and annoyed. The thought that Falk could see a future monster in him was far from flattering. His reaction could be seen in his face because Falk continued, 'that wasn't what you wanted to hear, was it? But it's important that you understand it. If I hadn't intervened, you'd probably become a bitter, sad man. Unfortunately, bitter, sad men have the habit of spreading more sadness and bitterness, and some of those people are particularly successful…I know what I'm talking about'.

Falk gazed into the distance as he spoke. There was a sadness in his face before his features softened and he turned to Ahren again.

'Our work as Forest Guardians will repeatedly lead to confrontations with the Dark Ones. How will you fight a Grief Wind if you haven't learned to subdue your bad experiences?' Falk didn't wait for an answer but continued.

'You're a good person and you can become a good Guardian. If I hadn't stepped in, you'd be at the very least, a sad person and certainly no Forest Guardian. Wasn't that a good enough reason?'

Ahren nodded shyly. He was grateful to his master, but the thought that he had been selected in order to prevent a greater evil remained.

Falk could see that his apprentice was not completely persuaded, but decided not to press further. The young boy had little reason to trust people, and his little speech had undermined the boy's self-confidence even more. He decided to change the subject. 'Have you ever actually held a real bow in your hand? I don't mean that old thing with the practice arrows from the Harvest Festival. Your last shot yesterday was really very good. The bow tautened, raised, aimed and released in a single flowing movement. I had a look at the bell this morning. It wasn't just a glancing shot. It was a bull's eye'.

The Guardian's words had their effect. Ahren's face lit up and youthful vivacity came flooding back into him. Of course, the fact that he'd just finished his fourth bowl of stew might have helped too.

'No, I've never shot with a real bow and arrow. But it was all so easy somehow, once it was calm in my head and I'd swapped hands'. He looked down at his right hand which held the soupspoon.

'We'll have to work on that, boy. There's nothing wrong with using the left hand, that's just superstition. Does your father come from the Low Marshes?'

Ahren nodded, carefully took the spoon in his left hand and answered deep in thought. 'He grew up at the edge of the Border Lands. He wanted to get away from there like so many others and move further in to the

Midlands. There is no more peaceful kingdom in the Midlands than Hjalgar so this is where he settled'.

'Yes, the people there have strange ideas. Their proximity to the Pall Pillar has made them too cautious and superstitious if you ask me'.

Falk pointed at Ahren's hand, which was holding the spoon rather clumsily. 'It'll take you a while to get used to it. Then everything will be much easier, believe me'.

Ahren looked up with curiosity. 'And what was that, the...Void, I think you called it yesterday'.

The Guardian nodded. 'Ah yes, the Void. That's the trick I showed you. That's where you concentrate on emptying your mind. I'm surprised it worked so well. On the other hand, I've heard that some people in extreme situations were able to do it in no time at all. But don't expect it to work so quickly the next time'.

'Oh', said Ahren, disappointed.

'I'm not saying you won't be able to learn it, but it takes time. Anyway, I had to improvise yesterday. The tree house probably won't last as a focus point for too much longer, unless you're more attached to it that I thought'. He smiled at the youngster.

'A focus point? What do you mean?'

'The picture you concentrate on when you're trying to reach the Void. But we'll deal with that later. Do you have any other questions?'

Ahren looked down at the knife that was sheathed in his scabbard in front of his chest. Before he could ask his question, Falk said quickly, 'Oh no. That will stay where it is for the moment. The knife is only to be used in absolute emergencies unless I say otherwise. In our line of work, you've made a terrible mistake if you get so close to an animal that you must use it to defend yourself. First, you have to get to know the forest, and really take in everything that I teach you about it. We can also train your left hand at the same time. Then we'll see how it's going'.

Falk stood up and opened the lock of the chest, using a small key which hung on a leather strap around his neck.

'Why don't you make yourself useful and do the washing-up while I assemble the things we need for the day'.

Ahren stood up obediently and carried the bowls out to the stream. When he returned to the hut a few minutes later, Falk had a bow in his hand and a big rucksack on his bag.

'Today I'll carry everything while you try to keep pace. Let's go'.

As he spoke, Falk walked quickly towards the forest and Ahren hurried alongside him. The first day was promising to be really easy. He'd been in the forest so often before and would have no problems keeping up with a heavily laden older man.

An hour later and Ahren was flat on his back again, gasping for air. Falk was squatting beside him with an amused look. It had taken only a few minutes after the start of their march for the penny to drop with Ahren. Falk was going to keep up the fast pace he was using. That in itself wouldn't have been a problem. Yet neither the trees, nor the uneven ground, nor the undergrowth nor even the little streams would slow Falk down. The same couldn't be said for his young companion. He had never been clumsy in the forest before but the speedy pace ensured that he couldn't avoid the branches in time and he also stumbled over roots and got caught up in the brambles.

Now he understood what Falk had said earlier when he had spoken about Ahren's old clothes and how they would be in tatters. The buckskin protected him from thorns and the whipping branches. His old clothes would have been torn and useless within minutes. And as for his skin, Ahren shuddered to think what state it would have been in by now.

He stumbled behind Falk, keeping pace after a fashion, gasping for air and cursing to himself whenever he managed to get enough air into his lungs. As soon as the Guardian stopped, Ahren collapsed on the spot. It was a mystery to him that Falk hadn't sent him back to the village there and then.

'That will do for the moment. Once you've got yourself together, we can have a look at the plants that are growing here'.

Ahren nodded gratefully and listened intently as Falk showed him the various plants in the clearing.

After a quarter of an hour he said, 'Right then, up you get! We've a long way ahead of us.'

Groaning, Ahren struggled to his feet and followed his master into the forest. And so, the day went on in this fashion. An hour's march. Then a quarter hour break, during which time he learned to recognize the different plants. Falk always seemed to seek out the places where many different varieties of plants could be found.

By the time they were returning to the cabin in the late evening, Ahren could hardly place one foot in front of the other. Falk took off his rucksack and said, 'so my boy, let's see what you've remembered'. He produced many bundles of green plants and laid them out on the grass. 'Tell me which ones you recognize and what they're called'.

Ahren could hardly believe his ears. His legs were no longer his own and he had an overpowering desire to curl up into a ball and fall asleep. As he looked at the plants lying in front of him, he realized he couldn't identify a single one. Falk was silent and let the boy think. Ahren considered them for a long time as he really wanted to name at least one of them. His eyes wandered again and again over the various branches, grasses, berries and mushrooms. Finally, his eyes settled on a reddish plant. He pointed at it and said uncertainly, 'Wolf Herb?' Even to his own ears it sounded more like a question than a statement.

'Can you identify another one?' asked Falk.

The young boy shook his head. His ears were red. First, I spent the day trudging and panting my way through the wood as if I had never been in the open air before, and now I can only identify one measly plant, thought Ahren forlornly. He was downcast. Of course, Falk would send him back. Would explain that he'd made a mistake. That Ahren would never evolve into a good Forest Guardian.

But his master merely nodded, gathered everything up and placed it into the chest. 'That was very good. It took me three days before I could even recognize one. My master was at his wits' end'.

The young boy looked up in amazement. It seemed absurd to him that his master could ever have struggled with the same problems. Surely Falk was only softening the blow.

His disbelief must have been written all over his face because once Falk had stored all the plants, he looked up and chuckled. 'It's only natural that you don't believe me. You should just keep in mind that I've had a much longer time to practise than you have. One plant is a good result for your first day'.

Falk fell silent and Ahren thought that his master must be finished, but then he continued and fixed Ahren with a steely look and spoke with an intense urgency. 'You must think in small steps. One plant after the other. One step after the other. There are so many things to learn, so many things you don't know about yet. Things that are second nature to me now. I'm sure it seems like an impossible task to you. But there's only one rule that's essential for your training: never give up. You can make mistakes, you can learn incredibly slowly or be clumsy all you like, but you cannot give up. If you don't, you'll learn everything from me that I know. And in all honesty, that's not quite a lot'. The grin reappeared on Falk's face and he slapped his apprentice on the shoulder.

The young boy could only stare at his master in silence as he thought about everything he had heard. Never give up. His master had reduced all his fears and doubts into this simple rule, and this had an incredibly soothing effect on Ahren.

Because a promise resonated through Falk's words, one which deeply moved the youngster: As long as he didn't give up, then Falk would not give up on him either.

After they had polished off the rest of the stew from the morning, the youngster lay down on the mattress and fell asleep immediately. His quiet, deep breathing filled the hut and Falk noticed that his apprentice was smiling in his sleep. The old man couldn't possibly know this. But it was the first time in years that Ahren was at peace in his sleep.

Chapter 4

Whatever had Ahren smiling in his sleep, the next morning was hell. He was woken up by his master's low humming, as he warmed up an herbal soup. The delicious aromas permeated the little cabin and the boy's stomach started to rumble. He moved to get up, but groaned hoarsely and clenched his legs. The least movement and he felt as if he were being pricked with needles.

Falk turned around when he heard the groans of his apprentice. 'Good morning, Ahren', he said with a chuckle. 'Are you hungry?'

'The soup smells good master but it would taste even better if you had a new pair of legs for me'. Ahren sat up clumsily and pulled his legs slowly under him so that he could stand. It took all his willpower not to groan again but he gave a clenched smile to his mentor.

Falk nodded knowingly. 'That's good. You're fighting your way through. Don't give up. Come here, the soup will help you. Some of the herbs will ease the pain and others will help your muscles to get through the day'.

The boy walked unsteadily to his stool and looked at his companion in horror. 'We're running again today?'

'No, we're not', said Falk with an impassive look.

'Great'. A wave of relief came over Ahren and he flopped down on the stool.

'We'll go at the same pace today as we did yesterday. I think that we'll wait with the running for a bit'. The old man's demeanour remained the same but Ahren truly believed that his master was enjoying every second of this.

Resigned to his fate Ahren grasped his spoon and tried the food. The soup was strong and thick, the taste was intense and spicy, and Ahren had swallowed three bowlfuls within minutes. As he reached for the bowl again, Falk shook his head.

'That's not a good idea, boy. Any more and you'll get sick as soon as we leave the house. Your body needs to regain the energy you lost through the healing but it has to be done slowly. Why don't you wash yourself and get dressed while I prepare everything for today's march?'

Ahren recognized an order, even if it was formulated politely, and stood up obediently. To his surprise he realized that the stiffness in his legs and the pains had become distinctly more bearable. Whatever was in the soup had had an immediate effect. He clamped his leather clothing under his arm and left the hut while his master began tidying up. When he came back a few minutes later, Falk was already dressed and was equipped with the same rucksack as the previous day, although it looked distinctly heavier today.

'Ready. Then let's go'. Falk tossed something to Ahren, which bounced off the surprised boy's chest and rolled across the floor. He bent down to pick it up and saw that it was a leather ball, not quite the size of a fist. He looked over questioningly at the Guardian, who gestured to him to throw the ball back. 'With your left', he said firmly.

Ahren threw the ball somewhat clumsily to his master, who then left the hut and strode quickly into the undergrowth. His apprentice followed him into the warm summer's day with a sigh and resigned himself to his fate. He trotted a while to catch up with Falk when suddenly the ball flew at him from the greenery. He just managed to pull his hand up –

otherwise the thing would have hit him in the face. As it was it just bounced painfully off his hand – his right one.

Falk's voice echoed through the forest. 'With the left, boy. And don't just stand there. The way is long today. And I'd like the ball again!'

Ahren rubbed his hand with a curse, picked up the ball and ran wearily into the forest.

The hours passed as they had done the previous day. Except that Falk would throw him the ball again and again, and Ahren would have to catch it with his left hand and throw it back again. This meant that the apprentice not only had to keep up the pace, avoid the branches, and look out for the roots, but also keep sight of Falk, as he never knew where the cursed ball would fly from next.

Ahren was spurred on by the realization that the leather ball really hurt when it hit his face, which happened regularly at the start. Any time he dropped the ball he would have to follow it and then catch up with his master, who didn't wait of course. Ahren never thought he would hate anything so much in such a short time as this small piece of sewn leather.

It was almost noon. Falk had just placed the plants in front of him, which he brought with him in the rucksack instead of plucking them again. He looked at the position of the sun in the sky and said, 'now we should be there soon, so be on your best behaviour'.

'Be where soon?' asked Ahren in surprise.

'At Vera's of course. Don't you know where we are?' Falk sounded genuinely surprised.

Ahren looked around and recognized that they were in an offshoot of the forest that was known by the villagers simply as *Herbal Grove*. Vera, the village Healer lived here, and Deepstone itself was only a few hundred paces away. They must have been running in a wide curve. Ahren hadn't been paying any attention to his surroundings on account of his exhaustion and perpetual concentration.

'What do we have to do here, master. Are you ill?'

'Don't be silly. Who do you think she gets her herbs from if they grow in inaccessible places and can't be raised in her garden?'

Now that his master had mentioned it, he remembered hearing that Vera had been helped by the Guardian. The woman was over 80 summers old and couldn't walk so well any more, but there wasn't a family in the village she hadn't assisted, healing an ill family member or saving domestic livestock. For this reason, she always had a steady stream of visitors who supplied her with everything she needed. She also loved chatting and listening, which made her the best port of call, along with the tavern and the village well, if you wanted to hear the latest news – which only increased the willingness of the villagers to give her a helping hand.

Falk looked at the boy sternly. 'This will be your first appearance as my apprentice. Be polite, speak as little as possible and don't get in the way'.

'Yes, Master...' Ahren stammered.

He knew Vera. The old woman was always friendly to him and Falk's harsh instructions seemed over the top. Unless he's ashamed of me, he thought quickly.

Falk seemed to realize what Ahren was thinking and he said in a milder tone, 'the Healer's house is a hot bed of rumours, I don't want you to say anything that could be taken the wrong way. The beginning of your training was dramatic enough, and the bonding ritual I performed with you was unusual too. We don't want to add grist to the mill'. And with that the Guardian threw the leather ball at Ahren, who had been staring at his master but instinctively raised his left hand and plucked the ball out of the air. He tossed the ball back to his master in triumph.

'That's a start', said Falk and nodded.

They went a little further and came to a small clearing that lay directly at the forest's edge. Only a few trees separated the small, thatched log cabin with its large tidily cultivated herb garden from the first houses of the village. A well-worn narrow brick path snaked its way between them. Everything was neat and tidy. The herb garden was surrounded by a thick wooden fence and there was even a luxurious flower bed just before the front door, wafting beautiful smells in the late afternoon sun.

Ahren had only been here twice before and that was in autumn and winter. It looked so different now and it took him a few seconds to recognize the place.

Falk gave him another stern look as they reached the front door. They could hear voices from the inside conversing cheerfully. Obviously, the latest morsels of gossip were being exchanged and Ahren understood now why his master had insisted on a note of caution.

Falk knocked on the door, the voices fell silent within and they entered the house. A friendly woman with a smile on her deeply wrinkled face was sitting in her rocking chair. Although it was warm, her legs were wrapped in a woollen blanket. A young woman had just risen from the stool and was picking up a basket. It was Senja. Her mother was the village weaver and she was the eldest daughter. 'I'd better be going now, I've wasted too much time already', she said. She nodded to the herbalist, smiled uncertainly towards Falk and Ahren and darted out before hurrying away quickly. The boy looked after her thoughtfully. Was he mistaken, or had she been afraid of them?

'Now, now, don't be brooding', said the old woman instead of a greeting, and smiled at Ahren. She seemed to see right into him with her clever eyes.

'You two with your leather gear and your knives are well capable of giving a right fright to a pretty young thing'. Falk snorted and bent down to give Vera a kiss on the cheek. 'The boy worries too much about what other people think of him, but I'll drive that out of him'.

She smiled up at him and patted him on the cheek. 'Don't be too hard on him or he'll run away from you yet'.

Ahren was totally taken aback by his master's friendly, even affectionate behaviour.

'That would be pointless', said Falk. I'm a Forest Guardian, I'd find him. Anywhere'.

At least that sounds like the Falk I know, thought Ahren. He positioned himself in a corner of the room and tried to be as unobtrusive as possible, while looking around with curiosity. The house was one-roomed just like the Guardian's lodgings, and the beams in the roof were festooned with bundles of herbs. They were hanging from them at differing stages of the drying process. There were shelves on two walls, with pots, jugs and little jars, all labelled in tidy handwriting. A cooking area and a narrow bed filled the other walls. A table with two stools, as well as the large rocking chair Vera was sitting on, stood in the middle of the room.

Falk began to empty his rucksack and to spread out the herbs he'd gathered the previous day on the table. Vera looked at him as he worked with a contented smile on her lips.

'They'll do for a while. You've brought an unusually large amount of plants today, even some I have here in the garden, although I have only a few of each sort'.

Falk pointed with his thumb towards Ahren. 'Basic training'.

Vera nodded. 'Typical Falk. Why give one task when you can do two or three at the same time'.

The Healer waved Ahren towards her and pointed at the plants on the table. 'And? Do you recognize any of them yet?'

As Ahren approached the table he felt Falk's penetrating look and immediately began to sweat. He took up the red plant that he had identified the previous day and said 'Wolf Herb'.

'Good. Keep going'. The old woman's gentle eyes seemed to radiate total confidence in his abilities so that he felt unable to explain that he'd only heard of medicinal plants the day before.

Instead he looked down at the table and tried to remember. Low Herb and Blue Head. And this one had to be Sharp Thistle. Ahren was pointing at the individual herbs which had individual characteristics or striking colours. He had tried to concentrate on the plants that had stood out during the break earlier in the day, and this was now helping him. But there were another thirty bundles in various shades of green on the table that said nothing to him. His two older companions looked at him fixedly. Vera patiently and Falk sternly.

A gust of wind carried the sumptuous aromas from the flowerbed at the front door into the house and this gave Ahren an idea. He bent down over the table and immediately two intensive scents filled his nostrils. 'Stink Weed, and Sneeze Root'. He had identified two further plants.

Falk snorted contentedly and Vera gave a smile of encouragement.

'You've found yourself a clever apprentice, you old fox', she chuckled.

Ahren beamed with pride and looked up at this master – only to be surprised by the leather ball, which hit his nose. He shot his left hand up far too late and only managed to give himself a blow under the chin.

'A start', said Falk drily while his apprentice angrily chased the leather ball and cursed silently to himself, using every bad word he had ever learnt.

When he stood up again and turned around, he saw that the old woman had a very serious look on her face.

'Be careful out there, and take care of the boy. One of the woodcutters saw a deer last week that had literally been torn to shreds, as if by a Blood Wolf'.

Ahren held his breath. Had he heard correctly?

Falk snorted. 'You know what the woodcutters are like, superstitious to the last. They're always seeing things that aren't there'.

'It won't do any harm to take a little care, though', Vera added.

Falk responded in a calm voice. 'Blood Wolves rarely venture this far east. The last one I saw was over twenty years ago. And anyway, they're unbelievably territorial. If there was one here, then there would be dead wolves and bears lying all over the forest'.

Ahren gave a strangled gasp and Falk turned to look at his apprentice. The boy had gone pale with fright and was staring wide-eyed at Falk.

'Look what you've started with your idle chatter. The boy is totally shocked', grumbled Falk. He went up to the terrified boy and put a hand on his shoulder.

Ahren looked up at him and stammered. 'Can a Blood Wolf really kill a bear?'

Falk led him to the table where the old woman was sitting and looking at the boy keenly. He gently pushed him down onto one of the stools and sat beside him. 'This was really only supposed to be discussed much later on in your training but as the subject has now been broached, we might as well get it over with'.

Falk shot the herbalist an angry look, but she looked back at him serenely. 'What do you know about the Dark Ones? Falk asked in a quiet voice.

Ahren's mind was racing. His head was full of the old stories that were told around the camp fires or late at night during the Winter Festival. 'They…they can turn themselves into smoke, they eat the souls of their victims, and before you die, they make you go mad. They're full of hate and teeth and claws and they're the servants of HIM WHO FORCES'. He could only whisper the last few words.

His master gave an amused look before becoming serious again. 'That's all true but not all Dark Ones possess all those powers. Otherwise the Adversary would certainly have won that time. There are more than twenty different Dark Ones that we know of. Each individual one has his own unique powers and they all serve HIM'.

Vera slowly got up from her rocking chair and shuffled heavily to one of the shelves. From there she fetched a bottle and three beakers and placed them on the table. She filled the beakers with an amber liquid while Falk continued. 'About a dozen of these Dark Ones are really relevant to us Forest Guardians. And only very rarely does one of them come into this neck of the woods.'

Vera passed them their beakers and sat back on the rocking chair with her own. She closed her eyes and took a sip.

Ahren carefully smelled at his beaker and his nostrils filled with the sweet pungent smell of honey mead. He looked at the beaker in awe. Only the wealthy villagers could afford this drink and then it was normally served in thimble-sized cups. Ahren had never been near a full beaker before. For a moment he even forgot his fear as he admired the priceless treasure.

Falk absently raised the beaker to his lips and continued. 'Blood Wolves were once normal ice-wolves, the largest wolves that exist in nature. The Adversary forced them under his control. He made them larger and stronger. The more blood they drink, the mightier and angrier they become. In the Dark Days, the first rule of thumb was to kill the opposing army's Blood Wolves, before they had torn apart too many of their enemies and their frenzy had become almost unconquerable'.

Ahren listened in fear and gripped his beaker of mead. Without thinking, he took a drink and felt a warm burning sensation spreading down his throat and into his stomach.

'An adult Blood Wolf can easily defeat a bear, and that's why I'm certain none has entered the forest. I would have heard it long ago and seen its path of destruction'.

The mead was slowly having its effect and Ahren's head began to feel light. His fear of the Blood Wolf disappeared in a gentle fog that seemed to envelop his thoughts. He had relaxed considerably. Vera gave a grunt of satisfaction as she saw the change in the apprentice's appearance. Falk gave him another encouraging tap on the shoulder as he glanced darkly at the Healer.

'It was completely unnecessary to upset my apprentice like that. A lecture on the Dark Ones is definitely not for the second day of training'.

Ahren emptied his beaker. The deliciously sweet yet spicy taste of the mead, and the feeling of drowsiness and fearlessness that it gave him, gave rise to a leaden heaviness in his arms and legs, and he could feel his eyes closing.

Suddenly there was an almighty bang that startled him, his eyes shot open and he saw the stern, weather-beaten face of the old Forest Guardian a mere hand span away looking at him. For a moment Ahren was back in his father's dark hut, and as he screamed and shot his arms up in an effort to protect himself, he threw his body backward, his stool tipped over and he fell back in a tangle of arms and legs.

He stared up at his master in a fog. Falk's hand still lay flat on the table where he had let it fall in order to wake the boy. Vera clicked her tongue disapprovingly and Falk scratched his beard with an embarrassed look on his face.

'I think we're going to have to get to know each other a little more. I'm really sorry, boy. That's how my master used to wake me up, whenever I dozed off doing my exercises. I still forget that you've grown up differently than me'. Ahren picked himself up off the floor, his heart was pounding and he could only nod, because he didn't trust himself to be able to speak. Neither of them could utter a word and so the two Forest Guardians only looked at each other in embarrassment.

Suddenly a high squeaky sound could be heard that broke the awkward silence and both of them turned around to Vera in surprise. She was giggling into her shawl. 'You almost managed a summersault and your feet rubbed off the herbs hanging off the ceiling', Vera spluttered, overcome by a fit of giggling and pointed upwards. Falk and Ahren looked up in surprise at the slowly swinging bundles of herbs and burst out laughing themselves. Their mutual embarrassment was punctured by the hilarity of it all.

Falk shook his head, finished his mead and stood up. 'That didn't exactly go according to plan. You were supposed to learn something about herbs. Instead we frighten the life out of you with stories of the Dark Ones, pour alcohol down your throat, and you almost break your neck by falling off the chair'.

Vera giggled again and also stood up. 'Before we leave, I just want to ask if Ahren can drop by now and then and learn how to make the most important creams and compresses. That will give me the chance to do

84

parts of my job which he can't participate in yet and then he'll also have the odd day when his body can recover'. He smiled in Ahren's direction.

Vera nodded. 'Of course. The boy is a bright spark and I'm always happy to share my knowledge. It will only be enough to learn the basics, though. If he wants to learn more, I'll have to keep him for one or two winters.' The three of them stepped out into the late afternoon sun, where Vera and Falk gave each other a quick hug. Ahren gave an awkward nod of farewell and noticed the Healer whisper something to his master before breaking away from him. Falk nodded and strode quickly away with his apprentice in tow. The old woman stood in the doorway and, lost in thought, watched them leave.

The return journey to Falk's cabin was surprisingly short. Ahren's master reminded him to remember the direct route so that he would be able to find his own way to Vera's hut the next time. Again and again he pointed out the way markings to the boy. These would help him to orientate himself. He also showed him how the position of the sun in the sky could also help determine the correct direction. He didn't use the ball at all on the return journey, much to Ahren's relief.

They arrived at the cabin just as dusk was falling and Falk ordered him to go in and light the fire in the hearth. The night was drawing in and they were sitting at their evening meal when Ahren asked a question that had occupied his mind before he had become Falk's apprentice.

'Master, where do you actually come from?'

Falk looked up from his bowl quizzically and grunted, 'What do you mean?'

'Well, everybody knows that you arrived in Deepstone a long time ago, but there are lots of different opinions about where you came from'.

'Is that so?' His older companion's face seemed to darken.

'What opinions have you heard?'

'Most people believe you come from the Knight Marshes. That you spoke their local dialect in those days. Others think you picked up your knowledge of the Dark Ones in the Border Lands. Still others are of the opinion that you lived among the elves of Evergreen', said Ahren as he divulged the most popular theories.

His master didn't seem to take too kindly to his question but Ahren felt he ought to know as much as possible about the man in whose house he was now living.

Falk was just about to rebuke him sharply but then thought better of it. 'All those theories have a grain of truth in them but none of them hits the nail on the head. I received my training in Eathinian as part of a punishment. That's what we call the territory of the forest elves and you should remember that. Evergreen is a very crude translation. The same as if an elf called Deepstone 'a heavy thing that makes a clunking sound and falls a long way down'. It's not only inexact but it's not in the least aesthetic, it makes you sound like a complete idiot to them'.

Although this little insight into the language of the elves was fascinating, Ahren was interested in something completely different. 'Your training was a *punishment*?' That would certainly explain his training methods, thought Ahren drily.

'Not what you're thinking. I was a drifter when I arrived in Eathinian. I lit a fire in the forest where it was prohibited, I slaughtered an animal that was protected and I relieved myself in a river that provided drinking water to an elf village two miles further along. Even one of these misdemeanours could cost your head among the elves, or, if they were feeling charitable, result in banishment. Quite a few of them wanted to see me dead, but when I was brought before the priestess of HER THAT FEELS to receive my sentence, it turned out she had a finely tuned, if very dark, sense of humour. I had to bear my guilt in the forest until I had undone the damage I had caused. My fire had destroyed an old tree that had stood there for many decades. The animal I had slaughtered had been vital for the maintenance of the balance between predator and prey. The elves take such things very seriously. And so I spent many years learning everything about the forest to make good for this one tree, and to bring the wildlife back into balance, which is much harder than I had thought, certainly if you go by elf standards. Any time I thought I had done the right thing my mistress would point out to me what the consequences of my actions were. In the end and with her help I had made good for the tree and restored the balance and in the meantime, I had become a Forest Guardian. I didn't want then, and have never wanted since to be anything else'.

Ahren stared at his master in silence. He tried to reconcile what he had heard with the man who was sitting in front of him. Falk nodded contentedly when it became clear that his apprentice wasn't going to ask any more questions. 'Now you know a little bit more. You're going to have to earn the next personal question'. He stood up abruptly, almost as though he regretted having been so open.

'I'm going to sleep. Clear up, quench the fire and go to bed too. Tomorrow's going to be a demanding day for you'.

With those words, Falk went out into the darkness leaving a very thoughtful apprentice sitting at the table asking himself what Falk meant by *demanding*. How, he wondered, would his master describe the last two days?

Chapter 5

Ahren lay on his mat the following evening wishing he were dead. Or that the forest would flee. Or that the bailiff would come and take away his master for unnecessary cruelty to apprentices in general and to Ahren in particular, and then lock him up in a particularly dark and damp dungeon. This thought almost made him smile – but even that was sore. With a groan and all the energy he could muster, Ahren managed to turn on his side and slurp a little more soup from the bowl beside his bed. It was supposed to calm his maltreated muscles. It was his fourth portion in the last two hours but his body still felt as if a millstone had rolled over it. A particularly large millstone. With prongs.

They had headed off early in the morning and within a few hundred paces after entering the forest, Falk had led him to an imposing king oak tree that stretched about thirty paces into the air and had enormous sweeping branches. It really was a magnificent tree and Ahren had looked up at it in amazement until his master said, 'up there in the tree top is a red towel knotted to it. Can you bring it down for me please?'

Ahren had been delighted. This probably meant there was no running around on the agenda today and he could give his legs a bit of a rest. He had always liked climbing and he had a knack for it. But his master knew that already so why was he testing him again?

With a shrug of his shoulders and an 'of course, master' he set to work. He scampered up the first few paces in no time at all. There were many places to hold on too, the branches were wide and secure and there was plenty of room to turn easily. It was the perfect tree for climbing.

It wasn't long before Ahren was up in the top quarter of the tree. But the further he climbed, the harder it became to get a good grip *and* a secure standing position. Ahren stretched his neck to see where the cloth was tied. Yes, there it was, a red ribbon, fluttering in the breeze about four paces above him.

With considerable effort Ahren pulled himself up the final few paces and at last he reached the piece of cloth, knotted to a branch. Ahren had to clasp this branch with his right arm while balancing on a thin branch. He carefully raised his right hand towards the cloth and started loosening it. It took him a minute to finally untangle the knot and stuff the material down his leather jerkin. He had an unimpeded view of the tree top and saw that under the cloth was a rope tied around the branch. It wound its way in several dozen loops towards the top. Attached to the rope at regular intervals were very small, thin strips of material of various colours. The rope finished a hand span away from the tip of the tree. Confused, Ahren studied the construction for several heartbeats before making his way back down. His master, after all, had only mentioned the red cloth.

Getting down the tree proved to be very easy and it wasn't long before Ahren was standing in front of his master with a self-satisfied grin. The master took Ahren's trophy with an indifferent look.

'The cloth was only for orientation so that you could find your task. I want you to loosen as many strips of cloth as you can during the day and tie them down here around the branch. And only one strip per climb, do you hear me?'

That wiped the grin off Ahren's face in no time at all. The climbing was fun and hadn't been particularly strenuous but there were at least fifty strips of cloth up there, if not more. That would be some slog!

'I'm glad we understand each other', grinned Falk. 'There's a water skin over there and a piece of cheese; you'd better ration it. In the meantime, I'll go hunting so we have food for the table again. We're in dire need of some because of the rate you gobble it down. I'll check up on you every now and then, and if you're not climbing, I'll bring all the strips you've brought down back up again!' And having issued his threat he left the boy alone and disappeared into the undergrowth.

Ahren stood there for a moment and considered this mammoth task until a loud 'now, Ahren!' echoed from the forest and he scurried up the tree.

He only had a cloudy recollection of the rest of the day. The first few rounds weren't all that difficult but the continual repetition extracted a high price. He realized soon enough that the higher the strips were hanging, the more complicated the knots were. This meant longer stretches of the body, and longer periods of keeping his balance, not to mention increasingly complicated movements with his left hand while his muscles became more and more tired. Ahren had never suffered from a fear of heights, but he became acutely aware, with every new scaling of the tree, that there was a real danger he would fall and break his neck.

Around noon he started taking little breaks in the tree so that he wouldn't be surprised by Falk on the ground. Once he'd caught his breath, he would groan or curse and reach for the next branch. He thought of taking more than one piece of cloth at a time. But it wasn't only Ahren who had a wonderful view of the surrounding forest, there were also many treetops from which *he* could easily be spied upon. Ahren had no doubt at all that Falk threw an eye on him from time to time, even if he was out hunting.

Ahren was close to tears when his master finally stepped out of the undergrowth. He'd been clinging to the lowest branch of the tree for about an hour, but no matter how hard he'd tried, his arms didn't have enough strength to pull him up to the next branch. He slid clumsily down the tree and collapsed beside the strips of cloth he had collected that day.

Falk silently counted the strips and hunkered down opposite Ahren. 'You got as far as the blue ones, no?' his voice was warm and friendly and he looked proudly at Ahren.

The boy closed his eyes and nodded tiredly before answering in a quiet, shaky voice. 'The blue ones were hanging so high and the knot seemed to have only one end, just like the ones you made for our tree house, and I still haven't got used to my left hand. I went up three times and tried as hard as I could. Then I climbed down to the lowest branch to have a rest, but in the end, I couldn't pull myself up again'. The last few words were little more than a whisper.

'So, you've climbed up and down this tree more than thirty times today? No wonder you're tired. I thought you'd only manage to get as far as the green ones, but you've brought them all down'. Falk's voice was still warm and friendly, and his obvious compassion as well as Ahren's exhaustion were all too much for the boy. He fell into the arms of his stunned master and began to sob uncontrollably. Falk patted him awkwardly on the back and mumbled, 'it's alright, calm yourself. The first time is always the hardest'. The apprentice reacted with a jolt and gasped, 'the first time?'

'Of course. This was no test at all. Here we're training all the muscles in your body. Coordination, endurance, dexterity and will power. The ribbon tree was a staple of my basic training too'.

Falk released himself gently but firmly from Ahren's embrace and saw in front of him a youthful and angry face. His tears had left light streaks on the boy's face which was smudged with earth and tree bark. But as Ahren was rarely angry, his unpractised grimace looked comical rather than threatening.

The old Guardian decided to ignore the silent rebellion and with slow deliberation packed away the empty water skin, the ribbons and the waxed cheese-cloth. Then he turned around to face the boy, who was still looking at him darkly.

'That's enough now. If you continue to look daggers at me, I'll send you up the tree in double quick time and you'll have to tie up all the ribbons again'. The boy looked quickly up at the tree top, then at the ribbons in Falk's hand before turning on his heels and trudging uncertainly away.

Falk smiled, turned away from the tree too and followed Ahren into the forest. The boy had been so angry that he hadn't noticed that he'd headed the correct way to the cabin without having asked the way. The old man looked down at his hands, still with the three dozen unknotted ribbons, nodded to himself and whispered, 'a start'.

Ahrend groaned and turned on his back again. The soup bowl was empty. He had made his way back to the cabin in brooding silence, had tortuously taken off his leathers and curled up under the blanket. Falk too had remained silent, prepared the meal, and patiently placed one bowl after another beside the mat, but now his master was outside. The glow from the dying fire gradually faded and the inside of the cabin was bathed in a soft red shimmer, making the contours of the room appear softer and somehow more fluid. Ahren mulled over the injustice of the world and how he had to end up with the worst possible slave driver of a master, before his exhaustion overwhelmed him like a black wave, and between one breath and the next, he was in a deep slumber.

The low snoring coming from inside the cabin told Falk that the youngster had fallen asleep and with a sigh of relief he leaned against the tree where he had set up his place for the night. He massaged his forehead and was glad he had weathered the day. What had he been thinking of, taking on an apprentice? The reasons he had listed out to the young boy were all true of course, but he of all people training someone? He had spoken more in the last four days than he had in the whole three months previously, and he would have to be a little more careful. The boy would only have finished his thirteenth summer by autumn and in Falk's case, he had completed his training as a well-drilled adult.

And there were other advantages he had enjoyed that he didn't want to think about now. That was all such a long time ago and really belonged to the past. Damn it, the boy was even disturbing his peace of mind.

He stood up and walked a few steps into the forest.

Following a custom going back decades he whispered as he did every evening, 'Selsena, is that you?' He waited a few heartbeats, then turned with a sorrowful look. He had only taken one tired step when there was a rustling behind him.

Falk froze in mid movement, didn't stir an inch. Nothing more than a whisper escaped his lips, a quietly whispered word, permeated with a wild, frustrated hopefulness. 'Selsena?'

The leaves behind him rustled again.

Falk didn't turn around but collapsed into himself where he stood, like a puppet whose cords had been cut. Nobody could see the tears rolling down his weather-beaten skin.

'The years without you were very long', he said, his voice breaking.

The leaves were no longer moving, but they didn't need to. Falk tilted his head low as he always did when she spoke with him before answering,

'Yes, I know. It was my fault. What has changed?'

A few seconds passed.

'The boy? Really?'

Falk still didn't turn. His eyes were closed and he felt a large body coming closer behind and towering over him.

'I'm speaking out loud because I'm out of practice. After all, it's been many years.'

He reached up and stroked the soft fur.

'Are you staying?' Falk hated himself for the frustration evident in his voice, but she could read his thoughts anyway so it really made no difference.

The answer wasn't the one he had hoped for but at least it was so comforting that he gave a quick laugh. She had always had a sharp sense of humour.

'Good, so nearby, until the boy has made himself at home. Otherwise, he'll end up running away from us screaming'.

Us.

The word echoed within Falk and suddenly all the dams burst. The irony wasn't lost on Falk that he was now behaving like his thirteen-year old apprentice, who only this afternoon had thrown himself at him and sobbed uncontrollably. It didn't bother him.

The night concealed him, the forest embraced him, and Selsena was back.

All was well.

Chapter 6

The weeks flew by. Falk went with Ahren two or three days in a row through the forest, carefully increasing the tempo over the period. It was still more of a quick walk than a slow trot but the would-be Forest Guardian hardly stumbled anymore and he was certainly able to keep pace. On top of that, it had been a while since he'd dropped the ball. Ahren was now using the left hand quite instinctively for a wide range of activities and so Falk had begun to incorporate both hands in the training. He thought if the boy had trained his secondary hand for all this time, it should be possible now for him to attain a level of limited ambidexterity.

Following the forest run there would always be a day at the ribbon tree and then one with Vera where Ahren could recover from his physical exertions. Instead, he would learn about compresses and creams for scratches, cuts, burns and inflammations. The old woman was always very kind and whenever Ahren spent a day there, at least a dozen visitors would arrive, either bringing or picking up something, and there would always be an exchange of stories and gossip. They always had a friendly word for Ahren and he began, quite unconsciously, to think of himself as Ahren the apprentice Forest Guardian, and not Ahren, the drunkard's son, whenever he was speaking to the others.

After his day with Vera, the cycle would begin again and by the end of the summer Ahren had got used to his constantly aching muscles. Falk had no mirror and Ahren was far too busy to notice what the others could see – that his shoulders were slowly becoming broader, and his arms and legs sinewier. The strong soup prepared by Falk, laced with healing herbs and full of the vital substances which helped Ahren's growth spurt, was so completely different from the watery broths that he had subsisted on when he was in his father's care.

And so, the first days of autumn arrived with their bad weather and the cool winds that had long ago driven Deepstone into the shelter of the forest. The forest marches were less fun than ever, the ground was slippery because of the rain and when Ahren arrived in the cabin at night he had to spend an hour cleaning his gear so that the leather would keep smooth and supple and the dagger protected from rust. Falk also began to leave the smaller household chores in his hands and soon he was getting up as early as his master so everything would be in order before the old man gave the order to set off for the day. The ribbon tree was much harder to climb now, when the branches were wet and slippery. After the first autumn storm Falk had silently given him a pair of leather gloves with the fingertips free. Ahren was puzzled by them until he tried scaling the wet higher branches with his bare hands. It wasn't long before the gloves were like another hand and he began to imitate Falk's stoical attitude to the weather. Sometime in the middle of autumn, it was the evening of a surprisingly mild day, there was a knock on the door of the Guardian's little cabin. The two occupants looked up from their leather work in surprise and Ahren gave his master a questioning look.

'Don't ask me, I'm just as clueless as you', grumbled Falk and stood up. Falk opened the door and as soon as Ahren realized who had granted them a visit, he leapt to his feet and the leather jerkin he had been fixing flew to the ground along with the awl and string. Likis was standing in the doorway with a broad grin on his face. He was wearing the classical merchant's tunic, and two parchment scrolls were sticking out of his breast pockets. A little slate was hanging on a thin chain from his belt.

'Likis, it's wonderful to see you'. With arms outstretched, Ahren ran to greet the merchant's son, almost knocking over his master in the

96

process, who was too slow to get out of the way. Falk was about to give out to them but on seeing the boys hugging each other in joyful reunion he simply shrugged his shoulders, sat down and continued with his repair work.

Likis held Ahren firmly by the shoulders and looked at him critically. 'Boy, but you've grown – and filled out! What's he feeding you?'

Ahren shifted from one foot to the other in embarrassment. He had spent his whole life comparing his size with Likis and now he was suddenly aware that he was taller than his friend by a head, and it had only been half a head four months ago.

He answered without thinking. 'A lot of soup and stews with game and herbs. Wolf Herb for the muscles, Life Farm for regenerating stamina and Red Leaf as a protection against illness.' Even as he was speaking, he realized that he sounded like old Vera rattling off a prescription for a healing ointment. His friend looked at him in bafflement, until the two burst into laughter.

'A start', commented Falk stoically in the background, and Ahren laughed even harder.

The pair squatted down on Ahren's mat and spent the evening telling each other what had happened over the previous months. Likis rhapsodized about his work in the shop and the merchants from Two Waters who delivered merchandize to them and also brought the latest news from all over Hjalgar. Apparently, a band of robbers had settled in the slopes of Greyjags and were holding up travellers. Quite a few mutilated wolf and bear carcasses had been found. When Ahren heard this, he looked up to his master and was about to speak, but Falk gave him a warning look and shook his head and so the boy said nothing.

The night was drawing in and there was no sign of the boys finishing their conversation so Falk cleared his throat noisily and said, 'Likis, it's not that we're not delighted about your visit, but you really need to be making your way home now'.

The wiry boy leapt to his feet and clapped his hand against his forehead.

'Of course, I nearly forgot. I'm here in the name of my parents to invite you to a meal on the eve of the Autumn Festival'.

Ahren was a little surprised. 'Is it that time again?' As he no longer took part in the daily life of the village, he had no idea what date the village council had set for the Autumn Festival.

'Yes, two weeks from today. Vera has forecast an early and hard winter'. The Healer had a sixth sense for the pulse of nature. In one of her lessons she had explained to Ahren that there were many clues for the upcoming weather in the behaviour of plants and the clouds. Falk said the same was true for the animals, but when he had looked for more information, Falk had stalled him with a shake of his head.

'You're not even six months with me out here. Ask me in five years again', was his sobering reply.

'That's why I came here today, to invite you', said Likis cheerfully. 'And, are you coming?' he looked expectantly from one to the other. Ahren looked pleadingly at his master. It was traditional on the eve of the three-day Autumn Festival to invite friends and family to take part in a relaxing, peaceful meal before the hurly-burly and excitement of the Autumn Festival. It was considered rude to turn down such an invitation.

But Falk was neither particularly diplomatic nor sociable, so you never knew.

Ahren need not have feared. Falk nodded and grunted, 'tell your parents thanks and that we will come. Now get out of here or my apprentice will be unbearable tomorrow for want of sleep'.

The two boys grinned at each other in anticipation of another evening full of each other's stories, not to mention the good food. Now that his friend was going, Ahren realized how cut off he was out here, and how much he missed his chirpy companion.

'Take care of yourself', he said sadly.

'It's only two weeks', said Likis in a comforting tone and gave him a quick hug. Then he gave Falk a wave and disappeared out the door.

Ahren went to the window and watched his sprightly friend until he was soon swallowed up by the night. Falk's cabin was on the outer edge of Deepstone but tonight the apprentice felt that the entire wood separated it from the village community. With a sigh he went to his sleeping area and curled up under the covers.

Falk worked on at the leathers for another few minutes, then tilted his head as if listening to someone and after a few heartbeats nodded. 'You're right'.

He put down his tools and clothing, looked again at the outline of the sleeping boy and went out into the forest.

Chapter 7

The next two weeks couldn't go quickly enough for Ahren. Falk noticed Ahren's impatience and upped the practice tempo considerably in order to distract his apprentice. The practice ball was constantly flying here and there between them. His master would deliberately throw it off course forcing Ahren to hop, duck, dive, or throw himself around abruptly so that he could catch the wretched thing in mid-flight and he was picking out more difficult terrain. They had to creep through undergrowth, clamber over fallen trees and climb up and down steep slopes.

Ahren was shattered every evening, such as he hadn't been since the early days of his training, but with his new found knowledge in the herbal arts, he was able to help himself and his body prepare for the following day. Soothing compresses, healing teas and strengthening condiments did the trick.

Falk never commented on this but Selsena could sense the master's pride, bright as a beacon in the dead of night. She often stood there in the darkness and kept watch over them both. Something old and dark had come into the forest again and soon blood would flow. She was determined to buy them as much time as she could.

At last the eve of the Autumn Festival was upon them and even the Forest Guardians were caught up in the village preparations for the coming festivities. Falk had gone hunting and, unusually, left Ahren alone in the cabin so that he could learn from the old book of herbs Vera had given him. It was true that the boy couldn't read but with the help of the pictures he could go over what he had learned.

But Ahren had other plans today. His master was hardly out of sight, when he raced off towards Vera's cabin. The old woman would be far too busy for him but that didn't matter. It was what was waiting for him behind her house that was important. He carefully made his way through the undergrowth to the back wall of the cabin. Yes, lying neatly there for him were a dozen boards and two thick ropes. During his last lesson with the herbalist he had made sure that a message requesting these things had been delivered to Master Velem.

The Autumn Festival was also the time when all villagers became a year older officially and so everyone gave each other presents and wished each other another healthy winter so that they could experience the next summer.

Ahren was determined to make his master a present. The old man was a slave driver, a curmudgeon and sometimes a man-made thunderstorm, but in spite of all that he had saved him from a bleak future and was investing a lot of time and effort in Ahren's education. The problem was giving him a present that he would like. His master lived very frugally. The present would have to be practical and of everyday use.

Ahren gathered together the items and could hear lively chatter and laughter coming from within and in front of the cabin. Half the village seemed to have gathered here in order to honour the old woman and to collect herbs and spices for the feast dishes or to get tips on how to prepare them. Suddenly the remoteness in which he and his master lived didn't seem so bad and with a grin and a shake of his head he started heading back to their cabin.

The trees had started shedding their leaves in the previous few days and a cold wind was spinning a red and gold kaleidoscope among the trunks. A few birds were stubbornly holding on to their memories of summer and whistling their defiance to the world at large. The boards were heavy and the ropes cumbersome but Ahren was now in top condition and it didn't take long before the cabin was in sight.

He checked quickly that Falk was still out, carried the paraphernalia into the house and began putting it together. He had worked everything out already in his head so the construction wouldn't take long if he could manage the Elfish knots. The same sort he had tackled with his teeth for two months on the ribbon tree. It had transpired that the blue ribbons that had comprehensively got the better of him on that first day had been knotted in the Elfish manner and were extraordinarily difficult to unknot, especially with one hand. The one positive from his months of frustration was that he had now mastered these knots perfectly. It took him less than an hour to tie the beams and planks together into two platforms, one above the other and supported by struts. Then he placed the sleeping mats, his own and his master's on the two platforms and his simple bunk beds were finished. There really wasn't enough room for two sleeping areas in the cabin and so he thought this was a really practical present made with the simplest of materials. The only flaw was that he had to ask Vera for the materials.

But she simply smiled and said, 'this is my autumn present to yourself and Falk'.

Ahren spent the rest of the day sprucing up the cabin, polishing his leather gear and looking forward to the evening. Every now and again he ran to the window so he could catch his master at the door. When Falk appeared at last coming from the trees with an enormous stag on his shoulders Ahren ran towards him to help him with his load.

'Thanks, son', gasped the Guardian. 'He's a big morsel, and I had to drag him further than I would have liked. Something was frightening the animals and hunting was a lot harder than usual'.

They put the booty down in front of the window and Ahren stood so his master couldn't see inside. His hands were sweaty with anticipation and he was surprised at how much he wanted to cheer up this grumpy old man. He must have become fonder of his master than he cared to admit.

Falk entered the room and Ahren called out, 'a healthy winter and a merry new summer', the traditional greeting when you handed over an autumn present.

His mentor stood there and stared critically at the wooden construction for a few heartbeats. Then he walked up to it and examined the knots carefully, tilting his head all the while as if listening to something. Then he turned around and said, 'that's a very good present and I'm very proud of you'. He sounded a little stilted as if somebody had fed him the lines. But Ahren knew that this wasn't his strong point and anyway he was far too happy to take any notice. Falk turned to the wooden bed and said, 'you sleep on top because your young bones could do with a bit of climbing'. After a few seconds he continued with a grumble, 'If I'm lying there and the thing collapses, you're going to spend the next two weeks climbing the ribbon tree...*and* you'll sleep on it'.

Well, that didn't last long, thought Ahren but answered with a smile, 'yes, master'.

The wooden bed had held together, much to Ahren's relief, and so now he sat with a full stomach beside Likis in his parents' sitting room and enjoyed the happy, unforced conversation with his friend. Two dozen candles were situated around the room, filling the space with a warm glow, and the candle scents intermingled with the aromas from the opulent feast that they had all had just finished eating.

The adults were talking about some feudal lord in the Knight Marshes who had been trying to claim a small border area of Hjalgar for himself. They were so deep in conversation that the two boys were completely undisturbed. They glanced at the large sand timer on the mantelpiece from time to time. The autumn presents were traditionally handed over during the night before the Autumn Festival, and that's why there were these enormous sand glasses which were turned over just before dusk. Once the sand had run through a few hours later it was time to thank the THREE for another year lived, and it was also time for the presents.

At one point in their conversation, Likis became very serious and whispered to Ahren, 'are you happy out there, alone with that curmudgeon. I sometimes ask myself if you've just jumped from the frying pan into the fire. We heard nothing from you for ages but Vera assured us you were fine so we didn't interfere'. Likis gave Ahren a questioning look but his friend gave him a reassuring smile.

'There's nowhere else on earth I'd rather be'. And he added in a whisper, 'I've even mastered a few tricks of the Elfish trade'.

His master had expressly forbidden him from mentioning this as he didn't want the rumour-mill to go into overdrive, but he really had to tell his best friend.

He squeaked in surprise, 'elves?' And the look Falk shot his apprentice suggested an awkward conversation later.

Ahren quickly steered the conversation into safer waters and asked what Holken, Sven and the others were up to. He'd probably run across them during the Autumn Festival and he wanted to be forewarned if there was anything in the air concerning the village boys. He had discovered that Holken had transformed himself; he was now a model youth under the bailiff and was getting lots of praise heaped upon him. Sven, on the other hand, had somehow managed to take over control of the boys and their pranks were getting meaner and more dangerous.

'There was even a fire in the old barn last week but no-one could tell who caused it. A horse was killed and the matter hasn't been closed. I think Sven and the other good for nothings were behind it but I've no proof so I'm going to stay mum', said Likis, finishing the conversation. The two boys were silent for a while until they noticed the adults stirring. One look at the sand clock and then everyone was on their feet.

The sand had run through and Velem and Falk stepped through the door into the antechamber only to return shortly afterwards with a heavy bundle each. Ahren felt a thrill of anticipation as he watched Likis unpack a blue velvet cap with yellow braiding and then joyfully thank his parents. This status symbol showed that he could now make small transactions on his own in the name of his merchant's house, something which made him burst with pride. He put the present on his head and turned to face Ahren, who had to control himself in order not to guffaw. The thing looked completely ridiculous. You'd be spotted two miles away in the forest. Ahren realized that Falk's personality was beginning to rub off on him.

He beamed for a second at his friend to show how much he was there for him today, then hurriedly stood up straight and faced his master. Without saying a word Falk presented him with a long bundle wrapped in oilcloth. Ahren pushed the heavy material aside with trembling fingers and a slender curved bow appeared along with a buckskin quiver containing a half dozen arrows. The boy whooped for joy and would have thrown himself at Falk were it not for the stern look and the warning furrowed eyebrows of his master.

'You've made excellent progress until now so it's time for us to teach you the basic skills in shooting with arrows, hunting and stalking'. At which point he brought down one of his calloused hands on Ahren's shoulder so heavily that the boy balked. 'The bow will only be used in my presence and with my express permission, or it will be turned into firewood'. Ahren nodded and stroked the smooth wood with his fingers. It was shining in the candlelight and you could see how carefully the surface had been polished. A faint, undulating pattern ran the length of the bow, disappearing behind the handguard, only to reappear on the other side. 'That's the Elfish sign for the apprentice bow', whispered Falk before placing a conspiratorial finger on his lips.

The boys spent the rest of the evening mostly just looking in silence at their presents until the lateness of the hour brought proceedings to a close. They promised to meet each other at one of the tables on the festival square and Ahren and Falk stepped out into the night air. The wind had calmed down and it was cold but clear. The waxing moon was in the sky and a few wisps of cloud were visible, drifting by. The forest was bathed in pale moonlight, giving a hint of the varied colours playing off each other in the fabulous autumn landscape. Ahren glanced quickly at the squat house of his father but there was no light to be seen. Then with a shiver he followed his master, who was taking the direct route through the forest to their cabin.

When they reached half way, Falk stopped, stared into the darkness of the forest and said in a loud voice, 'a healthy winter and a merry summer'. Then he tilted his head sideways for a moment, smiled and went on. Ahren asked himself if this was perhaps an Elfish tradition or if Falk wanted to pay his respects to the forest. He had also heard that old men could become strange in their ways. He shrugged his shoulders and trotted behind, hoping he would learn all the important things from Falk before he became too strange.

The following morning Falk was awakened by the clattering of wooden bowls and the smells of an herbal stew. He opened his eyes a tiny bit and smiled under his blanket as he secretly watched his apprentice preparing everything for breakfast. The rucksack had already been packed, Ahren was fully dressed, his bow and quiver standing by the door. He'd intended on stringing the boy along for another while yet. After all, it was another hour until sunrise, but Selsena gave him a mental nudge and so he opened his eyes and swung his legs out of the bed.

'Good morning, Ahren. I see you can hardly wait'.

The young boy glanced guiltily at the bow beside the door but then he pulled back his shoulders and said, 'if we're going to the Autumn Festival this afternoon, we just have a couple of hours to practise. I wanted to get everything ready here so we could head off as soon as possible'.

Falk was afraid that Ahren would choke on his breakfast, he was gulping it down so quickly. In the end the old man gave up, pushed his half- eaten bowl to the side and said, 'Alright then. Tidy up here, I'll get ready quickly and then we'll be off'.

Soon they were trudging in the early morning light and Falk picked out a clearing that was far enough from the village so there would be no fear of accidents. Then he began teaching his protégé how to handle a bow and arrow and the ground rules of archery.

Ahren devoted himself to the job at hand with full concentration and what Falk had suspected, that time on the village square, was now becoming crystal clear. The boy really had a natural talent with the bow. First Falk pointed out the most common beginner's mistakes but within an hour he was hitting a tree trunk four out of five times from twenty paces' distance. It was thirty paces by noon, and by the time the old man suggested stopping, Ahren was in sparkling form. His arms and chest had strengthened considerably due to the climbing of the previous months, so tensioning the bow was effortless. His muscles were aching now but he felt he could go on for hours.

He asked cockily, 'master, may I give your bow a try?'

Falk thought for a moment. 'Why not, nothing would surprise me today'. He handed Ahren his bow, which was considerably higher than the boy's head, and one of his long arrows. His apprentice struggled mightily until eventually, with trembling arms, he managed to extend the bow about half way. But his arms were too short and when he was finally forced to let the arrow fly from the bow string, it flew uncontrolled and awry off into the trees.

'Well, we won't find that one again'. Falk scratched his beard and took back the bow. 'You should really only try a long bow again once you've grown a head, both taller and broader'. Ahren nodded hesitantly and picked up his own bow again.

'I think we should go back now. I'll let the others know this evening that this is now to be called the practice zone, and tomorrow I'll bring a few targets that will be more difficult to hit. Then you can come here whenever you like and practise on your own. You're very good with the bow but you still need practice. I'll give you the hard lessons once you're able to hit all the targets without thinking about it. Tell me when you think you're ready and then I'll have a look'.

The happy boy followed his master with a spring in his step as they left the clearing, and he looked around him so that he would remember where his practice area was. He was imagining where Falk might put the targets, when something attracted his attention. There was something large and silver-grey on the other side of the clearing and between the trees. But when he looked more closely, the phenomenon had vanished. His master cleared his throat and turned around, and Ahren ran to catch up with him. He kept looking back over his shoulder but the forest lay still and deserted. The being had disappeared.

That afternoon the whole village was gathered on and around the festival ground and the tavern was filled to overflowing. Tables and benches were placed around the oak tree and a large fire was blazing to the left. Groups of revellers were sitting together and there was much to-ing and fro-ing between the bar, the attractions and the benches. It all resembled a complicated dance.

Ahren watched the confectioner spinning candy floss with the help of a bellows, and the blacksmith with his anvil had hammered some horseshoes out of shape. Some of the revellers were testing their strength by trying to get the horseshoes back into shape with as few hammer blows as possible. Two competitors would take up the challenge each time, egged on or mocked by the excited spectators.

Or you could take part in arm-wrestling, apple bobbing (for the small ones), ring tossing, and of course drinking competitions.

Ahren steered well clear of the tavern, where his father probably was, and wandered past the stands, exchanging pleasantries with the villagers and keeping an eye out for Likis.

At the ring tossing he squeezed past two revellers who were unsteady on their feet and promptly crashed into a delicate creature who was just composing herself before her throw. The wooden ring clattered to the ground without having touched one of the stakes around which it should have landed. Ahren quickly mumbled an apology and to his surprise found himself looking at the daintily featured face of Lina, the miller's daughter, and sister of Sven. She put her hands on her hips and looked at him with a mixture of indignation and curiosity. Ahren found himself drawn to Lina's finely worked festival dress, and as he gazed at it, it dawned on him that the person standing opposite him had also gone through some physical changes over the previous months – and somehow this made him more nervous than he already was. He wanted to disappear into the crowd when he was stopped in his tracks by the sound of a laughing voice. 'Not so fast, my little friend!'

'You owe me a throw'. Lina looked him up and down unashamedly. Ahren felt as if his head was as big as a watermelon and his face went a deep red.

'You're Ahren, isn't that right? I didn't recognize you at first in your leather outfit. You used to be smaller and a lot weaker'. Her statement may indeed have contained a compliment but her merciless description of his earlier self was hardly flattering. He mustered a heroic 'ehm...' and stared at her.

'I wanted to win this cute little stuffed monkey, and now you've spoilt everything', Lina complained with a twinkle in her eye. 'So, what are you going to do about it?'

Ahren was far too inexperienced to understand the rules of this particular game but he could certainly handle the ring tossing. Relieved to be on familiar territory, he turned to the carpenter who was in charge of the stand that day. He'd been following their conversation as cool as you please and a grin spread across his face with its bushy whiskers.

'The first try is free, any ones after that are a penny'.

Suddenly Ahren remembered that he hadn't had any money in his hands for months, nor needed any. Falk looked after the shopping and almost always paid with game or plants. He'd have to be lucky, first time out.

'Which stake do I aim for to win the monkey?' he asked, all the while feeling the rings. He was looking for the smoothest and best balanced one. The carpenter winked at him.

'That one over there, second from the right'.

Ahren was relieved. It was hardly two paces away and the stake was a little bigger than the ring. According to the rules, the wooden ring had to come to rest sitting on the stake. The hardest part would be ignoring Lina's presence. She was standing right beside him with an expectant look and a mischievous smile on her face.

Ahren took aim and the ring landed effortlessly on the stake. Pleased with himself, he handed the stuffed monkey to Lina, who smiled back at him. She linked arms with him and asked him questions about his education and about Falk as she strolled with him across the square. Ahren was so taken by her that he forgot to be sensible and started to prattle non-stop. About his training, about the elves and the Dark Ones, anything that came into his head and that would make him look good. The effect on Lina was enormous. There were plenty of juicy anecdotes in what he said. The rational side of his brain, meanwhile, tried unsuccessfully to make him focus on the fact that Sven had been watching them for some time and was looking daggers at Ahren. Ahren's master didn't seem happy about his indiscretions either and Likis could only shake his head sadly as he saw his friend parading around without a care in the world. The bell for the devotions finally ended the young man's boasting. Lina parted from him with a light kiss on the cheek and ran back to her family while Ahren floated in seventh heaven to his master.

Suddenly Likis was beside him, intoning in a loud voice and with sweeping gestures, 'and then I slew three dragons with one blow of my sword, while strangling a manticore with my foot…' Ahren heard no more of his friend's teasing for he suddenly felt a rap of his master's knuckles on his head. His pride severely dented, Ahren looked from one to the other and was asking himself what he had done to deserve this treatment when the bell stopped ringing and Keeper Jegral stepped in front of the fire where all the villagers had gathered.

The priest held his autumn devotions but Ahren heard only the half of it because he was too busy trying to see Lina in the gathering. He knew where she was standing, but every time he caught a glimpse of her, Sven would push himself in front of her and stare darkly at Ahren. When the prayers were over and everyone had drifted away to continue their festivities, the Keeper approached the two Guardians.

'Ahren, Master Falk, may the THREE be with you'. Falk nodded and gave him his hand, and Ahren gave a small bow. He was still in awe of the priest. After all, it was his miracle cure that had changed everything, including the direction of his life. The Keeper looked at him kindly at first before raising an eyebrow thoughtfully. 'I could always rely on your presence in the past. You *did* promise me, don't you remember?'

Ahren cowered and gave his master a guilty and pleading look. He too looked contrite and answered on Ahren's behalf. 'That's partly my fault. He did tell me about that, but I forgot. Although he should have reminded me'.

Once again Ahren had drawn the short straw. Why did it always end up the same way? The boy was just apologizing with a sigh when Falk interjected. 'Now that we're on the subject, my apprentice is unable to read and he's missing a bit of education. Could he attend the Godsday School? Then he could go to morning prayers and take part in lessons afterwards'.

Jegral beamed and said, 'What a wonderful idea. He would be welcome of course'.

The two shook hands on it, the Keeper smiled warmly at Ahren and continued on his way, to remind other young lambs of their spiritual responsibilities. Ahren thought about this new development with mixed feelings. One day's training less per week meant, in all probability, the other days would be an even harder slog, and that would mean less time for archery. But when he saw the stony reaction of his master all thoughts of protesting evaporated.

'From what I saw earlier, you urgently need to mix with your peers. If every tomboy makes you lose your head, then a Wind Whip or even a Grief Wind will kill you in a second'.

The mention of Dark Ones deflated Ahren completely. Falk had explained to him in one of his brief lectures that these beings manipulated the feelings of the Adversary against them. Ahren couldn't figure out how this worked exactly, but now that he thought about it, he had to admit that his flirting with Lina earlier wasn't a shining example of steadfast behaviour. He then nodded, resigned to his fate.

'Good. Go off and amuse yourself now', said Falk cheerily. 'Although I'd advise you against any further amorous adventures today or that scoundrel over there might attack you with a knife'. He pointed over at Sven, who was standing barely ten paces away with two of his cronies, watching Ahren's every move. The apprentice agreed, 'good idea'.

He turned quickly around to look for Likis when he spotted Holken. Ahren may have grown but Holken must have been stretched on the rack! His muscles were more impressive than ever, and now he was approaching. The would-be Forest Guardian looked for an escape route in panic, but the big boy was already in front of him. He wore the bailiff's uniform and he had a dangerous looking truncheon on his belt.

'Hello Ahren, I was hoping to see you here today', he began, and Ahren instinctively flinched half a pace backwards. His blond counterpart stuck out a hand and took Ahren's in a vice-like grip. 'I couldn't apologise that time for the blow I gave your injured hand, and I wanted to do that now. You just didn't want to give up and the rules were clear'. He shrugged his shoulders in embarrassment.

Ahren studied his face to see if this was just a mean trick but he only saw genuine regret. Surprised, he shook hands, partly because he hoped Holken would let go again. And he answered, 'Forgive and forget. To tell you the truth, that blow opened doors for me. I don't think Jegral would have just healed a sprained hand in front of everybody, and then I would have failed Master Falk's challenge.

Holken did let go of Ahren's hand, only to lay an arm across his shoulder and pull him along. Ahren might as well have been fighting with an ox, so he gave in.

'Come on, let's look for your wiry friend and have a drink. I was paid today, so the drinks are on me'.

The idea of a drink was tempting and Holken's presence would guarantee protection from Sven and his cronies.

'Sounds good, let's go', said Ahren with a bit more enthusiasm than he actually felt, and the two made their way between the tables.

Later that evening, Ahren rose from the table at which he, Likis, Holken and three other boys from the village had been celebrating and made his way unsteadily to the toilet. He had over indulged on the wine and now he was feeling the effects. His master had left an hour earlier but given him permission to stay on. And so, he had carried on celebrating and come to realize that Holken was much friendlier now than in the past, even if he was still a bit slow on the uptake.

Ahren stepped out of the light and between the trees in the forest. Falk had taught him the best place in the forest to pass water without leaving any traces, and Ahren was making use of this lesson now. He giggled over this creative use of his education, swayed and buttoned up his trousers when suddenly a sharp pain exploded in the region of his kidneys.

As if struck by lightning he collapsed with a scream to the ground and felt several feet landing kicks on him. He rolled up into a ball and protected his face with his hands but his attackers kept finding places he couldn't protect. It seemed like an eternity before Ahren heard worried calls and hasty footsteps approaching. Some of the revellers must have heard the commotion and his tormentors finally stopped kicking. Someone spat in his face, and the battered boy could just make out a silhouette looming over him in the darkness of the forest. Then the attackers were gone and within a few seconds the first villagers arrived. Ahren's whole body ached and he could only stand with the help of others.

Holken and Likis held him under his arms and hauled him home. As soon as they'd entered the cabin, Falk was up and questioning Ahren's friends but they had seen nothing, so he thanked them and sent them home.

Falk helped Ahren get undressed and carefully examined his wounds. Then he clicked his tongue and said, 'A blessing in disguise. You have so much flesh and muscle on your ribs that there's nothing broken. You'll be right as rain soon enough'.

He spent the next hour putting on bandages with herbal essences, always asking Ahren which herb he should use and why. His protégé was shocked that he should be asked these questions in the condition he was in but he understood that he would not forget these herbs and their medicinal effects for the rest of his life.

The rest of the Autumn Festival was very boring for Ahren. He had to stay in bed and rest his ribs while Likis and Holken would drop by from time to time and bring some of the Feast Day roast or treats from the baker's. Witness statements proved fruitless and of course Sven claimed not to have anything to do with it. The boys were convinced that he was behind the cowardly attack, but for the moment their hands were tied, and if that wasn't boring enough, Falk became even more reticent than before and hardly came into the cabin.

When Ahren complained to his friends about this, Likis answered, 'I think he's blaming himself for not having been there to protect you'. That seemed plausible somehow, seemed to fit with his behaviour and that reassured the young boy a little.

Ahren was allowed to take up his training again to a limited degree. The weeks passed with their normal rhythm except that Falk, with dogged determination, had moved on to training him in the art of close combat. The economical feinting movements and flowing attacks looked simple but were so difficult that Ahren wondered if he would ever master them. The second change to their daily routine was of course Godsday which Ahren, with newly starched shirt and linen trousers given to him by Keeper Jegral, now spent in the priest's charge. The Keeper taught him about the entity of the THREE and especially about the love of the MOULDER. He also taught him reading, writing and simple arithmetic. Ahren could always relax at this point, for through Likis' friendship he had already learnt everything the priest knew about numbers.

Reading was another matter. Ahren just didn't understand why anybody would go to the trouble of writing things down when he could speak the story so much more quickly. He asked the Keeper about this and he responded, 'You are right there, it does go more quickly. But think about it: the other must listen and understand everything correctly – or some of the knowledge will be lost. He cannot alter what he has heard for his own benefit – or the knowledge will be falsified. Then the student must pass on what he has learned – or it will be forgotten. There is knowledge in these books that has survived for centuries, unfalsified and unforgotten. That's a miracle in itself'.

From then on Ahren looked at the texts from a fresh perspective and developed a thirst for knowledge that filled the Keeper with happiness. He rewarded Ahren in the best way he knew how – by willingly answering every question as well as he could.

Time passed and winter set in over Hjalgar. The days were shorter and Falk began to introduce Ahren, in the early morning and the long evenings, to the arts of the Forest Guardian that didn't need daylight or much room. He learnt how to pack a rucksack without water, dirt or little animals getting in, which foods you could bring with you and for how long, and a dozen other practical things.

However, most of the dark hours of the day were taken up with the study of 'the Void'. During the autumn Ahren had learnt how to hit fourteen of the twenty targets Falk had positioned in the clearing. His master had rammed a stake into the ground at one end of the clearing. This marked Ahren's shooting position and he had drawn small white circles of varying sizes and at different heights on the trees opposite. Most of the targets were no problem, but some of them were the size of an apple and more than thirty paces away.

When it became clear that he would make no further progress without instruction, Falk lit a candle and told Ahren to sit with legs crossed in front of it.

'I want you to breathe in and out for as long and as slowly as you can and just concentrate on the flame. Think of nothing else, place all your concentration on this one spot of light'.

The wick of the candle had been pared back and the flame was small and weak so he couldn't blind himself. Strange as it seemed to Ahren, these exercises proved the most difficult of any he had done in his apprenticeship. He always thought of something else: of the following day, the lessons just completed, or how pointless it was to stare at a candle. Sometimes he managed to persevere for a few minutes but then horrible pictures would push their way towards his inner eye. His father and the way he had beaten him, the battering he had experienced at the Autumn Festival.

When he told Falk this, he responded, 'that's normal. When our reason is at rest, it loosens the bonds with which we control the conflicts that badger us the most. The elves call this phenomenon 'the Spirits of the Void', that's a rough translation. Everyone has to come to terms with the Spirits in their own way. Some learn to ignore them as one would the rustling of the leaves. Others confront their conflicts and try to get rid of them. The third way is to let go and make peace with them'.

'Which variation have you picked, master?'

'You don't have to decide on one. Some conflicts cannot be resolved, some cannot be ignored, and inner peace is by no means my speciality area'. He tilted his head and smiled weakly. 'I have confronted each vision individually and overcome them in whatever was the most suitable way. In the end you are fighting with yourself, so you have to decide the best way on your own'.

Then he left Ahren alone again with the flame and his thoughts.

The shirt collar pinched his neck horribly, the plain wooden bench was too small for his legs, as was the wooden desk he was squatting in front of, with the leather-bound book on top. Ahren was in a sweat, bent over his book of exercises in the overheated priest's study. He looked around furtively. The heavy bull-glass panes were free of ice although icy cold was lurking on the other side of the wall. Deepstone hadn't experienced such a cold winter in years.

Sweat was running down Ahren's face. The others didn't seem to share his problem. Likis obviously felt as fit as a fiddle and Holken used his spiritual inertia to his own advantage. Lina sat beside him at every lesson in order to help him with his reading and to make eyes at him.

Ahren turned to his book again but there was the Keeper, standing in front of him, looking at him with friendly yet reprimanding eyes, something he was particularly skilled at.

'Now, it seems Ahren wants to read something out to us, isn't that right?'

This was the priest's preferred punishment for lack of concentration. Ahren sighed inwardly. The only good thing about this was Ahren could always pick out a text he had questions about.

He leafed to the front of the book and began hesitatingly, to read aloud.

'At the beginning of time there were three gods: HE WHO IS, SHE WHO FEELS, AND HE WHO MOULDS. They argued with each other about who could create the most splendid things. Their pride prevented them from working together and so each of them began bringing their own creations to life. But each of them was incomplete without the other and in no position to create something harmonic.

HE WHO IS created the Golems: beings without feelings, coarse in form and lacking intuition.

SHE WHO FEELS crated the Wind Whips. Beings consisting of thoughts and emotions, without substance or constancy.

HE WHO MOULDS created the Transformers: beings without a core, many-shaped and fickle in spirit'.

Ahren stopped at this point and asked his first question. 'Keeper, if these beings were so incomplete, why did the gods let them continue to exist?' A murmur of agreement filled the air and Ahren realized he was not alone in wanting an answer.

The priest nodded and smiled as he always did when one of his students asked a good question. He answered with a counter question. 'Ahren, do you consider yourself perfect?'

As always, his gentle mocking hit the spot and even Likis nodded his head silently. Jegral could, with few words, awaken humility in anyone. Ahren wished he knew how he managed that.

The bald-headed man continued. 'So, you are not perfect. Or one could also say, incomplete. Would you like the gods to put an end to your existence?'

All the students shook their heads energetically in answer.

'That's what I thought. Those first beings may not have been complete but they existed now. They weren't to blame for their nature. And the gods knew this. If you create something, you are also responsible for it. You should make note of that'.

He turned to Ahren and said, 'carry on'.

The boy cleared his throat and continued. 'The gods saw that their attempts were not whole and complete and none of their creations reflected their dreams. They saw that they would have to help each other and so they laid their disagreements aside.

The union of the THREE was born.

A coming together of the gods, three wills with one goal. Each awakened a people according to their plans, supported through the powers of the other gods. For it was only together they could give their creations a harmony through essence and stability.

HE WHO IS created the dwarves: a people of unbelievable strength, stamina and stubbornness. Hardly flexible but firm and clear in form and with deeply rooted feelings.

And HE WHO IS was pleased and thanked his brother and his sister.

SHE WHO FEELS created the elves: spiritually adept creatures of fragile form, adaptable and instinctively seeking harmony with their surroundings. Alone of the peoples they tried of their own free will to make friends with the first incomplete beings.

And SHE WHO FEELS was pleased and thanked her brothers.

HE WHO MOULDS created the people: creations of adaptability and creative spirit which far surpassed their substance and ability to feel. It was due to this, that they did not live long and were volatile in their actions but were capable of great beauty.

And HE WHO MOULDS was pleased and thanked his brother and his sister.

Inspired by their success, the gods now wanted to create a world in which their creations could grow and flourish. Their joy and desire were so big that they created a world of enormous size, far larger than planned. They constantly had new ideas and could not stop themselves.

HE WHO IS placed himself in its core and gave it the foundations, from which a part of himself and his substance would flow into every living being.

SHE WHO FEELS became at one with the wind and whispered to every living being their task and their place in the world so all would be in a harmonious whole.

HE WHO MOULDS laid himself in the water, formed through his strength the mountains and rivers, made the land fertile and gave to all creatures of the world the desire to change.

They determined to call the world JORATH, which means *perfect* in the language of the gods, for that is what it was in their eyes.

But the creation had exhausted them.

They wanted rest to replenish their strength.

It was for this reason they created the Custodian, who would guard their creation as long as they were resting. The Creation was complete and the long sleep of the gods began'.

'That's enough for now', said Keeper Jegral firmly. 'Some parts of this story shouldn't be told in the dark part of the year. We shall continue at the Spring Ceremony'.

A heavy silence had descended on the room and Ahren was disappointed. The important part was yet to come and he had so many questions.

'Off home with you now and think about what I have told you'.

All the children said goodbye to each other outside the chapel and quickly went their various ways. Nobody wanted to stay out in the cold any longer than necessary, partly because their Sunday wear under the heavy winter coats offered little protection from the cold.

Ahren was in a ruminative mood. He looked at the chapel in its stillness with its covering of snow which covered the shingles that adorned the building. The wooden walls were painted white, the precious windows were warmly lit by the bright fire that burned within. The large engraved symbol of the THREE over the double doors seemed to look down on the boy who realized much to his own surprise that he really looked forward to the Godsday visits in spite of the lessons and the uncomfortable clothing. The sense of community was particularly strong at these times and the other boys were at last treating him as one of their own.

It had begun to snow again. A fine, light veil of crystals, which lent an air of peacefulness to the fading light of the winter afternoon. Thick heavy blue-grey clouds hung low in the sky and promised a heavy snowfall in the coming night. Ahren pulled himself out of his reverie and stamped with crunching steps through the blanket of white which almost reached to the top of his boots. If he went carefully, he could avoid getting his impractical linen trousers wet. He went through the silent village cautiously, his classmates having long since disappeared. Nothing spoiled the dreamy picture. Smoke was rising from the chimneys of the wooden houses, and Ahren could see light flickering through their closed windows. In the past, these images had made him melancholy, but now he was happy to be going home.

Home. When had he started seeing the Guardian's cabin as home? Lost in thought, Ahren walked past the back of the tavern to take the short cut through the forest when he saw a black bundle on the ground, about as big as a man. It was lying motionless a few paces from the back door at the foot of a tree. Ahren looked around carefully and approached it cautiously. He'd learnt his lesson about treacherous ambushes and wasn't going to fall into that trap again. As he approached it, he realized the bundle *was* a man, who had curled up and fallen asleep. He was already covered in a fine layer of snow and it wouldn't take long before he was completely covered. No-one would have noticed him – until it was too late.

Ahren bent down to help the poor unfortunate up but recoiled when he saw his father's sleeping face. He almost hadn't recognized him. The nose was laced with red veins, the pouches under his eyes hung heavily, his face was gaunt and he was covered in a stubbly beard which had been roughly cut into shape with a knife.

Ahren plucked up courage and bent over him to pull him up, only to be met by an unholy stench. Apparently, he hadn't had a bath in quite some time. He wrinkled up his nose and pulled the sleeping man up into a sitting position. He was so drunk that he barely woke. After a lot of effort Ahren finally succeeded in pulling him up the trunk of the tree until he was more or less in a standing position. He blinked but didn't seem to recognize his son. Ahren threw his father's arm over his shoulders and stumbled with him painfully slowly towards his family house.

His linen trousers were now soaked from the snow, his shoulders were aching from the weight of the drunkard, and Ahren had to breathe through his mouth because of the stench. After what seemed like an endless battle, they finally arrived at the low cabin that had been his home for so long. Ahren shoved open the door and dragged his father to his bed. The house was extremely warm as always, so there was no fear of his father catching the Blue Death. He took off his father's wet coat and laid Edrik down under his blanket. He stoked the embers, put some timbers on it to re-start the fire, which would last a few hours. Then he went to the door, turned around again to look at the room and the sleeping person. He had saved his father's life today. The onset of darkness and the falling snow would have sealed his fate. A life for a life, Ahren remembered, quoting to himself the old saying about earthly judgement. He turned on his heels, closed the door and didn't look back.

Once he'd arrived back at the Forest Guardian's cabin, he told his master what had happened. Falk looked at him earnestly. 'You did the right thing', he said, 'and I think what happened is partly my fault'.

'How do you mean?' Ahren was confused.

'I hadn't planned on telling you, but your father accosted me on the second day of the Autumn Festival. Said, if I was using the old customs against him, then I should really follow all of them. He demanded compensation. Apprentices used to be bought from their parents. He wanted a guinea'.

Ahren gasped in surprise. Guineas were made out of gold and were extremely valuable. A good horse would cost at least five guineas!

Falk continued calmly. 'I gave him three, divesting him of his pledge so he would never bother us again'.

Three golden guineas! Where did Falk get so much money? His father could live off that for two years without lifting a finger. No wonder he had drunk himself into oblivion. He had more than enough money for the tavern now.

Falk sighed. 'Well. Sometimes the quickest way to destroying a man is by giving him what he thinks he wants.'

Ahren thought about this for the rest of the evening and decided to be more careful with his wishes in the future.

Bright sunshine and a crystal clear, if bitingly cold sky had lured Ahren into the stillness of the clearing and away from the house. There was no breeze on this winter morning. The conditions were ideal and he could work on the targets that were still getting the better of him. He hung his quiver on the stake that marked his shooting position and looked at the strips of material he had hung on one of the branches. The red strip hung limply. No wind and a clear view.

Quickly and confidently he shot the arrows at the first targets. These had been as easy as pie for him for a long time but Falk's instructions had been clear. An arrow would have to hit every target before he would teach him the next lesson.

'Carelessness and hubris have killed more Forest Guardians than lack of skill. Nature rarely forgives arrogance', he added.

Ahren had learnt how to cut his own arrows in the meantime so he used these for the easy targets and kept the ones that Falk had given him for the more difficult exercises. He still hadn't quite mastered the fletching so he used the six perfectly balanced projectiles very sparingly and always retrieved them if he missed the target.

A few minutes later and everything was ready. Fifteen arrows had reached their targets. Five had yet to be hit.

Ahren took one of the good arrows confidently and breathed in deeply. The spirits of the Void had become a lot fainter since his last encounter with his father, and he found it easier to briefly inhabit the trancelike state before his subconscious would distract him and he'd have to start again.

But two seconds were an eternity in archery and he wanted to use them well today for his purposes. He concentrated on the image of the faint candlelight with his inner eye and emptied his thoughts while breathing slowly and regularly. He looked at the small, head-sized circle that Falk had painted on the trunk between two stems. From where he was standing, he calculated he would need to shoot the arrow perfectly through the gap between the two branches or the arrow would ricochet off one of them. As he felt his body relaxing and his eyes focusing exclusively on this small white target, he extended the bow, aimed and shot. The Void vanished immediately. Tension, the thrill of anticipation and fear all combined within him as he watched the arrow nearing its target. He let out a cry of joy as the tip bored into the upper third of the circle. Not perfect, but good enough.

Satisfied he reached for the next arrow and took aim at the next target. This one he liked least. The chalk outline was big, almost as big as a pig, proudly revealing itself way up at the top of a conifer – like a white eye looking at him mockingly. This shot was treacherous because Ahren knew that if he missed the target, the arrow would fly one or two hundred paces beyond the tree and land in a dell that he would have to search. So far, the pressure not to fail had led each time to him doing just that.

Quietly cursing his dastardly master, Ahren tried to conjure up the Void. After three futile attempts he was finally ready. The arrow left the bowstring, went in a perfect arc, missed the target by a mere handspan only to sink into the valley beyond. Now Ahren cursed aloud and briefly considered the option of leaving the arrow to itself, but then he imagined how Falk would look if he noticed one of his presents had been lost, so he set off. Half an hour later he found the projectile, which had become trapped in a thorn bush. He collected it and was closing up his quiver when he noticed a red spot in the dirty white drabness of the forest floor.

Ahren was curious and went closer. It was blood, fresh blood. The trail led to another thorn bush, which looked quite battered, as if something big had run through it.

Perhaps an injured stag, Ahren thought excitedly. Falk would certainly be proud of him if he were to come home with some wild game. And an injured animal would have hardly any chance of surviving in winter and that way they could spare a healthy one. Ahren stood stock still and listened. He could hear faint breathing sounds from behind the bush. He moved forward very slowly and carefully, just as he had learnt, and tried pushing his way noiselessly through the thorny branches.

There was a light wind blowing down here and he was convinced that it was coming from the right direction, he was downwind. So far so good. The stag wouldn't be able to smell him. Ahren lay down on his stomach and the cold snow sucked the warmth out of his body in an instant as he slowly elbowed his way forward.

Finally, through the branches he saw a stag lying at the foot of an enormous boulder. There was blood everywhere and the entrails of the poor animal were hanging in shreds from the surrounding bushes and shrubbery. Ahren looked in shock at the scene and tried to comprehend which animal had attacked. Then a thought struck him. The deer was clearly dead, but he'd heard breathing coming from this direction. He listened intently but the blood was pounding in his ears with excitement and he could no longer hear it.

His heart was beating wildly as he stood there stock still, not moving an inch. Feverishly he wondered what animal could have done this damage and he could only think it must have been a rabid bear. This thought put the apprentice into a state of panic. He forced himself to take deep, regular breaths as he tried to reach the Void. He didn't quite get there but at least he was thinking clearly again.

He was slowly crawling backwards when the black rock, where the stag was lying, began to move! A huge paw became visible and the enormous black wolf, which had been curled up beside its prey, stood up in one flowing motion. The animal was at least one head taller than Falk and as long as a horse. Its fur was so black that it seemed to swallow all light. The monster stood up on its hind legs and stretched its nose into the wind. As it was sniffing loudly, Ahren noticed that its right front leg was damaged and the creature was holding it close to its chest. The boy could see a furry pattern running between the fore-paws, a strangely convoluted spiral of dark red fur. It stood out like a brand on the rest of the jet-black body.

The creature's eyes burned a fiery red, no pupils, nothing. Only two half-moons that stared at him as the Blood Wolf slowly turned its head – and looked him directly in the eyes. Ahren spun around, ignoring the thorns that were scratching his face and injuring him, and broke through the undergrowth. Behind him he could hear a blood-curdling howl, deeper and more ferocious than any wolf he had heard before. He redoubled his efforts. He had managed about ten paces when he heard the Dark One crashing into the thorn bush. Another eight paces, a quick look behind, and he could see that the monster would break free any second and have a clear run. For a split second he thought of using the bow, but if he wanted to stop it, he would have to shoot the beast through the throat or through one of its eyes as it was charging on him. That may have sounded exciting and heroic in the old stories but Ahren really didn't feel like betting his life on it. The surrounding trees were too small to offer protection, so he wouldn't be able to climb to safety.

The clearing! If he could manage to get there, there were enough trees that were high enough. The prospect of an escape gave him the courage to run on. The distance between himself and the murderous beast was at least forty paces once it had freed itself from the thorn bush and it began to run. It had a limp! It obviously couldn't move its crippled foreleg, and that gave Ahren hope. At least until he risked another look over his shoulder after a few more paces.

His hunter was gaining three or four paces with every one of its bounds and would catch him within a few heartbeats! Ahren raced as fast as he could, straining every sinew in his body. He leapt over bushes and ducked with agile movements under low hanging branches. His arms worked like pumps to keep his forward momentum going at full pelt. He practically flew through the forest and a small part of him now understood how his master's varied lessons were coming together to work as a whole. But most of his thoughts were concerned with the fact that he could only enjoy this realization for a few brief seconds until the Blood Wolf tore him limb from limb like a little rag doll.

His nerves were completely frayed by now. He tried to make use of his smaller size by constantly feinting in order to ensure there were as many tree trunks as possible between himself and the Blood Wolf. This tactic only slowed him down and the distance between them was shrinking mercilessly. A hundred more paces to the incline, and on top of that was the clearing with the practice targets. Ahren calculated that he would manage about half the distance before he felt the fangs of the wolf on his body.

Still he ran on. With sweeping strides, he leapt up the hill but he could already feel the beast breathing down his neck. With a yell he stormed onwards, at the same time drawing his knife. Were the creature to grasp him, he wasn't going to give up his life easily. It was only a few strides to the top of the hill and the familiar edge of the clearing appeared before him. Any second and he'd feel the hard claws boring into his skin and the long teeth would finish him off. Ahren grasped his knife harder and was about to spin around to see his killer in the eye, but suddenly an enormous silver-white spectre appeared over the crest of the embankment and came hurtling towards him.

He flung himself to the side and caught a glimpse of horns, white fur and swirling hooves. With his nose in the earth he heard a deafening crash as the Blood Wolf and Ahren's mysterious saviour smashed into each other. He picked himself up quickly and saw a furious ball of black and silver-grey fur rolling down the embankment. He could hardly

130

believe his eyes, and not wanting to push his luck, he ran on as fast as he could until he finally reached the safety of the cabin.

Falk leaped up when his apprentice stormed in, closing the door behind him with a crash. Ahren doubted that this door made of flimsy wood could really stop the Blood Wolf but for the moment he was happy with the illusion of safety. He collapsed into a heap and for the next few minutes couldn't stop shivering. He wanted to warn his master but his teeth were chattering uncontrollably. He tried uttering 'wolf' a few times before eventually giving up. Falk knew a case of shock when he saw it and poured a beaker of calming tea out for him. He still needed help in drinking it and managed to spill half of it. Once the brew had performed its task, Falk let his apprentice relate the story right from the start. At first, he thought the apprentice had encountered his first wolf alone in the wild and hysteria had done the rest, but when Ahren began describing the animal, he became very tense. He had often experienced how victims of an animal attack would exaggerate their attacker's size and danger, but the boy had certainly not imagined the red eyes.

'Alright then, that must have been a Blood Wolf. Now we have to find out how strong the beast is' Falk began to put on his gear and took up the bow. 'Was the fur dark red or reddish-black?'

'Neither. The fur was jet black. It didn't even reflect the light', the young boy blurted.

'That's not good. The wolf isn't just fully grown but also very old. The more they kill, the redder the fur. Then the red becomes darker and darker and at some point, it's black'. By now he was fully equipped and opening the chest. This, Ahren knew, contained his master's most prized possessions.

'Then at least it's not so mighty', said Ahren relieved. 'It had a red area between the fore-paws'.

At this, Falk spun around and grabbed the startled boy by the shoulders. 'What a strange place. Describe it'.

'An elaborate spiral, thin and…bright red', blurted the boy.

Falk let his apprentice go and started cursing loudly.

Ahren stared wide-eyed at his master, who was letting forth a torrent of abusive language.

Once he had calmed down, he sat down on a stool, hung his head and said, 'I'm sorry, but that was necessary. If the monster is this size it must be at least four hundred years old. The patterns develop only over time and after countless victims have died. Don't get me wrong, but actually you should be dead' He looked at Ahren doubtfully.

'It only had three good legs. One fore-leg is crippled', argued the apprentice.

Falk only grunted.

'But it would definitely have caught me if it weren't for the grey thing', Ahren added.

His master sat bolt upright. 'What kind of grey thing?'

Ahren shrugged his shoulders. 'It suddenly appeared and jumped on top of the wolf, something with horns and silver-grey fur. I couldn't tell exactly what it was'.

Falk leapt up so quickly that he knocked over the stool. All colour had drained from his face and he gasped, 'Selsena!'

Before Ahren could figure out if this was an Elfish curse or a name, the old man had stormed out of the door without saying another word. The young boy was torn between fear and awareness of his responsibilities, and sat frozen on his stool. After a few moments he jumped up with a 'damn!' and ran after his mentor and directly towards where the Blood Wolf might be lying in wait for them.

Branches were once again whipping his face and his chest was rising and falling like a bellows, but this time, the gods be cursed, he was running in the wrong direction! His master was a silhouette in the afternoon light and no matter how fast Ahren tried to catch up with him, he simply couldn't. Branches, roots of trees, bushes and twigs just seemed to slide off him, his every movement was efficient and precise, just sufficient to avoid obstacles without ever slowing his tempo. Ahren would have admired this sight under normal circumstances but at the moment he had neither the time nor the nerve.

Every so often Falk would cry out, 'Selsena!', and Ahren was sure now it must be a name. It seemed that he must know the creature that had saved him and was more concerned for its safety than for his own.

Or for my safety, thought Ahren for a moment.

Then he realized how selfish this thought was. This creature, whatever it was, had saved his life.

The practice clearing appeared in front of them and Ahren began to grow seriously afraid again. His steps became slower and more hesitant and he dropped further back. His master had reached the middle of the clearing and stood there, rooted to the spot. He was murmuring something so quietly that Ahren couldn't understand it. The Forest Guardian tilted his head sideways as his apprentice had seen him do so often in the previous few months. Then he nodded and said something again.

Ahren trotted over to his master and caught his breath by putting his hands on his knees. Luckily, Falk seemed to have calmed down, he didn't seem to want to run any further, but was looking intently at the far side of the clearing. There, only a few paces further, was where the two creatures had clashed. For a few moments nothing happened. Then, an animal came slowly out of the undergrowth, and approached the two of them with its head hanging. A bloodied head and flanks, and even Falk drew his breath in sharply. He took a step forward, tilted his head again and nodded. His shoulders relaxed.

Ahren saw his rescuer approaching, and now he could make out details. At first, he thought the animal was a large horse, but now he saw the massive bone plate that covered its head and the three horns protruding from it. The top one was long and spiral with a tapered tip. The middle and lower ones were identical. Small and curved with a serrated edge. The creature had a broader chest than any horse he had ever seen and its fur shone a soft grey, emitting a mysterious silver shimmer wherever it hadn't been soaked with blood. A thick mane and mighty hooves rounded off the picture.

It came to a halt about a pace away and raised its head so that its silver eyes seemed to stare directly at Falk. He reciprocated the look, cleared his throat and said, 'Ahren, may I introduce Selsena to you?'

This information came as no surprise to Ahren at this point. He was sure this must have been the name of his rescuer, but one thing wasn't clear. What was it doing here?

He had a suspicion, but that was absurd.

'Is that a unicorn?' he asked in the silence.

Falk winced and the animal snorted scornfully as if it wanted to answer.

'Please don't say that', his master rebuked him. 'You sound like an idiot to her. The correct title would be Titejunanwa, which roughly translated means 'One horn, two daggers, three hearts, four hooves protect the forest' People made that into the word "unicorn"''.

134

As he was speaking, he began to carefully examine the creature's head and flanks. 'I could just call you 'A' from now on because the rest is too complicated for me, and that wouldn't be half as insulting as 'unicorn''.

Then another disparaging snort came from the enormous nostrils.

'Just call her Selsena', said Falk as he finished his explanation while he gently stroked the bloodied areas with the flat of his hand.

The blood simply flowed to the ground and not a drop was left on the hide!

The animal was completely clean again within two dozen heartbeats. Apart from three long bruises on the flank where the Blood Wolf had injured it with a paw swipe.

Ahren looked in amazement at the pool of blood in the snow.

'Nothing sticks to her hide', explained Falk. 'And so, for example, she cannot be poisoned by the spittle of a Grave Frog'. He bent down, examined the cuts and continued, 'which probably explains the fairy tales about purity, maidenhood and all that nonsense'.

Ahren had slowly taken a step forward and looked Selsena directly in the eyes. A happy feeling came over him, just as if he were seeing Likis again, and he smiled, in spite of himself.

Falk stood up straight and said, 'they are empaths, and can sense feelings and transmit them. Let me also make one thing clear: if a Titejunanwa gores you, then you're dead, virgin or not, whatever any of the stories might claim'. Ahren pulled back instinctively but a merriment immediately spread within him as the Elven-horse snorted.

'Is she laughing at me?' asked Ahren taken aback.

' Of course she is. She's cleverer than you are', said Falk with a smile. He tilted his head and added, 'Cleverer than both of us'. He patted the animal's neck and another feeling of joy passed through Ahren. It was strange but fascinating at the same time.

The old man understood his look and said, 'you'll learn quickly how to ignore them, unless she wants you to know something. By the way, we can head back to the cabin now, she says. The Blood Wolf has fled'. His master turned around and went back beside Selsena and with a spring in his step, started walking towards the cabin.

This news was music to Ahren's ears and with a last, anxious look over his shoulder, he followed the pair. He stayed in the background on the way home and watched the unlikely couple. Falk stayed close by Selsena's side and from time to time whispered things into her ear. Sometimes he would tilt his head to the side before answering. Ahren could feel joy, excitement and sometimes annoyance coming from the animal.

'She can talk to you, can't she?' he asked. They both stopped abruptly and Ahren realized that he had asked the question out aloud.

He blushed but his master only nodded. 'Yes, that's right. A certain…situation…has made it possible for us to talk to each other. She can hear what I think and vice versa. Except that I'm a bit out of practice and I have to ask my questions out loud to muster the necessary concentration'.

'So, if you tilt your head, then she's talking to you?' Ahren was very proud that he had figured this out for himself.

'Do I do that? I never noticed', answered his master thoughtfully. 'Another crutch I can hopefully get rid of soon'.

'Why are you out of practice', Ahren wanted to know. Falk scowled and said, 'we had different opinions…about something very important. We didn't talk to each other for a long time. I was in the wrong. That's all I'm going to say'. At that, Selsena snorted.

The rest of the journey passed in silence although Ahren was dying to ask dozens more questions, but Falk kept his head tilted the whole time, and judging by his face he was on the receiving end of a long and detailed lecture from Selsena. Ahren was comforted by the irony that his master was getting a dressing down for a change, and he smiled to himself.

All thoughts of the Blood Wolf, which was lurking somewhere out there in the forest, were forgotten for a few precious minutes.

Chapter 8

'I don't understand why I didn't notice the monster earlier. There were practically none of the typical tell-tale signs in the forest. No massacres of wolves and bears, no swathes of destruction in the undergrowth, no woodcutters ripped apart'. Falk threw his arms in the air and looked questioningly out the window to where Selsena was standing.

Ahren listened and shivered but didn't say a word. Talking about the Dark Ones wasn't half as terrifying anymore since he had faced the monster the previous day. Nothing could compare with the raw presence of the massive body with its black hide and muscles, which meant certain death.

Ahren got up and began to clear up the breakfast which had ended once his master had finished his exclamation. Speaking had been kept to a minimum the evening before. Selsena had settled down comfortably outside the cabin and Falk had assured Ahren that she would keep watch. It had been obvious to Ahren that he wasn't going to get any more answers that night and it seemed that they were safe for the time being, so he lay down and promptly fell asleep.

To his surprise he had slept well and deeply and without dreams. He had woken up refreshed and rested and not, as he had expected, bathed in sweat in a rumpled bed. He had then gone to the window and seen Selsena looking at him with her soft silvery eyes. A deep feeling of peace had spread inside him and he understood that the animal had guarded not only the cabin, but also his sleep.

Yet all three were restless now. The time had come for his questions so he ploughed on. 'Why didn't Selsena just kill the Blood Wolf? They did fight and she seems to have won'.

All the scratches on her flanks were almost completely healed and only recognizable as thin red welts on her hide.

Falk looked at his apprentice in disbelief and snorted. Then he thought better and explained the situation. 'Selsena caught him off-guard. An attack from close range with the main horn. Her speciality, if you like. She struck it on the shoulder and the two of them hurtled down the incline while the wolf tried to bite her on the throat'. Ahren looked over at the mythical creature anxiously. He vividly remembered the long fangs of the wolf and had no doubt at all that they could have torn apart the neck of the magical horse with one bite.

'She got free and got away from it. Had she engaged in combat for even one more second, then she'd probably have been killed'. The Elven horse gave a quick snort and Falk tilted his head, then said, 'No false pride now, you know that's the truth'.

Selsena looked away.

'The beast ran into the undergrowth, where it has an advantage over her, and for that reason she didn't give chase. We have to look for it', said Falk into the silent room.

Ahren nodded wearily. He had seen that one coming. After all, this was the main function of the Forest Guardian. Otherwise he would simply be a common hunter.

Falk proudly observed the stoic response of the boy and his look softened. 'The Blood Wolf is wounded and crippled. It is alone and there are three of us. Selsena can sense its anger if it's nearby. These advantages should even up the hunt a little'.

'Do you still think it's four hundred years old?' asked Ahren doubtfully. This was an unbelievable length of time that a young brain simply couldn't comprehend.

'I said at least four hundred yesterday. Based on Selsena's description and its quick reaction to her attack, I would guess that he had fought already in the Dark Days'.

Ahren was flabbergasted at this news. This creature had fought in wars that he had read about in the legends during his Godsday lessons!

Falk looked at his apprentice earnestly. 'It's important you understand we're dealing with an old and experienced brain here. Without Selsena's equally long experience in battle I'd have to drum up half the village, there'd be some massacre, and even then, victory would be far from certain. Think about it, the more blood it spills, the stronger it becomes'.

Ahren looked at the creature outside the window. She was just talking to Falk and the apprentice watched her thoughtfully. These eyes had seen things for more than seven hundred years. What wonders and sorrows must she have experienced?

Falk laughed out loud and the thought was gone.

'She says it's not polite to talk about a woman's age. Better that we change the subject. The first thing we need are battle arrows. Our hunting arrows won't even penetrate the Blood Wolf's fur. I'll take care of that. You run over to Vera and get the Earth Paste'.

Ahren nodded. This was a logical step. Earth Paste could camouflage individual human scents and made hunting easier. It was very difficult to make, expensive and was only used when hunting dangerous game.

Perfect for hunting Blood Wolves, thought Ahren grimly.

The old man continued. 'Selsena, you comb the forest and see if you can find its whereabouts. But in the name of the THREE be careful'.

She answered them both and a feeling of comfort filled the boy. Then she spun around on her hind hooves and disappeared into the forest in the space of two heartbeats.

Falk looked after her with concern, then looked over at his apprentice.

'What are you still doing here? She says the coast is clear but once she's gone from us, we won't know where the wolf is hiding, so stop dawdling and get back here in double quick time'.

Ahren didn't need to be told twice. He threw on his woollen coat and quickly went out the door and into the silence of the drifting snow, which had fallen during the night and was now sticking. Within two hours he had two sealed jars of Earth Paste and was on the way home. Vera had asked him why he needed this expensive cream, but as Ahren wasn't sure what he was allowed to say, he didn't say anything but suggested she talk to Falk. The old woman could be very indignant if you kept information from her, so Ahren left quickly before she could grill him. He would have to spill the beans sooner or later.

Falk had already returned when he got back to the cabin. It turned out that Ahren could have told Vera about the Blood Wolf. His master had not only ordered three dozen battle arrows from the blacksmith but he had also informed the village council that entering the forest was forbidden and he had even sounded the bell in front of the Village Hall to lend his words more weight. The village would now be in a state of emergency until Falk rang the bell again. For the moment no-one could leave their house without good reason, and all activities in the forest were suspended.

'The blacksmith said the arrows would be ready this afternoon. I have something else to take care of and will bring them with me when I return. You look after your equipment and especially your bow. I want you to string it with as much tension as possible. It's not going to help us if you hit the target, but the arrow simply gets stuck in the thick hide'.

Before Ahren could give an answer, Falk had disappeared again in a cloud of tumbling snowflakes.

He did as he was told and looked after his things. His master still hadn't returned by the evening, and the boy was becoming nervous. Selena wasn't back either and he began imagining the worst. What if the wolf had caught the magical horse? Or Falk? Or both? Once darkness set in, Ahren was in the grip of his own fantasies. With his inner eye he saw the whole village, lifeless and still. Doors had been torn off with brute force, the villagers slaughtered on the spot. Ahren was the only one left and a pair of red eyes were focused on his cabin, while in the darkness the Blood Wolf circled ever closer as he crept towards his prey. Ahren was beginning to flinch at every noise and caught himself holding on to his bow and arrow for dear life. He put both aside, lit the candle and tried to find the Void.

His master found him in the same position when he arrived back in the late evening. The candle had almost burned down, which meant that Ahren must have been there for several hours. The boy's head had sunk down to his chest and he was snoring. The old man closed the door with a frown, then carefully wakened the boy by placing his hand on the boy's shoulder and gently shaking him.

The apprentice looked up at him sleepily and said in a daze, 'you're back late'.

'The blacksmith took longer because he had never made battle arrows before. I decided to wait so that we're ready whenever we need them'.

Ahren noticed two bundles on his master's back. One was a fresh oilskin, slim in shape and undoubtedly held the arrows; the other was an

142

enormous, filthy leather bag, lumpy in shape which made a clattering sound whenever Falk moved. He placed both on the table and sat down.

'Did it work?' he asked, indicating the candle.

Ahren nodded first, but then shook his head. 'Not really. I did calm down but I didn't achieve the Void. The spirits are strong now that the wolf is among them'.

Falk gave an understanding nod. The boy's subconscious would be full of images of the beast they would soon be hunting. This was down to what he'd just experienced. It was quite an achievement that he had been able to calm himself to the extent of falling asleep on his own.

'A start, said Falk and began unpacking the bundles.

One of them contained the reinforced arrows, as Ahren had predicted. He picked one up to look at it more closely. The shaft was stronger and broader than the usual hunting arrow and the tip was a dangerous looking triangle with its tip ending in a barb. The weapon was at least four times as heavy as the arrows Ahren was used to. He shuddered at the thought of being struck by one of these monsters. The idea that somewhere people would be shooting these at each other in a war was unbearable and unimaginable. He quickly put the murderous instrument aside and looked with interest at his master, who was now emptying the second bag.

Armoured neck collars, underarm protectors and leg guards appeared, everything made from a strange whitish material, and elaborately adorned. He reached forward to touch one of the pieces but Falk silently tapped him on the fingers and gave him a stern look. The master began to smear the pieces of armour with ash from the fireplace until they looked grey and dirty, almost like neglected iron that was just becoming rusty. Then he placed them carefully on a shelf and took the last piece out of the bag. Ahren gasped in surprise. It was a broadsword and scabbard. Broadswords were a rarity in Hjalgar, and as far as Ahren knew there were none in Deepstone. He never would have thought that his master possessed one.

'Left over from a war I'd rather not think about'. That was all his master had to say about the matter. The rest of the evening passed by in silence.

The snow fell more heavily that night. Selsena returned in the morning and informed Falk that she hadn't been successful in her search. He stood at the window and looked out at the white landscape with a frown.

'The snow is already knee deep. A hunt is out of the question for the next few days. The villagers won't be happy that work will be impossible during this time', complained Falk. 'But Selsena will keep on looking. The good news is that the Blood Wolf doesn't seem to have made its lair in the vicinity. That's certainly lessened the probability of immediate danger'.

He turned around to his apprentice. 'We'll spend the whole day practising with the battle arrows and when your arms are exhausted, we'll practise stalking. I want you to be as prepared as possible'.

The whole of the next week was taken up with this routine. Now and again Selsena sensed the rage of the monster and began to encircle its hiding place. Meanwhile Ahren grew used to the new weaponry and his master taught him more about the art of stalking. The villagers waited patiently but on the fifth evening one of the most senior of the village elders came to their door and asked how long the danger was likely to continue.

Falk knew that this situation could not continue indefinitely and when Selsena reported on the evening of the ninth day that she had found the creature's lair, Falk announced, 'right, regardless of the snow, tomorrow we hunt the Blood Wolf'.

Chapter 9

The weather at least was reasonably kind and so the three headed off under clear skies to confront the Dark One who was threatening their village community.

One thing was bothering Ahren. 'Why is Selsena helping us? Couldn't she just gallop away? Or can you control her with your thoughts?'

Falk rubbed his beard and answered. 'Firstly, she's been my companion for more years than I care to remember. We'd go through hell and high water for each other and have done that many times. Secondly, SHE WHO FEELS created the Titejunanwa to protect the forest and all its inhabitants from the Dark Ones. It's her vocation to help us'.

Ahren had to digest this information first. In the humans' stories, unicorns only appeared as protectors of maidens, or proved the purity of a heart by boring into the subject with their horn. If it remained whole, then the person was without malice.

Then there were rainbows. In every story with unicorns, you had rainbows. The creature standing before Ahren, and all that Falk had told him about, didn't fit into the legends that he had heard.

When you looked at Selsena carefully, she appeared almost stocky. This was down to her broad chest which contained the three hearts. The breast cage under her hide seemed to be made of a continuous breastplate although Ahren couldn't be sure. The one on her head could be clearly seen and gave the animal a much more martial air than what was described in the legends. They walked further northwards, far further north than Ahren had ever marched with Falk.

'That's why I hadn't noticed the wolf', Falk realized. 'Since you've been with me, I've rarely come to this part of the forest. The wolf's lair is

146

still further north. It's too far to get there and back in one day. We're going to have to sleep in the open after the hunt'. He then pointed at the heavy rucksack on Ahren's back. The apprentice was heavily weighed down today because they had taken far more equipment than usual, including many healing creams and bandages.

Ahren swallowed and tried to think of something else. He was carrying the lion's share today partly because his master was wearing the pieces of armour that he had produced from the dirty bundle. Ahren's theory was that he had hidden the bag somewhere in the forest but the old man had refused to confirm this. The neck piece protected the lower part of Falk's head, and the metal pieces enclosed his underarms and lower legs. He'd tied the sword to the middle of his back so that his movement would be as free as possible. The snow was up to the middle of Ahren's thighs and he followed in his master's wake on a path that had been ploughed in the snow by Selsena's quiet steps.

Selsena stopped around midday and Falk listened to her. He nodded and said, 'this is it. Somewhere within a thousand paces is the lair, and the Blood Wolf is there. Let's put on the Earth Paste'. Ahren fished out the two little jars as silently as possible and they began applying the brown paste, which oozed the smells of the forest. Meanwhile Falk ran through their strategy one more time.

'Selsena will draw the beast out into the open. I'll try and land one or two arrows. Ahren, you stay in the background. Only shoot if one of us gets into distress, you just have to hit it so that it's distracted, then we can regroup. If we're lucky my first arrow will do the trick and it'll all be over in ten heartbeats. Then we can head back home'. He tried to smile encouragingly but he could only manage a grimace.

'Understood?'

Ahred nodded and Selsena snorted.

'Right, then. Let's get this over with'.

They moved forward slowly. Step by step, then stopping and listening. The Elven horse corrected course a few times, whenever she located the wolf more precisely.

After what seemed like an eternity she stopped and bowed her head so that her horn was pointing towards an enormous, fallen tree. The roots of the colossus had ripped a huge clump of earth out of the ground, which now stuck up into the sky like a little mountain, laced with its pattern of roots. Below this was a dark cool hollow, shaded from the sun and prying eyes. Something dark rose and fell at regular intervals and Ahren knew that this was the wolf's chest.

Slowly they separated. Falk moved to the left, Selsena to the right and Ahren stayed where he was until they had formed a semi-circle above the hollow, each ten paces from the next. With shaking fingers Ahren took an arrow and lightly tensed the bowstring so that he would be quick off the mark when the time was right. It was biting cold and yet his hands were damp with sweat and he could hear the blood roaring in his ears. He felt at the mercy of the murderous creature – something he had never felt before. If Falk and Selsena were to fail, then he too would be killed by the Blood Wolf. He felt as if he was handing over control of his life, which was almost more frightening than the death machine they were about to attack. If he hadn't trusted his master quite so much, he would have fled by now. Instead, he looked one last time into the calm grey eyes of the old Forest Guardian, who looked back at him before deliberately selecting an arrow and setting it in position. A short nod of his grey head and it began.

Selsena stood on her hind legs and let forth a loud neigh which contained within it a wave of defiance which she communicated through empathy to her partners. Ahren felt the strong impulse within him and ground his teeth in agitation.

The wolf reacted immediately. In one flowing movement it was up, throwing its head back and answering the challenge with a loud, nerve-wracking howl. Snow fluttered from the trees and Ahren's teeth hurt.

So far, so good, he thought and held his breath. The creature had reacted as they had expected and already Falk let an arrow fly, which headed straight for the wolf's invitingly upstretched neck. The arrow landed with a horrible crunch and Ahren was on the point of cheering when the wolf spun around and tried to bite the arrow, which hadn't seemed to have done it any harm.

Falk shot again, this time straight at the eyes, which the wolf had fixed on him. Again, there was another horrible noise as the arrow hit one of the burning red half-moons, extinguishing it forever. The angle was wrong however, and the arrow lodged downward behind the cheek instead of boring into the brain.

The next part of the plan involved an assault by Selsena, who was to land on the wolf's back and distract it. She was already racing for the Dark One but the wolf turned around and plunged with incredible speed towards Falk. Falk fired another arrow, which hit the Blood Wolf in the breast and a second later the monster took an almighty leap while letting forth a furious howl of pain. The black body of fangs and claws was on top of Falk in a fury of blood lust before he had the chance to shoot off another arrow. With a furious growl the fangs sank in and it began to bite.

Seeing the situation, Ahren screamed with all his might as he prepared an arrow, but he was afraid to shoot in case he hit Falk. Selsena was still at least five paces away when the Blood Wolf raised its head, the left arm of the old man between its powerful jaws, and it tossed its head from side to side so that Falk was thrown about like a rag doll. Branches were

149

smashed and his master's body, which was being tossed wildly around the place, was rammed at least once into the trunk of a tree. Then Selsena, who was less hesitant than Ahren, attacked. With a neigh of fury, she rammed her horn all the way into the wolf's flank and threw it down. Falk was thrown, screaming upwards in an arc before landing with a thud on the forest floor. Before the beast could catch Selsena, she had jumped away to prepare herself for another assault.

Now Ahren understood what his master had tried to explain to him. The Blood Wolf was much faster and stronger in close combat. No matter how terrifying the ramming attacks of the Titejunanwa might be, she would have practically no chance of defending herself once the wolf had her in its grip.

An evil intelligence flashed forth from the Dark One's remaining eye. It made no move to follow the magical horse but turned to the injured Falk instead. In frustration Selsena emitted another challenge, but this time it seemed to have no effect on the black animal. Without hesitating, it fell upon Falk again, who had turned on his back and was laboriously trying to draw his broadsword, as his arrow had been snapped by the wolf in the first attack.

Ahren saw in horror that the wolf would be faster, much faster. Without thinking, he tensed the bow as far as he could and let the heavy arrow fly. The missile struck the wolf on the right shoulder, just as it was looming over Falk. More surprised than injured, the monster turned its head. The Blood Wolf hesitated, unsure as to whether it should finish off the prey that was lying there invitingly or if it should make for the second archer. Ahren shot a second arrow, which landed harmlessly in the beast's hide while he screamed incoherently, less as a challenge and more as a way of counteracting his rising panic. The wolf made a decision and prepared to spring forward, which would have brought it effortlessly on the defenceless apprentice, but Falk finally pulled the broadsword out of its scabbard.

'Paladinim theos duralas', he called and the Dark One threw itself in a rage at him.

Falk plunged the sword into the beast's chest but because he was half under the animal it didn't penetrate far. He couldn't release his hands from the grip without losing his final weapon and didn't have enough strength to push the blade in deeper. The wolf lowered its head past the steel which was sticking into it and was about to rip Falk's head off. Sobbing, Ahren set another arrow in order somehow to help his master, when Selsena came galloping up. A flash of light from the low setting sun shone through the branches and caught the horns of the silver animal before the armoured head smashed into flesh and bones and with an almighty crash, the wolf was thrown forward and down into the old Forest Guardian's broadsword blade. Smoothly the sword slipped as far as the hilt into the wolf's breast.

With a final howl, and as if struck by lightning, the wolf collapsed in a heap, pulling Selsena with it, as her horn was stuck in the creature's spine. An unnatural silence filled the air for a moment, broken only by the irregular panting of the terrified apprentice, who was rooted to the spot, afraid of what he might find in the hollow.

It was only when the body of the wolf gave a sudden jerk and he heard a muffled, 'boy, a little help would be great', that he came out of his paralysis and hurried to help his trapped master.

Selsena, who must have been stunned for a moment, rose unsteadily and loosened her horn with a disgusting, squelching sound from the flesh of her enemy. Her bony head was spattered with blood and bits of the wolf, and Ahren looked away with a shudder.

Whoever made up these stories about unicorns had never seen a Titejunanwa in action.

He got down to work with a groan and started pulling Falk out from under the wolf's corpse. Sometime later and with a combined effort they succeeded in freeing the old Forest Guardian. Once he was up on his feet again, he pulled the blade out of the cadaver, wiped it dry on the hide and murmured to the sword, 'you haven't let me down yet', before slipping it back into its scabbard.

'Master, what was that you called out earlier?' asked Ahren curiously. The wolf had reacted to the call immediately and violently.

'We've just slain a Dark One that has been wreaking murderous havoc around the world for half a millennium and you want a lesson in Elfish?' his master replied humorously.

Ahren realized that he wasn't going to get a sensible answer today.

Instead, Falk gripped his hand and said, 'yes, thank you, Ahren. Things would have turned out very differently without you'.

The boy was bursting with pride, at least until his master tousled his hair as if he were a child. The old codger could really spoil things at a moment's notice. A feeling of happiness surged through his thoughts when Selsena started laughing at them both, and one heartbeat later they were all laughing their heads off, glad to be still alive.

He awoke with a start, wide-eyed and his face bathed in sweat. An old oath had been renewed; spoken by a voice he had thought lost forever. He looked over at the complicated network of lines, spirals and convoluted signs, which almost covered the marble floor completely. He could still hear the singing reverberating in the air. Quickly he spoke a simple spell while with a gruff movement of the hand he shooed away the servant, who had rushed to him when he had awoken. With full

concentration he stared at the barely visible lines that led towards the
west. He smiled and began adding a new sign to his magic web.

Now he knew where he must look.

A short time later they had lit a fire, but Ahren was still shaking like a leaf. Falk watched him sympathetically and said, 'Your body has to become used to the excitement. You'll feel better soon'. Ahren wasn't sure if he ever wanted to get used to the feeling of being in mortal danger but kept the thought to himself.

Falk rubbed his left shoulder absentmindedly. His movements were still stiff. After all, the wolf's attack had almost ripped his arm off. Only the old man's athletic constitution and the under-arm armour that the wolf had bitten into had prevented him from being torn apart - literally.

'Have you decided yet which part you want?' the old man asked abruptly.

Falk responded to Ahren's questioning look by pointing with his knife at the spread-eagled shape of the Blood Wolf. 'That is a Dark One. Tradition grants you the right to a trophy and you've certainly earned one'. The boy's thoughts turned to the grey Fog Cat cloak that Falk wore at any traditional occasion. Falk could never be considered a pompous person and so he had wondered a few times over the preceding months why he owned such a cloak at all. However, the great satisfaction that came with conquering such a powerful opponent explained the Forest Guardian's desire to display tangible proof of such an achievement.

Ahren walked slowly around the cadaver, half afraid the Blood Wolf could come back to life. If this encounter had taught him anything, then it was respect for the opponent.

He circled the mountain of fur and was considering whether he could use one of the fangs as a dagger when he heard a curious little whimpering sound. He turned around and went gingerly towards the source of the sound. It seemed to come from a part of the pit where the wolf had been lying. Although he watched out where he was walking, he kept stepping on dry bones which cracked and snapped under his boots. The skeletons of older prey lay all over the place and there was a strong smell of old blood emanating from the back of the lair. Ahren was about to turn back when he heard the sound again, which he now identified as a weak whimpering. A little puppy was lying among the bones, curled up in a protective hollow, with its snow-white fur. It looked up at the boy with its golden yellow eyes while it weakly called for its mother.

Ahren was overcome by a feeling of guilt mixed with an instinct to protect and he sank to his knees, unaware of the blood from the remains of the slaughtered animals which soaked through his leggings. He gingerly stretched forward a finger, ready to pull it back at the least sign of aggression.

But the little thing just sniffed at him, whimpered timidly again and looked past Ahren towards the entrance. Before he had a chance to regret the decision, he pulled off his cloak, wrapped the whelp in it and took the bundle in his arms. The little thing didn't protest, just snuggled into the boy's chest and closed its eyes.

Selsena had sensed the turmoil within the apprentice and warned Falk that something wasn't quite right. The pair had stood up and were waiting at the edge of the hollow for him. The old man looked down at the boy with a stony expression. 'Ahren, what do you have there?' The tone in his voice could have cut through rock.

'A whelp, master', said Ahren carefully and pulled back the cloak a little so that the little head became visible and blinked its eyes at the bright world. Ahren turned so that the animal couldn't see the body of its mother, and climbed out of the depression.

154

Selsena pranced nervously on the spot, threw her head back, and the wave of emotions that she let forth, a mixture of hatred and pity, were as disturbing as those he felt himself. She gave a neigh of protest and galloped off, disappearing into the undergrowth. Falk looked angrily down at Ahren, reached a calloused hand out towards the whelp and pulled out his dagger with the other.

Did he really want to kill the whelp? The boy retreated several paces, Falk in pursuit.

'Give me that!' The order was like the crack of a whip.

The little thing whimpered and Ahren shouted defiantly, 'no!'

Falk rolled his eyes and checked himself with difficulty. Holding the dagger in his hand, he said calmly and slowly, 'that is a Dark One. We kill Dark Ones'.

Ahren turned away so that his body was between the blade and the little ball of fur that was snuggling into him for protection. He couldn't, he wouldn't give up the whelp. His head and his heart told him that there couldn't be any relationship between the horrifying beast that had only a few short hours previously tried to slaughter them, and this needy little creature. He looked at the little face with the pointy ears and pink tongue which was now licking his chin.

'But he doesn't have red eyes', he argued stubbornly. All Dark Ones had, like the Adversary, who imposed his will on them.

'Not yet', responded Falk heatedly. 'But his master will call him at the first new moon, and if he falls into a rage and tastes blood, then they'll turn red. And then he'll be ten times as difficult to kill. He might even tear apart one of your friends. What do you think now?'

Ahren was filled with a deep-seated rage. This whelp had to pay for the sins of its mother, without having the chance to live its own life, free from the sins of the past. He saw himself, locked in his father's hut, with

155

no hope of rescue. Until Falk came. He had saved him. And now he of all people was adamant that this living creature couldn't be saved. To Ahren it seemed like a betrayal. He stood up straight and said in a firm voice. 'I claim this whelp as my trophy. I shall save him and he shall live'.

Falk was about to say something but then shrugged his shoulders and put his knife away. A deep sadness was etched on his face.

'Good, then I won't hold you back. Sometimes the younger generation has to learn the hard way'. Then he sat down by the fire and stared into the flames. Ahren sat down warily on the other side of the fire and held the whelp close to his chest.

For the rest of the evening the master and his apprentice sat in an uneasy silence. This silence continued as they made their way home the following day. When they arrived at the cabin that afternoon, Ahren was in a dilemma. He could hardly take the wolf with him into the village as long as everyone was in a panic and waiting behind their locked doors for the whelp's mother to attack, but he had to get food or the little thing would starve. That meant he would have to leave the whelp alone with Falk. The apprentice chewed on his lip before finally saying, 'I want you to swear that you will do no harm to the little one'.

Falk grumbled, as though he had expected that and said, 'Alright then. I swear by the THREE that I will not harm this animal either directly or indirectly until its eyes are red. Then I will kill it'.

That was more than Ahren had expected and he had to admit it was a fair condition, so he simply said, 'Thank you' and put the whelp down on the floor of the cabin.

Falk raised his eyebrows and nodded silently. The whelp ran over to him as if to sniff his hand and the boy could have sworn that the old man was on the point of stroking it before deciding to wave it away.

156

But he didn't want to push his luck and said nothing more but set off for the butcher. As the door closed behind him, he could hear his master complain, 'if the little boy pisses in the cabin, then you're going to clean it up with your Godsday suit, do you hear me?'

Ahren smiled all the way to the village. Falk had regained his gruff nature and that was a good sign.

The following days were a tough struggle as Ahren tried to improve the whelp's health. He had to work out the correct mixture of water and cooked meat pulp so that the little thing could keep his food down. He used all his knowledge of healing herbs so he could add the correct plants that would help the young animal to survive the adaptation. By the sixth day it was clear that the wolf would make it and that lifted a load off Ahren's mind.

His master kept his promise but did not help the boy. The old man spent a lot of time outside with Selsena, who refused to come nearer than twenty paces from the cabin. Ahren felt her attitude didn't help the situation but it didn't throw him off continuing to raise the whelp.

Falk had been paying him the apprentice wage since the Autumn Festival. Ahren hadn't touched it up until this point but now he bought everything he needed that would help provide for his little, furry friend. The new moon was ten days away and then his master would realize that Ahren had been proven right. The boy wouldn't even consider the possibility of failure and its consequences.

The two Forest Guardians were acclaimed as heroes among the villagers, as they had driven away the shadow of the evil one from Deepstone. There were a few doubters who claimed that the wolf had never existed and this had just been a trick to curry favour among the community. Falk nicked this rumour in the bud by unceremoniously dumping the head of the beast in the village square. Ahren could imagine who had been spreading these malevolent rumours but he was too preoccupied with looking after the whelp and anyway he didn't really care.

Ahren played as much as possible with the young wolf, held him close every night and fed him with such earnestness that it nearly brought tears to Falk's eyes. The tragic end was fast approaching and he could only hope that the boy would get over it. The animal became ever more restless as the new moon approached. It snarled for no reason and snapped at Ahren a few times when they were playing. The boy reacted with stoic equanimity, cut a few strips off an old cloak, wrapped these around his arms, and continued playing.

Falk respected his apprentice's determination and remembered the previous year's Apprenticeship Trials when a timid young boy with a broken arm stubbornly defied a far stronger opponent.

The day they had both been fearing finally arrived. The young wolf was irritable and tried to leave the cabin at every opportunity. Ahren became more and more frustrated. Falk finally took pity on him and decided to give the young boy's plan a chance. 'What do you intend to do?' he asked.

Ahren jutted out his chin and said, 'I'll chain him up if necessary'.

'That won't work', said Falk. 'That's already been tried. The frenzy ensures that he'll snap the rope, or the animal will strangle himself on it'.

'It's been tried already?' Ahren was stunned.

'Not just once. A hundred times. Without success. I'll admit, most of the animals were a little older when they were found. You've had an unusual amount of time for him to get used to you. But no, it has never worked. Either the animals escaped, or killed themselves in the process, or ripped apart their minders. First there's the frenzy, and if they then drink a drop of blood, it's too late. The eyes change colour and a new Dark One has been created. Herbs are useless during the frenzy too, so you can't drug them'.

A heavy silence hung over the room. Ahren could think of only one way out. 'Then I'll hold on to him for the whole night'.

Falk looked doubtfully at the young animal, which was pacing the room and growling. The wolf had grown to the length of his arm over the previous ten days.

'You want to hold on to a wolf in frenzy for the whole night and stop him from getting one drop of your blood into his mouth?'

'Of course'. Ahren was warming even more to the idea. 'I'll stuff my arms with material, hold his head in an arm grip and I'll hold his tummy in a grip with my other arm. I'll always stay at his back, so he can't bite me. He won't be able to strangle himself in my arms, the stuff is too soft and I can adjust the strength of my grip. Then he won't be able to escape either'. The boy beamed at his master.

Falk rubbed his eyes wearily. 'Ahren, that might work for an hour, then you'll get tired and make a mistake'.

But his apprentice was already gathering together the strips of cloth he had worn when playing during the previous few days. He tied them tightly to his arms with strips of leather and lay down beside the young wolf, who tried to jump to the side. He quickly had him in the grip he had described to his master and now he was lying on his side, the animal pressed closely to him. The whelp was growling quietly but not moving. The young boy's face filled with a triumphant grin and he called out, 'it's working!'

Falk stared at him, too tired and sad to discuss the matter anymore. 'Alright. We'll do it like this. You hold on tightly, I'll sit over there on the stool with my dagger. As soon as your insane plan fails, I'll do everything I can to save your life'.

The finality with which Falk described the failure of his plan was like a slap in the face. He avoided making eye contact with his master for the rest of the day and concentrated on perfecting his arm protectors while the night slowly approached.

'Ahren, it's time', said Falk in an unusually soft voice. Dusk had settled over the forest and the sparkling landscape of snow outside had transformed into a collection of faint grey shapes. Soon there would be the total darkness common to new moons.

The whelp had been standing in the corner for some time shaking and growling at the two of them. Ahren gave a tentative nod and then strapped the padding to his arms. The old man watched him for a while and finally started giving him advice. The construction of cloth and leather straps had to be snug to the arms without cutting off the blood supply but not so loose that the wolf could use the wriggle room to twist around in the apprentice's arms and rip out his throat.

Ahren moved slowly towards the young wolf, speaking reassuringly to him. Meanwhile, Falk was tensely chewing on his lips. There were two major weaknesses in Ahren's plan: there was the danger that his strength would not last, and the wolf might succeed in turning. The frenzy would last until sunrise and this was a night in the middle of winter.

For Falk the result was not in doubt. The padding and the leather jerkin would, in the eyes of the master, only protect the boy until he intervened. And that would be at the moment the animal was lost to the great Betrayer. He had tried to persuade Ahren to wear a neck guard to protect against a throat bite but the stubborn boy would hear nothing of it because if his neck were stiff, he wouldn't be able to keep a constant eye on the animal.

At last the apprentice picked the whelp up quickly and carried him to his bed. He lay down with his back to the wall so he could use the stability of the wood and crossed his arms over the front of the wolf, one arm bent around the animal's neck, the other around the stomach, just above the hind legs. The wolf began to defend himself and snarled dangerously but Ahren continued to speak soothingly to him.

Falk was close to tears as he saw the heart-breaking inevitable conclusion that was drawing nearer. He took the stool and sat two paces away and in full view of Ahren. He had pulled out his dagger, but held it hidden. 'I'm here boy', he said in a hoarse voice, 'as long as it takes'.

Ahren looked up in gratitude to his mentor. The wolf wasn't as strong as he had feared and he had no problem preventing his attempts to escape. This gave him courage.

The light faded noticeably and Falk placed a big log on the fire, which would burn for many hours. He could see from his stool with the flickering light of the fire how the young animal was struggling harder to escape from Ahren's grip. The growling was becoming deeper and more threatening and the young boy's body was swaying from side to side with the animal's movements.

Beads of sweat appeared on Ahren's face as he noticed that the wolf was producing more strength then he could have imagined. His arms were beginning to hurt and he had to keep reminding himself not to injure the whelp by squeezing too hard.

The evening moved on inexorably and it was now completely black outside the cabin. The animal was struggling incessantly in his arms, snapping the air, trying to twist and turn, scratching with his paws. Ahren tried to keep pressed against the wall so he could preserve his strength. The padding on his arms was holding, as were the leather leggings but the kicks were painful nonetheless. Any time he thought he had adjusted to the wolf's resistance, the whelp would increase his efforts. The burning in his arms had now spread to his shoulders and back. He was panting and much to his consternation the little body in his arms didn't seem to be tiring, but rather gaining in strength.

Falk stood up and came towards him slowly with the drawn dagger.

'No!' the boy screamed at the top of his voice and gripped harder. Then he saw that his mentor was holding a goblet in his other hand. He approached Ahren from above and poured some water laced with herbs down his throat, being careful not to come too close to the wolf's fangs. At first Ahren hadn't wanted to drink anything for fear it was a sleeping potion but then he smelled the Life Fern and Wolf Herb. He drank down the herbal tea greedily, knowing it would give him strength and ease the pain. He tried to reach the Void although all the muscles in his body were tense.

Soon the herbs did their job and he fell into a sort of trance. The whelp struggled in his arms but the boy was steadfast. After some hours, with the night already half over, the wolf suddenly became limp and gave up all resistance. Bathed in sweat Ahren smiled at Falk and said, 'That wasn't so…', then the little body nearly exploded.

Falk could see from his stool that the animal's eyes had rolled completely to the back of the head. His mouth was foaming, and it was obvious that the wolf wasn't just content with escaping anymore. Its claws were seeking out the body of the boy, every movement was aimed at injuring him and sinking his fangs into the Ahren's flesh. Falk sat as taut as a bowstring on the edge of his chair, ready to intervene as soon as this drama was over. He only hoped he would be able to save the boy.

Ahren was now sobbing uncontrollably and using every sinew in his body to resist the attacks. The wolf's claws were tearing deep channels in

162

the material protecting his arms, and the leather on his legs was beginning to wear away under the onslaught. The Void seemed to have blown away and Ahren couldn't find the necessary concentration again. His whole body was in pain and a wave of exhaustion overwhelmed him. He caught sight of his master's face, which reflected what he already knew. He was going to lose. His strength would give way and at some point, he would make a mistake.

And then Falk will kill the little fellow to save me…this thought reignited Ahren's resistance. Sobbing uncontrollably, he held on to the whelp, who relentlessly carried on with his work of destruction in Ahren's arms.

Countless heartbeats passed by, but the paroxysms continued. Paw swipes left their first bloody gashes on his legs where the leathers had worn through and soon his arms would suffer the same fate.

Falk looked on sadly as his protégé's resistance weakened and he quietly prepared to bring the whole thing to an end. He stood up, but instead of moving to the distraught boy, he walked to the window. He tilted his head and opened the heavy wooden shutters that kept out the winter. The world beyond the cabin was pitch black, a thick carpet of cloud hid the stars. An impenetrable wall of darkness was before him, as if nothing else existed except for the cabin and the hopeless battle raging behind his back. A cold blast of air came into the room and then an outline appeared from the dark night. The light from the fire in the cabin shimmered on Selsena's hide as the Titejunawna approached and looked through the window at the scene playing out in the room. Falk stepped aside to take up his watch again.

Ahren kept control of the wriggling body with whatever strength he had left. There were tears in his eyes and blood on his arms and legs. Now he had to keep his eyes on the wolf's head with even more concentration. One lick of his lifeblood and all would be lost. Ahren's determination was beginning to crumble and the morning was still so far away.

Then Selsena was standing at the window and her inscrutable, grey eyes were locked on to his. Peace arose within Ahren like the mist rising in a forest clearing on a warm spring morning. Serenity and an unshakeable quietness flowed through him and gave his limbs renewed strength. The whelp on the other hand seemed to be quietening down. The animal's efforts were still hurting Ahren but he seemed to have lost the determined ferocity which had marked his earlier behaviour.

Falk looked dumbstruck from one to the other, the dagger still in his hand, and for the first time was uncertain about what the next few hours would bring.

Chapter 10

Falk awoke with a start the following morning. He was still sitting on the stool and had a stabbing pain in his back. He must have dropped off at some point. The last few hours of the previous night had crawled painfully slowly. The struggle between the exhausted boy and the similarly spent wolf had lessened to no more than brief twitching of the muscles. The closer it had come to morning, the quieter it had become in the cabin, and at some point, the effort must have taken its toll on Falk.

Selsena was still standing at the window, looking at the boy. Up until now, Falk had avoided viewing the scene, fearful of what he might see, but when he turned around, he was met with an astonishing sight. The two bodies were lying entwined on the blood-soaked mat. The apprentice's arms and legs were covered in cuts and scratches, his clothing and padding hung in shreds, or lay scattered across the bed. The boy's face was pale and drawn with dark rings under his eyes. His chest was gently rising and falling, much to Falk's relief.

The whelp was breathing too so there was only one more thing Falk had to do. With his knife drawn, he glanced at Selsena, then crept closer and bent over the young wolf. With the tip of his knife a finger's width away from the animal's heart, he carefully lifted an eyelid of the sleeping creature.

The whelp's pupil was golden-yellow! Falk recoiled as if he had been hit. Ahren stirred in his sleep and snuggled up closer to the soft fur of the whelp, who grunted contentedly. Falk stood up and stared down at the sleepers. Then he turned to the window and said to Selsena, 'sometimes it's the older ones who need to learn new things.' He patted her on the neck and the laughter and the joy of the one, echoed in the soul of the other.

Ahren slept the whole day through and the following night, as did the little wolf. Early the next morning he was woken up by a rough tongue and an animal smell as his new companion licked his face devotedly. He sat up with a giggle and waved his hands around wildly. For a few heartbeats he was quite woozy. Then he began to remember what had happened and his aching body did the rest to remind him of the events that had just taken place.

The whelp jumped up at him, let out a high whimper and looked at him with loyal golden-yellow eyes. Ahren picked up the little thing and noticed that his arms had been bandaged. He pulled back his blanket and his thighs too had been expertly covered in white linen. He smelt at the bandages and recognized the scent of Red Leaf, which promoted the healing of cuts and scratches.

The whelp sniffed the dressing curiously, gave a big sneeze, then jumped from the bed and glanced back over his shoulder at the boy with an offended look. Falk wasn't in the room so Ahren stood up to mix together the meat stock for the wolf. Ahren's stomach was grumbling with hunger. He poured the rest of the stock into the bowl, added a few herbs that he had cut up and put it down in front of the little nipper's paws. The whelp sniffed at the bowl and within an instant had devoured it all. Then he looked up at Ahren and began whimpering again.

The boy scratched his head and said, 'we have a problem'. The food was all gone and now there were only vegetables in the house. The snow storm and the hunt for the Blood Wolf had put paid to food hunting, and so he couldn't make any more of the meat stock for the pup.

Ahren made a practical decision and heated the stew that was still hanging over the fire. It filled his own stomach and he tried to make a few carrots as tasty as possible for the hungry rascal. That was only partially successful. He finished his own food as quickly as possible so he could rustle something up for the hungry whelp. He was getting dressed when the door opened, and Falk came in weighed down by a large bundle. 'Good, you're awake', he said in a deep voice, then dropped his bundle on the table.

The wolf circled him and started jumping up at him, whimpering.

Then Ahren realized, he wasn't jumping up at Falk, but up at the table.

The master quickly took out a packet with waxed paper and threw a large chunk of meat at the wildly wriggling wolf, who immediately got stuck into it.

Falk nodded and said, 'just as I thought. I didn't think he'd be happy with the stock since the Frenzy. This meat has been well cured – we don't want to provoke anything – but I think the danger has been averted'. It was only now that Ahren noticed that his mentor had a firm grip on the dagger so he could draw it quickly.

Ahren was about to speak angrily but his master interrupted him.

'Boy, this is absolutely uncharted territory. Never before has a Blood Wolf survived the Frenzy in the company of people', he said severely. 'And never before have the people who kept guard over him survived', he added drily.

Ahren closed his mouth, hesitated, and then asked cautiously, 'what does that mean?'

He was afraid of the answer, but Falk smiled. 'Selsena says the aura of the Adversary is gone and also the latent rage. After she had calmed down, it was this anger that had kept her away from us over the past few days, but when she saw the danger you were in, she wanted to help'.

Ahren strained his neck to look out but there was no sign of the Elven horse. He really wanted to thank her because without her, at least one of the three who were in the cabin at the moment would no longer be alive.

Falk indicated with a look and said, 'she's wandering around the forest and recovering. Projecting such strong feelings over such a long period demands a lot of energy'.

The whelp had eaten everything up and was jumping up at the table again.

Falk groaned and produced another piece of meat, which quickly found its way into the creature's mouth. 'Now I've got two gluttons in my cabin', he complained. 'From what I can see, you've got a common Ice Wolf here, except that this one will probably grow bigger than most others.'

'Does that mean he'll grow as big as his mother sometime?' asked Ahren in amazement.

Falk laughed. 'Probably not. Don't forget, she was five hundred years old and her longevity was a side effect of the rule of HIM, WHO FORCES'.

A shiver ran down Ahren's spine. In the Midlands the name of the Adversary was rarely mentioned and only on formal occasions. Even if HE had been conquered, his name was considered a bad omen which attracted Dark Ones, and the Border Lands with the Pall Pillar in their centre were too close to be taking that risk.

He caught Falk's searching look, which was trained on the wolf, and he realized that this had been another test to see if the animal would react to hearing the name of the being that had put a curse on him.

But the only reaction was a contented grumble coming from the bundle of fur.

The two sat there in contented silence, watching the second piece of meat disappear like the first one, into the whelp's stomach.

The animal turned to the table again with pleading eyes and Falk produced the last piece, which was fresh and bloody. The Forest Guardian looked at Ahren intently.

'No point in putting it off. This is another test. After this one, the little thing is welcome. Agreed?'

He stretched out his hand over the fur-ball, who was still jumping.

Ahren's heart was in his mouth. Dumbstruck, he could only nod as he gripped his master's calloused hand. Falk firmly grasped his hand and dropped the piece of meat.

Ahren held his breath as the young animal attacked the tasty morsel - only to chew at it half-heartedly and with little enthusiasm. He threw them an offended look with his sad, soulful dog eyes.

Falk loosened his grip on Ahren's hand and burst into a hearty laugh. 'It seems we have a gourmet among us. He doesn't seem to enjoy the taste of blood. I take everything back', he stuttered and snorted and laughed. 'This is no normal wolf but a shrinking violet and that's fine by me'.

Ahren got down on his knees and embraced the whelp.

'Master, what's the Elfish for 'saved'?'

'Culhen' came the answer.

Ahren placed the whelp's head between his hands and the pup looked back at him with loyal eyes.

'Welcome, Culhen', said Ahren ceremoniously.

And he was answered by a wet tongue licking him across the face.

Chapter 11

Thankfully, the rest of the winter passed without incident and normality returned to the daily lives of the Forest Guardians. Culhen displayed such a joyful trustfulness that even nervous villagers were persuaded that he wasn't dangerous and once Keeper Jegral had intoned the blessing of the THREE over him, all doubt was vanquished.

The only snag was Sven. If cowards can sense anything, then it's the weak point of their enemy, and so it came to pass that he made several attempts to trap the whelp or to entice him away. Ahren knew what Sven was up to and he raged when he imagined how Sven might torture the whelp.

Falk approached the issue in his usual practical manner. 'The little thing will soon be able to take care of himself and then the problem is solved. And anyway, he has to learn that he must always stay by your side. Otherwise he'll be good for nothing when you're working and from the spring on, he'll have to stay in the cabin'.

And so Ahren began to train the dog hard under Falk's watchful eye.

'He's extremely intelligent for a wolf. Of course, he's inherited that from his ancestry', said Falk. 'This is your one opportunity. His brain is like a sponge that soaks everything up because he's so young. He can learn things now in a week that in the future will take you months or even years, and with a lot of effort, to teach him'.

The boy needed no motivation to spend as much time as possible with his new companion, and so they would practise from dawn to dusk. Stalking, hiding, reading tracks. His master even turned archery into lessons for boy and whelp. He would paint the tip of the practice arrow with a discreet scent and whenever Ahren's shot went astray, the little wolf would have to find the arrow and bring it back. It went without saying that Ahren was over the moon about this and by the time spring arrived, both apprentices, boy and wolf, were a very good team.

Vera doted on Culhen and with her help Ahren gave him various herbs to eat with his food, just as he had done with the meat stock that time. The young wolf had become familiar with the flavours when he was a whelp and so he could tolerate the aftertaste, although he only ate the prepared meat if he got a piece of cured beef as a reward. This was his absolute favourite food, the first food he had been allowed to eat *that* morning. And so Ahren always made sure he purchased some from the butcher, even if it cost all of his apprentice's wage. Ahren was intent on making Culhen big and strong as quickly as possible so that Sven would pose no danger for the animal. The combination of fortifying and stimulating herbs along with a big portion of feed was a resounding success, and the miller's sons' efforts eased off considerably, the bigger and heavier the wolf became.

Spring returned to Deepstone at last, and with it the Spring Festival which marked the end of winter and the beginning of new life. It only lasted for an afternoon and was characterized by religious ceremonies. It was the smaller counterpart to the Autumn Festival. Keeper Jegral was the focus of the community at this time and knew how to use his position to improve the community spirit within the village. The villagers cleaned up the chapel, they spruced up the square, and did little favours for the needier citizens. A friendly but firm word from the priest and a table might be repaired for free, or a hole in a roof filled in with no money changing hands.

On the day of the festival itself, there was a long ceremony of prayer and the names of those who had not survived the winter would be read out. Then the new arrivals, who had been born during the long winter and would experience their first summer, were named. It was always considered a good omen in the community if the second list were longer than the first.

The final part of the ceremony was dedicated to all those entering their sixteenth summer. They would place their hands on the triangular rock that jutted out from the chapel altar and swear to protect the community and to respect the THREE. And with that they would become fully-fledged members of the village, capable of making their own decisions.

The previous year Ahren had yearned for this moment with every sinew in his body, but now he was indifferent to it. He stretched secretly on the wooden bench to look down at Culhen, who yawned as if in response. The boy smiled affectionately at the wolf and then began daydreaming. Next year he would be standing up there swearing the oath but nothing would change and that was good. He was contented for the first time in his life and he was grateful for that.

He tickled Culhen between the ears, and the wolf laid his snout on Ahren's thigh. Everyone streamed out once the prayers were over except for the Godsday scholars. Unfortunately, the Spring Festival fell on a Godsday this year and so they had to attend lessons while the others celebrated outside.

Likis strolled over to Ahren and ruffled Cuhlen's head. Ahren was relieved that his best friend and the wolf were getting on famously. The merchant's son secretly slipped out a bundle from under his jerkin and within a heartbeat the chunk of meat, which the slender boy had smuggled into the chapel, had been gulped down.

'I thought he might be hungry', he murmured with a crooked grin, 'this is going to take another while yet'.

Culhen was now giving Ahren a begging look and looked every inch the loyal if starving wolf but Ahren only grumbled, 'greedy guts!'

The wolf had already grown up to his knee and had the corresponding appetite. Falk had now been roped into helping to get food – the wolf easily devoured every portion placed in front of him.

'Students, gather together', called Keeper Jegral and the seven young people and the wolf obediently marched forward. Luckily Jegral liked the reformed Blood Wolf too and so the animal was allowed to stay by Ahren's side during the lesson. The priest indicated to them to sit – today's lesson would take place in the chapel. The sound of festive laughter could be heard from outside and occasionally the unenthusiastic pupils looked wistfully over their shoulders to catch a glimpse of the world outside.

The Keeper cleared his throat and waited until he had the undivided attention of the group. The spring sunshine lit up the inside of the Godshouse and the play of colour reflecting from the Keeper's silk gown scattered dancing flecks of light around the space, which was painted a simple white. The pupils sat in the first row of the pews, which occupied the whole room. Jegral stood in front of them, and behind him was the simple block of white rock that served as the altar, and the triangle made from ordinary grey material, which represented the rock of the gods. Every community possessed such a rock.

'As I promised you before, we will now delve more deeply into the story of the long sleep of the gods', said the Keeper in a serious voice.

'This part of the story is rarely addressed but you should at least get the chance to ask questions about it'.

He grasped his book that had been lying on the altar and began to read aloud from it. 'The gods created the Custodian and then fell into a deep sleep.

The Custodian began to perform his task loyally. He kept watch over the creation, just as his rulers had ordered. But after eons and eons of

173

watching, the Custodian began to feel jealous. He became jealous of the peoples he had been guarding, for he had never received a word of thanks.

Jealous of the gods who had realized their plans and were now lying in a deep slumber. Jealous of the fact that he too wanted to create a people and beings with his *own* will but knowing he did not possess the power for such a creative act.

And so, he fell into a rage and turned against his creators.

He took to himself some animals and FORCED them into a new form. He put them under his power by substituting their free will with his own will. But the peoples of the gods rose up against these abominations which had no place in the harmony of creation, and began to hunt the false creatures, which they now named *the Dark Ones*. And so the Custodian's rage grew greater and he began a war against the peoples of the creation. The Dark Days had started.

He forced even more creatures into a new form and altered their purpose. Even among the thinking peoples he did not desist and controlled the weak-willed amongst them within his power. The peoples looked with horror upon their enslaved brothers and sisters and named them *the Low Fangs*. He raised powerful armies of Dark Ones to destroy everything that resisted his will.

And he was named HE THAT FORCES'.

There was a deathly silence in the room. The laughter and music from outside seemed out of place, almost surreal. The students looked at each other nervously. No one wanted to ask a question about the terrible events the priest had just described.

174

Ahren would have had a question last year, but since then he had found the answer. After his fight to free Culhen from the curse of the Adversary he had been so exhausted he couldn't think any more. The gods had created a whole world. Was it surprising that they had ended up making one mistake? Once it became obvious that nobody was going to ask a question, the priest sighed and said, 'then let us continue'. He raised his voice and carried on. 'The peoples fought against HIS army of Dark Ones but the Custodian's power was too great, the enforced shapes of the enemy too ruthless.

And so, the peoples pleaded to the gods for support. For it was clear they would be defeated. The gods heard their cries of pain in their sleep but they were unable to awaken. And so they dreamed and gave to the priests the gift of magic.

The priests selected those who had a gift for magic and taught them too how to bend creation. And so, the magicians were born.

With the assistance of the magicians, the Betrayer's army was held back but the victory was only short lived. HE WHO FORCES touched the spirit of some of those who knew magic, and he brought them under his control and so he then had magicians fighting within his ranks.

And so, the triumphal march began again.

Again, the peoples pleaded for support but the gods were exhausted and their sleep became deeper, so deep that the priests could hardly make contact and many prayers went astray, until finally the gods heard.

HE WHO MOULDS selected those people with a special gift, and granted them the ability to protect their innermost from the force of the Betrayer. He gave them immortality so that neither age nor hunger nor thirst nor sickness could harm them, only the vulnerability of the body remained.

175

SHE WHO FEELS gave each of them a soul-animal to accompany them, as companion and custodian, as protection against the conflict of the coming days. She combined the disposition of Paladin and animal into one spirit so that their love for the creation would never be torn asunder.

HE, WHO IS gave them weapons and armour, forged from the depths of his flesh so that they could defend themselves and protect their vulnerable bodies from death.

Thirteen were chosen, and their power was as great as the Custodian's, and it was divided equally amongst them, so they would not succumb to the same temptations as HE WHO FORCES had done.

And the peoples called them *the Paladins*.

The strength of the gods weakened further, and their sleep became deeper and deeper'.

The youngsters became restless, each of them had heard stories and legends concerning the heroic deeds of the Paladins, who had fought in huge battles and dark caves, many hundreds of years earlier when the Dark Days had been at their worst. These men and women had turned the tide in their favour and thwarted the certain destruction of the Creation. The youngsters were now calling for Keeper Jegral to relate some of these tales but he only smiled gently. 'I'm sure the elders will be only too happy to tell you the stories later this evening around the bonfire'.

In order to calm the chatter, he read on. 'The years passed and slowly the peoples of the gods gained the upper hand.

But the way was long, for a large part of the world lay in the darkness of HIS dominion.

The centuries of strife exhausted the souls and minds of the Paladins, and the gods again showed their mercy.

With all their remaining strength they dreamed up the soul-mates until their sleep became a dreamless blackness and the people were left on their own.

Whenever the spirit of a Paladin was at breaking point, they selected a soul-mate with whom they entered into an eternal bond.

And as soon as a child was born, then the Paladin began to age so they could pass on their task to their daughter or their son and find peace after centuries of battle and sacrifice.

Generation upon generation fought for victory against HIM, WHO FORCES and the war was successful. Paladin followed Paladin and each one carried their burden with pride.

After three hundred years HE, WHO FORCES was surrounded, his troops defeated.

But on the eve of victory, HE sent forth his mightiest servant and put all his strength into a mental attack on the spirit of a soul-mate.

He sent her images of slaughtered children and promised to protect her son if she surrendered to his power'.

Sobbing could be heard from among the pupils but the Keeper continued relentlessly. 'Her spirit broke, torn between her love for her partner and her fear for her son, and so she took a dagger and stabbed her partner to death in his sleep.

And so, the thirteenth Paladin was dead and with him each succeeding child of each Paladin. His companion disappeared into the night and was never seen again.

When the new morning broke, the will of the Paladins was broken. Only as thirteen could they destroy the power of HIM WHO FORCES and so the mightiest magicians of the peoples with the help of the twelve

Paladins cast a spell on the weakened Adversary, he having used up all his strength in the night of blood.

The creation was saved and the enemy spellbound. And so, the Paladins have kept guard until the present day. They left their companions, for their vulnerability through their soul-mates had been revealed, and remained behind alone and ageless in the world'.

Keeper Jegral closed the book and now spoke without notes. 'These great men and women have made an enormous sacrifice to protect those they love, and all of us. After all these centuries they are still out there, guarding us. Their names have been forgotten, just as they had wished. We only know of a few today, and they have made their own way'.

Ahren had already heard of the War Emperor from the South, who, according to rumour, was a Paladin. But from what had been reported, he didn't exactly sound like one of the gods' defenders, and so he had put it down to mindless gossip.

The priest looked around the group and saw he could not expect a discussion after such a heavy lesson.

'The THREE be with you', he intoned and dismissed them with a wave of the hand.

The darkened mood was instantly forgotten and with a cry of joy, the boys and girls tumbled outside and into the festivities.

Ahren set off home to the cabin that night in high spirits. The food had been delicious and he had joked around with Likis and Holken and exchanged glances with some of the girls. Falk and he had achieved hero status and the white wolf at this side attracted looks.

He danced around Culhen playfully and the wolf, for his own part, ran barking and jumping between his legs. The light from the village shone from behind them, as the celebrations were still in full swing.

Suddenly the wolf pricked up his ears and stared into the darkness. Three shapes appeared out of the darkness in front of them. Sven and his cronies, armed with wooden planks, spiked with nails.

The three moved menacingly forwards and Sven snarled, 'it's payback time'.

Ahren almost burst into laughter. He'd been expecting something like this and his master had always drummed into him, 'know the methods and goals of your opponents, and you have a big advantage over them'. Ahren had only drunk a little. This wasn't like the Autumn Festival. He wasn't going to make the same mistake again. He strode fearlessly up to the three boys, Culhen by this right leg. After the events of last winter, he wasn't afraid of the three.

The attackers looked at each other uncertainly. They hadn't expected such a reaction. The first one raised his arm somewhat hesitantly to prepare to strike but Ahren kicked him in the standing leg and the bully landed in the dirt, his cudgel clattering harmlessly on the path.

The attackers froze for a moment, then Sven and his other crony tried to attack him simultaneously, but Culhen was snarling and baring his teeth threateningly. In this way he kept the second attacker in check, so that the trainee Forest Guardian could concentrate on Sven.

The coward dropped back a step and prepared to strike but Ahren was already too close. He grabbed the hand holding the cudgel and twisted the miller's son's arm swiftly behind his back. He could only form a strange looking o-shape in his mouth as he was forced into a summersault and landed with a crash on the trampled earth. Ahren calmly picked up the two cudgels and turned to his last opponent, who was staring scared-stiff at Culhen.

'Well?' asked Ahren and threatened him with a weapon in each hand.

The rascal gave a quick scream, dropped his cugel and took to his heels.

Ahren flung the piece of wood into the undergrowth and walked calmly onwards without looking back at the groaning boys.

He had hardly gone twenty paces further when he heard a voice among the leaves. 'Good work, boy'.

Ahren looked quizzically at the edge of the forest and Falk stepped out of it. 'Master, you're not still celebrating?' The apprentice had headed off earlier and had left Falk, deep in conversation with Mistress Dohlmen.

'I'd been keeping an eye on those three and it was obvious they were up to something. Just wanted to see if you needed help'. Falk shrugged his shoulders.

He walked beside Ahren with an arm on his shoulder and so they continued towards the cabin.

<u>Chapter 12</u>

*He found it difficult to maintain the necessary concentration as he
awaited with suspense the return of the magician he had sent forth some
weeks previously. He hated having to wait so long but caution made more
sense now than unbecoming haste. Better a slow and certain result upon
which he could build.*

*At last the air above the magic net vibrated and the trance within
which he found himself enabled him to draw immediate conclusions
regarding its source.*

*In Hjalgar then. The chalk drawing was becoming ever more crowded
and complex as he added new lines.*

The net was closing in.

Ahren's training continued and the boy and his wolf grew in body and
spirit. Falk had now moved on to training his apprentice in using bow and
arrow while in motion, and they were now camping more often in the
wilderness as their trips often involved more than a day's march.

The summer was wet and often very cloudy but Ahren only noticed
this in passing. He was now catching his own game and was able to
exchange this for Culhen's favourite meat. The lessons in bare hand-to-
hand combat were now expanded as he learned fighting techniques with
the dagger, which up to now Ahren had been carrying with him unused.

The time for picking new apprentices had passed by and not a single
craftsman or woman had registered. The boy was doubly delighted that he
had been chosen the previous year and threw himself even more into his
training. This didn't go unnoticed and so Falk made the lessons even
more challenging. Falk didn't beat around the bush but now set him tasks

that he would have demanded of himself. Every evening Ahren fell into bed exhausted but happy, while Falk lay in front of the cabin under a tree and had hushed conversations with Selsena.

What are you thinking about? she asked silently one dreary summer's evening.

About the Blood Wolf, answered the Forest Guardian tersely.

Why? The animal is dead and the young one is developing splendidly, was the impatient answer.

Falk wasn't sure if she meant the wolf or his apprentice. His reward for this thought was an uncomfortable head butt from the horse.

It makes no sense, said Falk in his thoughts. *She was crippled and pregnant, that's why we noticed her so late. She was old enough to be careful and have regard for her weaknesses.*

The Elven horse rolled her eyes. *We've gone over this ten times already. It wasn't your fault. Her behaviour was completely untypical.*

Falk responded, *that's not what I mean. There were at least a dozen better hiding places between the Pall Pillar and this forest. Why here of all places?*

You think too much, Selsena calmly replied.

Falk stared out into the forest and hoped she was right.

The year went by and soon autumn was coming to an end. The Autumn Festival came and went. At the end of his fifteenth summer Ahren got new leather gear because he had outgrown the old set, and he gave his master a carving of the Blood Wolf they had killed.

'You never took a trophy with you that time. Now you have one, master', Ahren said proudly.

'Should I be running around the place with one of his mother's fangs?' said Falk with a knowing look, pointing at Culhen, who had pricked up his ears immediately and tilted his head to the side. Then he ruffled Ahren's hair and said, 'thank you, that's good work'.

The Autumn Festival had been a pleasant distraction but was soon a distant memory. Ahren had laughed a lot and drunk a little with his friends. He and Sven avoided each other. He had seen nothing of his father, but he had heard that he was continuing to exchange his unexpected fortune for alcohol, with grim determination. Perhaps that was the only form of peace that the troubled man could achieve.

The winter was mild and stormy, a somewhat colder version of the previous summer, and Falk now let the boy spend the occasional night in the forest so that he could put what he had learnt into practice. When the spring returned, Falk grunted contentedly, 'keep going like this and the year after next you can do your Long Week'.

Ahren was happy to hear this. The Long Week was the final test to become a Forest Guardian. The subject was taken into the wilderness where he had to survive for a week with only his dagger, bow and a quiver with five arrows. If the apprentice returned, he was a Guardian. And he would receive a distinction if he brought a trophy back with him.

But two years was a long time and Ahren wanted to learn as much as he could. Who knew, perhaps his master would send him away then.

The winter finally came to an end and the weather improved considerably. The Spring Ceremony began with great joy, for the villagers were thankful for the unusually mild winter. There had been no deaths this year.

Ahren sat in the front row of the chapel along with Rufus, Likis and Holken. They were beginning their sixteenth summer and now it was time for them to swear on the Gods' Rock. Likis wore a garment in the colours of the merchants' guild, while Rufus had simply chosen his Godsday costume and had attached a pin cushion to his sleeve. Holken and Ahren both sat in the leather gear of their professions, for the oath, according to tradition, had to show the villagers who they were accepting among them and how seriously the person taking the oath was taking his or her responsibilities.

Falk grumbled from the second row. 'These festivities aren't really my thing, but this way they'll get used to the fact that someday it'll be you guarding the forest. I'm not going to be there forever'.

Before Ahren could react to this morbid thought, the Keeper indicated to them to stand up. The four youths obediently climbed up to the altar.

Keeper Jegral intoned, 'do you swear to protect the community of the peoples and to respect the THREE?'

'We do swear it', they responded.

'Do you swear allegiance to the THREE against all false images of life?'

'We do swear it' was the ritualistic response.

'And do you swear to take on the tasks which the THREE have prepared for you, and to fulfil them however long they take?'

Ahren found this last question very pompous. Tradition demanded that each of them came forward individually and placed their hand on the bare triangular rock which symbolized the rock of the gods.

Holken thundered in a resounding voice, 'I do swear it'. And he reverently laid his right hand on the rock.

Rufus followed his example with a more hesitant exclamation. The poor boy's voice hadn't completely broken yet and he didn't want to show any weakness.

Then Ahren stepped forward and raised his right hand. It floated over the rock but then he shrugged his shoulders and changed his mind. He

184

placed his left hand on it. Falk smiled approvingly before his face suddenly grew serious.

For an almost imperceptible glow came from the rock as Ahren called out,

'I do swear it'.

A blinding flash of light filled the inside of the chapel and everyone shielded their eyes with their hands. A heartbeat later and the Godshouse was back to its peaceful self as if nothing had ever happened. There was confusion among the congregation. People looked at each other in bewilderment, looking for an explanation for what had just occurred.

Keeper Jegral raised his arms reassuringly, his silk gown was still sparkling and seemed to have trapped the lightning flash. It looked as if the robe was glowing in silent celebration. The priest's movements scattered a dozen little rainbows throughout the room.

'Surely just a stray shaft of light from the window', he announced with a firm authority in his voice that nobody dared to contradict.

He indicated to Likis to continue, who banged his hand on the rock and spoke hurriedly, 'I do swear it', and then pulled his hand back as quickly as possible as if he had touched a poisonous, rather than a lifeless object.

Meanwhile Ahren was looking down at his hand, which tingled a little but was completely uninjured. He looked over at the Keeper in the hope of getting some help but Jegral simply ignored him. He spoke the closing words and the ritual came to an end. The four young men left their places in the front row, went back to sit down among the congregation and heard murmuring around them. Ahren looked at Falk, who alone among the people was motionless and seemed to be looking through his apprentice as if he didn't exist. His face was pale and lifeless, and he looked as if he had been shaken to the core.

His cursed bed had caught fire again! Of course, it was partly his own fault, for he had woven the bed itself into the magic net but he hadn't reckoned on this. *He looked at the charred mass that had once been the delicate carvings that had covered the four-poster bed. He had not wanted to miss the slightest movement of the netting and for that reason had slept within the catchment area. No goblin in Hjalgar could sneeze without him getting wind of it. His sleep had of course been somewhat disturbed, but this here? Snorting with rage he ripped off the burnt satin robe from his body and studied the ebony coloured skin that appeared beneath. No burns. That was lucky. His personal protective magic was still working.*

He climbed out of the smoking ruins and went out onto the terrace, while behind him the servants, eyes wide in shock and open-mouthed, began clearing the chaos. He had found the old man and his loyal mare with the help of the last net but could not make head nor tail of how he was connected with the omen. He was clearly no threat.

And so, he had held up the net and listened to everything going on within the Forest Guardian's orbit. With a flick of the hand all the magic threads, which were once his place of sleep and had almost turned him to ashes, became visible again. Green flames danced around black tendrils until a lurid flash of light destroyed the whole construct. That was unequivocal.

He let forth a long sigh and raised himself up into the wind with some words of power. He began floating to his destination and felt a cold blast of air tugging at him.

He would have to get hold of some clothing on the way.

Ahren stared into Selsena's slivery eyes.

'Now let me get past', he cried out annoyed, and tried to squeeze past the heavy body of the horse, but she pranced a step in his direction and knocked him to the ground.

The young man got up with a groan and eyeballed her again.

Falk had hotfooted it out of the chapel the day before and stamped into the cabin, slamming the door behind him. The Titejunanwa had been standing guard at the entrance since then, preventing Ahren from reaching his master. The apprentice was worried about his master's strange behaviour and didn't want to leave Falk out of his sight. He had slept outside, snuggled up to his wolf, and even missed the festive meal in honour of the new community members. His stomach was rumbling, and as he had slept on the bare ground, his back ached.

It was late afternoon and his patience was at an end. He turned around and with a few deft movements of his fingers he lit a fire. Then he took the smouldering branches and began throwing them in a wide arc through the cabin chimney. Nothing happened for a few seconds, but then he heard a loud cursing coming from within and two heartbeats later the door was flung open, hitting Selsena in the rump. She moved aside with a disgusted snort, and an angry Falk came into view.

The veins in his head were bulging and his face was a deep red. A smoking branch was still hanging on his collar as he roared, 'WHAT DO YOU THINK YOU'RE DOING?!'

'Welcome back, master', said Ahren in a friendly tone, determined not to be brow-beaten.

Falk threw his arms in the air and furiously stamped back into the cabin. Ahren slipped in quickly too, before the door crashed shut again. The bed was untouched, apparently Falk hadn't slept. Ahren furtively glanced at the old man. The angry red colour had vanished but now he was staring listlessly out the window. Whatever had been eating him, it was still there.

Ahren warmed up the stew and placed two full bowls on the table. Falk didn't react so he gobbled down both bowls himself. Then he swept the cabin, added firewood to the fire and began to groom Culhen, who stretched out and grumbled contentedly.

When it finally became dark, he lay down and watched the figure of his master, still standing there, before he finally fell asleep.

Sometime during the night Falk had left the house and was now lying asleep under a tree and snug against Selsena. She had her legs folded under her as she always did when she wanted to rest.

Ahren stood at the door early the next morning and looked at the two of them. Whatever was bothering Falk, Selsena was obviously helping him deal with it.

The young man decided to seek out Keeper Jegral. Perhaps he could help Falk or at least explain to Ahren what the story with the light was.

He ambled into the village and had a friendly greeting for everyone he met. Most reacted as they always had done but there were a few who seemed nervous and hurried away. There seemed to be more than one person brooding over what had happened. He found the Keeper in his reading room, hidden behind a pile of books.

'Good morning, Keeper', he said loudly to attract his attention.

The priest looked up and blinked owlishly when he recognized the apprentice.

'May the THREE protect you, Ahren'. There was an audible creak as the figure stretched unceremoniously. 'I take it this is not a courtesy visit?'

188

Without waiting for an answer, he continued, 'I'm looking for answers myself, you know, but I can't find any. This Spring Festival ritual just came out of nowhere a few hundred years ago. It was never mentioned in the yearly chronicles, and then, from one year to the next it was suddenly a part of the Spring Consecration. No explanation, no nothing. That's very unusual'.

Ahren could almost physically feel the priest's frustration. He wasn't going to get any answers here today. He said his goodbyes and wandered aimlessly through the village. He kept seeing uneasy eyes staring at him, and so, clenching his teeth, he made his way home again. Much to his surprise and delight, Falk was up and cheerful when he arrived. His master had packed an enormous rucksack and indicated to Ahren to put it on. The young man groaned under the weight and Falk strode silently into the forest. His apprentice followed him, swaying under the weight, and hoping that his master hadn't decided to take out all his frustrations on him.

Falk led him up to the most northern end of the forest, then down to the western border and then further down to the southern edge of the trees. He would frequently point out milestones to Ahren and give tips of what he should keep a particular eye on in various parts of the forest. The first few days were certainly hard going but the longer they were underway, the lighter the rucksack became. Falk clearly didn't want to delay the hunt and soon he hardly felt the bundle on his back. He constantly sensed Selsena as a silver-grey shadow flitting between the trees, yet she kept her distance. It was as if Falk wanted to get as much information as possible into Ahren's head before they finished their tour around the forest.

They were on the way back at last when Ahren summoned all his courage and asked, 'master, what sort of a light was that in the chapel?'

He held his breath, anxiously awaiting the reaction, for he had no idea what would happen now.

Falk stopped, paused and then turned to face the young man, who unconsciously took up a defensive stance.

You've certainly thrown him there. Selsena's voice rang out uninvited in his thoughts.

Falk ignored her and tried to think of a suitable answer for his apprentice.

'I saw something like this once before, many years ago. It means that I must leave Deepstone for a while', he said finally.

Ahren suddenly had an uneasy feeling in his stomach and could only stammer, 'What do you mean?'

Culhen pressed up against his leg and he held firmly on to his soft fur. The wolf was now as tall as the middle of his thigh.

'I have to seek out a very dangerous place now and the way there is long. I can't take you with me', he continued in a tone that brooked no dissent.

The young man recognized this tone and knew he wouldn't get anywhere, so he decided to play along for the moment, which would give him a chance to think out what tack he should take.

He nodded, knowing that his voice would in all probability have betrayed him.

'Good boy', grunted Falk and trudged onwards, lost in thought again.

The following day they arrived at their cabin again, which looked forlorn in the afternoon sunshine.

As they entered, Ahren noticed a carefully folded sheet of papyrus that somebody had pushed under the door. He recognized Likis' neat handwriting and wondered what was so important that his friend would leave something so valuable. Neither vellum nor papyrus were cheap and were mostly only used for official reasons or for profitable business dealings. Only the truly wealthy wrote letters to each other.

Ahren was able to read by now, and so he scanned the writing. Then he crumpled up the letter and threw it into the fire that Falk had just lit. The old man raised his eyebrows and looked at the youth. Ahren clenched his fist and said quietly, 'Sven is stirring it up again. He's spreading rumours that the thing with the rock is a sign from the THREE that they are angry because we are bringing up a Dark One. We're clearly not honouring the gods and other nonsense. The fact that we've been missing for a few days isn't helping things either'.

He shook his head and looked out the window.

Falk grunted and sat down on a stool. He hadn't seen that coming. 'Good, I'll talk to everyone tomorrow. Then I'll decamp'.

Ahren spun around. 'You're seriously going to leave me on my own to face this mess?' Reproach and disbelief were written all over his face.

His master answered in a pained voice. 'I'm leaving you alone with the whole forest, boy. The village intrigues should present no problem'.

Falk had dismissed the latest attacks by the miller's son so casually that it was clear his own problems had to be considerable. Ahren was far from sure he could persuade his master to stay. He decided he would ask Selsena for help early the next morning when Falk was in the village. His master would surely listen to her. He hoped.

An uneasy silence hung in the air that evening and Ahren went to bed early. The thought that this would be the last night together for a long time dampened his mood and followed him into his dreams. A shadowy black figure seemed to be following him in the wood and it kept coming nearer. He kept looking anxiously over his shoulder at it and pointed it out to Falk, who didn't seem to notice it. When the thing was very close, he said, 'I must go now', and disappeared with a boom. Black-boned fingers grasped at Ahren and pressed on his throat…

Then he woke up.

The booming sound was still there and after several heartbeats he realized that somebody was hammering on the door in the middle of the night. As he was sitting up, still in a daze, Falk jumped out of the bed cursing, lit a candle and stomped to the door calling out loudly, 'may the THREE have mercy on you if this isn't important!' He pulled aside the latch and swung the door open.

A small pitch-black figure stood in the doorway and said, 'they do and it is!'

Ahren thought for a moment that the monster in his dreams had come to collect him but then he saw that it was a small boy with ebony coloured skin, wearing a black robe. He held a smoothly polished dark crystal ball in his right hand which glittered in the candle light. Before he recognized what or who it was, Falk had already slammed the door shut with a cry of anger, not giving their unusual visitor a chance to step in.

'Very adult' intoned a sarcastic voice through the thick wood. The dry, sober tone didn't match the voice of a young boy and this made Ahren uneasy, as did his master's violent reaction.

Falk roared through the closed door. 'Get lost, I want nothing more to do with you'.

'I would rather come through an open door but come through I shall. What say you now, Falkenstein?'

Falk opened the door wordlessly and stood aside.

'Good decision', said the boy in a praising, almost fatherly voice, and he stepped inside.

Ahren quietly pinched himself in the arm to make sure that he wasn't dreaming. They obviously knew each other, but why did his master allow this smart-aleck to treat him like that?

'It's been a while, hasn't it?' the boy remarked. 'Where's Selsena hiding then?'

Falk snarled, 'if she's any sense and noticed your presence, she'll have galloped away as quickly as possible'.

'No need to be so rude, Falkenstein. If memory serves me correctly, you were the one who was much better at running away. Isn't that so?' was the calm response.

Culhen had hardly reacted to the boy, strangely enough, and was even allowing him to stroke him. The boy looked at the wolf curiously.

Ahren took the opportunity to observe the intruder in more detail.

He looked like a boy of perhaps nine summers from either the deep lands of the south or the jungles of the east where the people had dark brown skin. His head was completely shaven and his eyebrows had been plucked and trimmed to form two thin lines. His expression was majestic, a sharp, straight nose above a severe mouth. His bearing was that of an adult although he had the appearance of a child. He was wearing a simple, black robe, which lent his ambiguous appearance an air of something disturbing and ominous. The material shimmered, and Ahren recognized it as being made from satin. Whoever he was, he was certainly wealthy.

Falk had collapsed on a stool. The boy's last remark had obviously hit him where it hurt. 'You have no right to say something like that. Not you', Falk said in little more than a whisper.

The visitor now became animated for the first time. 'Oh yes I do. I've earned that right through all the years we spent doing your work while you all were in hiding or chasing your gossamer dreams. Do you know what Qin-Wa is up to at the moment?'

'I heard', said Falk darkly.

'Really? Here in the back of beyond? You don't know the half of it, Falkenstein'.

'They call me Falk here', muttered Falk and stole a glance at Ahren.

The apprentice looked bemusedly from one to the other and didn't understand the world anymore. Falkenstein was one of those flowery names used in the Knight Marshes. But if Falk was really called Falkenstein, why was he using the short form? Had his mentor done something wrong and was he now in hiding here? When he had spoken about his past, the word 'drifter' had come up. Apparently, he had concealed more from his apprentice than the young man had imagined.

The intruder looked directly at Ahren for the first time, deep blue eyes that bore into his own. 'Falk, hmm? Well, alright. It makes no difference at the moment'.

He snapped his fingers, and the wood in the fireplace lit up and blazed for a moment with a powerful flame. Blinking in the sudden light, Ahren tried to take in what had just happened when the boy bowed to him and introduced himself in a formal tone. 'May I introduce myself? Uldini Getobo, adviser to the emperor of the Sunplains, chief commander to the Ancients and beloved of the gods.' He then gave an extremely winning smile which revealed his teeth. He was the very paragon of charm and politeness.

'Ahren, delighted to meet you', mumbled the apprentice instinctively, and stared at the figure in front of him. So, this was the immortal magician who had once weaved the Bane Spell against the Adversary and created the Pall Pillar? Ahren decided that this would be the opportune moment to wake up.

He closed his eyes firmly and pinched himself in the arm. Unfortunately, this didn't change the scenario and the young boy was still there.

'Did you expect us to recognize you?' Falk's interjection was thrown into the room with more than a hint of gratification and malice. 'Any bard trying to earn a crust by telling stories about you, makes you into a benevolent old man with a big bushy beard. Nobody wants to hear about a shit-arse who can flatten whole cities in a pique of anger'.

Uldini looked over Ahren's shoulder at Falk mischievously and said, 'there you are at last, my old friend. I did miss you'.

Ahren couldn't tell if this was sarcasm or the truth and before he could decipher Falk's facial reaction, his master asked, 'well, what do you want here?'

'Don't feign ignorance, you know very well'. The magician stuck out his hand and the crystal ball that he had been holding floated upwards and remained hanging in the air between the boy and Ahren. The apprentice pulled further back into his bed but the ball simply adapted its position.

'Just stay still, it will only take a second and probably won't hurt', grumbled the dark-skinned boy and mumbled a few mysterious words. Green sparks danced in the air between the ball and Ahren before transforming into a bright flash of light that resembled the light in the chapel during the Spring Festival.

Falk slumped into himself and whispered, 'It's true then.'

The magician spun around to face him. 'Of course it's true. Anyone who wants to see it can see it. Do you think I came here just to perform this little trick? I just wanted to play it safe and make sure I was rescuing the right one of the four'.

Falk was really paying attention now, and then Uldini nodded. 'Exactly. A large pack of Fog Cats are on their way here and are going to destroy the whole village. We have to get out of here as quickly as possible'.

Falk leaped up and ran to his trunk. 'How many?'

'How do I know, two dozen or thereabouts. I didn't stay to count them', the wizard spat out. 'I let myself be carried here by the Wild Wind so I wouldn't be noticed'.

Ahren was completely confused now. Nothing made any sense and so he clung on to the information he could make sense of. The village was being attacked by Dark Ones and the villagers were in danger! He jumped out of bed and began to get dressed. Falk did the same without saying a word. Within moments they were ready. The old man had put on the armour he had worn when they had chased the Blood Wolf and attached the broadsword.

Uldini looked at him with his head tilted and asked, 'and where is the rest of the armour?'

'Later', said Falk tersely and walked towards the door followed by the others.

Selsena was standing in front of the house and neighed quietly in greeting. There was neither animosity nor rejection in her attitude. Whatever issue the Forest Guardian had with the magician, the Elven horse wasn't involved in it.

Ahren turned in the direction of the village and trotted off. Culhen trotted beside him with his nose in the wind, when the young man heard Uldini's voice behind him. 'Where do you think you're going?'

Ahren stopped, confused, and turned around. While Falk was looking uncertainly and Selsena was prancing on the spot, the little figure of the magician stood there, his clenched fists on his hips before pointing to the north of the forest. 'We're disappearing as fast as we can'.

'But the village needs our help!' Ahren was perplexed.

Then Falk spoke. 'Boy, I had my work cut out for me dealing with one Fog Cat, but combating more than twenty? That's suicide'.

'If he thinks he's such a great magician, he can help us, or am I wrong?' answered Ahren fiercely. He wasn't going to let his friends die!

'You don't know the first thing about magic. If I intervene, it will be like a magnet. There are far worse things than a few Fog Cats out there that can find us', warned Uldini.

Ahren looked to Falk for support, and it was clear from his master's face that he wanted to help. The Forest Guardian hesitated for a moment, then nodded to his student and ran towards the village. Selsena neighed triumphantly and joined the group.

Ahren and Cuhlen ran with wild determination beside the Forest Guardian and the four of them disappeared into the undergrowth leaving a flabbergasted master magician standing in their wake.

'Hell-fire and damnation, of all the…!' thundered the now strangely old sounding voice of the boy into the night. He broke off his tirade of curses and shook his head. It had never been easy with Falk, and the youngster seemed to have made these tendencies even stronger. This was going to be some amount of work. He raised his hands out from his body with a sigh until they were at a shallow angle to the ground, rose a hand's width up from the ground and floated after the others.

It wasn't long before Ahren and Falk had reached the edge of the village and all seemed quiet.

'Perhaps there's still time. We should sound the alarm bell. If we get everyone into the Village hall or the chapel and light as many fires as possible, we can sit out the night. The battle would be much easier in daylight', whispered his master.

Ahren nodded. Falk had taught him much about combat with Fog Cats. They had originally been lynxes from the Fog Forests before they were employed by the Adversary as trackers and assassins. They had matt grey fur and could melt into the shadows and jump in among them within a heartbeat as long as they had a clear field of vision. Fighting them in an environment of no light was almost impossible. Because of course they could see in the dark and they also had superior hearing. Falk had defeated Grey Fang that time by smoking him out of his lair with a smouldering fire at midday. As soon as the furious beast was forced to spring out into the sunshine, Falk had shot an arrow through him before he had a chance of reaching the shade.

Ahren looked around him and shivered. Yes, it was a starry night and the moon was shining brightly, but here on the edge of the forest were many places the light didn't reach, and no fires were burning in the villagers' houses at this time. Every residence was deathly black.

The two Guardians crept slowly forwards, Culhen stalked in the undergrowth and Selsena stood stock still and listened with her thoughts. They had just arrived on the village square when Selsena neighed shrilly.

'They're here', whispered Falk and looked searchingly around. Ahren did the same and saw spots of moving darkness, that were appearing everywhere between the huts. They were leaping from shadow to shadow and he saw in horror how some of them were jumping onto the roofs of the huts and staring down the chimneys. A heartbeat later and they were gone and terrorized screams could be heard from within the buildings.

Ahren felt sick. He raced over to the alarm bell in the middle of the square and banged it as hard as he could so all of the citizens of Deepstone became aware of the imminent danger. At the same time Falk pulled out his flint stone and ran with Culhen by his side. Selsena in the meantime had spotted one of the Dark Ones, hiding between two houses and charged at it.

198

The shrill sound of the bell resounded through the night and the heads of all the Fog Cats that were out in the open turned around. Ahren saw little red eyes narrowed to a slit, looking him up and down. Falk had quickly lit one of the large torches that were attached to the iron holders at the entrance to the Village Hall and was already lighting the second one.

Ahren yanked an arrow out of his quiver and shot at one of the shapes that was coming towards them slowly and furtively. The weapon would have hit its target but the animal leaped at the last moment into the shadow of a hut, where it vanished, only to re-appear two huts further on.

'Save your arrows until they're nearer and the light lessens their possibility of escape', shouted Falk.

Both torches were now brightly lighting Ahren and his fighting companions within a circle with a radius of five paces, which dissipated the darkness. Right now, Ahren could only make out the eyes of the creatures, which were jumping hither and thither and circling ever closer around the two Guardians and Culhen, who was running around growling but remaining within the light. From the darkness they heard a wrathful spitting sound that suddenly broke off, followed by a loud whinnying. 'Selsena's got one', said Falk grimly and set an arrow to his bow , taking aim into the darkness.

Torches began to flare up behind the huts. The inhabitants had been abruptly torn from their sleep by the ringing of the alarm bell and the screams of the dying.

Falk roared with all his might, 'Fog Cats! Stay in your houses, stoke the fire! Don't open your doors or windows!'

Ahren screamed the same but for some the warning was too late. They heard more screams coming from the darkness as windows and doors were torn open, allowing the night attackers a way in. With tears in his eyes Ahren shot another arrow but could only hear helplessly, how the unequal duels came to their bloody ends.

'We have to do something', he said, turning in frustration to his master.

Falk glanced at him before aiming once again into the darkness beyond the torch light. 'Count them all. We're holding at least half of them at bay for the moment and Selsena has already killed three'. Every time the Titejunanwa was victorious, Falk was filled with a wave of joyful euphoria. 'If everyone stays in their homes, we should be able to prevent further victims. As long as *we* survive', he added.

Meanwhile the Fog cats had slunk up almost as far as the blazing light and could now be made out as grey spectres. Falk let fly with an arrow and one of the shapes was spun around spitting furiously before it collapsed and was totally still. Ahren followed his master's actions and both began to fire off arrows as quickly as possible.

They had already hit five or six Fog Cats when the rest of them began moving together towards them, emitting a most terrifying caterwauling sound.

'They're calling on others for back up', said Falk between shots and pulled out his broadsword. 'Make a bit of room. You keep to the right and let Culhen cover your left side'. Ahren moved to the side and pulled out his dagger and gave the wolf a firm hand signal to follow the order given.

Seven of the animals now stormed into the circle of light and finally Ahren could see details. Time seemed to slow down as the wiry, slim, matt grey bodies jumped towards them. Their grey fur was patterned with thin black stripes and the broad heads of the feline predators had long pointed furry hairs at the tips of their ears, almost like lynxes that had been bereft of their colour, so that they looked like the embodiment of the night.

200

All this went through Ahren's mind within a heartbeat and then the attackers were directly in front of him.

With a roar Falk started swinging his broadsword in a complicated pattern and caught two of the cats in one go while Culhen jumped on another cat. Ahren saw as if through a tunnel, a grey face with bared fangs jumping towards him. He dropped his arrow, yanked his dagger upwards, went into a defensive position before the body of the creature crashed against him and pulled the ground from under him. As if in a frenzy, Ahren started stabbing in every direction, the priceless lessons of his master quite forgotten, while the claws of the Fog Cat tried to find a way through his leather clothing and the head lunged forward attempting to bite Ahren in the face. The Dark One seemed twice as big now as it had a heartbeat earlier. Its fangs were snapping shut close to his throat, the muscly body was clasping at him and into him with its claws, and with wild movements it threw him to the ground. The Fog Cat was now standing over him and had the upper hand. It would soon be all over for Ahren.

Strangely enough, this thought helped the young man to overcome his panic. He remembered one of his master's lessons and reacted with lightning speed. Instead of pushing his opponent away and thereby giving him room to manoeuvre, he wrapped himself around the Fog Cat's neck and pulled it with all his strength towards him, so that its mouth bit harmlessly into his shoulder armour. At the same time, he drove his dagger through the ribs and into the heart of the beast, which crumpled together and became limp.

Ahren looked around frantically and saw that Falk had killed another cat and Culhen had his opponent in his mouth. The wolf shook the Dark One until it was completely still. The other two Fog Cats had retreated to the darkness again and were pacing around them in a semi circle without starting another attack. Ahren shoved the body aside and pulled himself up. He had just regained his breath when another ten pair of eyes appeared.

Falk said in a serious voice, 'the good news is that the villagers are safe for the moment. Selsena says all of them are here. They want to overrun us as a pack'.

Ahren swallowed hard, his mouth was bone dry and his hands, wet with the blood of the Fog Cat, were shaking.

The circle of grey bodies was moving inexorably closer and emitting a low purring sound that bored right into Ahren's very bones.

'Killing gives them pleasure. The Adversary has corrupted them through and through', said Falk disgustedly.

Ahren tried desperately to calm himself. His bow was too far away from him on the ground, and Falk didn't have time to change weapons, to shoot another arrow and get his heavy sword into position again. Culhen stood attentively at Ahren's left leg and so the three waited for the remaining Dark Ones to attack. They were seconds away from being destroyed.

Then Selsena rammed through the darkness into a straggler, who died with a shrill spitting. This sound worked like a signal on the mob, which now stormed forward and were ready to pounce in a wave of claws and fangs and wipe the three fighters off the face of the earth.

But then the torches suddenly went out.

At least that's what it seemed to Ahren because the flame from the torches became so small that they emitted almost no light. A heartbeat later the stolen fire resurfaced again but this time *behind* the surprised Fog Cats, who hesitated for a moment. This short delay saved the Guardians and the wolf for in the next moment the round creation of swirling fire exploded into a fan that spread in a semi-circle, catching everything that lay in its path. The Dark Ones caught fire in an instant and were blazing fiercely while Ahren threw himself, his arms clasped protectively over his head, on top of Culhen as the wave of fire raced towards them. But just like a real wave, this one broke too and pulled back to its source, until it was once again a circular fireball in the night.

Ahren lifted his head and saw the little outline of Uldini. He was standing with the crystal ball in his raised right hand and chanting some words while the swirling fireball dispersed into sparks. The flames of the torches immediately grew back to their original size and blazed contentedly as if nothing had ever happened.

Falk had watched the magic unmoved and without batting an eyelid. He sheathed his broadsword once it was clear that the burning heaps, which only a few seconds earlier had almost spelt their doom, were not going to rise up again. 'What took you so long?' he growled at the magician.

Uldini approached the torch light and Ahren was amazed to see that the boyish figure was floating over the ground and moving as quickly as a running adult.

'I had to catch up with you and could only use a little magic or they would have sensed where I was and intercepted me. As it stood, I had the whole pack in one place and I only needed one conjuration to nab them all'. The magician's voice constantly changed between a furious hissing and a reproachful grumbling.

'I have however, made all Dark Ones within two hundred miles aware of us so we need to get out of here as quickly as possible'.

Their rescuer's voice was so full of suppressed rage by this point that Ahren retreated until he felt the wooden wall of the Village Hall at his back.

Uldini made a dismissive hand gesture in his direction and snarled, 'explain it to him. I'll go and heal a few wounded people and then we'd better go, before this place is wiped off the map'. Then he floated off to the cabins where the cries of pain were coming from.

Falk made a conciliatory gesture and nodded, then turned towards his apprentice, who was just checking Culhen for injuries. The blood that was glistening on him seemed to be all from the monster that the wolf had conquered.

Ahren let out a sigh of relief and embraced his true friend. He himself was covered in blood so it made no odds . He was just happy to be alive.

Falk squatted down beside them. 'We don't have much time, but you need to know one of the ground rules of magic. The intentions with which a magic spell is cast always have an influence on the spirit of the magic maker. If you conjure in a rage, then this rage recoils on you. This effect is all the greater, the stronger and more quickly the spell is cast. If you destroy or kill with your magic, then the whole thing is much worse'. He gave Ahren a firm look. 'Whenever he's the way he is now, then don't provoke him. It's hard enough for him to pull himself together. Many war magicians have fallen into a frenzy and have had to be killed by their own people'.

'Is he going to recover?' whispered Ahren. He didn't know how good a furious magician's ears were and he didn't want to take any chances.

'Of course, the feelings fade away in time. And constructive magic, which is created from pity or love, has the opposite effect. He's helping those who can be saved, and so he'll almost be back to his old self'.

His master slapped him on the back. 'Now go and bid farewell to everyone. He's right in one respect, even if I don't want to admit it. The sooner we're gone, the safer Deepstone is'.

Ahren was excited and sad at the same time. Falk would be bringing him along instead of leaving him here. There was something uncannily reassuring about this thought, but it was hard to accept that he would have to leave everything he knew behind him. His thoughts came thick and fast as he remembered his friends and it became clear to him that he didn't know if they survived the attack unscathed. Ice seemed to flow through his veins when he imagined Likis might have been slaughtered by one of these grey monsters, and so he jumped to his feet and ran off.

Falk looked after him with an understanding look and let him do as he pleased. The wolf would make sure he was safe, and he asked Selsena to keep Ahren's feelings in sight. He stood up slowly with a sigh and sounded the bell three times so the villagers were alerted that the danger had been banished.

Ahren heard the bell echoing behind him and as he ran between the cabins. Doors and windows were carefully opened and frightened villagers peered out into the darkness. Ahren kept calling out as he passed them by, 'the danger is past. Go to the square and see who you can help'.

It wasn't far, a few hundred paces, but he felt as if the village path was stretching out to eternity. As he trotted forward, he wiped the blood awkwardly from his clothing until a wet sheen on the dark leather was the only tell-tale sign of his encounter with the Fog Cats. Culhen was stalking alongside Selsena in the trees – the inhabitants were nervous enough without seeing an Elven horse and a bloodstained wolf.

Ahren reached the northern end of the village at last and saw the merchant's house. Light came from under the door and there were no cries of pain. In fact, it had been a while since he'd passed any houses that were dark, which revealed the disaster that must have befallen their inhabitants. It was clear that the attackers had attacked the village from the south and the northern part had remained untouched.

A quick sidelong glance at his father's house revealed nothing of his fate. Light could rarely be seen inside and Ahren was fairly certain that Edrik had slept through the attack in an alcoholic stupor.

He hammered on his friend's door and shouted, 'Likis, are you there? Are you all alright?'

'Ahren?' came his friend's voice from inside. Then he heard the scratching sound of the latch being drawn back and the curious face of his friend appeared. The merchants' colours were even on his night cap and Ahren couldn't help sniggering when he saw his friend, in spite of the situation.

Likis pulled the cap from his head and muttered, 'what's been going on?' Beside him were his parents with concerned faces. They were both holding daggers and spied over Ahren's shoulders into the night outside.

'We heard the alarm bell and wanted to go to the village square but then everyone started shouting we should stay at home. We heard the all-clear bell earlier but nobody stirred around here and we thought better safe than sorry, so stayed put inside'.

'Fog Cats, a whole pack of them', Ahren explained quickly. 'We've killed them all'. He thought he'd just leave it at that for the moment. The task he still had to perform was difficult enough, and he didn't want to frighten his friend to death.

'Listen to me. Master Falk has to leave Deepstone for a while and I'm supposed to go with him. So, it's farewell for now…' His voice had been cracking with emotion until it finally trailed off.

Likis stared at him in amazement and said, 'Now, in the middle of the night?'While his mother added, 'After an attack like that?'

Ahren decided to tell a white lie to prevent an avalanche of questions. 'We want to be sure that we got them all and find out where they came from'. He really was befuddled about the wizard's and his master's motives but that sounded plausible enough and the attack had somehow been connected with their imminent journey. At least that's how he understood it.

He hugged his astonished friend and said over Likis' shoulder to his parents, 'thank you for everything'. He couldn't say another word but it seemed to have been enough. They gave a nod, full of understanding and warmth. Once again Ahren asked himself what his life would have been like if he had had parents like that. Strangely, the question had lost its force, for the path of his life had led to Falk, and that had made up for a lot that had happened to him before, in spite of all the dangers. He let go of Likis and said, 'I'm sure we'll see each other again soon. Look after yourself and your parents and stay well clear of Sven. He'll be looking for a new target when I'm gone'.

'I'll take care of him, don't you worry about that', said his friend in a husky voice. 'And don't you go falling into the clutches of some Dark One'.

They both gave quick nods, then Ahren turned on his heels and disappeared quickly between the cabins so his friend wouldn't see the tears streaming down his cheeks.

Chapter 13

It was a sorry sight that greeted Ahren when he reached the village square again. Villagers were standing all around in various states of dress. Most had woollen coats thrown over their nightgowns. Here and there blood-stained bandages glistened in the torchlight and the sound of distraught voices was punctuated by sobs and quiet sobbing. At the other end of the square he could see a row of motionless figures, lying on the ground and covered by woollen blankets.

Falk pulled him away before he could go over. There was no sign of Uldini. He grasped his apprentice by the shoulder and said, 'you don't want to see that, believe me'.

'Who?' asked Ahren, flatly.

Falk listed off a few names but none of them were people he had been close to. He felt a mixture of relief and guilt, but then Falk continued, 'Rufus is lying there among them'.

Ahren felt a stabbing pain in his chest. Even though the unremarkable boy hadn't been a friend really, he had always been nice to him. Ahren had learned to value his calm, steady manner in the Godsday school. Now he recognised three of the names. Rufus' parents and his ten-year old sister were also among the dead. He could see the faces of the three in his mind's eye and he felt sick. He doubled over and supported his hands on his knees and breathed deeply while Falk whispered to him, 'I know it's hard but every second counts now. A horde of Dark Ones are coming in our direction right now, and the quicker we get away from there, the safer these people will be'.

'Uldini said the Fog Cats were after four people. He means us, doesn't he? Likis, Holken, Rufus and me. It's all connected somehow with the
208

light at the Spring Ceremony, isn't it?' Ahren spoke in a hushed voice but Falk motioned to him to be quiet.

'I'll explain it all to you later but our friend says the others are safe. The attention is focused on you, him and me'.

'Why?' asked Ahren insistently.

'Later. Now let's scram'. Falk grabbed his upper arm and led him through the crowd. 'I've already told the village council and Keeper Jegral and explained our future absence. Uldini is waiting with our four-legged friends so as to avoid questions being asked that we can't answer'.

They arrived at the edge of village square and melted into the thicket of trees before Ahren had a chance to look for any familiar faces among the villagers.

Falk began to march as quickly as possible off through the forest. Within a few paces Culhen was by Ahren's side and the young man gratefully stroked the animal's coat, which was now dripping wet. Culhen must have used the free time to have a bath in a stream. Ahren smiled mischievously. He suspected, and not for the first time, that his four-legged friend was rather vain.

Selsena was waiting for them further back in the forest, standing motionless under an enormous oak tree. Her silver skin was lacerated with countless red welts, where the claws of the Fog Cats had scratched through her hide. Ahren stopped in shock but a wave of calmness came to him from Selsena.

'It's fine. Everything will be healed by the day after tomorrow'. The dark shape of the wizard came forth from behind the tree and looked at her with a critical eye. 'Is everything sorted or do you still have to hold hands with someone or other', he asked in a biting tone. His voice was beginning to come back to normal but he still seemed to be suffering under the emotional recoil of the death bringing fire magic.

'How many were you able to save?' asked Ahren, partly out of curiosity but also in an effort to distract the magician. If healing magic could help to restore his balance, then perhaps the memory of it could too.

'Five villagers will live to see another day although it was a close call for two of them. And I had to put them all under a sleeping spell, so there wouldn't be a new village legend about a healing black dwarf'. The biting tone could still be heard in the magician's voice, although a little fainter.

'Make yourself useful and heal Selsena', growled Falk and glared at the little being.

He nodded in reply and said, 'another bit of magic won't make any difference, all the Dark Ones in the area got a whiff of us long ago'. He murmured a few words that Ahren couldn't understand and green sparks appeared around the ball, which Uldini was still holding in his right hand. More and more sparks appeared over the course of perhaps ten heartbeats before they soared up and then dived like a swarm of glow-worms down onto Selsena, who stood stock still. The sparks landed on the welts where they went out, leaving a faint green glimmer, which gradually faded and disappeared. A perfect hide remained where the lights had been extinguished, leaving no sign whatsoever of injury.

'Are we ready then?' The wizard's voice sounded tired rather than irritated. Ahren decided this had to be an improvement.

'Where exactly are we going?' asked Falk hesitantly.

'To look for the Einhan of course. First the elves, then the dwarves. And, of course we need our Finder of the Path.'

The wizard stood there hopping from one foot to the other and for the first time he really looked like a little boy. The young Forest Guardian had to keep reminding himself that the boy beside him was one of the Ancients, one of the wizards and wizardesses who had unlocked the secret of eternal youth for themselves. And he wasn't just anyone, he was the highest and mightiest of the Ancients. Everyone knew the story of the gods' darling, the Ancient who knew how to do magic like no other being on Jorath. But the legends had never said anything about a delicate nine-year-old. Ahren brooded and turned to Culhen who was standing on his hind legs with his tongue hanging out and looking from one to the other. Then it slowly dawned on him what the ancient boy had just said. Elves and dwarves? Ahren felt a thrill of anticipation in spite of all the horrors of this night. This journey promised to be exciting!

Falk said, 'Then we're going to have to stop here in the forest temporarily. Otherwise Selsena will attract too much attention to herself'.

Uldini looked critically at the Titejunanwa's horns and nodded.

'It's a detour of only a few miles, and we're definitely going to need the rest of my armour', continued the Guardian.

Uldini raised no objections and so Falk tapped Selsena on her hide and started off.

Ahren felt ignored and the events of the last few hours made him combative. 'I'm going nowhere until someone explains to me by the love of the THREE, what is actually going on here!' And he jutted his chin out, ready for a fight.

All turned around to the apprentice in surprise and Uldini asked, 'What did you tell him?'

Falk didn't answer, at which point the boy laughed angrily, making a most peculiar sound and said, 'he's *your* protégé. Good luck!' Then he pointedly walked on.

Falk glowered at Ahren, a piercing look that he reserved for occasions when his apprentice had behaved particularly stupidly. Then he waved the young man over to him and said, 'let's march on and I'll tell you what you need to know'. Contented with his partial victory, Ahren set off and the disparate group went on their way.

They went through the forest speedily, Uldini floated along again above the ground so he could keep up with the experienced Guardians in the darkness of the night.

Falk rubbed his beard as he always did when he was contemplating something, and finally said, 'It's best if I start at the very beginning. You know about the Paladins?'

Ahren answered mistrustfully, 'I know what was taught in the Godsday school and I know the stories that have been told around the bonfire and in the tavern'.

'Then you know that there used to be thirteen Paladins, who fought during the Dark Days until the Night of Blood when one of them was killed?' Falk's voice was cracking and Ahren nodded. 'There are some things that the peoples today would rather not talk about. When it became clear that HE, WHO FORCES, could not be killed on account of the missing Paladin,' Falk continued, 'a magic spell was woven as an alternative, which was supposed to prevent him from ever waking up again. But the Ancients were not gods, nor even demi-gods. They had to combine the magic formula with a condition which could dissolve it. Otherwise their power would not have been strong enough to cast the spell. Only HE WHO FORCES has been able to cast permanent magic spells – and it's through those spells that the Dark Ones were created'.

Ahren nodded and couldn't resist a quick glance over his shoulder. Tramping through the forest in the middle of the night so soon after a fight with a horde of Fog Cats wasn't good for his nerves. The uncontrolled shivering, which he had also experienced after his encounter with the Blood Wolf, had stopped in the meantime, which meant he was

212

gradually getting used to the sensation of danger. Falk had been right in that respect.

'Thirteen Paladins are needed to defeat the Adversary. For the THREE had invested exactly that amount of power into the awakening of the Paladins, which was the same amount of power that had gone into the creation of the Custodian. Not too much, not too little. They were the means needed to recreate the harmony of the creation'.

Falk was staring off into the middle distance. He sounded as if we were retelling something from his childhood.

'So, some of them thought it would be clever to connect the condition for ending the excommunication to the one thing that could kill the Betrayer. As soon as the Thirteenth Paladin was chosen, then the magic spell that held the enemy in the Pall Pillar would break. The election was powerful enough as a ritual to guarantee that none of his servants could evade the trigger'.

'Well, that sounds like a great plan', said Ahren, hoping the old man would continue.

'That's what everyone thought at the time, but a Paladin had never been killed before. No-one knew what would happen next. It was hoped that the Thirteenth Paladin would be born again within a few years, the Pall Pillar would dissipate, and then the three could unleash their powers simultaneously and kill the Adversary before he had a chance to recover from the effects of the enchanted sleep and before he had the chance to form a new army. But they had underestimated one thing'. They ducked under a low hanging branch as they travelled on and he continued to speak. 'The THREE were in a dreamless deep sleep and it was impossible to wake them or to plead to them in their dreams, as they had been able to do before, so for the moment there was no possibility that they could create a new Paladin until they had recovered somewhat, and no one

213

knew how long this would take. The world was caught up in a deceptive peace. The centuries passed and many came to terms with the Pall Pillar and declared the enemy to have been defeated. This is why the religious texts nowadays are no longer very accurate. Nobody wants to hear that the Dark Days could come again'.

Falk looked quickly over at Uldini who nodded back at him.

'To provide certainty that the arrival of a chosen one would be noticed by us, a ritual was created that found its way into the Spring Ceremony. Centuries passed and nothing happened, the peoples of the creation began to feel safe, and the importance of the ritual faded from memory, as did the threat that the sleeping spell of the enemy would not last forever. Nobody thought at that time that the gods would need more than seven hundred years to gather the strength to dream up a new Paladin'.

Ahren listened intently. Much of what he had heard was new, exactly as Falk had said. Keeper Jegral's official version of the events had revealed little of this.

Falk looked at him expectantly. He had stopped marching, as had the others. Even Culhen seemed to be looking up at him. Had he missed something?

When Ahren didn't react, Falk continued. 'The ritual allowed for the stone of the gods to show a sign if the Paladin-to-be touched it during the Spring Festival'.

A nervous silence descended on the group while everybody waited for Ahren to draw the necessary conclusions. Several heartbeats passed during which his reason simply refused to function or to follow the logical chain of events to its inevitable conclusion.

'You all think that I…' he finally managed to utter weakly before trailing off. The idea was too absurd and the consequences were too enormous.

214

Falk pressed Ahren to him, something he had only done once or twice before since he had known him.

'I'm sorry, boy', he whispered.

Uldini looked fixedly over Falk's shoulder at Ahren during this embrace and said, 'you are going to be the future thirteenth Paladin and save the world as we know it, or die trying. Maybe even before your Naming if we stand around here cuddling each other in a dark forest'.

Ahren shook his head. His thoughts were spinning around in a circle. He, a Paladin? Those two had to be crazy. 'What do you mean 'Naming'?'

Uldini took over the talking. He obviously wanted to get the thing over with so they could move on.

'The awakening of a Paladin involves three steps. Firstly, the birth. Secondly, the selection, in order to see if the successor is worthy. This used to be a formality, as the descendants of the previous Paladins were the chosen ones. Once the selection was made, the power of the outgoing Paladin would begin to pass over to the chosen child, and that was our dilemma. HE had killed the father *and* the son, so the power of the thirteenth was lost'. He cleared his throat. 'Thirdly, the Naming, once adulthood was reached. The Einhan requested the blessing of the gods for the aspirant and he or she received the gifts of the THREE: immortality, soul-animal and godly armour – and then we had a new Paladin. All were happy and the predecessor could die at last'. He looked at the apprentice with a twinkle in his eye. 'You've already passed two of the three steps. Unfortunately, the last step is somewhat more complicated, not least because you cannot receive your power from your predecessor. The selection released the power. It will be anchored in you when you are named'.

'What do I have to do?' asked Ahren curiously, although he feared the answer.

'You don't have to do anything apart from accompany us. We'll find the Einhan and take it from there', said Falk in a comforting voice.

There was that word again: *Einhan.*

'What are the Einhan?' asked Ahren. Every answer seemed to throw up a new question, something Uldini recognized too. There was scorn in his voice again when he answered.

'Each is a specific representative of people, elves and the dwarves, and they intercede for you before their god. Which, by the way, will never happen if we're caught by a pack of Low Fangs here in the forest'.

Falk nodded to the wizard and they all went on, the old man leading a dazed Ahren by the arm. Lost in thought he stumbled through the darkness and kept thinking over what he had just heard. Hours passed before they finally stopped. In front of them was a dense thicket of blackthorn, a particularly hardy plant, named after the dark hooks that could be found all over its resilient tendrils. Animals avoided these plants as they were practically inedible and difficult to penetrate. However, they usually stood alone and Ahren had never seen so many together.

'Wait here', grunted Falk and drew his sword. Ahren looked at his mentor in amazement as he began to hack down the thicket with fluid movements. Falk had always drummed into his apprentice a respect for nature and pointed out to Ahren how he should behave towards plants and animals. Now the old man was standing in front of him and slashing all before him. Once he had hacked the plants to pieces, he pulled out an enormous, heavy oilskin sack with a groan, and carefully began to undo it. He responded to Ahren's look of shock with a shrug of his shoulders and the explanation, 'I planted them to protect my things. The plants were in the wrong place here anyway and were beginning to choke the forest'.

'The elves have made you soft, old man' said Uldini.

Falk shrugged his shoulders and carried on. 'Why don't you throw out a magic net and see how near the danger is. This here is going to take a while but we'll be all the faster afterwards'.

The wizard paused, then nodded, and began murmuring quietly and staring into his ball, which started to emit warm yellow rays of light. Ahren sank down at the foot of a tree and gazed into the distance, thinking again of all the things he had heard and experienced. Culhen came to him, rested his muzzle on his knees and began to whimper until the young man started tickling him in the neck absent-mindedly. The familiar contact with his furry friend had a soothing effect on his nerves and he gradually nodded off.

How much time had passed before he woke up, he couldn't tell, but he knew what had awakened him. Falk and Uldini were just finishing a heated debate, the wizard's ball was still emitting light. A strange picture presented itself to Ahren. Falk had not only put on the familiar armour for legs, arms and neck, but also a light breastplate and a knight's helmet made from the same whitish material as the rest of the armour. The way the pieces all fitted, showed that they belonged together and made up one piece. The armour looked very old-fashioned and the helmet was engraved in the form of a stylized falcon's head. Falk was in the process of rubbing ash onto the new pieces so that they would look worn and worthless too.

Selsena however, had made the most dramatic transformation. A broad, white, leather saddle with matching saddle-bags adorned her back. The upper part of her body was covered with metal panels made from the same material as Falk's armour, and her head was in a metal helmet that enclosed her forehead and horns, so it looked as if these were features of martial equine body armour. The Titejunanwa looked like a strong but standard war horse in an exotic suit of armour.

Falk was finished with disfiguring his own armour and now approached the Elven horse. The chorus of disapproval she emitted grew louder and louder and was now physically palpable, as if a thousand ants were scurrying over Ahren's body. Culhen gave a low yelp and Falk shouted at the magical horse, '*you* wanted to go back into the story. You've been sulking since time immemorial and now you've found your will. So, stay still'. The feelings ebbed away and Falk, undeterred, began to transform Selsena's proud war horse into an impoverished nag and relic from a bygone heroic era.

Uldini was giving orders on how to improve things further and seemed to be enjoying the whole experience.

Ahren pulled himself up and walked over.

'What does all this mean?' he asked.

'We want to journey through Three Rivers and head up north from there, past the Red Posts as far as Evergreen. Falk is going to be a wandering knight escorting yours truly, an alumnus of the lesser nobility, while you and your 'dog' are our guides in this region'.

Mention of the places that Ahren only knew from the stories was like a slap in the face and the serenity with which he had woken up disappeared in a puff of smoke. The impossibility of the situation felt like a millstone around his neck and he heard himself asking, 'and what if I don't want to go with you?'

Forest Guardian and Wizard gave him a searching look and his master was about to issue him with a sharp rebuke when the little man raised his hand. 'No, old man, I'll take care of this. Firstly, no-one can force you. A Naming can never be made against the will of the chosen one. That would presuppose force and goes against the nature of the THREE'.

Ahren nodded. That was only logical. In all the stories where great victories were won against the Betrayer, free will had played a decisive part. Rule and force were the tools of HIM WHO FORCES.

The wizard continued, 'but it is nonetheless important that you understand one thing. The magic spell that is holding him captive is fading. That's a fact. It has been getting weaker since the day you were born, and this process has quickened since your selection. HE can only work through his servants and his orders are diffuse and poorly focused, but the more he awakens, the clearer they become. You can hide away or spend your short life on the run, but eventually the Dark Ones will find you and kill you, and the world will have no chance against HIM WHO FORCES'. Uldini didn't need to explain the rest. Ahren understood that he had no other option but to accept the role, and anyway, something inside him harmonized with the words of the master wizard, washing away all doubts regarding his mission.

Ahren knew that he had to fight, whether he wanted to or not.

They spent the rest of the night in the protection of the trees. The wizard's magic had shown that they were in no immediate danger and it wouldn't be long until daybreak anyway. Ahren hadn't believed that he would be able to fall asleep again that night but his decision not to run away from the future events had a strangely calming effect on him and he dropped off within a few heartbeats.

The two adults looked at the brown-haired young man whose face was free from all worry as he slept.

'You have a fine young boy there under your wing, old man', said Uldini softly. Falk grunted under his breath, 'I know, but don't let him hear it. He has a very long and dangerous way to go yet and it would be better if he kept his two feet firmly on the ground'.

'If we know anything, we know about long ways, isn't that right?'

'Yes, you're right there. What are the other Ancients up to? There's been hardly any news from you for centuries.' Falk looked at the magus with interest.

'I gave out a new doctrine in the third century after the Betrayer's fall when it became clear that the matter would take a while longer. The peoples were beginning to forget so we pulled back and didn't engage as much as in earlier times. In this way old wounds could heal more quickly and we could move about more freely. The others still like practising their little power games but I find things like that boring', answered Uldini.

Falk nodded knowingly. Of course, his counterpart wouldn't enjoy that. Who wanted to play a game that he'd already won centuries previously? The others had been tussling over second place since forever.

'You know you're going to have to come clean with him soon, don't you?' asked the Arch Wizard. 'He'll find out at the Naming by the latest, and that wouldn't be the best way'.

Falk nodded. 'I'll talk to him before that, but he needs to digest this first. We need to sleep for a bit too. Selsena will stand guard'.

The little boy figure nodded and the light in the crystal ball went out. The forest lay in darkness and soon all were asleep.

Ahren woke up to the sounds of an argument. The little boy and the old man were shouting at each other, their faces red. The newly awakened apprentice watched the two in amusement. They looked like a grandfather and a cheeky and disobedient grandson. When he felt the soft and amused waves coming from Selsena, he knew he wasn't the only one who found the scene amusing.

'It's a massive detour and you know that! If we follow your route, we'll have to go right across the Knight Marshes twice. That will cost us weeks', shouted Falk and waved his arms.

Uldini responded forcefully. 'You're just trying to delay the meeting with Jelninolan but that makes even less sense. If we go to the Silver Cliff first, then we also have to go to Kelkor to trap the Finder of the Path. Do you really want to go into Evergreen with a dwarf and one of the Wild Folk?'

Ahren sighed. He had hoped that after the previous day's revelations the conversations between them would make more sense, but he was obviously mistaken. Culhen yawned and stretched out beside him and then he began to sniff the rucksacks.

Uldini had brought their few belongings when they had left the village but there was nothing edible among them. The two were still squabbling with each other and so Ahren decided to make himself useful by going hunting. He slapped his knee once and Culhen was immediately by his side. Ahren looked into his eyes and Culhen sat on his hind legs and looked questioningly at his master with his head tilted to the side and his ears pricked. 'Culhen, search!' said the young Forest Guardian.

The white wolf spun around with a low bark and leaped into the undergrowth. Ahren followed him at a distance and watched as his companion ran zigzag through the forest, his nose sometimes in the air, sometimes to the ground. Then he found a fresh scent and began to follow it. Ahren ran after him and the hunt was on.

He returned to their temporary camp an hour later with three rabbits hanging from his belt. The yield was less than he had hoped for but Culhen and he had only hunted on their own three times previously and so they had been unsuccessful several times this morning. The fact that

Culhen with his white fur was more at home in the tundra and the frozen north didn't help matters either during the hunt.

But at least they had enough sustenance for the day and Ahren had also collected some herbs so that they had enough ingredients for a good stew. Ahren had bled out the third animal and given it to his four-legged friend who chewed around it fussily until it became clear to him that there was nothing else to eat. Then he gulped down the rabbit in next to no time.

The two squabblers had sunk into a sullen silence and hadn't noticed the young Forest Guardian at all when he returned with Culhen. Once Ahren had lit the fire and prepared the stew, they came back to life. The smells of the food drew them to the fire and Falk grunted, 'so you did learn something', as he filled himself a large bowl and began to eat.

Uldini smelled at the stew simmering in the little metal pot and raised his eyebrows in surprise.

'Well, if it doesn't work out with saving the world, you can always try your hand at being a cook'. Ahren looked at the little wizard in consternation. Uldini continued in the same lighthearted tone. 'Stop staring at me so wide-eyed. When you get to be my age, you've no choice but to develop this sort of sense of humour'.

Then he helped himself and also enjoyed it. Once they had all had their fill, Ahren asked, 'is Deepstone safe now?'

After the attack of the previous night and the wizard's bleak pronouncements on hordes of Dark Ones, he wanted to be sure that his home village would be left in peace, before he turned his back on the place.

Uldini seemed to grasp what he was getting at. 'No need to worry. I hid the two other boys that took part in last year's ceremony from the traitor's eyes. That was quick and easy as they were of no importance. HIS senses are still very groggy, otherwise HE would have recognized immediately who represents the real danger, and all the Fog Cats would have chased you and you alone. After my little firework display last night, we have now become the sole focus of the Adversary'.

This led Ahren into his second question. 'Why are you two so quiet now. It was a completely different story last night.' He shifted position nervously.

'I think we have to thank the old Blood Wolf for that. Your master only told me about her this morning. The magic web that I wove last night detected no Dark Ones in the vicinity. Falk and I think that the old woman drove everything away that could have been dangerous to her pup'.

'And the Fog Cats, where did they come from?' Ahren wanted to understand what exactly had happened.

'They were sent out the moment you were selected. That pack was probably the greatest danger nearby, and even they took over a week to get to you. I think we're safe for the next two or three days as long as I don't do any major magic which might reveal our location'.

'So, the Dark Ones can sense your magic?' Ahren pressed on.

'Only the very intelligent ones can, but they will then pass it on to their less intelligent counterparts. But HE notices the magic too, depending on what HE might be listening to at the time. HIS attention is just as groggy and somnambulistic as HIS sight. That's our greatest advantage for the moment'.

Falk cleared his throat. 'That's enough talk for the moment. We need to get cracking, or we'll never get anywhere'.

'Where exactly are we going?' asked Ahren curiously.

Suddenly there was a tension in the air as the Forest Guardian and the wizard stared venomously at each other. Uldini spoke in a remarkably diplomatic voice. 'First we can head towards Three Rivers. That's the nearest big town and we can pick up provisions and weaponry there. Three Rivers is a good starting point, no matter which way we go after that'. Falk was placated and nodded in agreement as the three broke camp.

Chapter 14

Ahren brooded to himself as he walked quickly beside Selsena, trying not to fall behind. They were on a wide dirt road, typical of the travel routes in Hjalgar. They had left the Eastern Forest and were now heading northwards. They were hardly clear of the trees when Uldini abandoned his normal floating.

'We don't want to attract attention', he said. Falk then mounted Selsena's back, picked up Uldini, planted him in front of him on the saddle and then they carried on without saying a word, leaving Ahren open-mouthed in their wake. He ran in pursuit, swallowing dust, and demanded an explanation but received none. And so, he ran beside them in a foul mood and with sweat running down his back. The sun shone brightly in a clear sky and intimated that summer was on the way.

After a while Falk relented and explained the situation to Ahren. 'We're playing our parts. I'm the paid escort, this is my charge and you're our guide in the wilderness. Only speak if you have to, leave the talking to us.'

Ahren could only nod, he was too tired to start an argument. He could understand the reasoning but it didn't make the role he had to play any easier.

He was surprised how effective their disguise seemed to be when they started encountering other travellers. Hardly anyone took notice of them. There were one or two curious glances at Selsena's and Falk's exotic armour but Falk had taken care to make it appear so dilapidated that everyone passed by quickly without exchanging a word.

Ahren seemed practically invisible and so he had all the time in the world to study the various figures they encountered. The travelling merchants made up the largest proportion, most of them on their own or in pairs on carts filled with all kinds of bundles and boxes or covered with canvas. They all shot suspicious looks and quite a few were armed with daggers, one even had a crossbow. The wealthier merchants had one or two guards with them who made the same impression as Falk did. None of them carried a broadsword, rather truncheons or short swords. There were several envious glances in the direction of the massive blade, now in the scabbard affixed to Selsena's flank.

When a pair of scruffy figures, who were travelling the road without any merchants, examined them particularly intensely, Falk mumbled, 'I don't like this. There should only be a few peddlers around here'.

Uldini answered quietly, 'you've spent too long hiding in the forest, old man. Highway robberies have become more common and there have been more forays coming from the Border Lands, be they Borderlanders or Low Fangs'.

Ahren looked up, shocked. The Border Lands was the large area which surrounded the Pall Pillar. The Adversary was lying there in chains cast by the magic spell, trapped in silence and smoke. Only the daring or desperate lived there. The rate of miscarriages and stillbirths went up, the nearer one came to the crater which had been blown up when the magic spell released its power and the physical manifestation of the Betrayer, who had been fighting and slaughtering to the last moment, was forced to the ground. No-one knew exactly how deep the crater was, for from that day smoke had been rising from the place where HE WHO FORCES now existed, and as Ahren well knew, bided his time. Nobody dared to enter, and anyone who had, came out again as the Adversary's servant. There were enough tales of bold heroes who had tried it, only to be horribly transformed into Low Fangs who hunted down their nearest and dearest. Ahren was on the point of asking how true these stories really were but he'd had his fill of unpalatable truths for the day and so he stayed silent.

Falk quietly answered Uldini. 'From what we know already, these ambushes are no surprise. The Border Lands will fall under HIS control sooner or later no matter what we do'.

The apprentice shuddered when he heard these words. Thousands of people lived in this area that no power had claimed for its own. No kingdom wanted the cursed place within their dominion. The travelling merchants who came to Deepstone reported that it was populated by eccentric wizards, maverick farmers or those who had been up to no good and couldn't return to civilization.

'Couldn't we warn them?' asked Ahren.

'They wouldn't listen to us. Nobody would believe our story of returning villains and there's no ruler we can speak to. We can hardly traipse from one farmyard to the next. We can only hope that common sense will lead them away from there before it's too late'.

Ahren remembered that his father had originally come from the Border Lands and suddenly he was grateful that his father had had the presence of mind to choose Deepstone as his new home. He trotted on beside Selsena and looked uneasily at the wayside as they passed through a little wood, afraid that a band of highway robbers might ambush their little group.

By evening Ahren was exhausted and bathed in sweat from all the running. Falk said to him, 'if you're in luck, old Giesbert's farmyard inn is still in existence. Years ago, they used to have sleeping quarters and good food. Not a real hostel but more luxury than setting up camp on the side of the road'.

Ahren nodded wearily and went on in silence. Even Culhen was panting loudly and his tongue was hanging out. Ahren patted him on the head in sympathy and they climbed the hill that their road passed over. From the top, the little group could see a shallow valley lying sleepily in the late evening spring sunshine. There were rows of fields, and canals that brought the precious water to every corner of the valley. A two-storey estate house dominated the landscape, surrounded by a variety of huts and barns. Ahren was astonished and Falk gave a whistle. 'They've certainly gone up in the world,' he said approvingly and directed Selsena onwards.

'Is that all one farm?' asked the surprised apprentice and Falk nodded.

'Absolutely. If the farm keeps growing like that, it's going to turn into a proper village. Deepstone must have started exactly the same way but without the trade road of course. The Eastern Forest provides for us instead'.

They approached the big farm with a feeling of contentment and then Ahren saw two lookout platforms. Standing on each was a sentry with a crossbow. They rode directly under one of the sentries, a red-haired woman who gave them a warm greeting and then turned her attention back to the range of hills.

Falk nodded, satisfied. 'We can certainly sleep here. It will do us all good'.

They stopped at the Main House and Falk dismounted and then lifted Uldini off, very much the hired mercenary and servant to a noble son and heir. The wizard behaved in such a regal manner that all the workers bowed before him as they hurried by. Ahren was invisible as always. He threw his eyes up to heaven and was about to follow the others when Falk looked over his shoulder to him and barked an order. 'Boy, take care of the horse!' Then he disappeared inside. The apprentice looked after his master blankly for a heartbeat, then took Selsena by the reins and went to the stables, which could already be smelt from this distance. He cursed quietly to himself. Selsena was empathetically convulsed with laughter and this made the apprentice even angrier. He led her into her box and took off her saddle and bags as well as the body armour, which was surprisingly light. Only her headgear stayed on, to hide her true identity. Then he quickly and half-heartedly groomed the mare. Her dirt-repellant coat made this work unnecessary anyway, and thanks to her three hearts, she didn't even break into a sweat when she was galloping. She transmitted her gratitude to him nevertheless and he gently patted her neck.

'I still haven't thanked you for Culhen's salvation', he whispered quietly. 'So, thank you very much'. Warmth and joy flooded through him and Culhen came running and barking into the box, as he scampered delightedly around her legs. Ahren was enjoying this moment when he heard a voice behind him.

'Are you a new stable boy?'

Ahren spun around in shock, brandishing his dagger, only to withdraw it sheepishly when he realized that the voice belonged to a girl, maybe one summer younger than he was. 'You really don't look like a groom', she continued, unfazed.

'I'm a Forest Guardian', he said before cursing silently as he remembered his cover story. 'I earn my keep as a guide in the wilderness', he added quickly as he scrutinized the girl opposite. She was small, certainly a head shorter than he was, and her clever eyes shone from her freckled face. Her simple linen dress suggested that she worked somewhere on the farm. She looked at him with equal directness and Ahren noticed a certain similarity to the sentry he had seen up on the wooden platform. Perhaps that was her mother, he thought to himself.

' You'd make a good groom. The horse is really shiny, even though you've just come in', she saw in amazement. She smiled at him and Ahren smiled back, a little embarrassed and a lot less elegantly.

'Ah', he said and thought, what's wrong with me?

She stepped closer. 'Can I stroke your horse? I've never seen a colour like that'.

Ahren wanted to say, 'that's not my horse, and the owner definitely wouldn't approve'. But what came out was, 'sure, why not?'

She beamed at him and put both hands around Selsena's neck, who glared at Ahren and made him very much aware of her displeasure.

'She's very soft…but, what about her eyes, they're really silver', remarked the girl.

Ahren winced. 'She's terribly old already and that's why her eyes are cloudy'.

Selsena was really angry now and he stepped back out of the box to be on the safe side. Luckily, the girl released her hold of the Elven horse and followed him. He closed the box hurriedly and leaving the irritated mare behind, he smiled awkwardly at the girl.

'What's your name?' he asked, in an effort to deflect attention from the so-called horse.

'Miriam. And you?' she answered gaily.

Smitten by her breath-taking smile, it took him a heartbeat to answer the question. 'Ahren', he said finally. He scrambled for something innocuous to talk about, but Miriam was already asking the next question.

'Have you travelled far?'

'No, this is my first job. I've only finished my apprenticeship'. He was quite proud of himself that he had stuck as closely to the truth as was possible.

230

'Oh, right', sighed the girl, disappointed, and looked as if she was about to go. The temptation to show off a little so she would stay was too great.

'But we want to go to Evergreen to the elves, and then on to the Silver Cliff, where the dwarves live'. His words were incredibly effective. Her eyes lit up and her wonderful smile reappeared. 'Then we'll head on to Kelkor. We're bound to run into one or two giants', he added in a deliberately casual manner.

'Why do you have to go there? That sounds like a terribly long journey', she said, agitated.

Now Ahren had to be careful. Everything he had said up to this point fitted in with their cover story. 'I'm accompanying a noble youth who wants to see the places he heard about in his favourite stories. He has a cranky bodyguard with him who's making my life hell'. That was partly true as well and he began to feel a little more self-confident.

'I know how that feels. I have to help out in the kitchen until I'm allowed to be a sentry. The cook, well, she's horribly mean to me', complained Miriam.

Ahren nodded eagerly. 'My master was exactly the same. One time he made me collect knotted ribbons from a tree in the pouring rain'.

And for the next hour they swapped stories of their experiences at the hands of their hard-hearted teachers and they laughed and complained in equal measure. Ahren was dimly aware that Selsena would tell Falk of the apprentice's less than flattering descriptions of his master, but the undivided attention that the charming Miriam was giving him, made it worth any future trouble. He felt happy and free from all his cares and the time just went flying by.

Eventually Miriam looked at the position of the sun, threw her arms around Ahren's neck and said, 'I really have to go now. Thanks for the lovely stories.' Then she gave him a kiss and ran out giggling. Ahren stood rooted to the spot and stared after her, overwhelmed by the unexpected kiss. He left the barn and looked after the red-headed girl until she disappeared behind a house. Should he run after her? Was this a complicated game whose rules he didn't understand? While he was standing there, he caught a glimpse of something moving in the corner of his eye. The redheaded woman on the lookout platform was watching him with a murderous look. Slowly she raised her crossbow until she zeroed in on him. He raised his hands and took two steps back until her line of fire was hidden by the barn door. He decided in a moment of wisdom that it would be best to wait here for the others. Meanwhile Selsena was flooding him with waves of mirth.

When it was early evening Falk marched into the barn with a surprised look. He brought with him a bowl of cheese, ham and hard -boiled eggs which he handed to Ahren.

'Why did you stay outside? I only sent you away as part of our disguise. Of course you can come in to eat', he said and glanced at the wolf. 'But Culhen had better stay with Selsena'. The wolf whimpered in protest for a second before trotting over to the box where he settled himself down.

'It was so nice out here', said Ahren lamely.

Falk breathed in through his nose deliberately. The air reeked of horse manure, stale sweat and leather. Then he tilted his head to the side and listened to Selsena's remarks. Falk was still laughing heartily after two dozen heartbeats and Ahren was blushing deeply. At last his master quietened down and clapped his protégé on the shoulder. 'Come on in,

I'll cover for you'. He threw his arm around his apprentice and pulled him out into the open. He caught the sentry's eye and nodded at the woman. She winked in acknowledgement and stared off at the horizon.

'You still have a lot to learn. We have to thank our lucky stars that the Adversary isn't a woman or we might as well give up now'. Then he started to laugh again. Ahren ignored him as much as possible. They entered the taproom of the manor. It was furnished with rows of long benches and tables running parallel to each other. It seemed as though tree trunks had simply been halved and smoothed and then hammered into place as table legs.

The room was populated by guests similar to the travellers he had seen on their journey here. The room was partially lit by two oil lamps at the back of the room and also by the evening spring sunshine which bathed the room in a warm yellow glow. The apprentice reckoned that there was enough room for half the population of Deepstone.

The Forest Guardian made a beeline past the benches to the woman of the manor who greeted him with a friendly nod. Then he led Ahren up a staircase at the back of the room. Once they reached the landing at the top of the stairs Ahren could see an enormous dormitory behind an archway, but Falk opened one of the two doorways in front that led left and right away from the dormitory. He indicated to him to go in. There was a small, plain looking room with two beds, a table and two chairs in front of a window. Ahren entered.

Falk closed the door behind him and said, 'it's a bit conspicuous, renting the two single rooms, but this way we can talk undisturbed. And anyway, we both still have bloodstains on our leather jerkins – and you still have some behind your right ear'. Ahren checked with his hand and felt a large crust, which fell off as soon as he touched it.

Falk pulled a bottle of wine from his jerkin and put it on the table.

'Eat something first and drink. You'll get water later to wash yourself and to rinse things. Don't you dare finish the bottle!'

Then the old man was gone and Ahren was alone and unobserved for the first time in ages. He enjoyed the feeling and decided to make the best of the opportunity.

Night fell and at last Ahren felt himself again. Of course, he had become accustomed to the hardships that adventuring with Falk brought with it, but it was a different story travelling along this dusty dirt road and becoming over tired and baked in filth. He had eaten and drunk well while Falk had tended to Culhen. Then he had washed himself and afterwards given his clothing a thorough rinse. Then he had mended the worst of the tears that the Fog Cats had made with their claws. Now he was lying on the bed and could hear the unfamiliar sounds coming from the dormitory. He had become so accustomed to the silence of the forest that he was very aware of the noise so many people in close proximity were making. He could hear snatches of conversation as he thought about his exciting conversation with Miriam. Where was she now and what was she doing? Was she thinking about him too? His thoughts swirled around in circles until he dropped off to sleep.

He woke up with a start. He could hear a noise which sounded like leather straps slapping off each other. It was pitch black and after a few heartbeats Ahren realized that the sound was coming from outside and was coming through the slits in the window blinds. Falk had returned at some point in the evening and was fast asleep in the bed beside his, and so Ahren slipped quietly from the bed and crept to the window. He peeked out through the crack between the shutters.

Wisps of cloud were floating across the night sky and the moon was shining weakly. Whatever this strange sound was, it was coming from above them. He tilted his head sideways so he could see upwards out the gap. The noise seemed to be travelling. Dozens of shadows seemed to be moving past over the manor and across Ahren's limited vision. He could see dozens of winged figures, which were making the sound. Ahren blinked and tried to make out the creatures' characteristics, but they were too far away, and the light was too weak.

Maybe bats…, thought Ahren just as a shadow flew directly past the shutters. Ahren saw leather wings, birds' claws and burning red eyes when suddenly a calloused hand grasped his shoulder and yanked him backwards. He was just able to stifle a cry when he recognized Falk, who pushed him under the table and hid himself too as best he could. There was a scratching on the window sill outside and then the shutters started to rattle. Whatever was outside, it was trying to get in. Ahren caught sight of the small wrought-iron hook that held the shutters closed. A beak had pushed its way into the gap in the shutters and was trying to push up the hook. To his horror Ahren could see in the weak moonlight, teeth flashing in the beak.

A metallic scratching sound to his left revealed to Ahren that Falk had drawn his dagger. His own, unfortunately, was on the other side of the room, lying on his carefully folded clothing. He looked back and forth between that thing that wanted to get in and his dagger, trying to decide if he should risk the movement. The noise of the heavy leather wings became louder as the attacker's attempts to get in became more frantic, and then suddenly, it was all over.

The sound died away, and the shadow disappeared with an angry hiss. Falk sheathed his dagger with relief and looked at Ahren.

'Swarm Claws. That was too close for comfort'. He pulled himself up and stormed out of the room. Ahren crept out from under the table and followed him at a considerably slower pace and remembered back to his lessons. Swarm Claws were birds that the Adversary had perverted in a most horrible way. They earned their name through the oversized, razor-sharp claws on their feet and because they always attacked in swarms of more than a hundred. They didn't have plumage any more but were covered in a leathery skin. Their beaks were filled with barbed teeth. A Swarm Claw on its own was dangerous of course, but as it was only the size of a hawk, it could be easily beaten. But when they were in a swarm, they became a veritable nightmare of flesh-eating beaks and claws. Ahren thought of the many black shadows he had seen in the sky. If the window had opened, they would be dead.

Hopefully Miriam is safe, he thought in a flash. But he hadn't heard any screams, and the swarm had moved on. He quickly suppressed the memories that instinctively came to mind, of Deepstone and the screams of the villagers.

A shudder ran through him and he hurried to catch up with Falk, who had stormed into the other room, which the wizard had to himself. Uldini was perched on the bed, his arms around his knees, and looked like a frightened little child. Until he opened his mouth.

'Close the door, old man', he hissed. Falk carried out his order as Ahren quickly slipped in. He didn't want to hear the conversation, nor did he want to be alone now. He hunkered quietly on one of the chairs and kept a nervous eye on the window.

'Damn it, Uldini, you said we were safe', scolded Falk.

'They were definitely beyond the reach of the magic net last night. They must have flown without a break tonight', said the Magus defensively. It was the first time Ahren had experienced the resolute Ancient on the back foot. 'You know how these things function. If I make the web too big, it's discovered and everything starts again. I was very careful yesterday', he continued.

Falk calmed down a little and said, 'the way they were flying, they were on a search mission for the three of us, so they were focusing their attention on human dwellings. That would suggest that at least Selsena and Culhen are safe as long as they don't attract attention to themselves. But imagine if we had set up camp in the open and they had caught us?'

He was met with an awkward silence. Ahren tried not to imagine being at the mercy of this wave of claws and teeth with no protection or possibility of escape.

'How do you fight against them?' he asked. Maybe it would calm him down if he knew they were beatable.

'With lots of arrows and casualties', answered Falk grimly.

That wasn't of much comfort. Uldini cleared his throat. 'Magic has also shown itself to be effective. Thankfully, there are only four or five swarms that we know of on all of Jorath'.

'They generally sleep throughout the day and only wake up with difficulty, so we're safe tomorrow during daylight, but we need to stay armed during the next few nights,' said the old Forest Guardian firmly.

The wizard nodded, and Falk opened the door to the hall without saying another word. The private conversation was obviously over and Ahren followed him to their bedroom. They went back to their beds again but falling asleep was difficult for Ahren. When he did eventually drop off, he found himself being buffeted about by bloody claws that were grasping at him in the darkness.

Chapter 15

They set off early the next morning. The farmyard was still and deserted. The residents were still too traumatized by the previous night's danger to go about their daily tasks unimpeded. Ahren craned his neck to try and spot Miriam and he was relieved to see her looking out the kitchen window. He waved good bye and they moved off.

The next few days passed by in a refreshing routine. Ahren learned it was better to go in front of Selsena to avoid the clouds of dust her hooves created. The weather, thankfully, was dry. Fighting their way through the mud would have been far more uncomfortable than avoiding dust clouds. They encountered the normal array of travellers, and there was no sign of bandits or Dark Ones. In the afternoons they would seek out a lodging house or a farmer and pay for shelter for the night. The Swarm Claws didn't return and slowly Ahren began to feel at ease.

The rapid succession of events and revelations had taken more out of Ahren than he had realised. He decided to take one step at a time, the enormity that lay before him was too great. He enjoyed the journeying as much as he could, teaching Culhen new commands, and practising his archery in the evenings until it got dark. His companions often huddled together and talked about things that had happened in the past and about people he had never heard of. The apprentice gradually lost the desire to put the pieces of the puzzle together. The only thing that was clear was that at some time in the past Falk had journeyed with Uldini, but he had no idea why, or for how long. They wouldn't answer any of his questions directly and so he let the matter drop.

He decided to concentrate on the immediate future and looked forward to Three Rivers. The trading town in the north of Hjalgar was the second largest settlement in the country and the travelling craftsmen and merchants who had visited Deepstone in the past would always sing its praises.

Falk announced that they would reach their destination the following morning and during the course of the day Ahren noticed the gradual changes in the surroundings. The farms seemed a little bigger, there were hardly any more small holdings, and here and there they would see a carpenter's workshop or a smithy, buildings you would normally only see in the centre of a village.

Dark clouds began to gather that evening and they quickly sought out accommodation. Firstly, they didn't want to be travelling at dusk, and secondly, the patina that Falk had put on his and Selsena's armour couldn't withstand a heavy fall of rain.

The woman who put them up for the night had been a charcoal burner but had given up that exhausting work. She preferred to take in travellers who hadn't made it as far as the town. It wasn't long before the heavens opened and daylight vanished with frightening speed. Lightning flashed across the sky and Ahren went to the window. A flash of lightning lit up the sky and he thought he recognized a very strange cloud made up of a collection of leather-winged bodies. Then it was dark again. He couldn't be certain of what he had seen, but now there was a nagging doubt.

He closed the shutters and bolted them, giving Falk a meaningful look as he did so. He nodded silently in response and did the same with the other windows. All the while, the woman was happily chatting away, pinching Uldini on the cheek and patting his bald pate, which the wizard put up with stoically. Ahren had to suppress a grin and snuggled up to Culhen. An uncomfortable draught blew through the little house and the wolf's pelt was a welcome source of warmth. The old woman offered them a home-made pie and once Ahren had had his fill he forgot about the threatening shadow outside the hut and started imagining how Three Rivers would look.

Ahren was splattered with mud. He stared down at the trading town in disappointment. This was the place he had heard so much about. He didn't know what it looked like in sunshine but now it looked stocky and functional. No banners or pennants, none of the towers or other features he had imagined. Only a grey circle of houses squeezed together behind a palisade. A river stretched through the town and the intersection of two streets in the middle of the settlement presumably constituted the market square. They themselves were standing on a hill that Falk had led them up, several hundred paces off the main road.

He placed a hand on Ahren's shoulder and said in an amused voice, 'you don't look happy, boy. Expected more, am I right?'

Uldini grumbled, 'why the detour? It's not exactly a stunning view and I really want to get out of my dripping things. And your armour is running'. The magus was in a particularly foul mood today and Ahren reckoned the noble youth didn't like getting wet. It had been drizzling constantly since morning and all of them were soaked to the bone.

'The boy is still being trained and I want to show him two things. Anyway, it's better if he gawks from here, so that all and sundry don't see through our disguise straight away', Falk answered calmly.

Ahren gave him a look of displeasure and then tried to look disinterested.

Falk pretended not to notice and then began speaking in the peculiar tone of voice he used whenever he was teaching.

240

'Whenever you visit a strange town, view it from the outside first if you can. Preferably from a raised position, as we're doing now. First, look at the city gate. Are there a lot of sentries? That means trouble. The same is true if there are no sentries. Then they're all busy inside the city or dead'. He pointed to the wooden arch which represented the southern city gate and where a huddled figure was standing, leaning on a halberd under a heavy oilskin awning, staring out at the depressing day. From where they were standing, they couldn't identify the other three gates. 'That's the ideal position. Bored normality', said Falk in a pleased voice. Then he pointed to the only lofty building in the city, a three-storey stone building with a wooden pole above it, whose function Ahren couldn't figure out.

'That's the signal mast. Similar to our alarm bell but visible from far away. The coat of arms of the mayor or the city lord or lady would normally hang there. The emblem isn't there now so he or she isn't in the city. A black flag would signal on outbreak of the Black Death, red would mean the town was on a war footing'.

Uldini cleared his throat loudly and Falk continued. 'I'll explain the rest of the signals later, but I hope you understand now why it's important to check before you enter'.

Ahren nodded. His master had drummed into him how to recognize the behaviour of the different animals and the features of different areas of the forest. It was only logical that the same would apply to the city.

The small group descended the hill and soon they were at the city gate. Ahren put on a particularly bored expression and tried to look as anonymous as possible. The bed stone of the palisade was roughly one pace high and the palisade rose up roughly five paces in front of them.

This was the first time Ahren had seen such fortifications, but it looked old and neglected. Some of the posts were askew or broken and there were cracks in the bed stone. The town watch who waved them through with a bored look completed the picture. The haggard looking man was wearing a leather jerkin, which looked as if it had been repaired many times, and a rusty chainguard. His halberd seemed slightly warped and the young man could see several nicks in its blade. Ahren's image of the heroic bailiff had been severely undermined. Then they were through and entered Three Rivers. Ahren realised that his first impression of the city was mistaken. He could see solidly built stone houses, not to mention thatched wooden houses that had a more stable look than any of the ones he had seen in Deepstone, with the exception perhaps of the chapel and the Village Hall of his home village. All the buildings were well maintained and clean. When he looked down, he noticed that he was no longer walking on trampled down clay but on large stone slabs that were dirty and greasy from the rain but prevented you from sinking into the mud. The few townspeople he saw may have been running around in their normal work clothes, but even to his untrained eyes, Ahren could see a difference between the quality and fashioning of their clothes when compared with the clothing in his own village. 'Is everybody here wealthy?' he asked Falk very quietly and tried to hide his excitement.

Uldini snorted and Falk answered hesitatingly. 'They have a certain affluence. Anyone who lives behind the palisade must have enough money for the privilege. Even if they've neglected the defences to a shocking degree'.

Uldini snorted again and said, 'The numbskulls have been practising trade for too long and that's why they've neglected their defences. Neither Kelkor nor the Fen Knights have done anything more than provoke a couple of inconsequential quarrels over the last century and that's made them careless. They've forgotten that the Border Lands are a mere five days hard ride away. And a single Glower Bear would be able to rip through the toothpicks they call a palisade in no time at all'. The wizard's disgust was palpable, but there was also great sadness in his face.

He's worried about these people, thought Ahren. The magus could be even grumpier than Falk when he wasn't happy about something, but he had also seen Uldini in a happy, almost mischievous spirit – it was difficult to make out this moody person.

The drizzle was setting in and Falk began to walk faster because the rain was washing the ash off the armour plating and it was become shinier with every minute. He pointed to a hostelry with stables and they quickly hurried over and sheltered with the horses. Falk looked down at himself doubtfully and took off the armour until he was down to his leather clothing. Then he took off Selsena's armour and hid it all under a woollen blanket in the Elven horse's stall.

'Take good care of it', he murmured to her and they went into the taproom. While Ahren was taking in the comfortable if simple furnishings, Falk sorted out a room with the happy, wide-eyed innkeeper. Apart from themselves there were a few workers in the room, who were sitting out the bad weather, as well as three daredevil types at one of the corner tables.

Ahren wanted to take a closer look but the ferocious glare from one of the fellows, a coarse-looking man with stubble made him look away quickly. He knew this look from Sven. He'd really rather not meet a grown-up version of the miller's son, who had back up and weapons with him. The young man may only have glanced at him, but the long swords were unmissable.

Uldini squinted over at them too and said quietly, 'let's have everything brought to our room. I smell trouble down here'.

Falk nodded and made the necessary arrangements. They sat together in the early afternoon, having cleaned themselves, warmed up, and eaten a full meal. Falk wanted to head for the marketplace again.

'We need something more hardwearing than the leather jerkins, and a few decent travel utensils. And we need another horse as well as a pack horse. Selsena has been giving me a pain in my head, complaining about all the weight she has to carry'.

'I'm not going with you', Uldini replied. 'I'll try to make contact with some of the Ancients. Maybe they can cast a really big and heavy magic net. A few diversionary tactics would definitely help us.' He made the crystal ball float in the middle of the room and pulled out a piece of chalk.

Falk nodded and gestured at Ahren to come with him. 'It means Uldini will be busy for a while, but his idea is good. I'd be a lot happier if we could walk the length of the Red Posts without having to watch out for Swarm Claws or Fog Cats. There isn't much protection out there'.

'What are the Red Posts, master?' Ahren had never heard of them before.

There had been another enormous debate over the route they should travel and Uldini had won out in the end. Falk had seemed strangely relaxed since then although he had lost the argument, as if he had resigned himself to his fate.

'It's a sort of trade route. You'll see it when we get there'.

Ahren shrugged his shoulders. He had learned to accept these cryptic answers.

The drizzle had eased off and now there was a dampness hanging in the air between the houses, which Ahren found uncomfortable. There were many more people scurrying around and the closer they got to the market place, the noisier it became. He could already see the colourful

244

stalls and visitors weaving their way around in a complicated dance as they went about their various tasks. The whole market place was a hubbub of stallholders loudly pitching their wares and haggling with customers.

Ahren couldn't help moving closer to Falk for protection. He found this crying, moving, sweaty smelling mass of people a little frightening somehow.

Falk could sense his apprentice's discomfort and put an arm around his shoulders. 'You'll get used to it. You've only known village life and the wilderness. It's louder in the towns. And this is nothing here. At some stage we're going to have to go to the Sun Bazaar or the Eternal Market. You'll find clever dealers at the entrances selling wax balls for your ears, so you can bear the noise'.

Ahren looked at the old man sceptically, unsure whether he was pulling his leg. Then they were in the market place and Ahren had to have his wits about him to avoid running into people as he looked around curiously. There were the usual vegetable, fruit and meat stalls of which there were many scattered around the marketplace. But he also saw stalls for wares that would at the very most only be sold individually in Deepstone by Master Velem if he had been lucky enough to get one or two. Rare cloths and priceless garments, decorative ironwork and even weapons were laid out on the display cloths for customers to admire.

They were turning a corner around a stall when Ahren stopped suddenly and several people crashed into the back of him. He was too stunned to hear the muttered curses behind him as he stared in amazement at a dwarf, hardly five paces away from him. He was offering sparkling gems, rings and necklaces for sale, all of which were displayed on a black velvet cloth spread out on the stall. The small sturdy creature was surrounded by four ferocious looking guards dressed in uniformed tunics.

They all had their hands placed on their short swords, which were hanging from their belts. With the help of their shields they had little trouble directing the stream of people, so that they created an island of tranquility, where two wealthy looking merchants were examining the wares.

Even Falk look surprised. 'That's strange. The dwarves from the Silver Cliff don't usually sell their wares this far away from home. You have to travel the length of Kelkor to get here. He could do business in the Knight Marshes or in the Realm of the Sunplains with the same effort and earn twice as much money. Come with me'.

Falk determinedly pushed his way through the crowd and got to the counter. Ahren followed him and the guards eyed them suspiciously. From the way they changed their body position it was clear to Ahren that they considered the pair of Forest Guardians to be a threat rather than customers, and the young man realized that they were possibly three heartbeats away from open conflict.

The dwarf gave Falk a threatening look from under his bushy eyebrows but then the Forest Guardian said something in a strangely muffled and rumbling language, all the while crossing his arms in front of him, placing his hands on his shoulders and bowing. The merchant grunted in surprise and repeated the gesture and uttered the same words but in an incredibly deep and resonant voice, which gave his words a surprisingly natural fluidity.

The guards relaxed and turned their gaze back to the two merchants who were studying the wares, and also on the people passing by. Ahren breathed a sigh of relief and studied Falk's partner with interest. He had never seen a member of the little people before and his expectations were not disappointed.

The dwarf reached as high as the middle of Falk's torso, yet his shoulders were at least as broad as the old man's. His arms and legs were squat, almost squeezed together but extremely powerful. His straw-blond hair with its complicated plaits giving him an air of wildness, fell as a thick mane down his back. His full bushy beard was similarly braided and grew down to his barrel-shaped chest. His clothing was indeed select and worthy of a wealthy merchant, but he also had metal arm and leg armour strapped on, and when he moved, Ahren could hear the rattle of chainmail.

Some soldiers have less protection going into battle, thought Ahren.

His mentor and the dwarf were engaged in a friendly conversation and when the jewellery merchant turned and pointed southwards at something, Ahren saw that he was carrying two vicious looking axes on his back, that couldn't be seen from the front. The two merchants who were still looking at the jewellery noticed them too. One of them immediately became ashen-faced and retreated into the crowd where he disappeared. The dwarf noticed this, said something to Falk and hit him on the chest with his fist, causing his master to stagger.

At first Ahren thought that the merchant was angry because of his lost business, but then he gave a laugh, so deep and loud that Ahren's bones shook. He couldn't help chuckling too and it struck him that he liked dwarves.

Falk finished his conversation and much to Ahren's disbelief, gave the little man a gold thaler. They both repeated the gesture they had made when they had greeted each other, and Falk indicated to his apprentice to follow him.

The old man was silent and contemplative for a while. Ahren continued to look at the displays while Falk, with practised efficiency, strode through the market and bought all the things they needed, telling the stallholders to deliver them to their lodgings. He hardly haggled at all and paid horrendous prices for the purchases.

They finally left the market and went towards the western gate. The palisades and the town watch didn't exactly inspire confidence here either. Ahren realised that the jewellery stall had better defences than the whole city. He pointed this out to Falk, who laughed.

'You're not wrong. But you have to remember, Ker-Korog is a guest of honour of the city, and the armed personnel were lent to him and are, in fact, the bodyguards of the city steward. Three Rivers clearly wants to improve its reputation as a trading city and for that reason sent out invitations to the merchants from the Silver Cliffs and Thousand Halls. Not a bad move if you think of what he told me earlier'.

Whatever it was the dwarf had told him, he clearly didn't want to talk about it in public, and Ahren was clever enough not to ask questions about it for the moment. They went out the gate and Ahren saw a paddock on his left with more than two dozen horses in it.

'Let's see which of them suits you', said Falk.

The next hour proved to be entirely painful for the apprentice. He had only been on a horse twice in his life and that was years ago at an Autumn Festival. He kept falling off or being thrown off and the horse wouldn't listen to him. Falk lowered his expectations dramatically. His apprentice may have been quick to learn and gifted as well, but his horse-riding skills were minimal.

In the end they settled for the most docile horse available, a chestnut mare who still had another one or two summers in her for carrying a rider until she became too old. Ahren was depressed and could see how disappointed his master was. Today he had made two new discoveries: he liked dwarves and he hated horses! Falk quickly bought a pack horse and instructed the dealer to deliver the horses to the lodgings the following

248

break of day. His apprentice's foul humour was written all over his face and so the old Forest Guardian pulled himself together and smiled weakly at the young man. 'You can't be brilliant at everything. That's a lesson you have to learn too. With a lot of practice and hard work we might make you into a passable rider.' Ahren heard the doubt in his voice and scowled. 'And now we'll get a sword for you, what do you think?' his master continued and immediately the young man's mood improved. Then Falk led him back into the streets of the city.

It wasn't long before they reached a two-storey stone building. A heavy dark oak door prevented entry and on it was posted the emblem of the blacksmiths' guild.

'We must be right here. Ker-Korog recommended this blacksmith and when it comes to metalwork, the little people have a gift for it', said Falk.

He hammered on the door and soon it was opened by the largest woman Ahren had ever seen. The women in Hjalgar were mostly considerably smaller than the men and so the apprentice could only stare rudely while Falk explained their request. The blacksmith was a finger's width taller than Falk and had the broad shoulders and strong arms typical of workers in this profession. White-blond hair peeped out from under her veil and her piercing blue eyes twinkled humorously at Ahren as she listened to the old Forest Guardian. Then she moved aside and let the two of them in while she looked the young man up and down critically.

'So, you need a sword for the little one, do you?' she asked. 'What do you have in mind?'

Falk hesitated. 'I'd like your advice first before I decide. My knowledge is a bit…rusty'.

Then the blacksmith approached Ahren, who flinched and looked up at her uncertainly. She snorted in amusement and said, 'I'm not going to eat you. Have you never seen anybody from the Ice Islands or the Brazen City, boy?'

He shook his head and his master said, 'he's fresh-faced from the village. It's all new for him'.

The big woman gave an understanding nod and began to measure the length of his arms and the width of his shoulders with a thread.

'Shoulders too small and arms too thin for hammer and axe. Or do you have time to build up a bit of strength?' Her dry analysis cut through Ahren. His training had begun to reap significant rewards and he had almost beaten Holken in arm-wrestling a few weeks earlier. A wave of homesickness came over him as he remembered, and he looked dejectedly in front of him.

In the meantime, Falk answered. 'No, we're heading for a dangerous area and time is not on our side'.

She nodded and made Ahren hop, stand on one leg, turn in every direction, bend and stretch. He thought she might be a little strange in the head, but Falk stood there quietly, leaning against a pillar and looking on serenely. The door to the actual forge was open and it was warm in the room. Ahren was soon sweating but then she indicated to him to stand still.

'Quick, nimble and wiry. You had him climbing a lot, am I right?'

His master gave a satisfied nod.

'A quick blade is best for him. We'll try him out with a rapier'. She went to a shelf which had long, very thin blades.

Falk frowned but said nothing. The smith looked at the thread she had measured Ahren with, then took one of the weapons. It was a thin piece with a three-cornered blade that ended in a basket hilt. The young man took hold of it carefully and the proprietress indicated that he should follow her. The three of them went outside and into a walled inner courtyard with three straw dolls which were obviously used for target practice. There were more, further back, made of wood and judging by their scores, those were used for trying out the heavier weapons.

He was told to stab one of the straw dolls and the two adults stood there watching and giving him advice. The weapon felt light and fragile in his hands and bent to an alarming degree when he stabbed. He felt awkward and inept in contrast and the quick steps his watchers demanded of him kept ending up as ineffective little hops.

'That's enough', said Falk finally.

The woman took the weapon from him and went into the house to get another.

The apprentice whispered, 'what sort of a smith is she?'

Falk chuckled, 'she comes from the Brazen City, I know that much. What she's doing here…I've no idea. It must be something serious like a blood feud or something. But let me make this clear, she's not just a smith. Anyone who works at the forge in the Brazen City is also an armourer. We were damn lucky today. No wonder that Ker-Korog recommended her. It wouldn't surprise me if the dwarves agreed to do business with the city because of her. I'll definitely have to talk to Uldini about it later'. He became silent as the woman came outside again, this time with a long, straight, two-edged sword in her hand.

'The classic one. The long sword. Timeless and versatile'.

She handed the weapon over to Ahren, who now had to perform completely different actions, as he hacked at the doll and stabbed it. He felt much more comfortable with the heavier weapon and carried out most of the instructions very well. These exercises took considerably longer and gradually daylight faded.

Finally, Ahren heard Falk asking, 'so armourer, are you satisfied? It looks good enough to me'.

251

The apprentice held his breath and turned around to where they had made themselves comfortable at a small table. Sometime while he had been peppering the straw doll, she had organized goblets and beer and the two were sitting there like two old warriors and were examining him critically.

She answered with a frown. 'Satisfied? No. Good enough for bashing about in the hurly-burly, but in single combat…there's no doubt he's talented, but he's really using only one blade'.

She thought for a moment, then stood up. 'I'll try one more weapon. Keep the long sword here, you can take that if worst comes to worst'.

She quickly disappeared inside while Ahren looked at Falk in consternation. The old man shrugged his shoulders and sipped at his beer. After a few heartbeats the armourer returned, holding an unusual blade in her hand that Ahren had never seen before. It was slim and light, like a long sword cut in two, but with only one cutting edge, the other edge was blunt. The blade was also slightly curved and ended in a little tip. Ahren was fascinated. Everything about this weapon was slim and fast, yet without the fragility of the rapier.

'Is that a Windblade? He heard Falk asking. I didn't think the Brazen City produced such weapons. Or are the Sunplains and the Eternal Kingdom no longer at war?

She laughed, a surprisingly bright and friendly laugh.

'The war has gone on for so long that it's probably only the Eternal Empress who remembers the reasons for it. No, you're right, but one of the few advantages of my new home is the fact that I can now decide for myself what I want to forge. Call it professional curiosity but I wanted to know if it's possible to manufacture these things in our forges'.

'And?' asked Falk stubbornly.

252

'It's difficult but possible. It took me ten tries to get this one right. It's a little top-heavy and I could only fold it half the number of times I wanted to. Any merchant in the Eternal Kingdom will be able to offer you a better piece', she answered.

'Well, you're being hard on yourself', said the old man, amused.

She shrugged her shoulders. 'I'm just being honest. We'll see!'

Ahren took the weapon and began the exercises she was showing him. He carried out the steps and the swings almost like a dancer, with economical thrusts and semi circles, using the sword to parry and attack.

His arms and back were beginning to hurt after the hours of training but all his movements felt fluid and gentle now. They stopped only after the sun had completely set.

'There you have it, Master Forest Guardian. He's holding the worst blade of the lot in his hands in terms of quality, but his movements are immeasurably better. That's the one he should take'.

Falk scratched his beard and frowned.

'Then I have to ask you a favour. Can you show him the ground rules so that he can practise them on the journey? I'm only trained in the broadsword, and that breaks bones when it cuts.'

She nodded and Falk continued. 'We need to head off tomorrow. I'll leave him here and you teach him as much as you can. And remember, teach him simple things that he can repeat on his own, without getting into bad habits'. Then he stood up and slapped Ahren on the shoulder. 'Have fun and grasp the opportunity!'

He was out the door before the apprentice could respond, leaving him with the practice dolls and the gigantic woman from the Ice Islands. He was a little afraid but soon he was too focused on the training to think of anything else. If he had considered Falk to be a hard taskmaster, then the following hours put pay to that. He learnt perhaps a dozen moves, not more, but the armourer made him repeat them with merciless determination until she was convinced that he would be able to perfect them on the road.

'You're only at the beginning', she said during a break, as he drank some water. 'If you learn bad habits now, they will be with you for the rest of your life, so I'm only going to show you the moves where you know immediately if you've made a mistake. Your master will notice any major blunders and correct you'.

Ahren continued the torture of learning the basic moves as the armourer relentlessly hammered into his head all the things he had to be aware of. When the first cock finally crowed, she relented and he rolled together into a ball and fell asleep on the spot.

Ahren woke up late in the morning. He was lying on a soft bedstead under a warm blanket. The armourer, who had introduced herself during the evening as Falagarda, must have lifted him up and put him to bed.

He sat up with a groan and stretched his stiff limbs. He chewed some herbs, an antidote to aching muscles which were in a little bag that he always carried with him. Only Falk, he thought grimly, could manage to turn a simple shopping spree into gruelling torture for him.

There was no sign of Falagarda and a quick glance out the window showed that half the morning was already gone. What was keeping his master? He stood up and found the smith standing in front of the chimney where she was working on an axe. She glanced over her shoulder and called over the clanging of her hammer blows, 'good morning, your master hasn't arrived yet'.

Ahren stood for a moment, puzzled. What if something had happened? He opened his moneybag and took out the solitary penny Uldini had given him in case they became separated.

254

'What do I owe you?' he asked.

Falagarda gave a dismissive wave. 'Forget about it, boy. You're a quick student and if you practise really hard, you'll be very handy with Windblade, maybe even a master. The blade's been lying around here for years gathering dust'. She thought for a moment. 'Mind you, you can do me one favour. If your travels take you to the Silver Cliff or Thousand Halls, tell the dwarves there that Falagarda Regelsten is interested in developing a trading relationship that involves more than precious stones'.

Ahren didn't quite know what she was talking about, but he nodded and said, 'that's a promise. And thanks for the training'.

She nodded back.

'Then go look for your master. And good luck on your travels'.

Ahren gave a farewell wave, left the forge, went through the showroom, out the heavy oak door and onto the street outside. The previous day's rainclouds had disappeared and he blinked in the bright sunshine and tried to remember where exactly their guesthouse lay.

The sun offered the necessary orientation and he headed off in what he thought was roughly the right direction, always picking the street or alleyway, which he felt would bring him nearer his destination. He had just entered a narrow alleyway, about two paces in width, and he was pretty sure the guesthouse was at the other end of it, when he noticed three figures loitering with their backs turned to him. The houses were packed close together, so he would either have to turn back or squeeze between the people.

He was hesitantly moving forward when one of them turned around and he recognized the coarse fellow that had intimidated him the day before in the taproom. His opposite number seemed to have recognized him too and pointed in Ahren's direction while whispering something.

The other two heads spun around immediately, and the apprentice could see a hard- looking man and a ferocious wild-eyed woman with pock marks.

All three made themselves bigger in the alleyway so getting past them was unthinkable. Each of them had at least one hand hidden under their cloaks and Ahren remembered the weapons he had seen them with the day before. The physical threat was almost palpable and Ahren was not so naïve as to go closer. If only he had his bow with him!

There must have been seven paces between them and he was sure that he could have shot two arrows successfully in the narrow street. When he didn't seem to be making any move to do their bidding, the strangers began to move towards him.

Ahren quickly went through his options. The bow was a non-starter, also dagger and sword - he was in the minority and under-trained. He thought for a moment of running away but these three surely knew their way around better and could split up to cut off his escape routes. Calling out for help was useless too - it would all be over by the time anyone came.

Another six paces.

What was left? He thought of his training, which wasn't much use here in the city.

Until he remembered the ribbon tree.

A quick sidelong glance revealed that the stone facades of the houses were rough and the window ledges afforded excellent climbing opportunities. Without giving the idea a second thought, he jumped up and clung on to a projection in the façade of one of the stone walls. He heard a roar behind him as the blackguards realized what he was planning. He quickly pulled himself up, cursing the hours of sword practice he had undertaken the previous night as his muscles protested.

He looked up and the next reachable grip was the narrow window ledge on the second floor, roughly one pace above his head. He tensed up his body so that every muscle, from his fingers to his toes, worked as one. Then he pulled his arms downward before pushing his body with full force upwards, just before his attackers could catch him.

His months of climbing practice now stood him in good stead. He found it remarkably easy to grasp the window ledge and to pull himself up again until he was standing on the narrow wooden board that was creaking dangerously under his feet. He risked a quick downward look and saw three angry faces as they began to climb up after him. The coarse fellow had major problems getting a grip, but the other two were making progress almost as quickly as Ahren. He concentrated again on the climb, but the rest of the way was child's play. He only had to reach up and grip, and he'd reach the edge of the roof, and after two heartbeats he was lying on the shingle roof of the house. The smooth slate tiles were dangerously slippery underfoot and the steep angle of the roof ridge made it difficult to stand up. Remaining bent over so that his arms were in contact with the shingle, he clambered over to the other side of the house.

The first pursuer's head was already above the roof edge, and Ahren quickly began his descent. The street was broader and busier here and one or two passers-by craned their heads to peer up at him. He ignored them and slid down as quickly as he could, tearing his hands on the bare stone. The burning pain was a small price to pay for his escape, for as he raced on towards the inn, he could hear loud cursing coming from the roof.

'Ralg, he's running to the others. Grab him!'

The young Forest Guardian sprinted with all the strength he had. Windblade, which he had only casually slung on his back, banged loudly against his body as he ran, sounding like a bell around his neck.

The street he was racing along now ran parallel to the street on which he had evaded the lowlifes. Both of them met up on the street the inn was on, which meant that he and his adversary had roughly the same distance to run. It was like a two-horse race in the dark, at the end of which was the safety of his accommodation where hopefully the others were waiting for him.

For a second, the idea that they might not be there flashed through his head. After all, Falk hadn't come to pick him up. But he tossed aside this thought as he hurtled down the street and rounded the corner. They wouldn't have left without him. At the very least Culhen and Selsena would be waiting for him in the stable, and the idea of having an Elven horse and a half-grown wolf beside him spurred him on.

But there were still a good thirty paces to the entrance of the refuge when the cutthroat, who the others had named Ralg, came around the corner and headed helter-skelter for Ahren. The young man ran on and saw something flash out of the corner of his eye. The fellow had drawn his dagger.

Ahren instinctively reached for his own dagger but it wasn't there. They'd only wanted to go shopping the day before. As he began his final sprint, he swore to himself that he would never go anywhere without his short sword again.

Ralg had a coarse figure and was unable to climb but he was a good sprinter and it seemed as though he would catch up with Ahren before he could reach his destination.

Two paces from the entrance to the taproom and he felt a calloused hand on his shoulder. Before the scoundrel could grab him and pull him around, Ahren ducked down and spun to the side. Ralg took the opportunity to position himself between Ahren and the safe haven behind the door. He squatted down into a combat position, the blade under his right forearm so as not to arouse suspicion.

'Got you!' he grumbled in a hoarse voice and Ahren tensed himself up to ready himself for the attack.

Then Falk was there. With speed and determination, he came out through the taproom door and was behind Ahren's attacker. Before he had time to notice the impending danger, Falk had smashed his fist against Ralg's temple, and the ruffian began to tumble to the ground with glassy eyes. Falk repeated the action, then caught the man, who had lost consciousness. The scoundrel's dagger clattered to the ground and Ahren saw some strollers scurry away from the scene. Falk leaned the limp body against the wall and began to frisk him with practised hands. He fished some parchment out of the unconscious man's jerkin and skimmed through it with a frown.

'We need to get out of here before the others turn up with reinforcements. Get Uldini and our equipment and I'll meet you in the stable'.

Ahren had a hundred questions but he knew that now was not the time to ask them. He hurried to their room, but the wizard had already packed and was coming towards him, heaving the heavy bundle of equipment behind him.

The young Forest Guardian wanted to say something but Uldini cut him off. 'Don't waste your breath, we've been discovered, that much is clear'.

They both raced down the stairs and towards the stable, leaving open-mouthed guests in the taproom staring after them in disbelief as they thundered past with their heavy equipment.

Falk was already there and saddled Selsena while Culhen kept watch at the entrance. Their new animals were waiting for them and they quickly loaded them with their equipment. Finally, Ahren swung himself uncertainly onto the saddle and Falk looked at him in consternation.

'I'll take your reins, we have to get out of here quickly and I don't want to have to keep picking you up or searching for you', he said with determination.

They left the stables and trotted towards the northern gate. Ahren, who felt as if he were a child again, hanging onto the saddle while Falk led him by the reins, asked the question that had been vexing him.

'What happened there exactly?'

'I found this on your friend with the knife', said his master tersely and pressed the crumpled parchment in his hand. He unfolded it clumsily as he hopped up and down in the saddle.

It appeared to be some kind of official document, many lines, often with complicated words. He was somewhat skilled at the art of reading but as he was still unpractised, it took him a while to understand it completely. The top half gave physical descriptions of Uldini, Falk and himself, and underneath it stated that they were imposters who had robbed the merchant guilds of several thousand gold thalers.

'It's an arrest warrant!' gasped Ahren loudly.

Falk turned to him with a scornful look and pulled the parchment out of his hand.

'Why don't you speak up a bit, the town watch didn't hear you', he said sarcastically. Luckily, they had already passed the northern gate and there were no other travellers in the vicinity.

Ahren spoke in a quieter voice, 'but why is there an arrest warrant for us? And who wrote it?'

'Why' is simple', answered Uldini. 'A Transformer had it issued to make life difficult for us.'

Ahren winced. Transformers were the first beings HE WHO FORMS had created – without the backing of his siblings. According to legend they were grotesque, ever-changing creatures, who couldn't hold onto any appearance for long. Appalled by their fate, they willingly aligned themselves with HIM WHO FORCES. In return for their services, He forced them into whatever physical shape suited him at the time. There were hundreds of horror stories about them. They were far and away the most powerful and fearsome weapons in the Betrayer's arsenal. Ahren was greatly disturbed by the thought that one of their number had brought unwelcome attention onto the travel party.

'The merchant guilds issued the arrest warrants', added Uldini matter-of-factly. 'A clever move if you ask me. Their arrest warrants are less powerful than regional documents but they're valid in all the kingdoms. We'll have reached the Knight Marshes in two days but that won't be much help to us.'

'And now?' asked Falk darkly. 'I suppose we can forget our plan to join up with a group of travelling merchants'.

The wizard nodded. 'I'd forget about that idea. One of the Ancients should have a look among the guilds. If the Transformer is still there, which I very much doubt, that will flush him out. Until then we'd be better off to continue on our own'.

They travelled the rest of the morning in contemplative silence. Falk handed the reins back to Ahren so that he could learn to direct the horse by himself. With the midday son beating down on them, Ahren asked, 'why does the Adversary want to stop us already? Would it not make more sense to wait until my Naming, when the magic spell is lifted?'

Uldini looked at him out of the corner of his eye before continuing his catnap. Falk answered, 'if you die now, HE WHO FORCES has enough time to wake up, because it took the gods over seven hundred years to replace the last Paladin with you. But it's also true that the longer we take to appoint you, the quicker the Adversary will awaken from his long Sleeping Bane. He can feed off the powers of the thirteenth Paladin, which were released when you were selected, and gain strength from them until they are embedded within you. Your powers are connected to the Pall Pillar, which means that the two of you are bound together. This binding will only be cut when you have been named'.

Now Uldini opened his eyes and looked earnestly at the young man. 'He will wake up more quickly if your power is diverted, and we must prevent this at all costs. The channels between you and the Bane Spell are at their most permeable during equinox, when day and night are equal length. He can suck out a particularly large amount at that time. If we manage to appoint you before the next Spring Festival, we will have a time-scale of two or three years before HE WHO FORCES rises up. If we manage it before this Autumn Festival, we will have perhaps even half a dozen years. If we need more than one year...' His voice trailed off and he didn't finish the sentence. Once again there was quiet as they sat on their saddles, each one lost in their own thoughts.

'Why didn't you collect me this morning?' asked Ahren finally, breaking the silence.

'We noticed the good-for-nothings, who were watching us and were waiting for the right moment to catch one of them and question him or her', answered Falk. You were in safe hands at the armourer's, so we left you there. None of us thought that you'd wander through the city on your own'.

Somehow it didn't surprise Ahren that he was being blamed again, so he changed the subject.

'What did the dwarf say to you yesterday?'

His master sat up straight and addressed his commentary to Uldini as well as Ahren. 'The disputes among the knights have increased and some very extreme views have been surfacing in the recent past. They don't want any elves or dwarves in the kingdom – complete nonsense really. And the trade between King's island and Silver Cliff has almost ground to a halt. It's good that we're only skirting Knight Marshes on our journey'.

'It's no coincidence', mumbled Uldini. 'This much is certain, the agents of the Adversary are trying to foment unrest. A squabbling enemy is an enemy defeated'.

And with that they all fell into a brooding silence.

At dusk they sought out a little wood on the side of the road where they set up camp for the night. Ahren was sore from riding and so he was delighted when Falk ordered him to practise his sword-fighting exercises while he prepared the evening meal.

Uldini was staring into his crystal ball which was floating and emitting a weak light, and he seemed to be speaking to one of the Ancients. Although Falk was not familiar with Windblade, he had a good general idea of the feints and foot positions needed and he didn't tire of pointing out every tiny mistake Ahren made. By the time it was dark, every muscle in Ahren's body was aching and he was only too happy to lie down.

He was asleep in no time at all and woke up the next day after a succession of nightmares in which he was chased by a ragtag of figures with knives and swords, who were constantly changing their forms. He was happy to be free from his dreams until Falk tossed a bundle of practice arrows at his feet and told him to tie them to his horse. Ahren got up with a groan at the realization that this was going to be another long day. They rode silently over the flat farming land that made up the northern border of Hjalgar. They stopped unexpectedly in the late afternoon and turned off the road to find shelter in some heavy woodland.

Falk began to polish up his armour and ordered Ahren to do the same with Selsena's plating. They scrubbed off the grey coating and polished the whitish material until it was sparkling bright, and Uldini changed his clothes. His silk robe disappeared into his rucksack and he put on expensive linen clothing instead, before slipping a tabard over it. The tabard was decorated with a falcon perched on a stone. The rock glowed in the conventional black and gold of the the Knight Marshes.

Falk took from the saddlebag the mysterious bundle that he had always stored in his trunk in their cabin. From it he carefully removed a similar tunic, which he now passed to Ahren. The material was thick and heavy and smelt musty. Ahren slipped the unfamiliar clothing over his head. He wriggled around and tugged at it until it was sitting properly on him. In the meantime, Falk had slipped on a heavy gold signet ring on his finger. It was set with an onyx stone and displayed the same crests as on their clothing.

All this was amazing to Ahren, but what happened next really took his breath away. His master actually took out a comb and began to comb his hair and beard in a most fastidious fashion. Ahren burst out laughing at the sight, and not even his master's warning looks could stop him. It was only when Uldini gave him a warning look and shook his head that the young man could contain himself again.

The results of their efforts were impressive. Falk's white armour shimmered in a brightness that was mother-of-pearl, as did Selsena's, and the Elven horse conveyed her happiness in waves to her companions. Falk's broadsword was now hanging between his shoulder blades and his bow was now on Selsena's saddle. The more Falk tidied up his appearance, the more authoritative he appeared. When his master was finally finished, Ahren saw a transformation in front of him. It was still Falk, but he was now every inch the knight. Uldini resembled a liveried retainer. And then the two of them set about working on Ahren. They pulled and prodded, they polished his leathers, they even combed his hair.

He felt deeply uncomfortable and embarrassed, while Culhen sat in front of him, and seemed to be laughing at him with his tongue hanging out. That was, until he was subjected to the same treatment and made to look prim and proper by the two of them. Ahren had to carry his sword open on his back too, with his bow fixed to his saddle.

Finally they were ready, and once they had ridden from the shadow of the trees and into the early summer sunshine, they presented a breath-taking sight. Falk was riding alone on Selsena, Uldini on the the saddled-up pack horse. His master and the Titejunanwa glistened in the afternoon light and looked for all the world like the dashing figures in a heroic saga. Instead of sitting hunched and humdrum on the saddle, the old man was sitting bolt upright like a knight on his warhorse. Ahren could only stare in wonder and Uldini laughed out loud.

'That's enough, Falk. Judging by the boy's open jaw, it's effective enough to get us over the border easily. Good that you're here again!'

The old Forest Guardian flared into existence again for an instant as Falk answered angrily, 'I'm not here again!'

Then he rode ahead in measured steps and the others followed the would-be knight on the road.

Uldini talked to Ahren all the way to the border, advising him on the role he was to play. He would be Falk's page.

I'm still the apprentice, even in disguise, he thought bitterly.

At last they arrived at a run-down wooden hut, which was Hjalgar's border post. Two border guards, sitting under an awning, squinted at them with tired and bored eyes and waved them through without bothering to get up.

'That was the easy part', mumbled the wizard and nodded his head in the direction they would follow. Wooden posts were stuck into the ground on either side of the road, presenting two undulating lines to a distance of several hundred paces in either direction. These had to be the border stakes. Beyond the border stood a high square stone tower, reaching at least ten paces into the sky. It was crenellated on top and there were at least three crossbowmen watching them in a relaxed yet attentive manner. There were three armoured guards on either side of the road, all equipped with heavy halberds. Swords were hanging from their belts The crest of the Knight Marshes hung on a large banner from the tower - a golden crown on a black background surrounded by a circle of many dozens of small, golden, square shields.

They were still three paces away when one of the guards – and judging by the plume of feathers on his helmet, he was probably the head guard – shouted out in a booming voice, 'halt in the name of Senius Blueground, king of the Knight Marshes, and name your purpose!'

Uldini responded in a voice equally loud and in an arrogant tone, 'Dorian Falkenstein, knight and Lord of Castle Falkenstein wishes to visit his homeland'.

The words had no sooner been uttered when the guards hopped to attention and their commander said, 'but of course. A thousand apologies that I didn't recognize you immediately. Have a good journey on the roads of Knight Marshes'.

The border guards saluted as they rode by and as soon as they were beyond the row of ironclad men, Ahren heard animated whispering behind him.

Falk maintained his lordly pose but there was a frown on his face.

266

'I knew it was a bad idea. They recognised the name', he hissed.

'Of course they did. We're in the Knight Marshes, they love their stories. Lots of names might have been forgotten elsewhere, but not here', answered Uldini calmly. 'We've gone through this already. The arrest warrants only have the name Falk, the Forest Guardian. This was the quickest and safest way of getting in. Your name would have surfaced sometime anyway, so at least we controlled when and how'.

'Master?' asked Ahren, who couldn't contain himself any longer. 'Are you really a knight?'

Falk sighed and answered in a weary voice, 'I was a knight once. Then I didn't want to be one anymore'.

At these words a wave of cold rage rolled through Ahren's inside and Selsena gave a loud and shrill neigh.

It must have been Falk's decision that had angered her so much and that was why she had stayed away from him for all those years. 'Not now', said Falk firmly and the feeling of anger ebbed away, to some extent anyway.

'I went to the elves and at some point I became a Forest Guardian. The best decision of my life, and even this stubborn woman here will have to admit that it did me some good over the years'.

There was no response from Selsena but Falk smiled and patted her neck while Uldini said to Ahren, 'welcome to the Knight Marshes'.

Chapter 16

Ahren had expected a completely different world when they first entered the neighbouring kingdom. There were no kings, armies or heroes in Hjalgar, there were only bailiffs, village councils and city administrators. Which meant that any stories that reached Deepstone and told of the knights of this kingdom were fairy tales and adventure yarns.

After half a day's travelling, Ahren's expectations were wearing thin. The trade road was laid with large stone slabs, and now and again they would spot a defiant castle or a moated tower soaring into the sky, but apart from those, it was row after row of farms. There were many border poles with different coats of arms proudly displayed on them, and any farmers that they saw seemed considerably poorer than their counterparts in Deepstone.

When he asked the reason for this, it was Uldini who answered, while Falk clenched his teeth and stared stubbornly straight ahead. 'It's because of all the fiefdoms and their knights and followers. In Hjalgar the farmer tills his field, he gathers the harvest and gives a few coins to the village council, and he keeps the rest for himself. Here twenty or thirty farmers are supporting at least as many liege men and women, also the knights of the fiefdom. Then they also have to cough up the tithes that their feudal lord has to give to the king. There's not much left over for themselves.'

Falk was scowling now and was on the point of interrupting but Uldini continued quickly, 'on the other hand, there are hardly any brigands or other riffraff and Dark Ones are extremely rare here. Apart from the skirmishes between the knights, the Knight Marshes is one of the safest places in the world – as long as you obey the laws.'

The old man seemed placated and nodded. Generally speaking, his master had been very distant since they had set foot in the Knight Marshes, and it wasn't just in the way he was behaving and moving. He was also less communicative than before. Ahren decided to put off asking further questions.

He looked at the bundle of practice arrows he had had to take with him and wondered how the arrows fitted into the disguise.

The old man saw what he was looking at and grumbled, 'they're for practising, not looking at. See if you can hit that tree trunk over there'.

Ahren looked in surprise and unfastened the bow. He had to spend the rest of the afternoon shooting at different targets while his mare walked on contentedly. Shooting arrows on horseback was a completely new experience, and because Ahren lacked practice and was not a talented rider, he fell from his saddle several times, and missed the targets more often than he hit them. Culhen, on the other hand, enjoyed the game, running playfully after each arrow. He brought most of them back and that evening Ahren calculated that there were only ten fewer arrows than there had been at noon.

They rested in a hostelry and Ahren was sent to the courtyard to do his sword practice while his master looked on and corrected him. This looked like an everyday occurrence to the locals, with the knight training his page, and so they fitted in nicely with their surroundings. Their training method hadn't changed much, except for their clothing, and Falk was even more critical and stricter in his judgments and in his analysis than he had been before.

They continued on for the next ten days, the little group moving further into the country, steadily following the path towards the northwest. During the day, Ahren would train in shooting with bow and arrow from the horse and in the evening he would continue with his swordsmanship. There was very little talk and Uldini would often retreat with his crystal ball in the evenings so he could speak to the Ancients alone. One evening Ahren cornered the master wizard in the hallway of the hostelry in which they were spending the night and asked him sheepishly, 'why is Falk so overbearing towards me and why is he so silent? Have I done something wrong?'

Uldini paused for a moment and then answered quietly. 'Your master has returned home after a very long absence and he must come to terms with parts of his past and his personality, which he has suppressed. This is what happens if you run too far from something and for too long a time. It comes back to bite you eventually'. Then he disappeared leaving the perplexed apprentice in his wake. He could never get a straight answer and his blood was beginning to boil. He stomped over to his master's room and found him there, sitting on a stool and studying a map. Falk looked up sternly. Before he had a chance to say anything, Ahren unleashed his frustration and anger at being kept in the dark. 'I spend all my time stumbling behind you, not knowing what's going on, but following every order you give me, and meanwhile you're becoming more and more of a stranger, and I'm beginning to believe less and less of what you are all telling me. Two years ago, I became a Forest Guardian's apprentice and now nothing is making any sense anymore'. Ahren had been hoping to sound grown-up and determined, but he knew he sounded like a frightened, wounded boy.

For a moment there was a flash of anger in Falk's eyes, but then his face softened and became friendly, as it always did when his master knew he had pushed his apprentice too far.

He pointed to the other stool and closed the door. Then he sat down again and said, 'you're clearly confused and it's hardly surprising. Let's try to untangle the knots a little. First of all, I've always told you the truth, only it hasn't been *all* of the truth. Some of it I will tell you now, some of it will remain my secret, until I feel you are ready to hear it. Agreed?'

Ahren nodded in silence. He knew when his master was asking a rhetorical question. And anyway, any morsel of information was better than hearing nothing.

'Right then', the old man began. 'I was born here in the Knight Marshes as the heir to Castle Falkenstein., a small fiefdom that now lies in the heart of the country. My mother was an important…knightess and from when I was knee-high to a grasshopper I was being trained to follow in her footsteps. I learned how to fight with a broadsword, I learned riding and how to use a lance, everything that went with the territory. It soon became clear that I was a born knight. It finally came to the point where I took over from my mother. I got to know Selsena and we were an unbelievable team, a natural talent on a telepathic horse. Everything went swimmingly and Uldini and I performed many tasks together. We slew monsters and suchlike. We were highly successful, until Dark Ones slaughtered my family and everyone I loved, while I was trying to perform a task that was imposible to fulfil.' Falk's voice faltered and died away, and Ahren was sure he wouldn't say anymore, but then the old man continued in a quiet voice and the pain was evidently still fresh. 'I abdicated my knighthood and wandered around the world. As you already know, Selsena was not happy with my decision. I let myself go completely. Alcohol and disreputable company, gambling and other things I'm not proud of. In the end I had to flee a clan from the Green Sea on account of some ridiculous bet and found myself without money or sustenance in Evergreen again'.

Ahren noted that his master had used the human name for the Elfish forest, but he said nothing, though it showed him how his companion was struggling to relate the story he was telling.

'It was only the fame of my former deeds and the fact that a Titejunanwa had been connected to me that saved me from execution. I was brought before the Elf priestess and you know the story from that point on. After my training as a Forest Guardian I went to Hjalgar to enjoy the peace I had found in the freedom of nature. Then you turned up, and with you, Selsena. She must have been keeping an eye on me the whole time and knew that you were something special. And now the circle has been completed and here I am again, in this armour. I have to bring that which I am now, into harmony with that which I was. It's much more difficult than I had anticipated'. Falk looked at the young man. He had obviously come to the end of his explanation. Before Ahren could say anything, the old man muttered, 'now, get out into the courtyard. I'll be damned if you think you're going to get away with not doing your sword practice'.

His apprentice turned away with a smile.

Old or new Falk, there were some things about his master that would never change.

After four days they arrived at a large crossroads where a cobbled trade road from deep in the middle of the Knight Marshes intersected with theirs. Here they found a two-storey guesthouse and a trading post with a warehouse. There were at least forty people bustling around noisily. Ahren saw many merchants with escort parties, at least three different knights, and some wild-looking people with leather hair bands and painted faces. These were talking loudly to the warehouse keeper. Falk made a detour around the crowd and they continued to the inn. Ahren

272

asked quietly, 'what kind of a place is that and who are the painted people?'

'They were Clanmen from the Green Sea', answered Uldini. 'This is where the northern trade route, which we're journeying to Eathinian on, meets up with a smaller trade route, which stretches from the Red Posts to King's Island, stretching across the whole of the Knight Marshes.'

Falk dismounted to purchase provisions and Uldini got them something to drink, for the day was hot and the air was still in the midday sun. Ahren stayed by the horses and watched the various people while tickling Culhen. Falk had purchased a leather collar for the wolf so that people would recognize that the animal was tame, but the wolf would always guarantee that Ahren could be on his own if he so wished. He squatted down beside him and whispered lovingly to his friend, while the wolf lifted his nose to take in all the unfamiliar smells.

Then the young man heard a voice behind him. 'That's a wonderful animal you have there'. He looked up over his shoulder and blinked in the sunshine. The speaker was towering over him, a black silhouette against the light. His deep, warm voice sounded very agreeable. 'Not everyone has such a true friend. Many have to go through life alone'.

Ahren straightened up and turned to get a better look at the stranger. Before him stood a thin man with a long thin beard and deep, sunken eyes ringed with shadow. They seemed to be looking sadly but wisely out into the world. He was wearing a strange red robe, shot through with long, golden stripes. His hands were folded in front of him on his stomach and he had a book under his right arm.

'What's your name, boy?' he asked.

'Ahren', answered the apprentice instinctively.

'That's a good name. Tell me, Ahren, do you sometimes feel lonely?' the man wanted to know.

273

This was a strange question, for everyone was lonely at some time, so he nodded.

'And if I were to tell you that you didn't have to suffer loneliness or fear in your life again, never again?' the thin man pressed on.

The young man gave a sceptical look and his companion gave a warm and sympathetic laugh.

'I know what you're thinking: big words, easier said than done. I would very much like to tell you of the Illuminated Path'. And he tapped the book under his arm.

Before Ahren could answer, Falk and Uldini came out and walked up to them. 'On the saddle with you, page, we need to get a move on', his master snarled brusquely. Falk and Uldini mounted their horses and ignored the stranger completely.

The man bowed slightly and said, 'another time, perhaps', before stepping away.

Ahren got up on his saddle too and they rode off.

'What did that odd fellow want?' asked Falk as soon as they were out of earshot.

Ahren shrugged his shoulders. 'I think he was a priest, but I'm not sure'.

'Be careful at the trading posts. They're full of madmen and charlatans', added Uldini.

That explained why his master had pulled him away from the conversation so coarsely.

They left the crossroads behind them and now they were climbing a small incline. Ahead Ahren now saw a line of red painted stakes in the ground that created an undulating line as far as the horizon. He gasped in amazement for it was a stunning sight. The red stakes were greater than a man's thickness and towered a dozen paces into the sky. The distance

274

from one stake to the next was twenty paces at most and so they created an impression of a threatening wall as you rode alongside them. This effect was even more impressive because of the contrast on either side of the stakes. To his right Ahren saw farms and fields and castles set in undulating grass. To his left, however, the grass had not been cultivated as far as the eye could see. The wind blew across the meadows and hills and the long grass billowed like the waves of a large lake. The landscape was sublime and somehow deeply moving and Ahren found himself stopping and staring at it.

Uldini laughed and said, 'There's no-one who sees the Green Sea that remains unmoved. There's a saying in the Eternal Kingdom: "A person has only lived, once they've seen the two seas, the green one and the blue". And I think that definitely true'.

They rode in a gentle curve along the trade road until it turned sharply just in front of the red stakes and then ran along them in a northward direction. From the edge of the road Ahren could stretch out his arm and touch the smooth wood with his finger.

'Better not touch it', ordered Falk severely. 'This is the border between the Knight Marshes and the Green Sea. Any crossing over without clansmen escorting you is punishable by death'.

Ahren pulled his finger back quickly, as if the wood was burning hot. 'Why are they so strict?' he asked curiously.

His master answered, 'the way it looks there now, it used to look the same three hundred lengths further east'. He had pointed first at the untamed wilderness and then at the cultivated countryside. 'The knight Marshes was a small coastal region which kept expanding inland. The clans protested and many agreements and promises were made only to be broken again by the knights. When they had taken control of half the land, that was the straw that broke the camel's back. The clansmen massacred any further settlers, painting their building timbers with their victim's blood, and put up the poles as a warning to never again overstep the boundary to the Green Sea. Of course, there were some more military operations to seize more land but there were no towns that could be laid siege to. Only nomads with fast horses and first-class archers. In the end, the knights realized that they could only lose and so the border was fixed, and because nobody wants to step too close to the red stakes, the border was turned into a trade route. Both sides are always eyeing each other up, and there are many armed guards patrolling the route. That's why there are so few assaults.' Falk paused and then said with force, 'Keep to the path. Never go between two stakes. You don't know who's watching'.

He pointed at the green hill and Ahren saw a painted head ducking out of sight in knee-high grass. The young man shuddered and guided his horse to the right side of the road to be as far away from the mysterious stakes as possible.

There were small, squat hostels in this section of the trade road, which also served as border garrisons. Ahren saw many armed border guards and also some knights, so the travel party preferred to stay in their room unless Ahren was practising. Falk's ranking as a knight ensured they remained undisturbed and Ahren made steady progress in his training.

They rode alongside the red stakes day in and day out, and Ahren began to grow used to their imposing size. His archery training only took place on the right side of the route now, but soon their days were following a steady routine.

The days passed by and the weather was, but for a few wet days, friendly, as the summer reached its highpoint. At home the master craftsmen and women would be setting their Apprenticeship Trials and for the first time Ahren felt something like homesickness. The world seemed enormous to him now, as had been travelling for weeks alongside

276

the vast plains of the Green Sea. He realized that his Deepstone world with all its problems had been very small indeed.

In an effort to distract himself from these thoughts, he threw himself into the target practice Falk set for him, and his archery skills on horseback made a marked improvement, even if his horsemanship still left something to be desired. The ever-growing Culhen revelled in playing fetch and his head was now up as far as Ahren's hips. He was now the size of a fully-grown wolf and Falk expected him to stop growing soon.

One bright summer's day during their fourth week in the shadow of the stakes, Ahren saw a long strip glimmering on the horizon. At first he thought it was just a mirage, but the phenomenon remained constant. Falk saw his apprentice's questioning look and said, 'that's Eathinian, eternally green, an enormous forest that stretches the entire width of the continent. An almost straight length of untouched nature tended to by the elves – from the very beginning'.

Ahren heard the yearning and joyful anticipation in his master's voice and was infected by it. At night he pondered what surprise awaited him in the land of the elves and he became increasingly curious and impatient. Their slow progress towards the forest felt like torture and Ahren reckoned it would be another good week before they reached the home of the forest elves.

One morning Ahren was daydreaming about elves when Falk suddenly shook him by the shoulder. It was a dull day. The low clouds were slowly moving across the sky and the darkness suggested the travellers would soon be soaking wet. The young man sat up in his saddle and gave his master a questioning look. He didn't return his look however but whispered out of the corner of his mouth. 'Don't arouse suspicion but untie your bow from the saddle and open the quiver. We're about to be ambushed'.

The apprentice was about to crane his neck to see the danger, but Falk hissed sharply without moving his head, 'leave that, or do you want us all to die?'

Ahren slumped back down and looked for all the world like a daydreaming young man, while he secretly prepared bow and arrows for action. The blood was pounding in his ears and it was taking him longer than usual because his hands were shaking. Knowing they were in imminent danger was bad enough, but not being able to look for it was pure torture for the young man.

Falk continued to speak quietly. 'Selsena warned me earlier that she's receiving a lot of hatred and anger. Whoever's lying in wait there must have a couple of really shady characters among them if she can sense their feelings over such a long distance'.

'I can't do much with magic', murmured Uldini. 'We've another few days of unshielded travel through open countryside and I'm glad that the Dark Ones have lost our track. The magic nets of the Ancients have done their job and caused the necessary distraction. If I cast a strong magic spell now, the enemy will be on top of us immediately'.

'Can you throw a small magic net so we know how many and where they are? asked Falk quietly.

Uldini nodded. 'But that's it then. Then I'll defend us with a few little sleights of hand, but I'll only intervene in an emergency'.

He closed his eyes, made a few quick hand movements under his cloak and said something in the foreign language he always used when he was weaving his magic. He opened his eyes again five heartbeats later and said, 'there are fourteen, three of them have crossbows, the rest have cudgels and swords. They're a hundred paces away behind that big rock'.

He pointed his chain at a rock formation which rose up to the right of the trade route. The terrain was still undulating grassland as it had been for the previous weeks, but here and there were fragments of rock that jutted up from the ground like the teeth of an ogre. They were dark on the surface and Uldini had explained to Ahren a few days previously that they had originally been parts of one enormous mountain that had been blown up during one of the major battles. The young man was terrified at the thought that such a massive mountain could be destroyed, and he looked at them in superstitious awe.

But now this feeling was replaced by real fear for his life. Fourteen opponents. Falk had taught him enough about the art of war for him to realize that this superiority in numbers was justification to flee. But instead, his master was proceeding apace and deliberately raised the bow in his hand.

'What are you doing?' asked Ahren, confused.

'They're not using the left side of the road', said the old man calmly. 'Which means they have neither experience nor courage enough to challenge the Clanmen. They've dug their whole group in behind one rock instead of dividing themselves up. That says to me that we're dealing with amateurs, and we know where they are, so the element of surprise is gone. We'll force them to leave their cover and then you and I will pepper them with arrows until they flee. We'll start with the crossbowmen'.

Ahren was flabbergasted. He had shot animals when they had needed food and Dark Ones who had wanted to harm them or others. But now he had to direct his arrows at people.

'Can we not just talk to them?' he asked fearfully.

Falk shook his head grimly. 'The feelings that Selsena is absorbing are pure bloodlust and greed. Those people don't want to talk, at least not with us.'

'But maybe we can persuade them?' Ahren persisted. If he was going to have to shoot at someone, then only after he had tried everything to avoid it.

His master nodded haltingly. 'Alright then. We'll give it a go. But I want to tempt them out anyway. Ahren, dismount and prepare your arrow. Loosen your sword just in case and if one of them shoots then drop down on one knee and shoot at anything that's moving in our direction. Culhen will give you cover. I'll take on the crossbowmen'

His master wasn't counting on Ahren to agree to this, that much was clear to the young man. But Ahren was clinging on to the hope that the imminent bloodbath could be avoided.

Ahren did as he was bidden, his loyal wolf crouched beside him and as he was organizing his arrows in the quiver to make them easier to pull out he heard the thunderous voice of Falk, who had nonchalantly placed an arrow on his bow which he had set up in position on the saddle in front of him.

'We know that you're there. Your little ambush has failed. Come out and be on your way. Then nobody will be harmed'.

The sudden authority in Falk's voice even intimidated Ahren. Hopefully the bandits would cave in.

First, nothing at all happened. The rock lay still in the morning light. A dozen heartbeats passed by and then a number of figures came from behind and walked to the front of the rock. Eight positioned themselves in the middle of the road, two of them had crossbows at the ready. Another five appeared from the other side of the rock, away from the road. One of them was pointing a firearm at them.

280

The ambushers were too far away to study in detail but Ahren could see men and women in varying degrees of neglect. He couldn't see their facial expressions but their body language suggested determination and threat.

A particularly burly man called from the middle of the road in a voice, raw from years of heavy drinking, 'as you see, there are more of us than you!'

The mob laughed and jeered before he continued, 'put your weapons down now and maybe, just maybe, we'll spare your lives'. The last words came out as a snarl and Ahren saw, even from this distance, that their opponents were bracing themselves for action. He suddenly realised that there wouldn't be much more talking before they came to blows. Panic was threatening to overcome him and so he instinctively sought the Void in the hope he could control his emotions. Falk murmured, 'try to get the crossbowman on the right'. Then he called out loudly, 'one more thing before we begin'.

Before the words had echoed across, he had already lifted his bow, drawn the string and let his arrow fly. Distracted by the sudden end to the negotiations, the bandits ducked a half a second too late and one of the crossbowmen collapsed with a scream on the road. Ahren was just as surprised as the bandits, who after the split-second shock, were now storming forward. The remaining crossbowmen started shooting and Ahren shot at the chubby figure to the right of the rock before he had a chance to shoot. His opponent threw himself to the ground to avoid Ahren's arrow and the bolt of his crossbow went askew, flying harmlessly into the distance. Ahren heard a whizzing sound and realized that the other crossbowman had just missed them. He broke into a cold sweat and his concentration faltered. He heard Falk mutter something and then shoot, sending the second crossbowman tumbling to the ground.

With shaking fingers, the apprentice set another arrow and dropped to one knee as his master had ordered. His corpulent opponent was lying flat on the ground trying to reload his crossbow. The analytical part of Ahren's brain, which was firmly anchored in the Void, was telling him that the more immediate danger was the four bandits who were now charging at him. The remaining crossbowman would have to shoot through his own people once he had his weapon loaded.

And so Ahren fixed his look on one of the rapidly approaching enemies and suppressed his strong feeling of repulsion. Human being or no human being, the faces of the attackers left him in no doubt of what would happen to him and his comrades if they were overpowered. He let the arrow fly and his target didn't stand a chance. Wedged in between his companions and running on uneven ground he couldn't take evasive action in time. Ahren's arrow drove into his chest with a terrible sound and he collapsed to the ground without uttering a sound.

Ahren could feel the Void fading at the sight and he shot another arrow before his concentrated calm left him completely. The stocky woman he was aiming at this time threw herself to the side, but the arrow grazed her throat and a fountain of blood spurted out of the wound. She covered it with her hands and let forth a gurgling sound.

The horror of the scene completely banished the Void and Ahren jumped up, stunned, and dropped the bow. He stared wide-eyed at his victim who made a few weak movements while the fountain of blood slackened until the woman finally died. He staggered backwards a few steps and frantically looked around him. Falk had been firing the whole time and another three bodies were lying lifeless on the ground. Uldini was sitting on his horse impassively, the crystal ball in his right hand and he was watching the fight with total concentration. The bandits were twenty paces closer now and having received a quiet command from

Falk, Selsena charged at the rest of the bandits on the road while he pulled out his broadsword.

Uldini meanwhile shouted at Ahren, 'draw your sword boy! In the name of the THREE, defend yourself!'

Instinctively rather than consciously, Ahren followed the wizard's instruction. Culhen was standing at his right leg, his hackles raised and snarling angrily at the approaching enemy.

Falk fell to work on the bandits with ruthless efficiency. Ahren saw for the first time the harmony between his master and Selsena as they rode into battle. Titejunanwa and rider moved in perfect harmony. What the one saw, the other knew. The effect was uncanny. The Elven horse rammed an attacker who had been too slow to jump to one side, and the poor soul was spun through the air like a rag doll with a gruesome jagged hole in his chest, splattering the surroundings with droplets of blood.

Falk was warding off swords and cudgels from the flanks of his war horse with his broadsword in a combination of graceful arcs and cutting thrusts. He cut down two more attackers almost casually and they sank to the ground with a groan, unable to stand again.

But all this was of no use to Ahren. The two remaining attackers who had come from the side of the path would be upon him any second. A man with ugly pockmarks and a long sword, was lunging towards him while a woman with an evil grin and a serrated dagger in her hand, was running towards the seemingly defenceless child, sitting dumbfounded on his pack horse. Ahren tried to push himself between Uldini and the woman but the man blocked his way. Ahren was still overwhelmed by his latest deeds and mechanically raised Windblade into the defensive position he had been practising for the previous few weeks while he kept looking over at the two motionless bodies who were on his conscience, and this action in all probability saved his life. He caught sight of the one remaining crossbowman, who had reloaded his weapon, aimed it at Ahren and shot.

The apprentice instinctively leaped to the side so that Windblade was in the firing line. The bolt whizzed within a whisker past them, and Ahren felt sick as the displaced air caused by the bolt cooled his skin. If he hadn't taken that evasive action he would now be just as dead as his two victims and Culhen too had barely escaped being hit. This realization roused him into action. He pointed at the chubby crossbowman and shouted, 'Culhen, attack!'

The wolf catapulted forward, as if spring-loaded, howled loudly and hurtled towards the unfortunate man. Ahren concentrated on his own attacker, and as the pockmarked bandit aimed his sword at him, Ahren practised one of the few manoeuvres he was familiar with. The assailant's sword was coming towards him in a flat arc about shoulder high so that it would injure his head or chest. Ahren moved towards the strike and held his sword with the hilt upwards and the blade slanted downwards so that the cutthroat's blow slid along the curved blade with a scraping sound and was deflected. They were now standing beside each other and the parried long sword harmlessly cut the air behind Ahren.

The second part of the manoeuvre was even easier. While the bandit was stopping his sword to initiate a backhand stroke Ahren only had to use his movement to good effect and take another step forward while he turned his body towards his opponent and swung Windblade in a downward motion. The impetus of his body turn gave his weapon enough strength to cause a gaping wound down his opponent's back, with blood spurting forth immediately. The pockmarked swordsman dropped his blade and collapsed into a groaning heap. Ahren looked down at his blade in surprise and saw the brigand's blood dripping from it. Before he could react to the sight, he heard a tumult behind him and spun around with his sword once again in the defensive position.

The woman with the dagger was throwing herself at Uldini and they were too far away for Ahren to do anything. He screamed a warning but the wizard had already reacted. He flicked the crystal ball from the palm of his hand with his fingers and it flew with high speed towards the woman's face, however, instead of shattering into pieces, it ricocheted with a dull thud and flew back into the ageless youth's hand. His attacker dropped to the ground as if struck by lightning, and on her face was an enormous crimson swelling.

Ahren looked around frantically but there were no more bandits in the vicinity. Culhen was chasing down the crossbowman who had sought safety in flight and was running between the red stakes into the area of the Green Sea. Meanwhile Falk rode at a gallop towards the rock, as the brigands lay motionless on the road. Blood was dripping from Selsena's coat and also off the armour of war horse and rider. The sight was terrifying and Ahren swallowed hard. Falk rode around the back of the rock and seemed to be hunting down the puppet master of the ambush, who Ahren hadn't set eyes on. There had only been thirteen attackers although Uldini's magic had revealed fourteen. There was a short scream, and Ahren was glad that the rock was hiding the action. Then Falk reappeared and looked searchingly around. Culhen had been chasing the last survivor and Ahren had a sick feeling in his stomach about this. 'Culhen, come here!' he shouted and his four-legged friend turned with an unwilling growl and trotted back to him. Ahren breathed a sigh of relief as soon as the wolf had come back between the border stakes, and a few heartbeats later he understood exactly why.

The chubby bandit was still running for his life, away from them. He was wheezing and could still be heard from this distance. He was ploughing his way surprisingly quickly for a man of his size through the knee-high grass. Suddenly a shape seemed to grow up from the ground beside him. The clan woman had waited in the grass until the runaway was beside her. The woman rose up and in a single flowing movement she sliced her dagger across his throat and ducked down into the high grass. The man took two unsteady steps forward before he noticed what had happened at all, then he collapsed and his death rattle echoed around the field.

Ahren looked at the scene of the drama in shock, but nothing could be seen apart from the gently waving grass. He stroked Culhen and swore that he would never wander into the Green Sea without permission. Meanwhile Falk had ridden up to them and was asking, 'everyone unharmed?'

Ahren didn't answer. The shock of the bloody battle was eating away at him, and the terrible images of the last few minutes were spinning around in his head. Uldini answered for him and said, 'It's not all his blood. Two with the bow and one with the sword. You've raised a real warrior there. Maybe we won't all die under the spell of the Adversary.'

The images in his head were all too much for Ahren and he threw up violently in the middle of the road.

Chapter 17

By the time Ahren's stomach had settled and his uncontrollable shaking had stopped, Falk had matter-of-factly wiped the bloodstains off himself and Selsena with one of the attacker's cloaks. He had also polished all the armouring so that there wasn't a speck of dirt on it, nor on Selsena's coat. Ahren surmised absently that it must have been Elfish craftsmanship and he envied his partners' spotless appearance. He himself stank of blood, vomit and the cold sweat of battle. He was on his hunkers in the middle of the road, his arms around his knees, unhappily rocking back and forth. Culhen sat down beside him, whimpered and licked his master's face. The apprentice couldn't help smiling at this, then buried his head in the wolf's pelt, took deep breaths and tried to stop himself from crying. Uldini looked down at the distraught young man and said, 'he's doing well. I've seen some run away at the first sign of battle and others frozen on the spot only to be hacked down without resistance. Once he's recovered from this, he'll have taken a terrible but vital step forward'.

Falk nodded. 'But we can make it a little easier for him, can't we?' Uldini understood what the Guardian was driving at and began to prepare a little spell as unobtrusively as possibly. Selsena, meanwhile, walked over towards Ahren and began filling his spirit with the peace and confidence he had felt once before, when he had torn Culhen from the claws of the Adversary. The young Forest Guardian lifted his head from his friend's pelt and Culhen placed his head on the apprentice's knee and looked at him with loyal, loving eyes. Selsena calmed Ahren's tumultuous feelings and suddenly a fresh breeze was gently touching his face. His nose was filled with the fresh smell of grass and he saw in amazement how all the blood stains vanished from his clothing until there wasn't a speck to be seen. Tears ran down his face as he absorbed the love and affection of the two animals and he revelled in the sensation of being clean. He looked at Uldini who dissipated the breeze and gave him a friendly nod. Then Ahren pulled himself together, gave Selsena a friendly smile and tickled Culhen behind the ears. Falk came over and gave him a searching look. 'Feeling better again?'

Ahren didn't trust his voice so he simply nodded weakly, glancing at the same time at the two bodies that had his arrows in them.

Falk looked in the same direction. 'It's only right that you feel terrible, a different reaction and I'd be worried', said his master in a serious voice.

Ahren looked up at him in puzzlement. He himself had seen his breakdown as weakness, and had been envious of the others and their hardness.

'There are people, dwarves and sometimes even elves, who see killing in a different way to you. Some snap, which is why we are all here for you'. Ahren had a lump in his throat, but he really didn't want to start crying again. The thought of facing the horror he had just experienced without the support of his comrades was terrifying. He tickled Culhen again gratefully, who grumbled contentedly. His master continued. 'No matter how tragic this is, those who enjoy killing are much worse than the tortured souls that have been destroyed by the experience of war. Most succumb sooner or later to a killing frenzy. Usually they are remembered as heroes, so long as their desires serve the general good, and they almost always die young. Lured by the siren song of battle, they end up surrounded by the enemy and die in a final bloodbath of violence'.

The thought of actually enjoying killing struck Ahren as grotesque and regrettable, and he suddenly felt relieved at the sadness he was experiencing.

'But the worst reaction anyone can show is the complete absence of emotion. Those who experience no feeling as they stride through the battlefield bringing death and destruction to their enemy are generally the most terrible opponents. Their coldness grows to the point where they recognize neither friend nor foe, but, driven by their own motivations, they will sacrifice a hundred good men and women to kill ten enemies if it serves their purpose.' There was a hardness in the corner of Falk's mouth and his tone suggested to Ahren that a memory was prompting these words. Falk cleared his throat and forced himself back to the present situation. He then finished with the following words: 'We all feel sadness when we kill, and that's how it should be. It's only this sadness that spurs us on to avoid battle if possible, or to finish it with a minimum number of casualties on either side. Uldini and I have learned how to deal with these feelings and know when to negotiate to prevent something worse. Come with me, all of you!'

The old man turned on his heels and strode towards the rock from where the ambush had been launched. Ahren had to step his way between the mutilated bodies of the brigands that Falk and Selsena had killed. He thought of the firm but friendly tone of his master and the generous spirit of the Titejunanwa and tried to reconcile them with what he was looking at, but it was beyond him. He walked more quickly and hoped that some day he would find the solution to his emotional dilemma.

Falk led them around the rock to another body. Ahren was stunned. He was looking into the lifeless eyes of the wandering preacher who had spoken to him at the trading post some weeks previously. His red robe exhibited a darker spot where Falk's sword had been driven through.

What was he doing here and how had he caught up with them, and why had his master killed a seemingly unarmed man? He was swamped with questions and he looked at his master uncertainly, who was now kneeling down beside the body. Uldini reached the spot too and hissed as he drew breath. Obviously Ahren had missed something that the wizard had spotted immediately. He followed the gaze of the youthful figure and saw something long and dark lying in the grass a few paces away. Full of curiosity he stepped closer and saw with horror that a thin tongue was lying in the grass. It was roughly two paces in length and ended in a moist, shiny spike. Ahren stepped back in horror and looked over at his master who pulled down the deceased priest's jaw, revealing the bloody area where his tongue had once been.

'High Fang', he said and gave Uldini a serious look. The wizard let forth a string of expletives and threw his arms in the air, at which point his crystal ball rose up and settled half a pace above his right shoulder. The wizard was so agitated that he seemed not to notice. 'You know what that means, old man. One High Fang means at least a hundred Low Fangs. The enemy wants to stop us at all costs and there's a horde of these wretches scurrying about somewhere. They're probably making the Green Sea nervous. It would take a whole clan to eliminate a horde, and you'll only find border guards here at this time of year. Which means they can strike at any time.' Yellow sparks crackled between the Arch Wizard's fingers.

Falk responded quietly. 'Relax, Uldini. If his horde were near him, he would never have been so desperate as to put a bunch of badly educated highway robbers onto us. He probably noticed us when he was on a spying mission and had to improvise. If we travel on quickly, we'll get to the elves safely'.

Ahren looked at the haggard face of the dead man and tried to remember what he looked like when he was alive.

'He looked so normal', he said quietly.

290

Uldini nodded. 'that's why we call him *High* Fang. That's how we classify the human servants of the enemy. Let's get out of here, I'll explain it to you on the way'.

Ahren looked tentatively over at the bodies but his master said, 'the feudal lord of this stretch of land will bury them. There's too much blood in the air for us three to put fourteen bodies under the ground undisturbed. Even a normal beast of prey from the Green Sea could be dangerous for us.'

They gathered the horses together and rode away from the gruesome scene. Uldini distracted the young man from the terrible sights by explaining to him, as he had promised, the rankings of the adversary's servants

'If a human, dwarf or elf comes into direct contact with the willpower of the Betrayer, whether willingly or not, there are several results. Most of them die, pure and simple. Their spirit breaks, their heart stops beating. All elves and dwarves react in this way, and also the majority of humans. The humans who survive are forced into another form that seems totally arbitrary. They are human to a large degree, but there are two-headed variations, some with several arms, legs, with claws, fangs, feathers, whatever you can imagine. They almost always produce sharp teeth, which is why we call them Low *Fangs*. Their spirits suffer greatly under the implanting of HIS will and their intelligence is mostly limited. They gather together into hordes of one hundred up to one thousand individuals and they travel through the country looking for prey. Those of a high intelligence and an outstanding will can withstand the pressure of transformation to some extent. Even if they are still under the control of HIM WHO FORCES, they maintain a large amount of their human form and an intact spirit in so far as that is possible, even if they all eventually succumb to some form of madness or passion. Their changes are mostly subtler, a third eye in the palm of their hand, or a hidden tongue of poison, as in our friend's case back there. We call these beings High Fangs. They are the ringleaders of the hordes - philosophers, spies or assassins. You're already well acquainted with the Dark Ones. Almost all of them fulfil special roles or are compliant stooges of the High Fangs. Now, above them all are the Transformers. They are the generals if you like. They obey only the Adversary'.

Ahren wondered at the wizard's words. 'What do you mean, 'willingly or not'?' he asked.

Uldini answered, 'the unwilling variation follows three different types. Firstly, chance. A few Borderlanders came under the wandering and dreaming will of the Betrayer. That could even happen outside the Border Lands at the beginning of the spell, but it was highly improbable and is impossible now because he is still sleeping too deeply. The same applies to the second variation. Someone had aroused HIS attention during the Dark Days and to such an extent that HE WHO FORCES went to the effort of searching after the troublemaker. Luckily, such a visitation can be easily avoided if one carries a sign of the THREE, usually as a pendant. Otherwise HE would have been able to destroy all the opposition in their sleep. The closer one is, the stronger the effect. That's why we have possibility number three, the most common one nowadays. It still regularly catches border guards who are careless and wander to within a length of the Pall Pillar, and then a medallion is of no use anymore. One of the reasons that the gods created the Paladins that time was their ability to withstand HIS willpower, even in direct contact'.

Uldini was now lost in his memories and stopped talking and so Falk took over the reins.

'The willing variation is very simple. You go to HIM and submit yourself to HIS will'.

292

Ahren was shocked. 'Who would do something like that', he asked, flabbergasted.

'You want power over other people, you see no point in your life, you are tired of taking independent decisions, you are running away from their consequences or you simply reject the THREE. Some of them only wanted to be on the side of the so-called victors. The lonely, the lost, the despised – they all ran to HIM and ended up as Low or High Fangs in HIS army. That's another reason. If you go to HIM of your own free will, then the transformation won't kill you. There was even the rumour that you could become a Transformer. People can be incredibly stupid'. Falk shook his head in disdain. The three rode along for a while in silence.

Then Uldini asked, 'The High Fang, what did he say to you that time at the trading post?'

Ahren thought hard. It had been weeks earlier and he hadn't attached much importance to it. Finally, he said, 'Something about me not needing to be lonely anymore. Something like that. Something about a shimmering path or an illuminating way, I think'.

Uldini and Falk were suddenly very uneasy and the magus asked carefully, 'was it the Illuminated Path, perhaps?'

Ahren thought for a moment, then nodded.

Falk looked grim and said, 'that was fast'.

The apprentice looked questioningly from one to the other and finally his master relented and offered an explanation.

'There was a cult in the Dark Days that taught the adoration of the Adversary. Their true god was buried under a heap of lies in order to lure the unhappy and weak. 'Never be lonely again, have no fear, abandon yourself to our community, be free of all doubts, all that rubbish. This all resulted in the poor souls freely putting themselves under HIS control. The name of this cult was 'the Illuminated Path''.

'It seems our enemy is organizing himself more quickly than expected', added Uldini.

'You think too vertically', said Falk in contradiction. 'Not everything is coming from HIM. I think the Transformers are preparing the ground for the harvest. Not that this possibility is much better'.

Uldini shrugged his shoulders. 'Whatever the case, I'm going to call on the Ancients to eradicate the cult in all the kingdoms before it can gain a foothold. Anyway, that will give them something meaningful to do'.

'Good idea', agreed Falk grimly.

They rode on in brooding silence and after a few lengths, the rain started – thick heavy drops that soaked through to the skin within seconds.

Uldini looked up at the heavens and said, 'Well, that figures.'

Ahren awoke, his breathing was fitful and his clothing stuck to his body under the blanket. Just as every night since the ambush, he only slept a few hours before he was woken up by nightmares. Culhen was beside him as always, his warm pelt a rock withstanding his master's constant and alternate surges of fear and guilt. Whenever he closed his eyes, he saw the faces of his enemies who had died at his hands. He was finding it impossible to shake off the memories no matter how hard he tried to justify his actions to himself.

At the start he had tried to calm his nerves by reaching the Void. But the ghosts of the dead were the new ghosts of the Void and so this refuge remained barred to him until he could find the opportunity to come to terms with his deeds. Logic told him that he had done the right thing, that he himself would have been killed had he not defended himself. But the very same logic told him that they had taken fourteen lives in order to save five. He was going around in circles and didn't know the way out.

294

Falk and Uldini were of no use whatsoever. His master would always say, 'the answers are already there, you just don't want to see them'. And Uldini spoke like an oracle. 'Each must find their own way to come to terms with it. Find the reason that justifies what you have done. Falk knows his and I have my own. Find yours and you shall find peace'.

This really didn't help the young man, but he struggled on, forcing his way through the days as the ribbon of Evergreen grew bigger and bigger until they could recognize individual trees with the naked eye. According to Falk they would be there in two days and slowly the feelings of guilt gave way to curiosity and excitement. Only at night was it impossible to escape from his conscience in the nightmares that plagued him. Culhen would sense his disquiet and so lick his face and hit him playfully with his paws and within a few heartbeats they would be tussling for fun until Ahren would collapse, unable to breathe because he was laughing so much. Then he would stroke the fur of his friend and fall into a dreamless sleep.

The following days passed painfully slowly. The trees of Evergreen were growing into the skies before them, but still they hadn't reached the tree border. He reckoned that most of the trees soared over fifty paces up into the heavens, and the green wall stretched unbroken from one end of the horizon to the other. He felt a sense of awe in the face of such an elemental force of nature. His master understood the expression on his apprentice's face, for he himself often wore it. He whispered to Ahren, 'wherever I go, Eathinian will always be my true home. It would take a person three years to cross it from east to west, and three months to travel from here to its northern end where the Icy Vasts await one. It would take you a whole lifetime to see all of Eathinian'. Ahren had never heard the old man gush like this, but there was always a painful undertone when he spoke of the forest of the elves. This part of their adventure was finally coming to a close and the following day they would enter at last into the safety of the Elfish forest in order to find the first of the three Einhans.

Chapter 18

The green wall of trees soared ever higher as they traversed the final lengths to the Elfish forest. Shortly before that, they had passed by the Knight Marshes border station, a strangely humble stone building with an elderly man sitting snoring on a platform. Ahren had expected an imposing castle or some other symbol of power through which the kingdom would assert its border with the elves, but he was obviously mistaken. Falk had seen his puzzled look and explained the reason to him.

'There haven't been any border conflicts for centuries. The trees are a clear divide. The elves live within, the people outside. Everything has been peaceful since nobody tries to fell the trees anymore. A strong fortification would only increase tensions, and the more harmonious the relations are, the more the trade road brings in. Money has always been a powerful motivation'.

The green giants were now soaring before the travellers into the sky and Ahren's first impression, that most of these trees had to be at least fifty paces tall, had proven itself to be true. Sweeping branches full of leaves created a green canopy above the forest floor. As he lowered his gaze to look ahead, he saw that the trade path was snaking its way between the massive trunks of the enormous trees, and its appearance had altered markedly since they'd passed the border post. The massive stone slabs had made way to a curious green growth that made its way like velvet, smooth and shimmering.

They rode closer and Falk said, 'Leave the talking to me.'

Ahren stretched his neck but could see nobody. There was no border post or guards, and while he was wondering what exactly Falk meant, two slim figures stepped out of the trees and onto the trade path from left and right and looked at them impassively. Ahren squinted his eyes in an effort to make out details, as these were the first elves he had ever seen in the flesh, but the distance was still too great.

Falk said quietly, 'we'll dismount here and lead the horses by their reins'.

Uldini grumbled but followed the others' example.

They slowly walked towards the two elves, who still hadn't moved a muscle. The whole situations seemed somewhat unreal to Ahren. They were still a hundred paces from the first trees but already they were stepping into the shade of the leafy canopy. Much to Ahren's surprise it had hardly darkened at all, but everything was lit up in a greenish lustre. He looked up and had to blink straight away. The leaves of the giant trees were strongly translucent and hardly stopped the sun at all. He was filled with a sense of security and peace, almost as if the canopy of leaves was keeping everything evil at bay and only the warmth and beauty of the world was allowed to pass through.

A light breeze ruffled the tree tops and the silent swoosh created a play of colours as shades of gold and green danced their way through the branches in ever changing variations as the sun found its way to the forest floor.

These sensual elements hit Ahren quite unexpectedly and tears of joy ran down his cheeks. He felt safe for the first time since he had left Deepstone. Selsena emitted a storm of joy and happiness, which proved to the young man that he wasn't alone with his emotions. His master was walking before him but the young man could tell from his trembling shoulders that the old man was equally overcome.

He blinked away his tears and concentrated fully on the elves they were nearing. They were a dozen paces away and he could now make out all their features. Both were slim and tall with snow white hair that fell to

298

their chests and down their backs in complicated plaits and coils. Their bodies were covered by unusual leather armour that Ahren had never come across before. The leather seemed to be made up of individually hardened leather pieces which were in a variety of curved shapes that made a complete, closed piece. Ahren could make out fine lines where the individual leather plates met up and he asked himself why anyone would dress themselves in armour like this with its dozens of weak points.

The guards were unarmed and looked at the travel party as they finally arrived with eyes that were calm yet penetrating. They didn't say a word to the arrivals and still hadn't moved, but still Ahren couldn't ignore them. The guards radiated a sort of quiet authority that warned everybody not to proceed without their permission. Falk cleared his throat after a few seconds of silence and said in a trembling voice, 'we wish to enter Eathinian in order to speak to Jelninolan'. He clearly wanted to say more but it seemed that the feelings that had surfaced on his return to the Elfish forest were overwhelming him. But there was something else. His shoulders were pulled in and he had sunk his head and was looking erratically from one guard to the other. His proud and unflinching master was coming across like a nervous and vulnerable Godsday student. This sight took Ahren aback, and he was even more dismayed when one of the guards said in a quiet but clear voice, 'we know who you are, Dorian Falkenstein. Your time under the Elfish trees was declared over. Turn around and return no more'. His master flinched at these words as if they had been accompanied by blows. Selsena gave a shrill neigh as a reaction to the emotional suffering her spiritual partner was enduring, and Ahren felt an anger building up inside him at the heartless way that these two elves had chastised the old man. Falk himself seemed to want to yield, and turned away, his face a picture of inner torment. Ahren was about to utter some scornful words when suddenly a crackling sound filled the air behind him. The apprentice spun around and saw Uldini. Ahren gasped and staggered backwards until he crashed into his horse, for he hardly recognized the wizard. He was floating a good one and a half paces above the ground and he was engulfed in an aura of flashes that was dancing over the ground and among the trees with a power that was almost tangible. His eyes were lit up in a painfully bright glow and when he spoke, his voice sounded like thunder,

'I am Uldini Getobo, beloved of the gods, supreme commander of the Ancients, weaver of the Bane Spell and protector of the Sunplains. I demand admission for me and my companions and an escort to Jelninolan. Now!'

The last word was accompanied by a tremendous blast that threw everyone off balance as it raced along the canopy of leaves and disappeared in the distance. The simultaneous whoosh of the leaves around them was deafening. Ahren had been in awe at the stillness of the guards, but the way the Arch Magus so easily made use of his absolute power was quite overwhelming. The elves were obviously of the same opinion for they turned without saying another word and led them into the Elfish forest. Ahren stared at the floating figure in front of him as if in a trance. The transformation of the childlike figure into this manifestation of light and willpower had stunned him so completely that he was rooted to the spot. Falk trotted in a daze behind the elves, still trapped in the painful suffering that the elves' rebuff had caused. Uldini floated forwards and whispered to Ahren as he passed him, 'now get a move on! You THREE, how I despise these sleights of hand'.

This comment was typical of the dry humour and Uldini's pragmatic nature that Ahren had got to know in the previous months and it broke the spell that the wizard's present appearance had on him. He was still in awe of the Arch Wizard's power play but he was no longer crippled with fear. He took his horse by the reins and hurried after the others. Uldini's aura hurt his eyes if he had looked at it for too long, so he concentrated on his surroundings instead.

The shimmering ribbon he had seen from the distance and on which he was now walking, turned out to be a thick bed of moss that felt soft and feathery under his feet yet provided a secure footing. Ahren could see no kerbstone, but despite this the bed of moss was always three paces wide and led them into the wood, curving here and there around the giant trees. He looked around but neither boots nor hooves left their prints on the cultivated moss. Ahren didn't know of any plants that were so robust, and his admiration for the elves increased. If the path leading them on was a minor miracle, then what wonders awaited them in the middle of the forest? He continued to study the scene around him and saw something moving in the branches high above him. A white-haired figure in leather armour and with a long bow in his hand was following them, hopping with fluid movements from branch to branch in the same way that Ahren used to jump from stone to stone as he crossed the little river at home. The grace and ease of movement almost distracted him from the danger the longbow above their heads presented. A quick look around revealed that at least six armed elves were keeping pace with them above and he was in no doubt that he hadn't spotted them all.

The apprentice wanted to talk with the others about them, but Falk was caught up in his own troubles and it would be impossible to have a quiet word with Uldini without going too near the lightning flashes that he was still emitting. The discharges seemed harmless enough as they were causing no damage to their surroundings, but the young man didn't want to risk his health on this assumption, so he said nothing and tried to ignore the armed escorts above them, concentrating instead on the elves who were leading them. High cheekbones and pointed chins gave their faces a somewhat triangular appearance. Their silver eyes twinkled forth from their finely drawn features. Their movements were supple and they almost came across as animals of prey that had been dressed in a human form. Now that they were moving, Ahren could see the functionality of their armouring. The variously shaped tiles of hardened leather floated on two levels, one over another and occasionally he could see leather strips, which connected the tiles, shining in the gaps between them. As he watched the elves move, he realized that this type of armouring offered total freedom of movement and the body was always protected by at least one layer of leather as the tiles harmoniously interacted with each other. Serpentine patterns were engraved on the individual tiles and so every movement of the elves presented a new combination of swirls and spirals that dazzled the eyes. He got a headache if he watched the patterns for any length of time.

Having satisfied his curiosity regarding his surroundings, Ahren glanced surreptitiously over at Falk. His master trotted, head hanging, behind the guards with Selsena close beside him. He seemed to have recovered some of his composure, but anguish could still be seen clearly on his face. The apprentice absently tickled Culhen behind the ears. The reformed Blood Wolf seemed to be in top form. Once they had entered the forest, he had been jumping with delight around the trees only to return every so often to be close to Ahren before running off again after a few heartbeats. The animal's joie de vivre was infectious and the peacefulness that Ahren had felt when they had all first entered the forest began to return.

The sun was a soft disc through the canopy of leaves and as the travel party moved silently on, it continued its upward journey in the sky. It was already almost midday when the scenery changed. Broad ribbons of woven cloth were stretched tautly under the tree tops between the branches and in this way created trails on which a few dozen elves went about their business. Ahren looked on in amazement as even elf children leapt fearlessly from material to material at heights of thirty paces in order to take shortcuts or to change their altitude. He could see little dwellings on almost every tree, made completely from the same woven material, slung artfully around the available branches. Intricate knots and designs transformed fabric into cheerful peaked roofs or round houses that resembled birds' nests, depending on the number and position of the supporting branches and the knots and folding techniques used.

Ahren took in the beauty of the Elfish settlement with wide-eyed astonishment. Not a single branch seemed to have been pruned, everything fitted harmoniously into the natural structures of the forest. The apprentice kept staring upwards and in the meantime more and more elves appeared, looking down on the new arrivals, mostly with curiosity, some grumpily. Only very few of the very young Elf children seemed afraid, all of the others reacted astonishingly calmly to the figure of Uldini, who was still spraying sparks around him as he floated.

Magic seemed to be nothing unusual here and soon Culhen was arousing more curiosity than the Arch Wizard. The elves, all of them white-haired and silver-eyed, were pointing down at Culhen and whispering excitedly to each other as the wolf rambled around the trees. Ahren gave a quiet whistle and Culhen trotted over to him before sitting beside him. The young man tickled Culhen's furry head in a deliberately exaggerated and intensive way to forestall any misunderstanding regarding his friend's nature and Culhen began to grumble with pleasure. Then he squatted down and let the wolf lick his face with his slobbery tongue. Giggling broke out from the surrounding treetops and the children hopped and climbed down the branches at lightning speed.

Within ten heartbeats Culhen was surrounded by his new playmates who were calling, teasing, feeding, and romping with him. The young Blood Wolf was overjoyed and soon he was buried under a pile of giggling and laughing Elf children. Ahren felt a calloused hand on his shoulder as he watched the fun and games, and he heard the voice of his master. 'Very good work, boy. Elves are very closely connected to nature and her creatures. You have brought a Blood Wolf into their presence, but one who is a friend and has been wrested from the influence of the Adversary. That will bring us further than all the magic Uldini can invoke'.

Ahren looked at Falk, who smiled weakly. The pain was still visible in the old man's eyes, but his normal stoic composure had returned, and that was a step in the right direction.

One of the elf guards disappeared while the other one indicated with a hand gesture that they should wait. The apprentice compared their attitude with that of the other elves and he could hardly believe that their ice-cold escorts were also part of this community. All hostility had vanished from the faces of the inhabitants once Culhen had been accepted. Many greeted Ahren with a friendly nod or waved at him. Some performed a strange formal gesture in front of Falk which he reciprocated, beaming with joy. The tumult gradually died away, and those whose curiosity had been satisfied, went off about their business. It was striking however, that none of the adult elves came down to them.

When he mentioned this to Falk, the old man responded. 'The forest floor is not part of the settlement. It's as if we were outside the city walls. We are only inside once we have been invited up'.

'What sort of a gesture was it that the elves made to you?' asked Ahren, inquiring further. Now that his master was open to questions, he wanted to make use of the opportunity while they were waiting.

'It's a welcome greeting. They're expressing their friendship in spite of the fact that I'm not supposed to be here'. Falk's voice wavered.

'Why did the guards turn you away? I thought you had already paid for your crime'. Ahren aimed for as gentle a tone as possible in order not to push his master too far.

But he responded in a surprisingly calm voice. 'It's nothing personal. Elfish laws permit visitors only a limited time under the trees of Eathinian. When this time has run out, you cannot return for a year. When I was serving my sentence in the forest, I exceeded the time span a hundredfold. So, when I left, I was told that I could only return after 237 years.' Ahren looked at him in amazement but Falk merely shrugged his shoulders. 'Elves have a different concept of time than humans.'

Before the apprentice could ask any more questions, the second guard was back, accompanied by an elf.

The female elves Ahren had seen in the trees may have resembled those in the stories – tall, slim, white-haired with finely drawn features – but the elf he was looking at now definitely stood out from the crowd.

The first thing that struck Ahren was her red hair, which framed a friendly face. Intense green eyes looked curiously up at him in a friendly manner. The elf was on the short side and rounder without being any less dainty. When she saw Falk, she smiled and Ahren's heart missed a beat. The goodness and warmth of her smile overwhelmed him and within a heartbeat he knew that he would defend this elf with his life.

Dazzled by her radiance, he watched Falk kneel in front of her with a serious face and murmur something in Elfish. She merely smiled in return, patted him behind the ears and pulled him to his feet.

'Speak so that all of us can understand you. Where are your manners?' Then she gave his master a hearty embrace and said, 'I was never angry with your decision, only with the way you treated Selsena. She's on your side again so I bear no grudges'.

Ahren thought the little elf sounded like a mother but the tone of her voice and her self-confidence suggested that her short statement could also have been a knight's dictum. He realized that this thought may not have been so far off the mark when he saw that the two guards had relaxed at last and were now grinning at Falk. The elf let go of Falk, who quietly wiped a tear from his eye, and she turned to Uldini, kneeling before him and stretching her arms out.

'Aunt Jelninolan!' screamed Uldini and jumped at her like a little boy. Ahren looked on open-mouthed as the elf lifted up the Arch Wizard and spun him around like a little child while he giggled uncontrollably. Her radiance had just as powerful an effect on his companions as on himself. But who was this woman?

Falk turned to him and gave a hearty laugh when he saw the young man's face.

He said in a cheerful voice, 'Ahren, chosen to be the thirteenth Paladin, allow me to introduce you to the Arch Wizardess Jelnilolan, high priestess of HER WHO FEELS'. The elf gave a little curtsy that seemed more playful than formal and smiled at him. The full impact of her radiance overwhelmed him as her green eyes bore into his, and he felt the full extent of her goodness and friendliness.

A feeling of security began to spread within him as she spoke. 'The blessings of HER WHO FEELS be upon you always. May all creatures under HER control recognize your heart and behave accordingly'.

she then placed a soft hand on his cheek. Ahren closed his eyes and enjoyed the comfortable feeling, above all else of being protected. A small part of his heart wondered if that was how it felt when you had a mother. As far as Ahren was concerned, he could have remained standing

306

there for hours, but suddenly he felt a push between his legs and heard an excited whimper. Culhen had freed himself from the mass of elf children and now pushed Ahren roughly aside so that he could push himself forward on his stomach towards Jelninolan, whimpering and wagging his tail and looking for her hand with his head. The elf priestess looked thoughtfully for a moment at the Blood Wolf, then smiled again and repeated her words, while she placed a hand on Culhen's head, between his ears. The animal was now completely silent and at the end of the blessing he tilted his head and looked up at Jelninolan with curious eyes. Everything was still for two heartbeats. Only the gentle rustle of the trees could be heard. It was only now that Ahren noticed that all the elves were watching them spellbound, without making a sound. Then Culhen sat up on his hind legs, tilted back his head, and uttered a long howl that reverberated loudly through the forest. Ahren flinched, but he was the only one to do so. All the others smiled and ruffled his fur or patted his head. He jumped away and into a crowd of squealing elf children who welcomed him even more enthusiastically than they had the first time. It seemed his friend had passed some sort of test without even knowing about it.

The high priestess turned and waved at them to follow her. Ahren trotted after the others wearily. The multitude of emotions he had experienced in such a short time was taking it's toll.

Culhen stayed behind and didn't react to his commands, but Falk simply said, 'Leave him be. It's better if the children keep him occupied than you having to control him. When animals receive the blessing of the goddess, they're full of beans for a few days.'

'It felt really lovely', whispered Ahren quietly as the latest experiences overwhelmed him again. Falk nodded and said, 'the blessing is reserved only for elves and a select few other creatures, or to be more precise, for highly valued animals and a handful of esteemed outsiders. It's only bestowed once, so treasure this in your memory.'

As they were speaking, they went around a massive tree trunk and began climbing one of the cloth paths which resembled a ramp and rose gently into the branches. Ahren was surprised at how securely his feet held their grip and how little give there was in the cloth under their steps.

His mastered continued, 'You and Culhen are part of a community that is respected by all natural, living beings. Every animal, every plant will recognize this blessing and as long as you remain in harmony with them, they will always consider themselves your allies'.

It all sounded very vague and Ahren was too exhausted to think about it so he just nodded.

Satisfied, Falk continued, 'one of the reasons we came here was so that you would receive this blessing. I actually thought Jelninolan would wait until the ritual itself, but elves are very spontaneous and sensitive to feelings by nature. It seems I drummed enough respect for nature into you to make them satisfied with what they saw in you'. He leaned forwards, 'and between you and me, rescuing Culhen from the claws of the Adversary has made you a lot of friends here in no time at all. I underestimated that reaction completely.'

They walked on in silence and finally reached the first level, which had a few dwellings. Ahren looked at one of them curiously from up close. Intertwined lengths of cloth were artfully arranged in patterns and shapes, creating here a wall, there a window, not to mention gables. He pressed his finger against one of the cloth walls but it only gave way half a finger length. He tried to follow the direction of one of the lengths of cloth, but failed. The patterns were so complex that his head hurt if he concentrated on them too much. His eyes began to water at the effort so he shook his head and gave up. Uldini popped up beside him and laughed.

'Leave it be. The human brain isn't cut out for this art. It took me three years before I understood the basics that time'.

Ahren remembered the emotional reaction when the Arch Magician greeted the elf.

'She's not really your aunt, is she?' he asked quietly.

Uldini laughed again. 'No, of course not. When I discovered the secret of eternal life, I was a nine-year-old slave boy in the clutches of a below average magician. I didn't know what sort of a formula I had deciphered and were it not for Jelninolan, I wouldn't have survived the following day. Had I told my owner, it would have been all over for me, but luckily, all Arch Wizards can sense when a new member has joined their ranks. She was outside my sleeping place when day broke the following morning and she bought me. I spent the following decades here and received a proper education in the magic arts.' The little figure sighed. 'Those were happy times.'

The news that Jelninolan was older than Uldini didn't surprise Ahren. He had expected elves to be age-old and wise, and it was comforting to him that at least one of his assumptions had been proven correct. Falk and Jelninolan were whispering to each other like old friends.

Ahren racked his brains trying to remember, and then asked Uldini quietly, 'wasn't Falk afraid of meeting her?'

The Arch Wizard chuckled gleefully. 'Before Falk came to Eathinian that time, he had decided not to work with me again. Selsena didn't agree with his decision and was angry with him. It all became loud and horrible and finally she galloped off in a rage and Falk had to make his own way through the world. When in the end he was in a degenerate state and running riot around Eathinian, Jelninolan intervened. She wasn't happy at his behaviour and let him know that in no uncertain terms when he was doing his compulsory labour in the forest. Ever since his exile, Falk has always feared another confrontation. Believe me, if he hadn't made up with Selsena, the reunion today would have been twice as loud and half as harmonious'. Uldini grimaced and placed a hand on Ahren's arm so that he stood still and looked the sorcerer in the eye.

'You've noticed this peaceful feeling when she looks at you, haven't you?'

The young man nodded and found himself smiling automatically at the memory. Everyone has had the same feeling in her presence, he thought

'And now imagine her angry and shouting at you'.

Ahren shrank back and looked doubtfully at the red-haired, roundish elf walking in front of them. Somehow, he couldn't imagine this personification of peacefulness and goodness becoming enraged, but he wouldn't give her any reason to reprimand him, just to be on the safe side.

Falk and the high priestess had stopped outside a large, angular dwelling, which could almost pass for a human tree house.

She turned around and said, 'this is one of our guest chambers. The first few days under the trees are always very disturbing for people. Rest yourselves and have something to eat. We'll talk again early tomorrow. In the meantime, I'll speak to the forest and listen to what she has to say'. Then she turned on her heels and left without waiting for a response.

Ahren looked after her and Uldini chuckled quietly.

'Like a strange mixture of motherly sternness and kingly authority, don't you think? I've learnt to contradict her only when it's absolutely necessary'.

310

Falk mumbled something to himself and took a fresh fruit from the bowl that was standing there ready. Ahren took one too and looked around him.

The dwelling consisted of a large room that, with the help of loosely hanging lengths of material, was divided into three sleeping areas, and one main room. Plump cushions for sitting on, were scattered around the floor, and naturally grown branches, which never seemed to get in the way, served as storage places for bowls, jugs and glasses. The three ate in silence and found themselves being enveloped by the same peaceful mood that they had experienced when they first entered the elf forest. Nobody wanted to talk much, each person dwelling on their own thoughts. Falk seemed more relaxed than he had been in weeks and Uldini was less serious. Ahren enjoyed the feeling of contentment and safety that radiated from everything around him. He closed his eyes, gave a contented sigh and fell asleep on the spot.

Chapter 19

Ahren woke up, fresh as a daisy. He lay there with his eyes closed and enjoyed the peace of the moment. The greenish light of Eathinian warmed his face and the rustling of the trees soothed his spirit. The silence around him could only mean that the others had got up before him, and the fact that Culhen hadn't licked his face, suggested that his four-legged friend was playing with the tireless elf children. After a while his curiosity concerning the Elfish settlement won out over the peace of his sleeping space.

He opened his eyes and stretched himself and noticed that somebody, in all likelihood Falk, had carried him to one of the separate sleeping areas and peeled him out of his leather clothing. Ahren smiled in gratitude, rotated his shoulders and stretched his back in order to loosen himself.

He pulled the length of cloth aside and stepped into the main space. As he had suspected, none of the others were there. Fresh fruit was laid out in the bowl that they had already eaten out of the previous day, and Ahren dived right in. He almost emptied the bowl, and as he was eating, he kept glancing outside curiously. It only dawned on him then that there were no doors to be seen. The entrance to their dwelling wasn't even hung with cloth and when he looked around, he could see that the same was true for the other cloth constructions in the vicinity. He only saw a few elves, and very few other new things. It seemed as though the guest quarters were chosen so that they were somewhat separate from the rest of the community. Ahren did have a fine view of the forest, but if he wanted to see anything else, he had to crane his neck or leave the house.

312

Unsure of where to go, he first returned a little on the path they had come in on the previous day. He peered curiously into every cloth house he passed. Most of them were empty; now and then there would be an elf sitting in one, eating, who would give a friendly nod. He wondered where everyone was, but soon he realized that the settlement stretched out over several levels and there would certainly be something like a village square somewhere. He had seen the elf children climbing up and down the cloth paths the day before and these connected the various levels. Ahren was on the lowest level, exactly at the height where the foliage on the giant trees began. He looked down into the depths and he was only too happy that he had a head for heights for there were at least two dozen paces between himself and the forest floor. He could make out above him at least two further paths among the branches that led to different heights. After wandering around for a little he came to the cloth ramp that led downwards to the forest floor. He hadn't seen anybody below him as yet, so he carried on walking in search of a path that led upwards. The cloth ribbon snaked its way between the tree trunks sometimes gently inclining or declining. Ahren could see that the wide cloth path that he was walking on was artfully wound around the branches at regular intervals as it led past them. He never had the feeling that he would lose his footing, and the path always gave him a feeling of stability. Whether that was down to the qualities of the unusual material, or the almost magical knotting and wrapping techniques used by the elves, he could not tell. For a while he wandered aimlessly. Here and there the ribbons would intersect, and now and then Ahren would take a turn in the hope that he would see a familiar face or find the path that led upwards. He called after Culhen a few times, but the Blood Wolf was undoubtedly enjoying himself with his new playmates and Ahren didn't begrudge him that pleasure. This was the first time since Deepstone that the animal found itself in a community that accepted him without question, and the young man was determined to allow his friend to enjoy this positive experience as much as possible.

He strolled on, taking in the idyllic peace and majestic beauty of the elf forest. The emotions that the enormous trees and the greenish light had stirred up in him the previous day had been tumultuous and overwhelming, but today they had a more subtle influence on him, like the steady sound of a noisy waterfall, just far enough away not to be a disturbance, but close enough to penetrate everything he was experiencing. The result was an inner calm and clarity, which lay over every thought that came to him.

At last he spotted a ramp among the branches that led upwards and into the distance. He smiled contentedly and walked purposefully towards it. As he approached the ramp , he noticed a group of trees that were even taller than the ones whose branches he was walking among. There were at least two dozen of them, leafy giants soaring at least a hundred paces into the skies. Ahren could see a large platform, seemingly floating between their mighty stems, and buzzing with elves. The ramp he was on led upwards to the platform and Ahren quickened his steps. The nearer he approached, the smaller he felt in the presence of the gigantic trees. He concentrated on the platform ahead and noticed after a time that it was not floating but was attached through a series of ropes that were variously attached upwards and downwards to the surrounding enormous trees. There were well over two hundred elves scurrying around the platform going about their business, and most of them seemed to be artisans. This had to be the centre of the elf city.

Ahren rapidly ascended the ramp, and he noticed that the layer of material, out of which the platform was constructed, was the thickness of his forearm and the material was intertwined in complicated patterns. He reached the top of the ramp and stopped at the edge of the circular surface

314

to get an overview of the scene playing out in front of him. There were elves everywhere, sitting or standing, performing the most varied of tasks, and strange sounds and smells permeated the air. There were some trades he recognized immediately: weavers, tailors, cooks and tanners. But he also saw trades that clearly involved magic. Two dozen paces away he saw a group of six elves who were working a lump of metal together. Where one human or dwarf would have used a hammer, an anvil and a roaring fire, here five of the elves sang to the lump of metal while the last she-elf formed the metal into a long blade with her hands, stroking the material again and again, warping it ever so slightly with each gentle stroke. Finally, the blade was finished and the song faded to a whisper. Ahren unwittingly moved closer, still wanting to hear the sound of the elf voices. The woman blacksmith now ran her finger nail over the surface of the blade and scored patterns and signs on both sides of the metal before she paused and the whispering ceased. Ahren was sure the workers were finished when suddenly the five singers held hands and began to sing full-throatedly. The woman smith held the blade on her outstretched hands and slowly turned around in the middle of the circle, looking each singer in the eye for several heartbeats. A silver shimmer covered the blade for a moment, then the singing stopped and all six sank onto the floor and into a deep sleep, the blade still resting on the hands of the woman smith. This seemed most unusual to Ahren and he looked around to see if anyone had taken notice of this unusual scene. With the exception of a few approving looks however, nobody batted an eyelid.

Ahren shook his head and walked on. He saw at least seven further elf groups lying on the floor and sleeping. Quiet song seemed to accompany all of the more difficult actions that were being performed here. Not alone did he see blacksmiths, but also potters, carpenters and bowyers, surrounded by up to a dozen elves who were giving them magical support. Now the young man understood the elf tales the other peoples had related. Magic seemed to come so naturally to them that they used it to make even the easiest tasks simpler. Ahren was actually quite thankful that his was the case. The thought of a blacksmith's fire on a platform made from cloth which was seventy paces in the air was quite terrifying to him. He strolled on, looking at all sorts of magical handcrafting, until he finally saw familiar faces. Falk and Jelninolan were sitting together in the middle of the platform and deep in conversation. They would probably send him away but he wanted to say hello at least and ask what was going to happen next. As he neared them, they looked up and their serious demeanours disappeared.

'Sit down, Ahren', said the elf priestess with a warm smile and Falk grunted in approval. Ahren did as he was told, all the while watching in fascination how an elf, three paces away, was manufacturing glass. He put his hands into a bowl of sand, while the other three elves overlayed a magic spell through their song. The first elf pulled out his hands, holding a lump of soft glass which he skillfully manipulated into a goblet. On the ground beside him were over two dozen other goblets, all exactly alike. Ahren pointed over at the trades-people and said in astonishment, 'nobody will believe the wonders I have seen since stepping on to this platform'.

Jelninolan chuckled and said, 'we must come across as very pretentious, showing off our magical abilities so intensely, and in public. If truth be told, there hasn't been an elf born yet that has had more than the most rudimentary skill in using a hammer'.

Ahren looked over at his master in puzzlement, who laughed loudly when he saw the young man's face.

'She isn't exaggerating. All elves are very talented in magic, but they are truly awful as classical hand-workers', he explained.

316

The priestess giggled again but then became serious. 'You have to understand we are a people guided completely by feelings. That's reflected in our magic and in all our dealings. If we feel the materials, we can create amazing things using our bare hands, but if we have to use a tool, we lose this direct connection and the results are…not very impressive. Magic is our tool. Our workers in magic always work in groups, as you can see'.

Ahren nodded towards the sleeping group. 'And what about them? I saw the same with the woman smith earlier. There are a lot of people sleeping, considering it's a workshop'.

There was a touch of disapproval in his voice.

The elf responded calmly. 'That's presumably why the rumour exists that we elves are lazy and lie around in the sun all day. Our magic is exhausting and we invest all our feelings into the things we create. It wouldn't work otherwise. It's energy-sapping and we get tired quickly. I think our average craftsperson works about two hours a day. But we create more in that time than others do in ten hours. So, we're quite satisfied with that'.

Ahren looked thoughtfully over at the sleeping figures until he was brought back to the present by Falk's calloused hand as it slapped the back of his head.

'Don't think now that you can be lying around in the sun too. Make yourself useful instead and go find your wolf. Time is running out and we should head off this afternoon', grunted the old man.

'Head off? Where?' asked Ahren, disappointed. 'We came here to find an Einhan for you' replied his master, 'and to take an elf artifact with us that we will need for the ritual. Unfortunately, it's not here, but deeper in the forest'. At this point Falk gave Jelninolan a poisonous look and she looked back at him scornfully.

'Don't look at me like that. It was the Voice of the forest that decided. You know full well I cannot go against the Voice'.

Falk harrumphed and looked away. It looked as though trouble was brewing between the two of them so Ahren stood up in order to look for Culhen. Then he paused for a moment and asked, 'who is going to be my Einhan?' Jelninloan smiled at him and said, 'I will be your advocate of course, And now go look for your wolf before he hides himself in the forest to escape from over-boisterous elf children. Take the ramp back there, after two hundred paces there's a descent to the ground. He should be around there somewhere'.

Proud that the elf priestess considered him worthy to become the thirteenth Paladin, Ahren turned around and followed the route indicated. Every so often he would stop and look in amazement at another wonder being created by the craft-elves. Now that Ahren knew the background, he found the process less mystical but all the more enterprising. The elves certainly knew how to compensate for their natural limitations through the use of magic. He was even more cheerful now he knew that Jelninolan would be accompanying them. Their task would certainly be made easier by the presence of another friendly soul to combine with Selsena's on their journey. He left the platform and soon found the ramp that led him downwards. Once he was on the forest floor, he immediately looked for signs of the wolf and found them immediately. The young wolf's paw prints, which were now very big, could be seen everywhere. It seemed he had been playing with some of the children again. The challenge was to find the tracks that indicated where he was now among the prints left by the children jumping here and there, not to mention the ones that simply went around in circles. Ahren followed a track that went around a tree in an ever-increasing circle before it led into the forest. After some minutes he heard an excited whimpering and yowling. He knew the sound. His friend must have flushed out some game which had retreated to the safety of a tree. That always frustrated Culhen and then he would make this grumbly whimpering sound, as if he wanted the world to know the injustice of it all - that wolves couldn't climb trees - although the best food was to be found up there.

Ahren reached the Blood Wolf within a few heartbeats. Culhen glanced briefly over his shoulder before fixing all his attention on the tree again and continuing with his grumbling and whimpering. The young Forest Guardian looked up the tree to see if he could find the cause of his friend's discomfort. Several man-lengths above him he saw something move. There was something dark perched on one of the lower branches and it seemed to be doing something to the stem. Ahren couldn't make out its shape and he whispered absently to Culhen, 'what have you flushed out there, my friend?' He squinted his eyes in an attempt to make out some details.

Much to his surprise, the potential prey seemed to have heard his quiet words. It turned its long, narrow head towards him and glanced at him with its smouldering red eyes. It had a hooked, blackish-red beak which ended in a razor-sharp point. It gave a short warning chatter before turning back to its original position and Ahren again saw its amorphous, black outline, which he now identified as a dull, leathery back.

He slowly went down on one knee and put his arm around Culhen in order to quieten the wolf, all the while trying to breathe calmly.

It was a Swarm Claw. He would recognize them anywhere, ever since the night in the hostelry. What was a servant of the Betrayer doing in the elf forest? According to Falk, they didn't dare come here. But here was one, sitting up in that tree and ignoring him. Suddenly a terrible thought struck him. What if the bird wasn't alone?

He began to check the surrounding trees for more of them, all the while instinctively holding his breath. He was terrified at the thought that he may have wandered into the middle of a swarm of them and that dozens of sharp beaks could rip into his flesh. It would be a pretty unedifying end to his brief career as a Forest Guardian.

Luckily, the bird seemed to be on its own. Ahren gave a sigh of relief and slowly began to move backwards. But Culhen whimpered quietly and remained rooted to the spot. Ahren gave the wolf an agonized look and then looked back up at the black outline in the tree. Of course, he should do something against the Dark One, but he had left his bow and armour at the lodgings. It had never crossed his mind that he would have to fight here in the elf forest. He only had his hunting knife. True to his word he had never left the house again without his short knife. He slept with it, ate with it, even went to the privy with it. The only problem was, if he wanted to take action, he would have to tackle an enemy with his knife. An enemy who was a dozen paces up and who could fly. He needed a plan and he needed more information. He circled the tree as slowly and as quietly as possible until he was to the side of the Swarm Claw and able to make out what the animal was doing up there.

There was a knothole in a massive branch of the tree, and the beak was constantly disappearing inside, hacking away at something. The Swarm Claw was on the hunt. Ahren watched for a few heartbeats and considered the situation. He was confused. According to Vera's books and Falk's lessons, Swarm Claws caught their prey by swooping on them in an ambush. They would skewer the smaller victims in their sharp claws and carry them away. They would bore through the larger prey with their beaks, mainly attacking the eyes and throat. This hunting pattern was unusual, as were the facts that the animal was here and alone. Whatever was in this tree, it was irresistible to this monstrous bird.

Ahren bit his lips and considered his options. It would probably take too long for him to go and get his bow. The same applied to looking for help. Allowing the Dark One to escape was an option but the thought of appearing before his master without having done anything was unbearable to the young man. Anyway, the Swarm Claw had seen him and if he got away, then all the Dark Ones that were hunting him and his companions would know exactly where to find the travellers. The Swarm Claw had to die, preferably before it killed its prey. At the moment it was pre-occupied but once it had what it wanted it would doubtless take flight. Ahren drew his hunting knife and weighed it in his hand. Falk had practised knife-throwing with him, but only over very short distances if he couldn't use the bow, and always as a last resort.

'Throwing a knife is the same as disarming yourself', his master liked to say. It was highly unlikely that Ahren could fatally injure a Swarm Claw with a top-heavy hunting knife at a distance of twelve paces, and in an upward direction. He would be more likely to hit it with a stone, but that would disturb rather than injure the Dark One. Maybe the bird would then attack him rather than flee. Both options were not particularly attractive to the young Forest Guardian. That left one other option – Ahren would have to climb up and take the animal by surprise. Not the best plan, but the only one. He couldn't climb up the trunk. The animal would see and hear him coming. It would have to be a neighbouring tree.

Ahren had a quick look around and found a suitable candidate. It was an older tree, its trunk nicely gnarled with plenty of grip, and one of its branches grew high enough for Ahren to be able to attack the bird from above with a leap. He quickly imagined all the things that could possibly go wrong in this enterprise, but a weak squeak from the knothole told him that time was running out. The Swarm Claw's prey was tiring. It was now or never.

A crouching run got him as far as the old tree and he climbed it quickly, always careful that the trunk would be between him and the other tree, where the Dark One was increasing its efforts to catch its prey. In little more than ten heartbeats, he was at the same height as the Swarm Claw. He climbed a little further up the trunk and then began to move around it as quietly as possible. Finally, he saw the branch he had selected when he was on the ground, and stretched his whole body so that he could pull himself up to it in one fluid movement. Squatting, and on his stomach, he slowly began to push himself forwards into the leafy, younger part of the foliage that grew at the end of the branch, which would bring him to within two paces of the Dark One. The aromatic, slightly resinous smell of the leaves wafted into his nostrils, and the comfortably gnarled, barky structure of the wood gave him a stable hold. The trees in this forest were perfect for climbing, and Ahren understood once again the deep love his master felt for this place.

These thoughts dissipated as soon as the prey squeaked again, and Ahren carefully stood up on the branch, now no thicker than his thigh. He could just make out the Swarm Claw's leathery skin through the leaves, about a man's length under him and one pace away. It had now stuck its head completely into the hole as it sought to finish the hunt. Without thinking of what he was going to do next, Ahren drew his hunting knife, prepared himself, and leaped, planning to land behind the Dark One on the branch, hold on to the branch with one hand, and stab with the other.

But when he landed on the branch behind the Swarm Claw, he realized that he had jumped too far. He fell on his knees, slipped from the branch with hand outstretched and was in danger of falling. With the greatest of difficulty, he managed to get into a squatting position on the shaking branch with the help of his free hand, and clasped the hunting knife with his other hand.

The bird had meanwhile used the time to pull its head out of the hole and turned with a light hop. It seemed to be mocking the young Forest Guardian as he tried desperately to find his balance. The Swarm Claw spread its leathery wings in a threatening manner and swung its razor-sharp beak with lightning quick movements back and forth. Any normal bird would have taken flight at this point but the Dark One was having none of it. Ahren squatted lower and eventually managed to regain his balance, when the Swarm Claw's beak lunged forward, almost catching his knee. He quickly brought his dagger between himself and his opponent. He forced himself to breathe deeply and fixed the bird with his watchful eyes, swinging the blade in easy circles here and there. For his own part, Ahren was being stared at by one fixed, red eye. The Swarm Claw had tilted its head to one side and was following the movements of the weapon.

The two unequal opponents watched each other cagily, each ready to pounce on the other's mistake. The attack on his knee showed Ahren the evil intelligence of the beast. The beak didn't need to reach his face or his neck. It would be enough if he fell. Many people had fallen victim to the Dark Ones because they had only seen them as wild animals, but the will of the Betrayer, who had forced himself on them, meant they were not only larger and faster, but also cleverer and more brutal. It was these differences that made these creatures so dangerous. Ahren had already experienced this during the fight with Culhen's mother, and also in the battle with the Fog Cats in Deepstone, but nowhere had he seen this so clearly and intensively as here, on this tree, in this duel of the eyes with a bird that would send him to his death if he made the smallest mistake.

Fifty heartbeats passed by and neither of them moved, only the arm with the knife weaved its defensive dance between them. The bird sat there as if frozen until Ahren had to shift his weight to relieve his protesting muscles. The blade swung to the side for a heartbeat as he turned his foot and suddenly the Swarm Claw was transformed into an explosive hail of beak thrusts. Ahren parried the attacks instinctively but had to endure two painful cuts to his left arm. Neither of them was particularly dangerous, but they bled enough to make his knife hand slippery and they would weaken him if the duel dragged on.

The Swarm Claw was stock still again and looking at him with its smouldering eye, waiting for his next mistake. The young Forest Guardian feverishly considered his options, but he just couldn't think of a way out of this dilemma. The Dark One was just as fast as he was, its small size was an advantage on this narrow branch, and even its beak was slightly longer than his blade, so his longer reach wasn't an advantage. And he also had to protect his knees, which stuck out towards the bird because of the way he was squatting. The cuts in his forearm were burning, and so he was left with only one option. He would have to stab once with all his might, right into the Dark One's breast and hope that the Swarm Claw wouldn't injure him to the point where he'd fall from the tree.

Ahren gathered himself together and sank his doubts and fears into the Void, then tensed every muscle in his body as he prepared for the lunge. His opponent noticed the change and slowly began to spread its wings to go into attack mode. Ahren knew now that the element of surprise was gone so he prepared for the worst and threw himself forward on to the Swarm Claw and towards its terrifying beak.

The bird was about to react but suddenly there was a most terrifying, bloodcurdling howl from the foot of the tree that petrified any animal within a radius of five lengths. Ahren too would have flinched but for the fact that he was already in mid-flight, and so it was only the Swarm Claw that reacted, looking briefly to its side at the howling Culhen. It hesitated for less than half a heartbeat, but that was enough for Ahren's blade to land with a heavy thud, and it bore into the monster's chest as far as the hilt. The beast swung its beak back but it was too late. Quick as a flash, Ahren let go of the grip and the bird fell from the tree, wildly hacking all around it and trying to hit out with its claws until it fell into Culhen's waiting fangs and was torn to shreds by the angry wolf. Ahren collapsed onto his stomach, his arms and legs dangling on either side of the branch as he slowly returned from the Void, breathing deeply and trying to calm his shaking body.

He looked gratefully down at Culhen who was busily tearing the Swarm Claw apart. He enjoyed the coolness of the branch on his cheek and the aromatic smells of the forest in his lungs. He silently thanked the THREE for the fact that he was still alive, then slowly picked himself up. Faint sounds and a tiny movement in the knothole reminded him that the Swarm Claw had been hunting something. It seems that its victim had survived. He pushed himself forward slowly. He had had enough confrontations with animals while balancing on a branch for one day. He turned his attention to the opening in the tree and he was struck by its frayed, irregular edging. He could see nicks everywhere and it took him a moment to understand what he was looking at. The Swarm Claw had widened the opening with its beak so it could push further inside. The actions of the monster were proving to be ever more peculiar and Ahren hoped that it hadn't been infected with a disease, now that a large part of it had ended up in Culhen's stomach.

He glanced down and saw that his friend was rolling around in the grass, trying to get the blood off before patiently starting to lick his fur clean. He then directed his attention back to the mistreated knothole and peeked carefully into it. Two curious eyes above a few shivering whiskers looked back at him. In front of him was a chipmunk with a nasty gash on one side of his fur.

An *elf* chipmunk, Ahren silently corrected himself. The fur was white, the stripes and eyes, silvery. SHE WHO FEELS had a weakness for this combination of colours, thought Ahren, amused. The little animal made angry noises at him and he placed his uninjured hand, which had no specks of blood, carefully into the hole so that it could become familiar with his smell. He wasn't sure how bad the injury was, but there was no way he was going to leave the animal there to die after he had just risked his own life in his fight with the Swarm Claw.

He decided he would leave out the chipmunk when he reported back to Falk and concentrate instead on maintaining the secrecy of their whereabouts as his reason for killing the Dark One. That sounded much more heroic and there would be less likelihood of his master and Uldini collapsing into fits of laughter.

The chipmunk sniffed around at his hand, then jumped without hesitation onto his palm and curled up. Ahren raised his eyebrows in surprise.

'Are you somebody's pet?' he whispered quietly. He slowly drew his hand back and looked down at the tiny animal. It was difficult to examine him up here and it was hard enough to climb down with an injured arm, let alone holding a chipmunk as well. With soothing sounds, he placed the animal in the inside of his jerkin and began his slow descent. His injured arm was painful and the blood made the tree slippery, and he couldn't lean against the tree-trunk for fear of squashing the chipmunk. It took him ten times longer than normal to get to the forest floor and by the time he got there he was bathed in sweat.

Culhen was waiting for him with his tail wagging, and began sniffing at his jerkin excitedly. Ahren couldn't help smiling and gently pushed his head away.

'Leave the tiny tot alone. He'll hardly want to see an over-enthusiastic Blood Wolf after being attacked by a Swarm Claw'.

Culhen sat down on his hind paws and gave the young Forest Guardian a reproachful look. Ahren became serious, went down on one knee and pressed his head into his friend's furry shoulder.

'Thank you for your help', he murmured. 'You saved my life today'.

Culhen turned his head and licked his master's face, then pressed his nose into Ahren's jerkin again. The young man shook his head and turned away, rolling back the torn sleeve on his injured forearm.

'Here, stop frightening our guest and make yourself useful'. Ahren held his cuts in front of the wolf, who sniffed at them for a moment before beginning to lick Ahren's forearm and hand clean. The animal's tongue burned like fire, but Falk and he had made the amazing discovery in the previous few months that Culhen's saliva had a cleansing effect on cuts and abrasions. Blood Wolves had a reputation for recovering quickly from wounds, but nobody had known how exactly they did it. His master was amazed to learn that there was something as profane as medicinal saliva. Culhen finished his work and began once again to sniff for the chipmunk. Now that his injured arm had been taken care of, Ahren reached carefully into his shirt and took out the shy animal, indicating to Culhen with his other arm that he should keep his distance. He held the chipmunk in front of his face and examined the cut he had noticed above in the animal's flank. There was one good thing about the Swarm Claws' razor-sharp beaks. The cuts were clean and the wound edges even. Normal claws would tear and fray the skin making treatment much more difficult and they would take longer to heal. A quick glance at his arms revealed that his wounds had already been transformed into fine, red lines, and a thin crust was beginning to grow on them. Culhen's saliva seemed to thicken the blood somehow, which enabled them to close up sooner. But that was as far as it went. Now the wounds had to continue to heal normally.

Ahren turned his attention back to the little animal in his hand. It was lying on its uninjured side and seemed to be very weak. All of its left side was soaked in blood. The cut was not deep but very long, from its hind leg up to its left ear. Ahren chewed the inside of his cheek uncertainly while he considered what to do next.

He then spoke in a determined and urgent voice.

'Culhen, listen to me now. You won't eat this little fellow, will you? I know he looks really tasty but it would be terrible to rescue him first only to gobble him up later, don't you agree? But you can sniff him and give him a good lick, what do you think?'

The Blood Wolf had tilted his head sideways and his eyes hadn't left the chipmunk while he licked his chops. The young Forest Guardian hoped that his friend would react at the very least to his stern tone of voice. He slowly put his protective arm to the side and held the injured animal in front of Culhen's mouth, still speaking to the Blood Wolf. If Culhen's saliva didn't seal the wound, then the little animal would die anyway, so it was worth the risk. Ahren had always asserted that the Blood Wolf understood more than simple commands even though Falk was sceptical. Now he'd find out if he had been right. The wolf sniffed at his potential prey and licked his chops again. Ahren spoke in a sterner voice and finally his friend's head shot forward and sank over the helpless animal. The pink tongue, just as big as the rodent, licked the stripy body a couple of times and then Culhen sat back on his hind legs and looked up at Ahren with his head tilted.

'Good wolf!' cried Ahren and tickled his friend euphorically behind the ears, while still looking at the little patient. The animal was either sleeping or had fainted in panic, but the cut looked good and the blood was already coagulating. He would have to nurse his patient back to health for one or two days perhaps, but then he would be able to let him loose in the wild again with a good conscience. Ahren stood upright, stroked Culhen's head again and headed back along the path towards the village.

The walk back was exactly as he imagined his entire stay in a protected elf forest would be. The singing of birds and the fluttering of leaves filled the air, a multitude of smells enlivened his steps and the soft forest floor turned the walk into a most enjoyable perambulation. The peace which he had felt inside him on their arrival was back again, and Ahren noticed that he had taken the longer walk through the forest, which led to the ramp bringing them to the guest quarters. He wanted to get changed anyway before meeting up with Falk and his little stripy friend urgently needed something to eat in order to regain its strength. He came to their dwelling with the sun well past its zenith and he knew that Falk would be getting impatient. He quickly put on a new jerkin as well as his leather armour and also took his bow, swearing to himself never again to leave the weapon out of sight, just because he thought he was in a safe place. His encounter with the Swarm Claw would have been over in two heartbeats if he had had his bow with him.

He opened his rucksack with a shake of his head and set about making a little nest out of his ripped shirt, which he put on top of his other things. He carefully laid the sleeping chipmunk inside and closed the rucksack again but without pulling the straps so that enough light and air could get in. As long as Ahren walked at a leisurely pace and didn't start to run with the rucksack, the little fellow would be warm and comfortable inside, and once he was strong enough, he could dart off whenever he felt like it. Ahren went over to the fruit bowl and scrabbled around until he found some nuts that had gathered at the bottom of the bowl. He laid them beside the chipmunk's nose, carefully closed the rucksack again, put it on his shoulders and went out into the sunshine. Pleased with himself, he hummed a tune and tickled Culhen's fur absently and wondered to himself where they would be going next. The guest lodgings had been emptied of everything except for his own belongings which meant that the others had collected their things already, since Falk wasn't reckoning that they would be returning there again. Now that he knew the way, it wasn't long before he was back on the central platform, where new groups of elves were now practising their trades. Ahren could see many of the morning's trade people slumbering peacefully on the floor. A vase was being created in a very impressive way beside where he was standing and he wanted to watch the whole creative process when he heard a sharp harrumph behind him. He spun around and there was Falk, his hands in fists on his hips and a face like thunder on him. There was no doubting his disapproval.

'Finished dawdling?'

His master was really angry and Ahren decided to play his trump card there and then.

'Culhen flushed out a Swarm Claw and I had to kill it before it could lead the other ones to us', he answered quickly.

Falk narrowed his eyes, his anger vanished and immediately he was in a state of high alert.

'We'd better discuss this in peace and quiet', he said and with a hand gesture indicated to his apprentice to follow him. The old man led Ahren silently to look for a free place. They walked through groups of

330

craftspeople who were working at their trades without seeming to follow any recognizable technique. Finally, Ahren saw the rest of his companions standing at the other end of the platform and looking at them expectantly. Ahren corrected himself, all of them except for Selsena. The Titejunanwa was visiting her herd as long as they were in the forest, and maintained constant telepathic communication with Falk.

Falk indicated to the group that they should follow him and so they silently descended the ramp and went a little further into the forest, the others continually throwing questioning looks at him and Ahren.

Finally, it was all too much for Uldini who stopped in his tracks. 'Alright you secret-monger, what's happened?'

Falk stopped too and turned around to the group. 'Perhaps Ahren should first explain calmly what he's experienced', he said thoughtfully and looked at the young man hopefully.

Ahren quickly recounted his encounter with the Swarm Claw and how he had slain it with his hunting knife while balanced on a branch and how Culhen had helped him.

After he had finished, Jelninolan gave him a supportive and congratulatory smile while Uldini patted Culhen's back and murmured, 'well done, my boy'.

Falk stared at his apprentice for a few heartbeats and then responded. 'You have a tendency to master a situation in the riskiest manner one can possibly imagine. We'll talk about that later. However, your decision not to let the Swarm Claw escape was correct. In fact, a whole swarm of the beasts came into the elf forest last night. The elves plucked them all from the sky, or so they thought. One of them must have given them the slip. I just don't understand why a whole swarm of Swarm Claws was sacrificed in order to determine our location. An attack in the elf forest is bound to fail. We're too well protected'.

'You forget that HE is in a deep sleep. HIS orders were probably quite imprecise', interjected Uldini.

Falk nodded hesitantly. Even if he wasn't quite convinced, he let it go at that. 'Be that as it may, we have to collect Tanentan, and then we need to move on'.

'Who's that?' asked Ahren curiously. At last he was going to find out more about their next step.

'Not who, but what', answered Jelninolan. 'It's an artefact of our goddess. In your language the name, roughly translated, means 'the soundless lute'. Our legends have it that SHE WHO FEELS taught the first elves with the help of Tanentan how they could live in unison with the world'.

Uldini joined in. 'The lute can manipulate feelings. I have a less romantic theory that the first elves were brought under control that way, until they had learned how to master their strong emotions. But the result is the same either way'.

Jelninolan gave Uldini a withering look, but the master magician rose in the young Forest Guardian's estimation, for he hadn't flinched when she had looked at him. Nevertheless, the little figure became silent and winked at Ahren instead.

'The problem is', continued Falk, 'that Tanentan was brought by command of the Voice of the Forest, to a safe place, which happens to be the Weeping Valley'.

Uldini groaned and rolled his eyes which made him look for all the world like a nine-year-old boy. He saw the questioning look on Ahren's face and explained, 'The Weeping Valley is the place where HE WHO FORCES first brought an animal under his control and corrupted it. Where the first Dark One was created.'

332

'The goddess was beside herself with rage and sorrow,' continued Jelninolan. 'In spite of her deep sleep, she furnished Eathinian with the protection that it has enjoyed to this day and ordered the elves to protect every animal living in the forest. The valley has lain shrouded in a light mist since that day and nobody is allowed to enter it. Unless the Voice of the Forest has given permission.'

Ahren was shaken by the story. It became clear to him that sometime, there must have been the first Dark One, but the fact that the location was known, made it somehow more real and more tangible. His encounter with the Swarm Claw and its cunning evil, which was hidden beneath its animal instincts, was still very much present. The thought that all these Dark Ones had once been normal animals that had been violently changed, filled him with a cold rage and a deeper determination to fulfil his task.

Falk had turned again and marched on, and nobody felt up to talking for a while. The sun had travelled a considerable distance before Ahren's curiosity got the better of him. 'Who is this Voice of the Forest, and why can't we simply ask for permission to enter the valley?' he asked.

Jelninolan gave a quick laugh and answered him in a warm-hearted tone. 'The Voice of the Forest is the mouthpiece of the goddess. HER wishes and feelings are passed on to us that way. She is the highest judge and at the same time the spiritual leader of all the elves. No important decisions are taken without her advice. Only rarely has it been elves, mostly they are animals, once it was even an old tree. Now it's a stag. The voice comes and goes as it pleases. No-one knows where it is at the moment'.

Falk added in a grumpy voice, 'You see we have a choice between wandering aimlessly through an enormous forest in search of a particular stag, or trying our luck with the Warden of the Weeping Valley. Seeing as time is not on our side, we've decided on the Warden.'

'A warden?' asked Ahren nervously. He didn't like the direction this conversation was taking one little bit.

'The Weeping Valley is one of the forbidden places for the elves,' answered Uldini while Falk and Jelninolan exchanged exasperated looks. 'These places are always protected by a warden, normally an animal that's under the special protection of the goddess,' he explained.

Ahren was silent as he digested the information, none of which made much sense. 'Why exactly do we need this lute at all?' he asked in a slightly annoyed voice.

Jelninolan looked at him in astonishment. 'You don't know anything about the ritual?'

There was such surprise in her voice that Ahren immediately defended himself. 'I know that we have to go to a certain place as quickly as possible, and we have to have a certain somebody with us. Oh, and since this morning, I've known that we need certain things as well.' Somehow his defence had turned into a complaint, but that didn't bother him. Falk's habit of keeping everything secret until the last minute was hard to put up with, especially when, like Ahren, you were the centre of everything that was going on.

His master was about to respond vehemently, but when he saw how stunned the elf priestess really was, he held back. 'It was just for his own protection', he finally mumbled and walked ahead briskly to create some distance between himself and the group.

The elf walked beside Ahren and put an arm on his shoulder.

'You poor fellow. Falk is so used to carrying so many secrets around with him, that he keeps everything to himself. I'll try to explain it to you'.

She looked at him from the side.

'You know that you were chosen?'

Ahren nodded. 'At the ceremony in the temple, which all the villagers considered an unimportant ritual'.

Jelninolan nodded. 'We thought that ritual out ourselves in order to find the missing Paladin. Imagine the Pall Pillar is gradually dissolving and no-one knows where the thirteenth Paladin is. We would have had to comb the world looking for you, and in the meantime, HE would be getting mightier and mightier. The Spring Ceremony was supposed to come across as irrelevant. Otherwise the Dark Ones would have been on your tracks even more quickly'.

Ahren shuddered briefly at the thought.

'In those days, the newborn of a Paladin would be touched with a godstone. It would then, through this so-called focus stone, begin to absorb the strength of the departing Paladin. The child would experience as happy a childhood as possible in order to preserve and nourish the goodness within. With the onset of adulthood came the Naming. This is the ritual that we now want to perform. The candidate had to present an advocate from the world of people, dwarves, and elves. This was necessary as only humans could be formed into a Paladin. The natures of dwarves and elves don't allow for such a drastic transformation, so a right to be heard was woven into the Naming ritual. No elf and dwarf advocate meant no Naming'.

Ahren nodded. 'The Einhan. Falk told me about it. And why are the objects needed?'

The priestess responded. 'In order that you couldn't just invite any old elf or dwarf to take part in the Naming ceremony, they had to present themselves with a holy artefact of their people to prove that they were worthy of being an Einhan'.

'Anyway, it's much easier to channel the blessings of the gods onto the chosen one if strong magical foci of the respective deities are present,' interjected Uldini with a dry smile.

Jelninolan spun around. 'Do you have to rubbish the romance and splendour for everybody?' she asked angrily.

Uldini raised his hands and gave a look of perfect innocence. 'Not at all, my dear auntie. I just wanted to make clear that some of the ritual comes from a certain necessity. Otherwise the next thing he would have asked would be if it were possible to leave out some of the formalities in view of the circumstances.'

Ahren held himself back from laughing. That question really had gone through his head and he winked at Uldini behind the elf's back. She had calmed down in the meantime and continued with her explanation.

'Anyway, where was I? Ah yes, the Naming. Uldini and his magic wand will be responsible for the human part, Tanentan and I will represent the elves. Regarding the dwarves though, that has me stumped. Dwarves are incapable of using magic, at least not in the proper meaning of the word, and I don't know any Arch Wizard I could contact. I can only describe the diplomatic relations between the elves and dwarves as indifferent coexistence, to put it kindly.' She looked over at Uldini with a questioning look.

He shook his head. 'I'm the Supreme Head of the council of seven. You know that they like wizards even less than elves. If I could do anything, I could try perhaps as an emissary of the emperor to obtain an audience with the King of Thousand Halls, but whether he'd listen to us…' Uldini trailed off, leaving the unfinished sentence hanging in the air and the two looked at each other in bafflement.

Suddenly Ahren burst out laughing. He hadn't laughed so heartily in a long time. He held his stomach and laughed until tears were streaming down his face. Culhen jumped around him excitedly with his tail wagging and seemed to be taking part in his friend's enjoyment, while the Arch Wizard and the elf priestess looked at each other dumbfounded.

'Maybe it *was* too much for him in one go', murmured Uldini and tapped his head knowingly, but Ahren waved dismissively.

Gasping for breath and trying to control his laughing, he managed to respond. 'You are a mighty wizard and an elf high priestess, both of you are ageless and on the council of the seven, but you're still as much in the dark as I am when it comes to Falk's plans. An old Forest Guardian is dictating to you how things are going to proceed and is leading you by the nose, just like he's doing to his young apprentice.'

His two companions looked so surprised and helpless when he said this that he broke into another bout of laughter. It could of course be true that all the events were too much for him, and that was why he was reacting hysterically, but by the THREE, it was good to know that even these mighty figures had their limits and could be kept in check by a grumpy, uncommunicative man.

Jelninolan smiled good-naturedly at Ahren and her face indicated that she understood the irony, but Uldini refused to let the matter rest. 'Falk!' he thundered in a magically enhanced voice, and with lightning speed he flew up to the Forest Guardian, who had been tramping ahead of them all this time.

Ahren managed to regain some control of his laughter and watched amused as Uldini gave his master an earful. He responded calmly with a short answer and then turned and continued walking. Uldini floated for a moment and stared at the Forest Guardian's back. Then yellow sparks started flying in all directions from it, blowing up dust from the forest floor. The wizard meanwhile returned to the others, all the while cursing to himself. As soon as a curse was uttered, a particularly bright flash would discharge on the ground. By the time he reached them, the flashes had disappeared but Uldini's eyes were still smouldering like yellow fire.

'What did he say? asked the elf.

'That we'd find out soon enough', said Uldini through gritted teeth.

Ahren was about to burst out laughing again when he saw Uldini's face. He knew, chosen one or not, that if he didn't pull himself together, he would spend that evening as a toad, so he bit his tongue and walked quickly ahead of them so that they would only see his shaking shoulders as he tried to suppress his laughter.

Chapter 20

They caught up with the old Forest Guardian that evening. He had set up camp beside a small pond. There were no insects on the water, and the fire had already burned down to its embers. Jelninolan raised her eyebrows quizzically but Falk pre-empted her.

'Only dead branches on the ground, it just burned for a short while, but we need the heat for our supper.' He took a bundle from the fire. Various vegetables that he had wrapped in the local leaves to protect them from the fire. Soon they were sitting together and eating in silence, each caught up in their own thoughts.

Ahren was ravenous and gobbled down his food, secretly glancing every so often at the others, while tickling Culhen, who was grumbling contentedly beside him. Nobody seemed to want to break the silence so Ahren decided to ask the first question that came into his head.

'How exactly are we going to get into the valley if it's forbidden? Are we going to fight with the Warden?'

Falk cleared his throat and looked over at him earnestly. 'It's not that simple. If we were to attack the Warden or to enter the valley illegally, we would have the elves on our backs. Not even Jelninolan can enter the Weeping Valley without the permission of the Voice. Only animals under the protection of the goddess are allowed in.'

'So, what are you planning?' Ahren persisted.

'We won't be going in, but Selsena will. She knows already and will be waiting for us there. She is under the protection of the goddess and so should be able to pass. Whether she can bring the lute back with her is another question. Hopefully this loophole in the law will be enough.

Otherwise she'll have to fight the Warden and we won't be able to help her'.

Jelninolan nodded, concurring. 'It would be a ritual duel between two creatures of the goddess. Nobody can intervene and everyone must respect the result.'

Falk spat into the embers. 'I don't like it. Too many hitches in the plan, and no way of supporting her should anything go wrong.'

The three began debating the issue again and they ended up going around in circles. Finally, they all settled down to sleep without having come up with a better idea.

Ahren was the first to wake after a restless night. He rubbed the sleep out of his eyes and quietly went over to his rucksack to see how his patient was getting on. The chipmunk was still there and had rolled himself up into a little ball of fur. He was fast asleep. Ahren could see that the cut was healing nicely. Half of the nuts had been eaten and it wouldn't be long before the animal would be well enough to fend for himself again. He closed up the rucksack, freshened up, and began, out of pure habit, to dismantle their sleeping quarters while the others slowly woke up. Falk nodded approvingly and then they had a cold breakfast of fruit before moving on.

According to Jelninolan they would reach the border of the Weeping Valley by midday. The morning's march was peaceful and quiet, each of the travellers mulling over things. The sun shone low through the leaves, there was a light mist hanging in the air like little spider-webbed flags fluttering among the trees. The air was aromatic and clear and Ahren was surprised again at how timeless this forest seemed to be. Spring, summer and autumn all seemed to combine into one season, keeping this forest in a state of perfect harmony.

Culhen jumped playfully beside him, running off into the forest every now and then when he got the scent of something exciting. Sometimes he returned with spoils, mostly not. Jelninolan didn't say anything, which suggested that he was permitted to hunt, as part of the endless natural cycle of hunter and prey.

They finally came to a slope which led down into a small valley. It was hardly more than a large depression, perhaps two hundred paces in diameter and didn't have many trees. Its surface was covered in a thick moss and several types of climbing plants were visible. A fine mist, hardly hindering their view, hung over the whole valley. It lay on the plants, and droplets constantly dripped to the ground from the leaves and branches. It was almost as if all the plants were in mourning.

'Before you lies the Weeping Valley,' said Falk quietly. 'Selsena should be with us any minute.'

The unicorn trotted up to them out of the undergrowth twenty heartbeats later and greeted them all with a friendly snort and a wave of welcoming joy. Ahren suspected that some of the tension of the previous few days had come about because Selsena hadn't been with them to exert her calming influence.

Jelninolan now spoke to the Elven horse. 'The lute is hanging on a tree in the middle of the valley'. She pointed at a speck and when Ahren screwed up his eyes and looked at the spot he could make out the outlines of the lute, which was hanging just three paces high on the trunk of a massive tree.

'It has a carrying strap you can wrap around your horn', the elf continued. Then she patted the Titejunanwa's flank and stood aside.

Falk looked her in the eyes. Whatever he was saying to her, he was communicating it silently. Selsena shook her head and snorted, then trotted down to the valley. Ahren instinctively held his breath and even

341

Culhen sat on his hind legs and watched their companion with his ears pricked, and his nose in the air as she went off. Everybody was stock still and after ten heartbeats, Falk slowly breathed out.

'So far, so good. Her presence doesn't seem to be presenting any problems. The critical point is coming now.'

The silver-white figure carried on until it arrived at the artefact. It was still quiet from within the valley. The only sound was the water drops falling from the plants to the ground. It was only now that Ahren noticed how quiet the place was. There wasn't a bird to be heard, not even in the part of the elf forest they were standing in now. Nor was there a breath of wind. As if the forest itself was holding her breath.

Selsena stood on her hind legs and stretched her horn against the trunk of the tree in order to slip the carrying strap onto it. Suddenly the ground around her moved.

Ahren wanted to shout a warning but the unicorn had already reacted. With two prancing steps she had escaped from the centre of the movement, and then Ahren saw what was moving. Moss was crumbling off shimmering green scales, where the Warden of the Valley of Weeping had been slumbering for years. Its tiny eyes on its large head were eyeing the intruder, and the enormous snake wrapped itself protectively around the tree and raised itself up. The animal was enormous. Its head alone must have been the same size as Ahren's upper body, and although more than half its body was entwined around the tree, the monster still towered four paces above Selsena and stared down at her. This monster made a terrifying impression but Ahren knew immediately that it wasn't one of the Dark Ones. Its whole presence suggested it was purely and simply a beast of prey. There was a purity and an animal vigour about this beast, unadulterated by the malevolent intelligence of a Swarm Claw or a Fog Cat. The sole point of this enormous snake was the protection of this

342

place and the eternal circle of hunter and prey. There was a certain dignity inherent in this clarity, and Ahren was sad that Selsena was forced into taking on this creature. It wasn't her enemy, it was just following its natural instincts. Selsena pranced towards the tree trunk and the snake's head immediately jerked down towards her and snapped. Ahren wasn't sure if the snake had missed its target or if it was just issuing a warning. He glanced at Falk and saw that his master didn't know either. Jelninolan had put a hand on his shoulder and Ahren was certain that it was only this silent reminder of the rules that prevented him from rushing in to help his companion. The Elven horse was now trotting around the snake in a circle, testing out its reactions and movements. The beast's head followed her every move while its scaly body wound easily around the tree trunk. Whenever Selsena tried to move as much as a hoof nearer, the snake's head would dart forward, warning her to keep her distance.

'Tell her she has to change her tactics,' muttered Uldini quietly. Falk showed no sign whether he had heard the advice, but two heartbeats later the Titejunanwa turned away and trotted back two dozen paces. Then she turned around and began to charge towards the snake.

Falk loudly drew breath and whispered, 'Risky, my girl, far too risky.' Soon she was within the enormous animal's reach. It had opened its mouth and revealed fangs the length of two short swords. Moss was being thrown up by the unicorn's hooves, the snake's head darted downward at lightning speed and for a moment it seemed to the onlookers that the two adversaries' forms had blended together.

Ahren screamed, for it seemed to him that the Warden had caught his friend. Then Selsena spun along the armoured body of the snake, gouging a deep tear into the green skin. Some of the scales came flying off and for the first time the snake emitted a deep, dangerous hiss. Selsena galloped on in order to get beyond her opponent's reach. The snake snapped after her, but the Elven horse was too fast for it.

'Very good. She's built up enough momentum to counter the Warden's speed, and the reptile can't bite her from the front without impaling itself on Selsena's horn.'

Ahren wasn't sure if Falk was trying to reassure his companions or himself, but he was thankful for his words because they gave him comfort and courage. Selsena turned again and prepared for another charge. The snake now extended itself to its maximum height and waited for her. The monster looked like an enormous swaying green tower eight paces high. Then it darted downwards towards the fragile looking unicorn. Once again there were scales flying everywhere, and once again Selsena shot out behind the massive body. Ahren could see the cuts his friend had scored on the scaly body with his naked eye. The longer of her two horns was dripping with blood and her whole bone-plate was a soaking red.

'How long can she keep up that speed?' asked Ahren quietly.

Falk looked at him with wild eyes. 'She'll manage it alright. The old girl can attack like that for four hours in a row without tiring.' He couldn't fail to hear the confidence in his master's voice and he began to relax just a little. The unicorn must have found a reliable method of defeating her enemy and now it was only a matter of persevering.

The snake, however, seemed to come to the same conclusion. Just as Selsena was about to launch another attack, it wound its way low between the trees and disappeared from the spectators' view.

'Damn it, where is it? A big animal like that can't just disappear into thin air,' called out Uldini nervously.

Jelninolan hissed at him to quieten down and responded, 'We're standing here at the very edge of its territory and the Warden is wounded

344

and testy. Perhaps we should try not to attract any unnecessary attention to ourselves.'

Falk instead answered the Arch Wizard's question. 'The animal has lived here for eons. It knows every tree, every bush, every leaf. Every natural pothole is a potential ambush and with these massive trees, every hollow tree trunk is a hiding place. Its scales are the same as the moss that grows here and if we're unlucky, it will have dug a few tunnels that we can't see from here. It knows now it has to catch Selsena by the side or from behind. Or from below. She has to get out of there as quickly as possible.'

Falk had automatically fallen into the dry tone he used whenever he was analysing the behavioural habits of a wild animal or a Dark One. The experienced Forest Guardian was speaking now, not the terrified companion. Ahren frantically asked himself how he or the others could help as he watched on helplessly and saw Selsena slowly and carefully approaching the tree trunk and the lute. There was no sign of the Warden and finally Selsena pushed her horn under the leather strap. She raised her head, the strap tautened, and she began to slowly raise the lute off the short branch from which the strap had been hanging. She was stretching just a little further forward awkwardly when suddenly Falk whispered quickly, 'There it is. It was waiting for this.' Then he gave a panic-stricken shout. 'Get rid of it! Get rid of it and run as fast as you can!'

The unicorn reacted immediately and lowered her head so that the instrument slid back into place.

At the same time the ground around the Titejunanwa exploded and the snake broke out from a shallow tunnel. Its head missed Selsena's neck by a hand's width but Ahren could hear the heavy thud as the massive head slammed into her left shoulder. Selsena neighed shrilly as the Warden tried to wrap itself around her.

Ahren looked on in horror at the terrible scene playing out in front of him. If Selsena couldn't get away from there immediately, she would be squeezed into a bloody pulp by the heavy body with its multiple tendons and muscles.

The unicorn leaped from a standing start over the snake's coils before it had a chance to tighten its deadly noose, but her hind legs crashed into the monster and hung there for a moment. Selsena gave a whinny of pain and flung herself around. She dashed away but it was clear she was limping badly. The snake immediately gave chase and it was obvious to all that the unicorn had lost her speed advantage. The Warden would catch her sooner rather than later

The Elven horse tried repeatedly to leave the valley but the Warden cut her off every time and the slope slowed the limping unicorn considerably.

Ahren looked pleadingly at the others but all he could see was pure frustration in their faces. His thoughts were racing as he dug his hands into Culhen's fur, so his friend could support him at this terrible moment. Then the young man froze.

'Jelninolan, only an animal blessed by the goddess can go down there?'

She looked at him sadly. 'That's right, we can't help her'.

Now he was really excited. Selsena didn't have much time, but he needed the right answers to know if his plan could be successful.

'And you're a high priestess of the goddess and you spoke THEIR blessing over Culhen on the first day so that the other elves would accept him, am I right?'

'Yes, of course, but he isn't big enough to last more than a few seconds against the snake', interjected Falk, his voice filled with frustration.

346

Ahren clapped his hands. 'But he doesn't have to!'

He whispered something to his friend and slapped him on the back. Like a white thunderbolt the wolf shot straight into the valley with Ahren urging him on frantically.

Falk stared at him flabbergasted. 'What in the name of all THREE are you doing there? You can't sacrifice *him*?'

Ahren didn't look away from his friend, even though, out of the corner of his eye he could see that the duel between snake and unicorn was coming towards a sad ending. Everything depended on his plan now. And on Culhen.

After a few seconds it became clear to the others that the wolf wasn't racing for the snake, but for the place where the lute was still hanging.

Ahren pulled himself back into the Void, took his bow from his shoulder and placed the arrow in position. He ignored the surprised protests of his companions and concentrated completely on the narrow strip of leather, that he could sense rather than see. The young Forest Guardian had only one chance and the timing had to be perfect. Culhen would need as much time as possible. Just as the wolf arrived under the tree and was preparing to jump at full speed, Ahren let the arrow fly and watched its path with bated breath. The wolf leaped up, turning his body in the air so that he could run back as soon as he landed.

If the arrow missed its target, it would injure his friend and the Warden would certainly catch the shot animal. Everything seemed to be happening in slow motion until the missile slammed into the trunk above Culhen. The leather strap broke with an audible snap and the artefact fell towards the ground, right between the open fangs of the leaping wolf. He snapped the throat of the instrument between his teeth, landed on the ground and began racing back to the edge of the valley, with the lute sticking out of his mouth like a grotesque version of a hunter's quarry.

'I don't believe it', groaned Falk.

Uldini and Jelninolan joined in with Ahren's encouraging cries.

The Warden's reaction was lightning quick and focused. It immediately abandoned Selsena and raced, sliding along the forest floor, towards Culhen.

The monster was indeed faster than the wolf with the cumbersome lute in his mouth, but on account of his manoeuvre under the tree, the wolf was already on the home stretch. The advantage that the young wolf had was enormous and he raced as quickly as he could towards his fellow travellers, who spurred him on with their cries.

Selsena in the meantime had retreated to the safety of the elf forest and limped out of sight among the trees. Culhen was now twenty paces away, with the snake another twenty paces further back. Ahren stood at the edge of the valley and pulled Jelninolan beside him. The distance between apprentice, wolf and snake was vanishing and Ahren prayed to all the gods, all the while calling to Culhen and beckoning him. He stretched his arms out to the wolf and when the animal was almost on top of them, he ripped the instrument out of his mouth and rammed it into the elf priestess's waiting arms. Culhen shot by him, the snake in hot pursuit.

Purposefully.

On its mission.

The young man threw himself between the snake and the wolf, stretched one arm out towards the Warden and pointed with the other one to the lute in Jelninolan's arms.

'STOP!' he roared at the top of his voice while the massive, scaly body swayed over him, filling up Ahren's entire field of vision. The head swung back, the body was coiled and ready to spring, a couple of hand widths from the valley's edge.

348

'STOP!' roared Ahren again. 'Your task is finished. The lute has left the valley and is now in elf hands!'

The snake hissed at him threateningly and soared like a wave of scales over him, ready to squeeze him into a pulp within a heartbeat. Then its silvery eyes slid slowly over towards the lute and then down to the valley's edge that lay between them. Then the Warden was stock still for three heartbeats, before it turned and slid slowly back down into the valley, as if the events of the previous few minutes had never happened.

Ahren turned in a daze towards the others and said, 'it wasn't a Dark One. It's nice when your opponent sticks to the rules for a change.'

Then he sank to his knees, threw his arms around the wolf and buried his face in Culhen's fur as tears of relief streamed down his face.

There was silence for a while, broken only by Ahren's sobs until finally he heard Uldini asking in a dry tone, 'Is the boy alright?'

'It will all be just fine,' he heard his master saying with amusement. 'The last time he fainted. This is a considerable improvement.'

Ahren couldn't help chuckling when he heard that, and he lifted his tear-stained face up from his friend's fur, the friend he had almost sent to his death. Culhen licked his face and wagged his tail. Ahren had to chuckle again, then pulled himself up and turned to the others.

Falk looked both proud and serious, before giving him an appreciative nod. Uldini smiled his typical half-smile. Jelninolan was completely wrapped up in her examination of the lute, which she held in her arms like a baby.

Ahren still didn't trust his voice, so he cleared his throat before asking, 'Selsena?'

Falk smiled briefly, and he answered, 'A few bruises and aching bones. Nothing that won't heal quickly, especially with her herd taking care of her. She'll be right as rain in a couple of days.'

Ahren breathed a sigh of relief and stroked Culhen's head again. Somehow, he just wasn't able to let go of the wolf.

Once it was clear that the young Forest Guardian was in control of his emotions again, Uldini asked, 'How did you know that it would break off its attack?'

Ahren shrugged his shoulders and answered. 'I figured it out. Culhen has been blessed, so he was allowed to enter the valley. He didn't attack the Warden so there wasn't any ritual duel between the two of them, which would have allowed the snake to continue its attack outside the valley. Its job was to keep the artefact from falling into unworthy hands. I was counting on Jelninolan being considered worthy, so the task was to get the lute over here quickly and within the restrictions that had been laid down. I never expected the Warden to leave Selsena alone immediately, I only hoped it would break off from the fighting once the lute was out of the valley.'

Ahren began shaking again and dug his hands into Culhen's fur. 'The rest was luck,' he whispered.

Falk scratched his beard and looked thoughtfully at Ahren. 'A damn big risk you took there – but I'm glad you took it. Although you bent every single rule to its limit. Hopefully the other elves will see the matter the same way as the Warden.'

Uldini added drily, 'we'll find out soon enough.'

Three slim figures in leather armour approached them with their bows cocked and stared grimly at the lute in the priestess's hands.

Jelninolan whispered quietly to her companions, 'We'll offer no resistance. Everything can be interpreted in our favour up to this point but if we attack the valley's Honour Guards, we lose all legitimacy.' Then she stepped forward and gave a little bow, before trying to reason with the three elf warriors with authority in her voice.

350

They listened with stern looks and answered briefly, but their bows remained cocked and aimed at the group.

The whole conversation was in Elfish and so Ahren didn't understand a word. He leaned over to Uldini and asked him quietly, 'I thought Jelninolan was the high priestess of the goddess. Why are they threatening her?'

Uldini kept his eyes on the four talking figures. 'They don't value titles the way humans do. They would never think of giving someone an advantage on account of their position, especially not if they think a wrong has been done. I would even say that they are stricter with dignitaries. Elves are emotional creatures and community is sacred to them. If someone in a vital position damages this cohesion, it has far-reaching effects on their society.'

Nerve-wracking moments passed as the elves continued their discussion. The three finally lowered their bows and divided themselves up among the travellers. Jelninolan turned to the others and explained the situation in a sad voice. 'They will accompany us back. According to them, the Voice of the Forest must decide whether we are in the right or not. I'm sorry, but we can't travel for now.'

Falk frowned and Uldini let out a quiet curse.

'What does that mean?' asked Ahren.

'It means,' said Falk between gritted teeth, 'that we have to sit here until a white stag gallops into town and decides whether we should live or die.'

The little group spent the rest of the day trotting back to the elf settlement. It was no surprise that the mood was grim. Nobody talked. Ahren tried to ask one or two more questions but he was fobbed off with one syllable answers. On one occasion he tried to get Culhen to slip away into the undergrowth so that at least his friend would be safe, but one of their elf guards immediately pointed an arrow at the wolf. It seemed Culhen's role in the recovery of the artefact was too crucial to simply let him escape.

Ahren shook his head in frustration. On the one hand, the elves were exactly as he had expected, openhearted and hospitable, with warm dispositions and full of magical skills. On the other hand, he found the passion with which they rigidly adhered to every little rule unsettling. When he thought of the way they had banished his master for centuries, he even considered these creatures to be cold and alien.

He found these contradictory impressions hard to grasp and he finally concluded with a sigh that he was trying to apply human qualities to a non-human folk. If he was ever to evaluate the reactions of these emotional forest dwellers, he would have to be far more open towards their otherness, if it ever came to it. He couldn't really imagine that the Voice of the Forest would condemn them to death, but it was bad enough that the elves were withholding the artefact from them, and so they couldn't complete the ritual in which he would be named Paladin. Mind you, he was basing this assumption on purely human empirical values and so his thoughts went round and round in circles until they finally set up camp for the night.

Everyone was chewing on the dried fruit the guards had handed out to them, and Ahren stared out into the forest, lost in thought. Darkness fell and the sparse snippets of conversation slowly petered out. Ahren was about to snuggle down under his blanket when he noticed a change in the lighting conditions. Something luminous was approaching them through the trees. He looked uneasily across at the others, but they were just exchanging curious looks.

'A Rillan?' asked Uldini and the elf priestess nodded.

'It seems to be for me', she said.

Ahren saw a luminous blue-white sphere flying directly towards Jelninolan. It didn't seem to bother anyone, not even the guards, so Ahren relaxed and looked with curiosity to see what would happen.

The elf raised her hand until her palm touched the outside of the sphere, at which point it dispersed leaving an iridescent pattern in the air. Ahren saw that all eyes were trained on the sign and it was being studied very carefully. It was clear to Ahren that it had to be some kind of elf hieroglyphics. It was a magic message!

Then the elf dropped her arm sadly and the message was gone.

'The Voice of the Forest was found by a hunter from the village. It seems it passed on in the cycle of life some weeks ago.'

It was clear to Ahren that these words were meant for him because everyone else had been able to read the message, but he didn't understand what it meant. His confusion must have been obvious because Falk cleared his throat and said, 'the Voice of the Forest is selected by the goddess in a seemingly arbitrary manner. Mostly it's an animal, sometimes an elf or even a tree. No matter who or what has been selected, the life expectancy or the living conditions of the relevant being remains as before. A tree can wither and die, an elf may cease to be, or, as in this case, a stag can be killed by a beast of prey. The Voice then passes over to another carrier. The problem is finding this carrier.' His master ruffled his hair. 'That will just delay things further.'

Ahren nodded silently. The more he found out, the clearer the picture of this strange culture became. If the goddess didn't even grant her mouthpiece a special place in the cycle of nature, why should the elves do it for their high priestess?

'I can send out a Call when we get back to the community, but our chances are slim. A young Voice reacts far less often to the Call than one who is aware of its role', said Jelninolan.

Uldini shook his head. 'The gods are being particularly uncooperative, deep sleep aside, when you consider that we're trying to protect the world from a new onslaught by the Adversary.'

He lay down in frustration and grumpily covered himself with his blanket before staring out into the darkness. Everyone followed suit and finally the exertions of the day took their toll, and all fell asleep.

Ahren had a restless night. Time and again he would wake up, bathed in sweat, his arms and legs contorted and entangled in his blanket. Rather than giving him energy, the short periods of sleep drained him. He finally gave up just before dawn and got up. He took Windblade, pointed demonstratively at it so that one of the guards would look over, then went a few steps to the side to show that he wasn't presenting a danger, and began his sword practice. His joints and muscles were sore and he realized immediately that he had been neglecting his training. He saw his weapon in a different light ever since he had killed the bandits with his sword and he found it very difficult to practise techniques that were capable of killing other living beings. He breathed in deeply and sucked the aromatic night air into his lungs, concentrating on the gentle sounds of the sleeping forest and admired the beauty of the faint moonlight shining through the leaves. Then he began again and concentrated on the simple movements the armourer had hammered into him in such a short time. In the end he was just as soaked through as he had been after his restless sleep, but this time it was because of his efforts. The feeling of being able to do anything at all was better than the helplessness that had held him in its grip the whole night through. His companions were still sleeping, and just as restlessly as he had.

The sun was taking its time rising, so he started from the beginning again and tortuously went through all the exercises again. When he was finished, his arms and shoulders felt like rubber and his back ached all over, but he felt better and less wound up. Wearily he went back to his sleeping place in order to catch another short sleep, but no sooner had he stretched out on the bed when the camp started coming to life. He only managed a short nap but at least he could lift his arms again and he'd be able to carry his rucksack. He was just given a little dry fruit for breakfast, and then they carried on.

Two hours later they had arrived at the edge of the settlement. Ahren had expected some uproar - angry and disgusted elves with perhaps one or two defending their actions. Instead, everything was normal. They were led to their lodgings and then left alone, none of the residents behaving in any way different than normally. Polite and friendly looks, sometimes a little bow, other times a friendly wave before he or she continued on their way. Nothing suggested that they had committed a transgression. Once they were alone, Ahren could contain himself no longer. 'Have they changed their minds? Are we free to go?'

The others shook their heads and Jelninolan answered, 'We decided a long time ago to submit ourselves in these cases to the verdict of the Voice. Controversies like this used to lead to horrible outcomes on account of our emotional natures, and we don't want this to be repeated. That's why no party tries to grab power, and why everybody behaves in as open and friendly a manner as ever. And no, we can't leave. Without an acquittal we cannot reach the borders of Eathinian. The treetop guards would detain us.'

'No, they wouldn't.' Uldini's face was a mask of scarcely contained rage. 'I can get us out of here and you know it!'

Jelninolan smiled and put a hand on his cheek. 'Of course you could. And you'd destroy half the forest as well, and conjure up a war between humans and elves at a time when unity is needed.'

Her gentle warning and her reference to the consequences were effective. The anger drained from his face and he sighed. 'This trip isn't doing me any good. I've become more used to commanding and ruling than I thought.'

Falk gave a deep laugh in response and said, 'That's exactly why this journey *is* good for you. At last we have a little humility in that ageless body of yours.'

Uldini was about to contradict him vehemently, which would have led to another fight full of taunts and jibes between them, but Ahren intervened by asking a question. 'So, what happens next? What about the Call you wanted to put out?'

Jelninolan took Ahren's bait gratefully. She didn't seem to want to experience another verbal dual between these two squabblers either. 'I'm going to have to ask about fifty other elves to give my prayer to the goddess, beseeching her for advice. That could attract the Voice, but as was mentioned already, it doesn't usually work with a young Voice.'

Ahren began peeling of his leather armour and putting the individual pieces on top of each other. It seemed they wouldn't be going anywhere for a while and he might as well make himself comfortable. While he was doing that, he asked another question regarding something Jelninolan had said earlier.

'You mentioned horrible conflicts among the elves earlier. What did you mean by that?' He'd wanted to break the oppressive silence with this question but obviously he'd picked the wrong topic. The elf priestess looked as though she'd bitten into a lemon, Falk threw him a disapproving look and Uldini covered his eyes with his hands and let out a groan.

The apprentice first thought he wouldn't get an answer, but then the elf priestess began to speak. 'In the Dark Days, the elves fought on the front line against the hordes of Dark Ones. Our losses were many and the horrors we suffered were worse than the other races, as they were less susceptible to strong emotions than we were. There were…differences of opinion as to how we should deal with the chaos and suddenly swords were being drawn, bows tautened, brother against brother, father against daughter, and that was in the middle of the war against the Betrayer. Two groups developed among our folk. One group began creating rules and rituals which would ensure harmonious living together, and they concentrated on supporting the war in a less aggressive manner. We began to play to our strengths as healers, scouts and path-finders and badgered our enemy with our archery regiment. But we steered clear of close combat so that we could maintain our emotional health. The Eathinian that you have come to know grew out of this movement and spiritual mentality.' Jelninolan took a deep breath and Ahren noticed that the less comfortable part of the story was about to follow. 'The other group believed that only with the full potential of all our emotions, both good and bad, could we enjoy victory over the Betrayer. They embraced the state of intoxication which our emotions could awaken in us, and they experienced euphoria and blood lust, sacrifice and atrocity as they reaped a bloody harvest in the ranks of our enemy. They began setting ambushes, then night attacks, they poisoned foodstuffs, and some of them even allowed themselves to be taken as slaves so they could sabotage the enemy armies from within. All of these deeds dramatically altered their soul and spirit until it was no longer possible to live together with them.

In order to prevent a bloodbath, they agreed to move away and find their own homeland. They travelled south and settled in a forest at the front so they would be as close as possible to the fighting. When the war was over, they swore they would roam in the Border Lands and keep guard against the enemy.'

Ahren was beginning to understand what the elf priestess was driving at. 'You're talking about the night elves from the Forest of Ire! They were normal elves? You're *one* folk?' He'd really meant to be more tactful, but every second horror story he'd heard was about the pale elves with their poisonous daggers who would move around soundlessly at dead of night, leaving corpses lying around that had been living and breathing the day previously. Jelninolan nodded in silence, then went to the entrance of their dwelling, stretched her face towards the sun, closed her eyes and stayed there.

Uldini went over to Ahren, laid a hand on his shoulder and whispered, 'maybe you could come to me if you have questions like that, what do you think?' Ahren nodded, embarrassed. Then he turned to put away his leather armour, which had been lying there unnoticed while the dark story had been related. He noticed the rucksack and he felt twice as guilty. His little foster child, the chipmunk! He hadn't seen him since the previous morning. Hopefully the little chap had made himself scarce at some point. He opened the rucksack and there the little animal was, a little white ball of fur with its silvery lines gleaming in the light. The nuts had all been eaten and he seemed in good health. He took the rodent out carefully and examined the cut on its side. If he hadn't known where to look, he'd never notice the fine line in the fur.

'Culhen really did a good job on you, isn't that right?' whispered Ahren. The rodent's little head turned towards him and the animal was making an angry noise when suddenly there was a clattering noise behind the apprentice. He turned around quickly and saw his master, sprawled on the floor beside the upturned stool he'd been sitting on, staring open-mouthed at Ahren. The young man instinctively wanted to apologise but then he noticed that Falk wasn't staring at him at all. Uldini looked over curiously too before uttering a brittle laugh, creaking with dry humour. 'Auntie?' he called over his shoulder, 'come in, please, you really have to see this.'

The elf came back into the lodgings, her eyebrows quizzically raised. Meanwhile Falk had picked himself up and righted the stool. The priestess was about to ask a question when she spotted Ahren with his little charge. She stood stock still, went white as a sheet and then walked over to him and stretched out her arms. 'Could I have a look at your chipmunk?' she asked with a nervous glance over her shoulder towards outside.

Ahren was quite intimidated by his friends' reaction and handed over the little animal, which was now chirping cheerfully and scrabbling about the priestess's robe.

'It's not mine,' explained Ahren quickly. He was sure now he had done something wrong and didn't want the others to be jumping to premature conclusions. 'I only nursed it back to health after the Swarm Claw had almost killed it.'

But all eyes were on the animal, which had calmed down, clambered onto the priestess's palm and was now looking deeply into her eyes.

Uldini took a deep breath and then let out a sigh. 'I think we're at fault here'. He turned to Ahren. 'Everything's been going so quickly and none of us wanted to put too much pressure on you. But…would the situation become clearer to you if we told you this: you recognize the Voice of the Forest, if it dwells in an animal, by its silvery-white fur and its silver eyes?'

Ahren felt faint and sat down. 'Are you telling me that...?' He couldn't finish the sentence. It was just too difficult to acknowledge that he had carried the goddess's sacred animal around in his rucksack. Mind you, he had saved the life of the elves' most holy animal and there was a very good chance that the Voice wouldn't sentence to death the person who saved its life and his friends.

'That explains the strange behaviour of the Swarm Claws too. They weren't after us. They wanted to kill the Voice,' added Falk when he noticed that his apprentice needed time to process the situation. 'Bestowing the Voice costs the goddess a lot of energy every time. If a young Voice like this one had been killed by a Dark One, the elves might have had to manage for years without leadership.'

' We'd have also been neutralized. At least with the Voice's rescue, the complaint against us should be off the table,' added Uldini resolutely. Falk and Jelninolan nodded in agreement, grinning cheerfully. Uldini turned to Ahren and gave a little bow. 'Young man, you've saved our skins twice in the last two days. One thing is clear. I don't need any ritual to tell me that you're worthy. I was giving out about the lack of support from the gods yesterday, but tonight I think I'm going to pray long and hard and apologise. I'll go and spread the news before I start getting all sentimental.'

As the little figure was going outside, Falk called after him in an exuberant voice, 'But leave out the bit about the rucksack. The fact that a human has saved the Voice of the Forest will be enough for them.'

Jelninolan was still standing deep in silent conversation with the little creature in her hand when Ahren suddenly leaped up. The first shock was over but instead of the joy he should have been feeling, he was uncontrollably angry. All the dangers in the Weeping Valley had been completely unnecessary! Had he been told everything earlier, he would have walked into the elf village the day before yesterday, he would have presented the Voice, he would have been hailed a hero, and he would have been handed the soundless lute with a ribbon around it and been congratulated with lots of backslapping!

An angry red mist had descended on Ahren. He drew himself up to full height and jabbed a finger into Falk's chest. 'From now on you won't treat me like a small child. Selsena and Culhen could have been needlessly killed yesterday because nobody bothered to tell me anything more than the bare minimum. But that's over now!' While these words were being uttered, Falk's eyes had narrowed to angry slits and his whole body-language suggested to Ahren that the old Forest Guardian was on the verge of getting into a fight with him. But he didn't care. Neither of them pulled back by even a hair's breadth and the tension in the air was palpable.

'He's right'. The elf priestess's words, spoken in a soft and gentle voice, brought the two back from the brink.

Ahren's anger evaporated with the understanding that resonated in her voice, and Falk nodded hesitantly. 'Alright then. You have free rein. From now on you can ask whatever you want, and you will get all the answers. We only wanted to protect you, but that didn't work too well, so we'll try it your way. But don't think you're going to be happy with all the answers.' He held out his hand and the young man took it. Falk gripped Ahren's hand firmly and said in a voice of steel, 'And don't forget that I'm still your master. If you turn on me like that again, I'll have you running up and down trees until you think you've turned into a squirrel, is that clear?'

Ahren nodded silently. Then his hand was released and he found himself in a bear hug.

'You've been brave and clever and I'm proud of you'. Falk said that so quietly into his ear, that he didn't understand him. Before Ahren could react, his master had released him and said loudly, 'and now go wash yourself, put on something clean and polish your armour. The elves are going to want to see you, and the hero of the hour can hardly appear looking like a snotty nosed kid in a filthy jerkin who doesn't know how to hold his bow.'

Ahren quickly grabbed his armour, went outside and marched to the nearby stream, which served all the village's daily needs.

The old man stared after him and Jelninolan came up beside him. 'He's not a boy anymore, but he's still not a man and has to deal with so many things. I understand why you acted the way you did.'

Falk glanced at her and answered. 'Still, we did overdo it. He has earned our respect and it's time we gave him more leeway.'

The priestess's voice then took on an amused undertone. 'Do you really want to answer *every* question he asks?'

Falk grunted and said quietly, 'I just have to make sure he doesn't ask the wrong questions.'

Only Uldini was present when Ahren returned to their lodgings. He was sprawled out contentedly on a large cushion. 'It's a good that you weren't here. It was all rather turbulent. Of course, all the charges against us were dropped on account of your heroic deed. I think two of the older elves almost had heart attacks when they heard the news that a little human child was their saviour in their hour of need while their tree-top guards were sitting around on their bottoms, oblivious to it all.' The Arch Wizard giggled sarcastically and rubbed his hands.

I'm not a child any more,' protested Ahren wearily. The wizard sat up and raised a defensive hand. 'Most of the villagers here are two hundred years old and more. What do you think they see you as?'

The Arch Wizard tactfully hadn't mentioned that he himself was considerably older than that, but Ahren got the message anyway. He sighed and began to get changed. It would be quite some time yet before everybody was taking him completely seriously.

'I'm responsible for you looking as impressive as possible, then we should go to the main square. The whole village is going to be there and a few representatives from the nearby settlements.'

'I thought the whole settlement was here,' answered Ahren in amazement.

Uldini gave a friendly laugh and said, 'Eathinian stretches across the whole continent. Do you think there are only three hundred elves living in the whole forest?'

Ahren wanted to protest but Uldini raised his hands reassuringly. 'There are about fifty thousand elves living in Evergreen, in settlements like this one, and in most cases, it takes many days to get from one to the next. We came to this one here because it was easy to get to by the Red Posts and Jelninolan was waiting here for us. She hasn't said anything, but rest assured she's been trying to make contact with the Voice of the Forest since she found out about you. Now we know why the old Voice never responded.' He drew his finger across his throat.

Ahren felt a little uncomfortable when he heard the Arch Wizard speaking so sarcastically and dismissively about such serious matters. But then it dawned on him that this little creature must have seen so many terrible things and that this was his way of dealing with them. Ahren himself had changed considerably in the previous months and his confrontation with Falk was evidence of that. Centuries full of responsibilities and change must take their toll on a person's spirit, even someone as mighty as the Arch Wizard.

Uldini's lifted his hands up to his face in feigned shock. 'Oh no! Are the green sparks there again?' he called and Ahren realized that he had been staring, lost in thought, at his companion. He turned away guiltily and hurried to finish his preparations.

The wizard sniggered behind him. 'I'm familiar with your reaction. You get used to it.'

Ahren wasn't sure if he was referring to his sardonic manner or to the distressing events of the last few days, and he came to the conclusion that the clever magus had probably meant both.

After a time Ahren turned around and said, 'I'm ready. We can go.'

Uldini tilted his head and scrutinized the apprentice with a critical eye. Ahren may have put in an effort but he was still an apprentice in tatty armour. The Arch Wizard produced his crystal ball and let it float around Ahren a few times while he quietly uttered some words. The young man looked down at himself and saw that his leather had taken on a bright sheen, as if it had been polished for hours. His clothes didn't have a speck of dirt on them.

'That's the best I can do. Almost everyone present has powers of magic, and any illusion that I create will only make you appear vain. Everything is so much easier in the Sun Court.' He stepped behind the apprentice and pushed him out into the light.

'Come on, the others are waiting. Let's get it over with, I'm hungry.' At that he lifted up and floated off quickly, so that Ahren had to trot along quickly so as not to fall behind.

Chapter 21

They met nobody along the way and once they saw the enormous trees in the centre of the village, Ahren knew why. The whole platform was full of elves, who turned as one in his direction as soon as he came into view. No sound emanated from the gathering and you could hear a pin drop. As they walked towards the silent community, Uldini looked over his shoulder and said, 'don't worry about it, it's their way of celebrating. They're all bound together on the same emotional level at the moment and they're jumping mental somersaults for joy. If you were an elf, you'd be participating and feeling fantastic. Just trust me. They're very grateful.'

Uldini's dry manner helped to calm Ahren's nerves and stepped onto the platform. All the elves were greeting him with quiet smiles and he managed to respond with a smile of his own. The crowd divided and Ahren went to the middle of the platform, trying not to think about the fact that there were five hundred people standing on a thin cloth platform high in the air. Although he was used to the cloth paths, this enormous flat surface with its knotted material still made him nervous. His companions were waiting for him in the middle.

Jelninolan looked the same as ever. Her small, round figure, her red hair and green eyes were even more marked, now that she was surrounded by these many tall, slim, white haired elves.

Falk was standing by her side, in full regalia with his gleaming armour and his fur cloak, and Culhen was lying on a fat cushion in front of them with a contented look on his face. He must have been thoroughly groomed because his fur shone like satin in the warm afternoon sun. He greeted Ahren with a joyful bark. Uldini floated beside the high priestess and indicated to him to stand in front of them.

As Ahren stepped closer, he saw the Voice of the Forest, who had rolled himself together between Culhen's front paws and was now looking at Ahren with sleepy eyes.

Jelninolan smiled at him and produced Tanentan. The artefact had been cleaned and polished but the impression it left was still that of a simple lute. The priestess began to sing in the Elf language and her fingers plucked the strings, but no sound came from the instrument. At first Ahren thought the lute was broken, but then he felt it was talking to him, as if the individual sounds were being generated directly within his spirit. The priestess wove her song out of this spectral music, and suddenly it became clear to the young man that although he didn't understand the Elf language, she was singing the story of his battle with the Swarm Claw.

He saw the images with his inner eye. It was as if everything was happening again, and when it came to the point where his dagger lunged into the Swarm Claw's chest, Culhen uttered a howl which was the perfect imitation of the one he had uttered under the tree, when he had distracted the Dark One.

Then the song was over. Jelninolan place her hands on the strings and the horrific episode vanished. Ahren was dazed and it took him a while to come back to the present. He blinked repeatedly to banish the memories. When he had regained his sense of orientation, he noticed that everyone present was bowing towards him and Jelninolan spoke in a booming voice. 'We thank you for your deeds!'

Then everyone straightened up again and a quiet murmuring could be heard. The elves were beginning to behave like individuals again and not as one large, indivisible group. The ceremony seemed to be over and the spiritually united bond had dissolved.

Uldini clapped his hands. 'That was refreshing. What is there to eat?' he called in a self-satisfied voice.

The magus was obviously familiar with the elf customs for a short time later there was a movement among the crowd. Cushions were artfully arranged, and baskets of food were brought from the surrounding lodgings. Soon all the participants were sitting around, scattered in little groups on the floor. Ahren and his friends ate in the middle of the platform which had filled up in no time. Soon there were elves sitting on all the edges of the cloth, their legs dangling in the air below. There was eating and drinking, the air was filled with laughter and the melodic language of the forest dwellers.

There were groups of singers scattered about and Ahren was amazed at how harmoniously the songs intertwined with each other. There still seemed to be some kind of unconscious union among the elves.

Ahren was starving and gobbled down everything he could lay hold on. Provisions had been pretty meagre the last couple of days and so he stuffed himself with bread and honey, not to mention mint pasties stuffed with meat, washing them both down with a sharp-smelling fruit juice, which tasted a little of apple and aniseed.

Chewing with his mouth full, he asked his master quietly, 'I thought elves didn't eat meat'.

Falk nodded. 'They only do it rarely. You could put it like this: they only eat what the forest has too much of. The rabbit population had to be reduced considerably this year, so that's why there are pasties.' He bit heartily into one, then continued, 'I remember one season when the river changed direction nearby and there was an explosion of blueberry bushes. For weeks afterwards all the meals had blueberries. As the gods are my witness, I avoided that fruit for years afterwards'. He laughed and slapped Ahren on the back.

He had rarely seen his master so happy and Ahren was painfully aware that this place really was the Forest Guardian's home. He chewed thoughtfully on his pasty, then he put it aside and asked Jelninolan, 'can I have a quick word with you?'

She gave him a quizzical smile and when he stood up, she followed suit. Ahren wound his way through the crowd until they got to a quiet spot near the edge. The elf priestess stood beside him and waited politely while he enjoyed the view and wondered how he should start.

'Everyone seems to be very happy that we saved the Voice', he began, awkwardly. The priestess smiled in amusement and raised an eyebrow quizzically.

'And you worked that out for yourself?'

Ahren sighed. He was no good at these things and it wouldn't get any better unless he came to the point. 'I wanted to ask if I could make a request, now that we've helped you.'

The elf hesitated and looked at him in surprise. 'You want a reward?' Jelninolan's aura had lost none of its power over Ahren and the disappointment that was revealed in her question caused him to flinch.

'Yes…no, well, not for me anyway,' he said quickly. 'I'd never be here without Falk. I'd never have learned how to climb or how to hunt Dark Ones or how to treat injured animals. Without his training, I wouldn't have been able to save the Voice of the Forest. Would it be possible for his banishment to be lifted?' His voice had been getting quieter and quieter and now it petered out. His companion looked at him thoughtfully with eyes narrowed and with a maternal sternness. Then she nodded and said, 'I'll see what I can do.' She turned around and went, leaving a somewhat baffled apprentice in her wake, who didn't know what to make of her reaction.

The elf priestess didn't return to the others and so Ahren went back alone. Every elf he passed gave him a broad smile, or proposed a toast in his honour, or even bowed slightly before him. When he arrived back to his friends, he saw that Culhen had an enormous bowl of rabbit meat in front of him, which he was holding between his front paws as he wolfed down the food, growling with enjoyment.

Uldini watched the wolf with amusement and then turned to Ahren. 'It seems our furry hero is perfectly content. The Voice has retired back into the forest. He was probably afraid our friend would eat him by mistake.'

Ahren laughed and then became serious and sat down on one of the cushions. Daylight was gradually vanishing, and a soft twilight was settling in on the forest. He took another sip of the strange drink and Uldini leaned over him.

'Be careful with that. You hardly notice it but there's some alcohol in it. If you drink too much and then go for another walk along the edge, well…'

He wriggled his eyebrows in an exaggerated manner and Ahren had to laugh again. The Arch Wizard really knew how to use his childish appearance to his advantage, whether it was just to make jokes or to highlight the difference between appearance and reality.

Falk was chatting to a group of elves some paces away and Uldini leaned closer towards Ahren. 'We're alone now and I'm in a talkative mood. Falk took off your muzzle today, so if you have any questions, now would be a good opportunity.'

The wizard's offer took Ahren by surprise, but then he asked a question that had been troubling him for a while. 'Why did you connect the reappearance of the Paladin with the eternal spell. Would it not have been better if all the Paladins were there before the betrayer wakes?'

Uldini's eyes lit up. 'A really clever question. We did discuss that at the time. We wanted to intertwine the problem and its solution. A balance of strengths if you so wish. None of the other ideas were implementable. The most popular suggestion at the time was: The Pall Pillar falls when the gods awaken. Sounds mad, doesn't it? But it wasn't. We would have had to connect the sleep of the gods to the Pall Pillar and thereby create a channel between THEM and HIM. Can you imagine how much power HE would have been able to draw from such a connection? Other alternatives presented the same problem. If HE or his servants had somehow managed to conjure up the end of the Bane Spell, then you'd have a world without a Paladin, so we decided to make things simple and fool-proof. First you appear, then HE wakes up. The Paladins were our best option. Half of us thought the thirteenth would never come back, the other half thought the new chosen one would be found within a few months. Then we would have gone with the little child to the Pall Pillar, we would have carried out the ritual of Naming and speared the swine without giving him a chance to bat an eyelid.' The Arch Wizard gave him a penetrating look. 'Nobody planned it to take this long for a new candidate to appear. We came up with the idea of the focus stones sixty years later when it became clear that there was no short-term solution in sight. But now, hundreds of years later, the situation has completely changed. We have to travel all over the place, picking up people and items for a ritual that in those days we could have done in a day, because everything was close together.' He paused for a moment to gather his thoughts. 'We enshrined the Naming of the Paladin with the eternal Bane Spell because the ritual of Naming has enormous power. No-one should have been able to remove the Bane Spell or evade it. That worked, but the powers of the thirteenth Paladin were set free with your election and now HE can tap into this power, slowly but surely – through the connection between the Bane Spell and your election. Now, the longer it takes us to perform the Naming, the more power HE can steal.'

Ahren gave an understanding nod. 'That's why he wakes up earlier if we dawdle. He'll become stronger, and I'll become weaker.' Ahren felt a shiver run down his spine at this thought.

Uldini hesitated. 'Yes, more or less. I've gone through all the calculations again. Ideally, we'll execute the ritual before the winter solstice. Then we have a few years before he wakes up in order to find the others and kill him with the united powers of all thirteen Paladins. But if we need longer than next winter solstice, he'll wake up in the following winter and we'll be done for.'

'So that's the reason for the delay tactics. The Swarm Claws that are looking for us and forcing us to travel more slowly, the bandits ambushing us and the attempt to kill the Voice of the Forest,' said Ahren slowly.

'Exactly. You recognise the pattern. HIS main aim is to kill you, don't believe anything else. But if HE can slow us down at the same time, that's almost as useful to HIM. Death by a thousand cuts.'

Everything was much clearer to Ahren and he was grateful to the wizard for his explanations. But there was one thing he still wanted to know. 'We have two of the three Einhans, but who is the third? Has Falk said anything yet?'

Uldini shook his head. 'We haven't had a chance to have a private conversation yet, but he seems to have a plan. I mean, he knows where to look and who to ask. That's comforting. We can ask him together later.'

Ahren squirmed with excitement. He was being included at last. ' Then we can carry out the ritual of Naming! What does that mean for me?'

Uldini raised his hand reassuringly. 'Almost. We sealed the place of ritual at the time with magic so that nobody could find it by accident. One of the Wild Folk will have to lead us there, but that's no problem, and no, not much will change for you, unfortunately. By rights you should get the talents of the THREE at the Naming, but because you're a special case, I'm not sure what exactly is going to happen. Only the MOULDER will definitely touch you and make you resistant to the Betrayer's influence. But I've been protecting you with my magic anyway since I've been with you, so you won't feel any difference.'

Ahren looked at the childlike figure in surprise. 'Thank you.' he said.

Uldini nodded and smiled drily. 'One does one's best.'

It was getting even darker now, and soon some of the elves were conjuring up spheres of light which were floating above them on their gentle paths and partaking in a ghostly dance. Ahren lay on his back and looked up enthralled, leaning his head against Culhen's overfull stomach. The wolf gave a disgruntled growl but was far too full to resist his friend. Ahren let the sweet night air take hold of him and followed the complicated patterns of the blue-white illuminated spheres which were moving across the sky like glow-worms. A solitary elf started to sing, then another and soon the harmonious singing was everywhere. A deep peace enveloped the young Forest Guardian and he let his fingers run through the wolf's fur. His questions were forgotten, and he surrendered to the peace of the moment. Ahren took another sip of the elf fruit drink and was soon lulled to sleep by the light, the song and the warmth of his wolf friend.

Epilogue

When Ahren woke up the next morning, he saw that he wasn't the only one had slept outside in the cosy warm embrace of Evergreen. At least half of the revellers were still lying around in small groups on the platform, their heads or bodies on the cushions. The sleep patterns and sleeping arrangements of the elves was as much a mystery to him as everything else about them. The missing doors in all their lodgings, the singing of the individual elves which always harmonised with the singing of the whole group, not to mention the previous day's ceremony, all showed the young Forest Guardian how closely-knit the elves were. He tried to imagine a human group living like that and he could only laugh. The bailiff would have a lot on his hands because their living together would be far from harmonious.

He stood up and Culhen stretched himself in gratitude. Ahren had misused him for the whole night as a pillow. The wolf shook himself off and sniffed his friend's hand.

'You can't be hungry again', Ahren chided quietly.

The large bowl that the Blood Wolf had licked clean yesterday wasn't two paces away and Ahren was convinced that half a dozen rabbits must have been in it. Culhen whimpered quietly and pushed against Ahren's hand with his nose again. He shook his head in disbelief and relented.

'Alright then, let's get you something to eat. You've certainly deserved it'.

Ahren tickled the wolf between the ears and then began to pick his way slowly through the groups of sleepers. There was no sign of the

374

others and Ahren figured that they must have returned to their lodgings during the night. He had no idea where he could find something to eat in the village and he didn't want to wake any of the elves, partly because he didn't speak Elfish, so he decided to go to the lodgings and ask Falk where he could fill up his greedy wolf.

Culhen trotted contentedly beside him, sometimes panting quietly and sometimes sniffing the ground curiously. The young Forest Guardian looked at his friend thoughtfully. In nearly two years Culhen had grown into an imposing wolf. His head was now above Ahren's hips, he was muscular and a little broader than normal wolves. If he kept on growing, he would be heavier than Ahren and no-one would take him for a normal animal any more. He tried to comfort himself by remembering what he had read in Vera's books. The tome stated that Northern Wolves - and Culhen's breed was descended from them – reached their full height at two years. Hopefully his friend would take after them rather than after his mother.

The truth was that Culhen was unique and would always put up with Ahren no matter what happened, so long as they could be together. He threw his arms around the animal impulsively, which resulted in his face being licked and being enveloped by the aroma of six eaten rabbits. He gave a groan of disgust and wiped his face dry with his sleeve. Then they went on towards the others.

Ahren arrived at the lodgings and found Falk, Uldini and Jelninolan at breakfast. The atmosphere suggested that they'd been having a friendly conversation and they greeted him heartily. He sat down beside them and Culhen made a beeline for the corner of the communal room where a bowlful of rabbit was waiting for him.

Falk looked over in amusement and said, 'your wolf will get fat if he carries on eating like that. Soon he'll only be able to howl at the Dark Ones because he'll be too heavy to budge.'

Culhen glanced back, the picture of injured innocence, before continuing to eat. Jelninolan smiled and responded, 'and he's vain. There was no need for his howling yesterday, the song would have brought forth the memory anyway. But he wanted to show off.'

The animal gave a quiet whimper but carried on eating.

Uldini shook his head. 'I'm telling you, he's slowly beginning to understand every word we say. It seems it's not only his tummy that's growing,' and he tapped his head.

Ahren was glad that everyone seemed to be in a relaxed mood. Their latest victory and the harmonious feast had done everyone good, and he himself felt full of derring-do this morning. Hoping he wouldn't destroy the mood, he asked, 'so what happens next?'

Falk answered calmly, 'First we have to leave Evergreen, then straight through the Knight Marshes to King's Island. That has the only harbour with a connection to the Silver Cliff. Then, from what I've last heard, there we will find a dwarf, who would be suitable as an Einhan'.

'Who is he?' asked Uldini curiously, but Ahren was hardly listening. He would ride through the length of the Knight Marshes, he would land on King's Island, a small island that contained a capital city of the same name! he'd also never seen the sea before, and they'd even travel by ship! He tried to hide his excitement.

Falk answered Uldini's question. 'At the moment he doesn't have a name. He's staying on a lonely sentry post, or Lonely Watch, as it's called.'

Uldini whistled through his teeth and Jelninolan snorted with disgust.

Ahren gave a questioning look, and much to his silent delight, Falk answered immediately. 'It's common among the dwarves to give certain, usually very difficult tasks to individual dwarves, who then have to fulfil them. Until they have done this, they are left on their own and don't have a name. They first get this back once they have performed the task, with a new syllable added in recognition of their service to the community. You can recognise the oldest and most decorated of them by their terribly long names.'

The elf priestess shook her head and Ahren understood why. It sounded tough enough to his own human ears, sending an individual into exile and without a name, in order to do something for the community. It had to sound like pure barbarity to elves with their understanding of harmony.

Uldini followed up with a question. 'Do you think he'll help us? You know what dwarves can be like.'

Falk nodded. 'I know him from before. He's the only dwarf I can think of who would be worthy, and would help us without too much persuasion. Besides, he's on the Silver Cliff at the moment. Trogadon's shield is stored there as well. That will do for our ritual and it's not important to the dwarves. It's only used for ceremonial purposes every couple of decades when a new master blacksmith is being appointed. That way we'll avoid having to go to Thousand Halls.'

Ahren racked his brains, trying to remember what he knew about dwarves. There were two dwarf settlements. Thousand Halls, the actual kingdom of the dwarves, lay to the south, beneath the Eastern Sunplains. The High King had his seat there and most of the dwarves' military might was based there too. The Silver Cliff on the other hand, was a small enclave, which specialised almost exclusively in trade with Kelkor and the Knight Marshes, and lay on the banks of Kelkor. Ahren could understand why Falk would prefer to go there. The journey was half as long and the Silver Cliff dwarves were considered to be much more open-minded than their southern cousins.

Uldini nodded approvingly and said, 'that sounds promising. Let's hope that your friend has finished his task by the time we get there.'

Falk shrugged his shoulders. 'Even if that isn't the case, the dwarves are a pragmatic folk. As non-dwarves, we can give him a hand, and usually it's only something like smoking out cave spiders or things like that. The dwarves don't possess any magic but you, Uldini, should be able to manage whatever it is he's supposed to do in a day.'

The Arch Wizard made a face. 'I hate spiders and now I feel like I'm being used.'

Falk responded calmly, 'It's time you made yourself useful.'

The verbal combat showed to Ahren that the informative part of the discussion was now over and he began to think over what he had just heard. The Knight Marshes, a voyage on a ship and visiting the Silver Cliff. It all sounded incredibly exciting and would ease the pain of leaving the elf forest.

He looked over at Jelninolan and a wave of pity came over him. She would have to leave the community of elves for a long time. Ahren was beginning to feel what this meant for an elf creature.

He leaned over to her and whispered, 'Maybe you could come later to some agreed meeting point after we've found the dwarf. You and Uldini could talk to each other using magic.'

She smiled at him and said, 'That's very nice of you but it really is time that I moved away again so as not to lose my connection to the outside world. We have a tendency to withdraw too much. Anyway, I have no intention of letting you out of my sight until you've been named.

Too many enemies are after you, and you're going to need all the help you can get.'

Grateful for her support, he settled down to breakfast, all the time listening to the playful conversation between his master and the Arch Wizard.

When he was finally finished eating, his master looked at him with eyebrows raised. 'We'll be leaving tomorrow morning at the crack of dawn, which means that you have the rest of the day to continue with your disrupted training,' he said firmly.

Ahren nodded guiltily, then took his bow and Windblade in his hand and went out to look for a quiet place to practise.

The day flew by. The quiet atmosphere in the forest and the familiar activity gave Ahren time to think and mull over the events of the previous days. Falk came by from time to time and gave him new tasks or asked him a complicated question at difficult moments in the training. Jelninolan provided him with company too, and tested his knowledge of the plants and animals in the forest.

Above all, he enjoyed Uldini's visit. The Arch Wizard entertained him with anecdotes about the Sun Emperor's court. Late in the afternoon his master gave him climbing exercises to complete until finally, shattered and exhausted but nonetheless content, the apprentice made his way back to the guest lodgings. A hearty stew was on the table and Ahren helped himself. Then he curled up under his blanket, relaxed his exhausted muscles and dozed off to the sound of his companions' quiet conversation. The day had almost been the same as in his earlier existence in the forest cabin, and as he drifted off, he thought of the wonders and adventures that awaited him and a smile spread across his face.

The three others looked over at the sleeping youth and Jelninolan said, 'he's come a long way in a short time. How long have you been training him now, two years?'

Falk nodded proudly. 'I'm glad we can give him a little breather now.'

Uldini chuckled quietly. 'Breather? We're going to travel through a kingdom full of feuds, go on a voyage half the the length of the eastern coast, and then we have to help a dwarf on his lonely watch. What could possibly go wrong?'

The journey continues in:
The Naming (The 13ᵗʰ Paladin Book II)

Dear Reader:

If you enjoyed this book, please leave a short rating in the shop, where you bought it. As I am an independent author with no backing of a publisher, every positive comment helps to convince others, to read my novels.

Acknowledgements

My thanks to everybody who supported me with my first novel.

A journey may always begin with a first step, but no-one said that you have to walk alone.

Made in the USA
Las Vegas, NV
11 August 2023